For Farrah ♡

ALL THE JAGGED EDGES

" Are you stabby, little Fox?
Or are you more blunt force
trauma? "

ALL THE JAGGED EDGES

Cover Design | Illustrations: Will Hatch
Editing: Taylored Text
Map Design: Virginia Allyn
Book Design and Typesetting: Enchanted Ink Publishing

ISBN: 979-8-9882516-2-0 (E-book)
ISBN: 979-8-9882516-4-4 (Paperback)
ISBN: 979-8-9882516-0-6 (Hardcover)

WWW.TALARATATE.COM

Content Warning

All the Jagged Edges is a dark, fantasy romance. While comical at times, the story includes elements that might not be suitable for some readers. Suicide, suicidal thoughts, graphic sex, bondage, bullying, drug and alcohol abuse, sexual asphyxiation, cheating, mentions of abortion, and excessive use of the F word are all aspects of this novel. Readers who may be sensitive to these triggers please read at your own discretion.

For my fellow depression-fighting, anxiety-riddled humans who wake up every day and find the strength to keep going–you're a fucking warrior. **This one's for you.**

Playlist

Vienna - Billy Joel
Charlie - Mallrat
Wish On An Eyelash - Mallrat
Teeth - Mallrat
Blue Jeans - Lana Del Ray
Cradles - Sub Urban
Underwater - Rüfüs du Sol
Fuck You - Silent Child
The Search - NF
If You Want Love - NF
Name - Goo Goo Dolls
Daydreamin' - Lupe Fiasco
Mother We Just Can't Get Enough - New Radicals
You Get What You Give - New Radicals
Sic Transit Gloria ... Glory Fades - Brand New
I Am A Nightmare - Brand New
Seventy Times 7 - Brand New
Mix Tape - Brand New
Tiny Dancer - Elton John
Strangers - Bring Me the Horizon
Blinded - Third Eye Blind
Rumors - NEFEX
What If It Doesn't End Well - Chloe Moriondo

*It's no use
going back to yesterday
because I was a different person then.*

Alice's Adventures in Wonderland
By Lewis Carroll

CALF

WILLOWBY

Elkwood Mounta

Oakland

MoleRail

Aspendale
West

Ravenwood Castle

Shit Shack

MoleRail

Dogwood Dell

Sticks River

Berkshire

Hideout

Mo

kelpie pods

ALL THE JAGGED
EDGES

TALARA TATE

PART ONE

ALL THE THINGS I LEFT BEHIND

CHAPTER ONE

HARPER

THE TACTICAL FLASHLIGHT IS A FUCKING supernova exploding in front of my eyeballs. My vision blurs from the tears forming, and I can physically feel my pupils constricting with all their might.

Fuck, I'm high.

"Well, Miss?"

Oh, he was speaking this whole time. I wiggle my tits a little and his gaze drops to follow the motion. *Scumbag.*

"Sorry, Officer, I didn't know."

It's as good an answer as any, and the right one apparently, because he moves the flashlight out of my face and points it at the ground. *What a waste of battery power.*

"You have ID on you?"

I pull my phone from the back pocket of my jeans. It takes me a second because the fucker is jammed in there pretty tight. Removing the phone case, I pull my driver's license out and hand it to him, my innocent sixteen-year-old face smiling back at me like the condescending bitch she is.

Officer Scumbag uses the flashlight to look at my ID like it's his reading glasses and shakes his head in disapproval. "It's your lucky day, Harper Elliott."

"Sir?" I blink up at him through long black eyelashes.

"You're still a minor."

I turn eighteen in two days.

"And I'm feeling like I'm in a generous mood."

Gross.

"So, I'll let you off this time with a curfew ticket." He pulls out his ticket pad thingy and turns away to write my information down.

I guess I should be grateful. After all, I was breaking and entering. A line of people not much older than me stands against the garage—arms up, legs spread and all that—of this random person's house, waiting to be fully arrested.

The truth is, I really *didn't* know. My lovely boyfriend dragged me here for a party and once again, my dumb ass was too drunk to ask questions. Speaking of ... where is he? My head swivels around and I catch him speaking to another officer in the street.

God, he's hot.

Tight jeans and a form-fitting, plain-white t-shirt. Over it he has a faux-leather jacket that matches his all-black sneakers. Dark hair peeks from beneath a backward hat. Last night he fucked me against the side of a house, party music blaring loud enough to drown out me moaning his name. He's nineteen, but knowing him, he'll swindle his way out of this. He always does.

"Miss Elliott." Officer Scumbag waggles his finger, calling me over to his shiny car. "Here's your ID. Do you have a way home?"

"My car is right over there," I say, motioning my head to the black Jeep Liberty across the street.

This fucker laughs at me. Actually chortles like the fat fuck he is. "I don't think so. You'll need a parent to come pick you up."

"Why?" I whine.

"Because I need to make sure you get home safely." He gives me a condescending look, but what he doesn't know is that my mom is probably blown out of her mind on Xanax. Plus, she'd freak if she found out about my curfew ticket. Which leaves me no other choice.

"And my boyfriend?" I motion my head toward Cole, cock my hip and put my hand on it like I have any leverage in the world, but fuck me, right?

The cop looks at me and frowns. I'm really testing that generous mood. "One of the guys here has a few felonies under his belt. We'll let you guys off this time."

This time.

They always say that. For now, they got their big, bad wolf, so they'll let the sheep go. Fine by me. I walk over to Cole, who is profusely thanking the officer for his time.

"Fucking pig," he mutters when the cop's out of range.

"They won't let me drive."

"Why?"

"Does it matter? They won't let me. I need to call my dad unless one of your parents wants to come whisk us away."

The look he gives me says *we both know you don't want that.*

And I don't. His parents hate me. The details of why and how that came about are a story for another time. Right now, I have to call my dad—the last person I want to deal with.

The phone rings twice before he answers, sleep lacing his words despite it being just past 11:00 p.m. "Harper? Is everything okay?"

"I'm fine, Dad," I say meekly. "Listen, I've gotten myself into a bit of a pickle."

The other end is silent. I'm pacing now in tight circles and nearly fall over, but Cole catches me. I'm too high to be spinning myself around like a goddamn dreidel.

"Dad?"

"I'm waiting for you to explain."

Right.

"I was at a party and the cops came." No reason to tell him that the party hadn't even started yet and we broke into some rando's house. "They're letting us off with a curfew ticket, but they won't let me drive my car, even though I'm sober."

What? Little white lies never hurt anyone.

"Text me the address, I'll be there in a bit." A click signals he's hung up, and Cole looks at me expectantly.

"He's coming," I say.

"And?"

"And what? You know him."

I squint at the address painted on the sidewalk so I don't have to waltz up to the mailbox. The numbers tilt and swirl in my vision, so I close my eyes tightly and try again. When I'm convinced I have it down, I shoot off a text to my dad.

"He's usually pretty chill," Cole remarks, leaning up against my car. I ignore his comment about my father. My dad is really chill, but ... it's too hard to put into words. Spending time with him brings out emotions I'd need more than once-a-week-therapy to work through.

My phone buzzes in my pocket.

> Dad: Be there in 10 minutes.

"We have ten minutes. Hey, where did Thomas and Reno go?"

He shrugs. "Dipped as soon as they heard sirens."

I frown. "Why didn't we?"

"Bunny, you're just not that good at climbing a fence." He pulls me closer and puts his smirking lips against my pursed ones.

It's stupid, but I actually feel bad about this fact. A year ago I was stressing out about passing an SAT exam that was two years away. Now I'm disappointed I'm not badass enough to run from the cops.

"I could be," I offer. *Dumb.*

Cole smiles at me. "We'll find an elementary school fence for you to practice on. It'll be fun."

I return the smile because all I want is to be next to him at all times. I want to live in his skin until he can't remember what it's like to breathe without me.

I kiss him and bite his lip, eliciting a groan of approval before shoving my tongue in his mouth. His mouth moves against mine for a few seconds, but then he pulls away.

"Harper, as much as I'd love to bend you over the hood of this Jeep and fuck you into oblivion, I don't think either of us needs to push our luck tonight."

I give him my best puppy dog expression, pushing my body into his and squirming a little. I can feel his cock hardening in his jeans, and few things make me happier.

"Fuck, Harper." Cole pulls me in tighter and cups my ass, sending waves of heat through my body like an inferno. He pushes his knee between my thighs and I grind against it. A soft moan escapes my lips and tumbles into his mouth as his tongue strangles mine.

"Hey! Knock it off, you two!" one of the cops yells from the driveway.

I spin around and salute with perfect posture. "Sorry, Officer, just waiting for my daddy to get here."

The officer's eyes widen as he stares at the lunatic I've become. A shit-eating grin plastered on my face and Cole snickering behind me has me almost convinced I'm happy.

My dad pulls up in a beat-up, cyan Nissan Frontier. I slide into the front seat, his sheepskin seat covers cuddling my exposed lower back.

"Harper," he says in a greeting. Cole slides into the pop-out seats in the cab. "Cole. Why am I not surprised to see you here?"

"Someone's gotta look after this firecracker, sir." Cole reaches over and squeezes my thigh.

I grin wildly at my father, my buzz fading, as he harrumphs and drives Cole home. The only noise in the car is Tom Petty playing quietly on the stereo. I want to turn it up and sing along, but I have a sneaking suspicion this isn't the right time.

Before Cole gets out of the car, he reaches over, kisses my cheek, and thanks my dad. I want to pull him onto my lap and never let go, but I settle for watching him get inside safely. Anxiety over the next time I'll see him bubbles to the surface, and I bite my lower lip in frustration. Is this what love feels like? I don't think it should be this painful, but what do I know?

"Should I be worried?" my dad asks as he drives us to my mother's house.

"Do you ever worry?" I snap back.

Thanking him would be the nice thing to do, but I'm angry. He's acting like he gives a damn, but the truth is, he's just pretending to play a role he thinks is the right one.

To no one's surprise, he doesn't reply and we sit in silence the entire way back. When we get to the security station for the gated community my mom lives in, I lean over from the passenger side and wave at Bert, the security guard. We have a love-hate relationship, and he grimaces when he sees me. I smile back because that's what we do. The gate opens and my father drives down the familiar path to a house I've never truly deemed as home. A few minutes pass and we're taking the winding driveway up to the gates of hell.

I'm being dramatic. It's a beautiful mansion, straight out of MTV Cribs. My stepdad helped invent the little black strip on the back of your credit cards.

I know, right? We're fucking loaded.

The house is Spanish style, with tan siding and warm sandstone walls. Terracotta shingles on the roof and a beautiful courtyard outside make it seem like it's been plucked off the set of *Blow*. A huge fountain in the center tinkles with the sound of falling water. It's supposed to be calming, but all I feel when I walk to the front door is a deep sense of foreboding. It's dark through the big arched windows, and I plan on sneaking through a back door to my room.

"Thanks, Dad."

"Hey, kiddo?" I stop with one foot out the door, literally. "I'm here if you ever want to talk."

Jesus fucking Christ. No, thank you.

I give him a tight-lipped smile and nod back.

The house is deathly quiet and every noise I make seems to echo off the walls, but my money is on both my parents being in a drug-induced sleep, their white noise machine blaring like they're trying to drown out the memory of having a daughter.

I have my own wing of the house, which sounds nice but is actually just really lonely. The second I step into my living room, I kick off my five-inch heels and unzip my jeans, wriggling them over my ass until I'm in nothing but a black lacy thong and a white crop top.

I still have to hide my weed from our maids because they love to rat me out, so I go into my bedroom and rip open the drawer next to my nightstand. It has a false bottom I built into it a couple of months ago. Just call me Bob the fucking Builder.

Sliding it open, I find myself staring at my college acceptance letter from Columbia University. It's something I should be proud of—they have one of the best creative writing programs in the country. The thing is, I don't deserve it. My writing isn't that good and I imagine a little word from my stepfather is the only reason I got in. I should burn it; I'm not interested in the future.

Instead, I pull out my pipe and pack a bowl. I'm so horny, and I had hoped to spend the night with Cole. Grabbing my phone, I shoot him a text.

> Me: I miss you.

I stare at the screen like he might respond within 5 seconds, but he never does. Keeping it glued to my hand, I plug in my earbuds and let Billy Joel's "Vienna" fill my head. Carrying my drugs and technological lifeline to the pool in the backyard, I light up, feet dangling in the warm water, music blasting.

I know what you're thinking: poor little rich girl; she has everything she could ever want, and yet, she's still complaining.

Well, you're fucking right. My life is pretty good. I have more money than I could ever dream of using, my boyfriend is ridiculously hot, and let's be honest, my tits are perfect.

So why do I hate waking up every morning?

I lift my dull, brown split ends and stare at them before my attention catches on the embers burning in the pipe in my hand. One by one they go out, and I'm left in the darkness.

CHAPTER TWO

##

I'M NOT SURE HOW I GOT HERE. THAT'S MY EXCUSE FOR everything these days, isn't it? It's not that I don't actually remember, I do. Brenna, this girl in fourth period, asked me if I wanted to smoke with her tonight. I don't really know her and wanted to say no, but it turns out the social part of my brain rules with an iron fist, so the exact words out of my mouth were, "Fuck yes."

And here I am, incredibly stoned and sandwiched between two dudes I barely know in the back of a shitty car on a quiet residential street by our high school. Brenna is making out with a guy in the front seat like his lips are the elixir of life and I'm worried that if I don't leave soon, this is going to turn into some weird orgy.

"Can I?" I nudge the guy to my left and point at the door. He stares back at me like I just spoke Portuguese.

"Can I get out?" I repeat, slowly and loud enough for his one brain cell that hasn't had a vacation in six years to hear me.

On my other side is a guy named Luke that I made out with once three months ago. He spanked me and told me to call him Daddy, so I immediately walked out.

I'm not nice. Nobody ever talks about me and says, *my friend Harper, she's so nice.* I like to think of it as a test. A first defense against the fragile people of the world. If you need warm and cuddly, I'm not it. Go somewhere else. Find someone different. The worst part is the colder I am, the more people are nice *to* me. It's as if their brain wants to see if it can come up with a way to make me respond like a normal human. It doesn't work. Or maybe I've become so unoffended by the mean shit people say that everyone seems kind.

No one is meaner to me than me.

One brain cell guy finally remembers he speaks English and steps out of the car, smoke billowing out like an industrial-era chimney. I fish my phone from my back pocket and squint against the screen's brightness—currently the only light on this street. After a few swipes, I put the phone to my ear and listen as it rings.

"Harper! It's Harper!" Emma screams so loudly, I worry for a few seconds that my eardrum has blown out. Pulling the phone away from me while music blares and people shout on the other end, I'm resigned to holding the mic in front of my mouth. No need to put it on speakerphone when she already sounds like a fucking banshee.

"Hey, can you come get me?" My throat feels like it's filled with gravel and I wonder briefly if smoking weed can turn you into one of those people with a hole in their throat.

"Yeah, obviously. Of course. Where are you?" The words are so fast I have to spend a couple of seconds thinking about her response.

I peer up at the street signs. "Larson and Manton. Wait, are you high?"

She pauses and then giggles maniacally, like an evil villain. "Can you walk to the school parking lot from there?"

"Sure, but did you hear what I asked?" I might have turned into a degenerate, but I'm not entirely stupid.

"I'll be there soon." The call clicks off and I'm left staring at my phone. My options are limited at this point: go find my friend who is already on her way or get back in the hotboxed car full of creeps.

So basically I have one option.

Deciding that they're unlikely to even notice I'm gone, I don't say bye and instead start walking toward our school. It's only a few blocks from here and the cool air feels good against my skin that's been smothered in the essence of sweat and marijuana. I'm in a nice neighborhood, so I feel completely safe despite the fact that I'm wearing tight jean shorts that barely fit over my ass and essentially a bra as a top. My shoes today are six-inch black leather platforms with sharp metal studs on the heels.

Impractical for a late-night stroll, but I look cute as fuck.

When I reach the parking lot, Emma is speeding to a stop in her white BMW SUV. I don't know what the model is because our other friends got drunk one night and ripped the decals off.

She's not alone, and when I hop in, the car lights nearly blind me. "Thanks for getting me."

I'm expecting Noah in the passenger seat, but Lindsay turns around with a Cheshire grin. "You're so welcome."

They're definitely high.

"Please tell me you're both only stoned. I could walk home from here, I didn't plan on dying tonight."

They both laugh these hyena laughs that I normally find adorable, but right now have my heart pounding.

"We're rolling," Lindsay exclaims and simultaneously all the doors lock.

Jesus fucking Christ.

"It's a two-minute drive. It's fine." Emma draws out the *I*'s in that last word like her life depends on it. Maybe it does, because I'm considering all the ways I could murder her once we get back to her house.

The music in here is too loud for any conversation, but that's fine because I'm pouting in the backseat.

Lindsay turns around and tries speaking to me, but all I can hear is "Crank That" by Soulja Boy blaring on the radio for the ten millionth time today. I swear to fucking God, if I have to listen to this shit one more time, I'll wrap my car around a telephone pole.

"I can't hear you!" I scream back at her, letting a little bit of my anger bleed through.

She turns down the music. "Where's Cole tonight?" she asks, and I try not to bristle.

I don't fucking know because he hasn't answered any of my calls and I keep glancing at my phone like I'm a forty-year-old man waiting for lottery numbers to be announced. I have to win because I spent all my life savings on tickets and this is my last chance before I have to foreclose on my house and my wife leaves me, is what I want to say, but instead, I look around like she might not be talking to me and say, "Fuck if I know."

"I heard he was hanging out with Annika tonight," she replies, turning around before I can grab her skinny cheeks in my claws and squeeze so tightly she bleeds.

"Why would you even say that?" Emma asks, shooting her a glare.

"Because she's a fucking bitch," I answer.

Lindsay whips her head back at me—her short, bright red hair dulled in comparison to the electric green eyeshadow she's wearing—and narrows her eyes at me. She's lucky I'm high and too lazy to smack her pretty little face. She's probably right about Cole, though. "No, I'm not a bitch, *bitch*. I just don't like him. You could do way better and he's a fucking loser."

Sometimes I think the same thing, but sometimes I also feel like if he wasn't around, I'd drown myself.

We pull into Emma's driveway, which is nearly as long as mine, but completely vertical. Her house is on stilts, like the Empire State Building. It's an absolute nightmare to back out of, but the view from her bedroom overlooks the whole San Fernando Valley. It's the only time this city looks decent and not like the heaping pile of trash it really is. I want to leave LA as soon as I possibly can, but something tells me I'll die here.

Music blasts through the whole house, rattling the windows. "Where are your parents?" I ask.

Emma shrugs. "Japan or some shit? I don't know ... London? Who cares?"

"Not here," Lindsay chimes in, throwing her hands in the air.

My head hurts.

As soon as we walk into the house, my nose is assaulted by a thousand different smells, most of them not good. The entryway is trashed. The air in the main living area is thick with bad decisions. I don't even want to know how long this party has been going on.

There's a couple basically fucking on the couch, someone is passed out underneath the coffee table wearing sunglasses, and another group of people are doing lines on the kitchen counter. The sounds of screaming and splashing pour in from the backyard, and I would bet my left tit that no one in the pool is clothed.

"Do you wanna play?" Emma asks, pulling me by my wrist into the massive dining room.

A group of our friends surrounds a big lazy Susan on the table, its surface bordered with full shot glasses. Everyone is talking so loudly that they don't notice us entering, and I pull a chair up to the table, pushing aside a half-drunk bottle of cotton candy Smirnoff. One of the shot glasses fizzes and then turns the same clear color as the rest.

This game is called Roofie Roulette. Yes, you fucking read that right. But don't worry, we don't mess with GHB. It's just ecstasy dropped into a shot glass and then spun around. You won't know if you're the lucky winner until twenty minutes later when your pupils have swallowed your irises and giving everyone a massage sounds like the best idea in the world.

Here's the kicker though: everyone wants to be 'the lucky one' so they just keep playing until they're all high out of their minds and ready to die of alcohol poisoning. I prefer to just pop the fucking stack onto my tongue, thank you very much.

With a snotty smile, I say, "I'll pass." They hardly notice though, and my bored gaze trails across the house. "Hey, where's Noah?"

Emma glances over her shoulder. "Probably blowing Damien upstairs."

Ew. The guy is a literal greaseball and why he's even a temptation to her is the fucking Rubik's Cube I'll never solve.

"Should we stop her?" It's a stupid question, I realize as the words slip out of my mouth.

Emma laughs and shakes her head, leaning forward to spin the lazy Susan. My friend is beautiful with curly, long, brown hair and eyes that match. She has the best sense of humor and a wicked body image disorder. You know the type—takes Adderall every day so she's never hungry but wears the same size jeans as the rest of us. "Noah is an adult. She can make her own decisions."

I snort, but don't argue. I'm not interested in fighting about it. Instead, I watch them get plastered for an hour, until eventually everyone starts making out and for the second time tonight I worry about getting pulled into an orgy.

Pushing out of my chair, I walk through the house when I happen to be in the perfect place at the perfect time.

"Look at what Cole just sent me! Dude's a fucking savage."

I walk over to a blond copycat version of Cole. If I'm being totally honest, all these guys look the same after a while. He's shoving his phone in another guy's face and I grab it out of his hand. It's a picture of someone—presumably Cole—fucking some girl from behind, and I can promise you that girl is not me. His fist is wrapped in her streaky, fake blonde hair and I'm so angry I want to vomit all over the guy standing next to me's shoes.

But I don't.

You know why? Because I'm a fucking lady.

Instead, I scream so loud that everyone turns to look at me. It's not good enough. I still feel terrible inside. So, I throw this guy's phone across the room and watch as it hits the wall, shattering into a million pieces. Five pieces. It shatters into five pieces.

"What the fuck, bitch?" blond, backward hat guy yells at me.

He has every reason to be upset. I just broke his phone, but do I apologize? No. I'm sick of fucking apologies.

"Bite me, asshole." I stomp off, but I don't get too far.

He grabs my arm, his grubby little fingers getting way too close to my boob, and spins me around.

"Hey, crazy bitch, you just broke my phone."

Everyone is staring now, and honestly, I don't mind. Glaring at him, I rip the phone case off my phone and slam three hundred-dollar bills into his chest and say, "Fuck off," before storming out to the backyard.

I need to be high—*now*. But when I reach into my back pocket, my weed isn't there. How I manage to not throw a lawn chair through the window is beyond me. I swipe a random shot glass filled with God knows what and throw it back, relishing the burn all the way down.

Deep breath, Harper. There are pros to being single, right? I was getting tired of the sex, anyway. But my organs feel like they're being ground into mush and I'm pretty sure my heart is suffocating, if that's even possible.

I hold back tears as I wander over to two random guys smoking in the corner. They're far enough away from the house that they didn't hear my little outburst.

"Hi," I say, sitting down next to them.

They stop their conversation and stare at me. I don't need to, but for fun, I adjust the straps to my bralette and their eyes follow the bounce of my tits.

"Hey," one of them says. The other one is too busy still staring at my boobs.

"Are you guys smoking weed?" I ask, adding a hint of awe.

"Yeah, we are, but this is our last bowl." Another guy I didn't see peeks out from out of nowhere ... or maybe I'm higher than I think. I know he's lying because the other two give him a look like he's the reason they're all still virgins.

"Oh, okay. I was just wondering because I've never smoked weed before." I smile as innocently as I can.

"What?" one of them chokes.

I nod my head and roll my lower lip between my teeth.

"We have more," the other one says, shooting who he thinks is his cock block an "I dare you to say something" glare. He doesn't realize his real cock block is my broken heart and the fact that he's wearing a neon blue polo shirt. *Gross.*

A few minutes later—sufficiently stoned and bored from making conversation with these idiots—I get up and walk away, ignoring their calls for me to come back. The party is still on full blast and someone splashes me as they cannonball butt-ass naked into the pool. The water is a rippling teal tinted yellow in the bright pool lights. I let my mind wander to what it would be like to sink to the bottom.

My phone buzzes in my pocket and it's a text from Cole.

> Hey Bunny. Sorry I didn't have my phone on me

I think my heart has an actual seizure. I just want to curl into a ball and cry, but I'm not sure I'm even capable of making tears at this point.

> Me: It's okay.

I type the words, and I want to send them. To pretend like I don't have the information I do. I just want to be fucking ignorant. But I'm not.

> Me: You're so lucky I'm nowhere near you because if I was I would make you choke on your own dick you cheating piece of shit.

Send. It almost makes me feel better. I almost smile. You know how they say that it takes more muscles to frown than smile? I don't know if that's true, but if it is then my face could be an Olympic athlete.

All I can do is stare angrily at my phone while my peers burn through their serotonin stores and force their livers through an obstacle course that would put *American Ninja Warrior* to shame. I want him to grovel and beg for my forgiveness, but I know he won't. He never does. And every single time, I say it's the last time. But the truth is that I'm just as much of a liar as he is.

CHAPTER THREE

HARPER

SO, I GUESS SOMETIMES I WONDER IF I ENDED IT ALL now would it be so bad? I mean I'm decently happy ... but I also know things could get a lot worse. Sounds kind of nice to just skip it all." I look up at my psychiatrist texting on his phone. He's old as fuck and if he squinted his eyes at the screen any more they'd be closed.

I stare at him blankly.

After a few seconds, he notes that I've stopped talking and pockets his phone, looking up at me. "Makes sense," he says, nodding his head like he didn't just ignore every word I said.

"Great," I say with a cheery smile.

"How is your writing going? Columbia University." He lets out a breath like he can't believe I got in either. "That's a big deal. Great school, Columbia."

"It's fine," I lie. I haven't written anything in months. Poetry used to be my outlet, but now my creativity has deserted me just like everything else.

"How do you feel on your medication?"

This ... this thing inside me began years ago when I started having panic attacks for no reason. Sometimes the anxiety would wake me up at night. Sometimes I wouldn't eat for days. I was fourteen. I didn't know what was happening to me. I thought I was sick. I guess in a way, I am.

Much to my mother's dismay, I started antidepressants three months ago. I'm pretty sure she's one of those people that doesn't believe in mental illness, but I've never been able to talk to her long enough to find out.

"Fan-fucking-tastic," I reply. I want to get out of here.

He frowns at my choice language and looks at his watch. I can see the relief etch itself in his features.

"Well, I'll see you next week."

I nod, grabbing my jacket sitting next to me on the couch, and leave his office. I read the three texts from my mom saying she's going to be late as usual. It's too stuffy in here, and if I didn't feel like killing myself before, the fake-ass smile the receptionist is giving me would do it.

Taking the elevator down, I step out into a lobby that looks like it's trying hard—and failing—to be some elite office space with a cheap fountain in the center and an empty concierge desk in one corner. The fountain isn't even running. It's just a pool of water collecting mold and dust.

I push my way out of the double doors and into the smothering heat.

Pulling my hair into a ponytail, I pace back and forth before deciding to call Noah.

"Hello?" she answers, sounding much more chipper than me.

"Hey, do you want to do something tonight?"

"Can't. I'm on my way to get an abortion and I'm usually pretty loopy after."

I nearly choke on my saliva. "You didn't tell me you were pregnant."

18

She makes a noncommittal noise and sighs. "Wouldn't be the first time. Anyway, tomorrow?"

"You sure you don't want me to come over after or anything?"

"Yeah, I'm sure. I'll just be asleep, anyway."

"Okay, tomorrow it is."

"Oh!" she yelps in excitement. "You should call Emma and see what she's up to. I heard Simon is having a party tonight, and it's going to be so fun. Dammit, now I'm jealous."

She's talking to me like she's not on the way to a life-changing event that would traumatize most people at best. I feel traumatized just thinking about it.

"Thanks, I'll do that."

"Love you!" she says before hanging up.

I stare at my blank phone screen. Sometimes I swear I'm on a different planet.

My mom pulls up in her white Mercedes Benz G-Class. I put my phone back in my purse and open the door. Cool air and the smell of mint waft around me as I climb into the passenger seat.

"Hurry, get in," my mother says through pursed lips.

She's classically beautiful, with daffodil hair and a rail thin pointed nose. I look literally nothing like her and it doesn't help my theory on not being from here.

"I'm getting in as fast as I can," I mumble.

She darts her eyes around like she's worried someone's going to see her. Oh wait, she's *actually* concerned about that.

"Mom, this is an undisclosed office building in the middle of Encino, and you are one of a million people who drive a Mercedes in this town. Do you really think someone is going to know you picked me up from a shrink?"

"I just don't understand why you insist on seeing him. Your father put you up to this, didn't he?"

Yes.

"No." I say with finality, hoping to end this very familiar conversation. It's bad enough I have to go with her to set up for a charity event she's throwing this weekend at the rec center.

She glances over at me, pulling down her sunglasses slightly, as if she can't believe what she's seeing through the lenses and needs non-tinted vision to tell her what I look like. She makes a noise of disappointment before speeding off.

"You're so pretty, Harper. Must you wear fifteen layers of eyeliner?" Backhanded compliments are her specialty. "And the black nails, really?"

I hold my palms up to myself and bend my fingers in to get a good look. I like the black. Yanking the sleeves of my shirt down to my wrist, I pray she stops her looking too closely.

My eighteenth birthday came and went without much hurrah. Well, I got blackout drunk and woke up next to a pool, but that's really par for the course. The only thing I did for myself was get a tattoo that twirls around my right forearm. My mother would probably keel over and send us hurtling into the canyon if she found out, but not before she took away my phone and my car.

Reaching into my bag, I pull out my eyeliner and layer another coat on top of the one I'm wearing. I smile at her, which earns me an eye roll.

"It's in right now," I say.

"It's trashy, is what it is. You'll take it off before the event tomorrow."

I want to say, *or what?* But I'm tired of arguing, so I just rest my head against the window, hot from the desert sun. The radio station is playing acoustic versions of pop songs and it's worse than someone water-boarding me while blasting Fallout Boy. I move to change the station and she slaps my hand out of the way, her perfectly manicured acrylics nearly slicing my finger off.

"I like this, and God knows you're only going to play that emo crap."

I don't know who taught her the word emo, but I'm too impressed to be upset. Stifling a laugh, I turn back to the exhilarating view of LA traffic.

Emma texts me while I'm in the car asking if I want to go to the party Noah told me about.

I reply yes and look at my mother. "I'm going to spend the night at Emma's tonight."

My mom turns to me and glares. She doesn't like my new friends. "Is her mother going to be home?"

I hate that she pretends like she cares what I do when she's gone six months out of the year and barely knows when I'm home. "I don't know," I say honestly.

"Well, why don't you guys do something at our house?"

"Fine," I give in, knowing that if we sneak out she'll be none the wiser.

I text Emma and let her know the change of plans.

The lull of the terrible Sirius XM radio eventually puts me to sleep. It's not until my mom slams on the brakes and my head careens into the dashboard that I wake up.

"We're here," she announces before getting out of the car and walking in without me.

I check my reflection in the mirror before stepping out, making sure my makeup hasn't smeared all over my face. It hasn't. Thankfully, it's just the same empty eyes staring back.

I SPEND THREE HOURS OF hell in the rec center, helping turn the sleek chrome and tan wood into a nineteen-twenties casino before we finally get to leave. Just when my faux-smile feels like it's sure to crack and my eyes can't stop themselves from rolling at the dull conversation, I'm in the car going home.

We don't speak the entire way. It's energy to force conversation and neither one of us has any to spare.

"Your sister would be ecstatic about tomorrow," she mutters as she pulls into the massive driveway.

"Maybe you should have flown her home then," I reply.

I don't care what my sister would or wouldn't have done. Everyone has made it abundantly clear that we're complete opposites. She's of the blonde hair, valedictorian variety. I'm the dark and demented little sister—the kind that watches true crime instead of MTV and sits in detention every other week.

Alina went to private school. I didn't get in. Alina has blue eyes. Mine are nearly black. Alina paints her nails pink and purple and shades of mauve. I bite mine until they bleed and then cover up the broken ends with black nail polish. If it's not obvious, we never got along, and when she went to college last year I saluted her goodbye. Happy to never have to deal with her friends who always looked me up and down with disgust. Fuck you, too.

"Don't think I didn't offer," my mother says.

"Well, sorry that you'll have to settle for me." I give her a sardonic smile.

"You could try," she says with a sigh.

"Try what?" I snap. "Try to be like Alina? I'd rather choke."

When will she learn that the harder she tries to fit me into a box, the more I'll fight? I'll file myself down until my outline is sharp and pointed. Until I shred the fucking cardboard and devour the pieces. I'll do it or I'll die trying.

"Spare me," she drawls and heads into the house.

I walk toward the yard, to my own back entrance. When I open it, the person standing inside makes my heart feel like it fell out of my ass.

"Hey, Bunny," Cole says.

I glare at him. "What are you doing here?"

To say I'm surprised is really underselling it. Cole is harder to catch in one place than fucking Sasquatch.

"You're not answering my calls."

My jaw nearly drops, but somehow I school indifference and cross my arms. "Why the fuck would I?"

"I didn't do anything wrong! You didn't even let me explain."

"I don't really want to hear your bullshit excuses. You think I don't know you're cheating on me?"

"I'm not! Okay … okay, maybe I *one time* hooked up with someone else, but that picture you saw was not me."

I can't believe my fucking ears. Is this an actual apology? The worst part is I think I'm actually considering accepting it.

Tell him to leave. But my mouth doesn't move.

"I'm sorry, Harper." He looks like a puppy dog. If a puppy dog was six feet, with a boyish grin, and perfectly tanned skin from summers by the beach. "I promise it won't ever happen again," he tells me.

His promises would be more useful if I could wipe my ass with them.

"Fine," I relent.

I know what we have isn't a real relationship. You know the kind that they write about in books and songs? The kind of relationship that helps you find yourself instead of losing everything you are. One filled with trust and respect. No, it's not that, but it'll do.

CHAPTER FOUR

HARPER

E MMA CHATS LOUDLY IN THE BATHROOM ABOUT something I haven't been paying attention to. Walking into my closet, she finds me sitting at the back in front of the mirror. Somehow, I've managed to put all of my makeup on without even realizing it. We look at each other through the glass reflection. My face is a golden pale color. But it's fake. The purple eyeshadow makes my already dark eyes look like black holes. I've layered my eyeliner so that it enhances the *don't fucking talk to me look* that peers out at people ... or so I hope. For the past five minutes, I've been staring at myself, trying to sort out how I ever got to be the creation looking back at me, but I'm coming up blank.

Emma groans. "Your hair is so pretty. I know you talk about dyeing it all the time, but this chocolate color is like *so* hard to get with dye. Don't fucking touch it. Promise me."

"What?" I blink at her through the mirror as she frowns.

"What's wrong?"

"Nothing, I just zoned out," I explain.

A knowing smile creeps onto her face. "Are you holding out on me?" She opens her hand, waiting for me to drop something into it. Drugs, I presume.

"I don't have anything," I say with a forced laugh. "Except this." I crane my body beyond its normal height and reach for the top shelf, pulling down a bottle of Grey Goose vodka.

Emma makes a show of licking her lips. "Gimme!"

Now seems as good a time as any to get wasted. I'm not driving, so I uncap the bottle and pour some of the contents into my mouth, relishing the burning sensation that runs through me and the nauseous heat that fills my gut. I haven't eaten all day, which we all know is a recipe for a magical night.

"Jeez, Harper. Share much?"

"You have to drive," I seethe as the vodka settles.

"Just a little," she begs.

I blink back the urge to vomit and breathe through my nose. Screwing the cap back on the bottle, I hand it to her and she promptly chugs half as much as me. Her normally curly brown hair is stick-straight, and she looks like a Maxim cover model in the tight, black dress she's wearing. It nearly shows off her entire ass when she walks, but I think that's the point.

"Fuck," she gasps. "Let's go!"

It's ten at night. We've let my parents know we'll be watching a movie in my room for the rest of the evening. I doubt they'll think twice about us again, so we tiptoe, heels in hand, out the back door and to Emma's car. When we drive out of the gate manned by the one and only Bert, I slink far down into my seat. With a giggle, Emma covers me with her jacket and waves enthusiastically to Bert as she leaves.

I pop from my hiding spot and laugh with her before digging through her glove compartment and finding some weed and a pipe. I pack the bowl and light it up, breathing in the earthy smell and savoring the way it makes my head feel light as a feather. When I pass it to her, she steers the car with her knees while taking a hit.

"Should we just go straight to Simon's house?" she asks, handing the pipe back to me.

I suck it hard, blowing smoke out the window as she races down the 101 freeway. If you've ever smoked weed, you know that the more you cough, the higher you feel. Don't ask me why. Science? As harsh air sputters from my mouth, my hypothesis is confirmed.

"Sure," I agree.

The lights from oncoming traffic blur in my vision; the mix of alcohol and weed in my system lets my mind wander into a familiar place where the pain of my existence doesn't feel so utterly bleak.

Go ahead, call me whiny and watch me not give a fuck.

"Do you ever feel like your life is meaningless?" The words come out slightly slurred as I drift in and out of reality.

Emma glances at me with a serious look. "Sometimes," she says quietly, turning the music down. "You alright?"

I shrug. "I'm fine, just ... having a hard time focusing on the future."

"Fuck the future," she says with emphasis.

I giggle even though her words aren't meant to make me laugh.

"Seriously, Harper. Fuck the future. Enjoy the now."

I don't have the energy to tell her that I'm not sure I remember how to enjoy anything anymore.

THE PARTY IS A RAGER worthy of the title. Mindless bodies dance to the loud bass and empty Solo cups roll into the pool. I've been offered and accepted cocaine thrice and music pumps through my veins like its own drug. There's even a chocolate waterfall with various fruits next to it, like we're at someone's wedding. I have not once, but six times, held my mouth under it while someone simultaneously drizzled vodka down my throat.

I haven't laughed this hard in weeks, but then again I can't even really remember the last ten minutes, let alone days ... so maybe that's wrong. As I sit on a pool lounger—giggling about God knows what to myself—someone sits down next to me.

"Something funny?" he asks, and his voice is all silky and sultry. He smells like weed and ... and ... I'm definitely going to vomit.

I run away from the stranger, but I don't make it very far, and puke in the bushes on the side of the house. With a pathetic groan, I wipe my lips with the back of my hand as the poison leaches its way out of my system. Who am I kidding though? All I am is poison.

The muffled sound of drums and singing grabs my attention. Lifting on my toes, I look through the window above my crouched position. A group of boys are playing instruments in the garage. I briefly wonder what it's like to feel happy without being numb before I yak up more liquid from my stomach. My head spins, but not in the way I enjoy, and the urge to lie down overwhelms me. I don't know where Emma is, and most of the attendants of this party don't go to my school. The ones who do are people I've only ever said hi to a few times.

In a blink, I'm stumbling through the house. I don't know how I got here, but I'm still alone and my head pounds like a bongo drum. I open up the door in front of me and someone screams, reeling back in the sheets as the guy on top of her falls to the side.

"Sorry," I mumble as I begin to back away before I notice who it is.

"Harper," Harper whispers ... wait, no ... I'm Harper. This is ... this is Emma.

"Fuck," Cole says as he scrambles up from the bed.

My brain takes a few seconds to gather what I'm seeing—my best friend fucking my boyfriend. Wait, is he my boyfriend? Yes, we definitely got back together ... right?

"Harper, wait!" Emma shouts.

I don't really know what she's talking about, but then I find myself in the hallway, clearly having left the room in a hurry. I stumble into a bathroom and glance in the mirror—onyx tears stream down my face, painting my reflection as some demon princess from another realm. I'm sad. This is sad. An onslaught of emotions pummels into me, and I fall next to the toilet, vomiting one more time.

I laugh into the bowl ... or maybe I'm crying. Crying and laughing. Laughing and crying. What can I say? I'm a Gemini.

"Harper!" Emma pounds on the door, but I at least had the sense to lock it.

"You can't come in here," I slur. "Pity party, party of one." I start laugh-crying again as the room undulates around me.

The grout in between the tile finds purchase under my nails as I curl into a ball on the floor. Someone screams. At first I think it's Emma and I silently tell her to shut up, but the shouting only gets louder ... more panicked, and something urges me to move. I rise from the floor and swallow my nausea as I walk into the hallway, the hurried yelling continuing from outside. Someone pushes past me so hard I have to grab the wall not to fall over. When I stumble into the back-yard, there's blood everywhere. Footsteps trailed in red, spots of crimson soaking into the terracotta tiles, dark black hues coloring the pool water.

Time slows as I look around and watch a group of strange men stabbing anyone who walks by. Is this actually happening? What is going on? I'm way too drunk for some fucking gang war.

"Harper!" A body slams into me and I scream in horror as time speeds back up. The voice belongs to a guy named Oliver in my AP Euro class. "Move!" he shouts.

When I don't respond, he grabs my hand and drags me from the yard. I clumsily follow behind him, catching the heels of his feet with the tips of my platforms every other step. He curses loudly, but I can't tell if it's aimed at me. "Do you have a ride?"

"No," I cry, remembering my best friend is a traitor.

"Fuck me, come on." He picks me up like a baby and runs down the sidewalk, the cacophony of panic fading into the distance.

"Did someone call 9-1-1?" I manage to say when he places me on the ground.

Sirens wail in the distance in answer.

"You need a ride home?" he asks me.

I nod sadly and then burst into tears.

"Jesus, stop. Please stop ... I don't ... everything is going to be fine." He pats my shoulder and opens the door to a white pickup truck.

It's not fine, but it'll do.

We get into the car and Emma's name, along with a picture of us sticking our tongues out, glows on my phone as it rings. I'm glad she's not dead, but I ignore the call. Like the gentleman he is, Oliver drives me home. I peer out at Bert when we get to the gate. He grimaces, and I slump into my seat. After thanking Oliver for saving my life, I hop out of the passenger seat and shut the door. His headlights sear big white circles into my vision as he reverses out of the driveway.

My head is trying to wrap itself around the events of the evening when I make the mistake of stumbling through the front door instead of sneaking around back. The security system announces my arrival in a monotone voice and within a few minutes, my mother is running wild-eyed into the foyer. She catches me trying to balance on one foot as I take off my heels. Her gaze doesn't catch on my sparkly, skin tight dress or the blood on my shoes. She doesn't care that there's vomit in my hair or that I reek of alcohol. No, her eyes zero in on the tattoo I have left open for the world to see on my right forearm. Like a viper, she yanks my arm and takes in the words.

The tattoo could be a beautiful image of us smiling at each other with the words "*I love my mommy*" etched in nice cursive. Or it could be a giant dick that says, "*suck me real good,*" in block letters. She wouldn't care which, so the symbol and words I actually got mean nothing to her and everything to me.

"What the hell, Harper?" she snaps, slapping me across the face.

I smile. The burn of her palm is nothing compared to the ravenous monster ripping chunks from my soul.

Her shocked face turns to horror. I hope I look like her worst nightmare.

"Leave me alone," I mutter, pushing past her.

"What are you doing with your life?" she shouts at me.

I spin, tip over, and catch myself on the entryway table. When I do, the giant mirror hanging on the wall above it displays the sad picture of me in its reflection. I'm so tired of it. I hate everything, from my stringy brown hair to my slutty dress to the black streaks down my cheeks. I hate the demon staring back, taunting me. Every day it reminds me of how worthless I am. How if I just disappeared, people would hardly notice.

"I don't know, I'm eighteen," I grumble.

"Better start figuring it out. You're throwing your life away," my mother screams. "A perfectly good life where everything has been handed to you on a silver fucking platter." If my mom is cussing, I know it's bad. "You've had every opportunity your sister has. I don't understand why you can't be more like her." As if me not being an exact replica of Alina is the greatest tragedy she'll ever know.

"I don't fucking know either. There's something wrong with me," I slam out.

"Guess so," she says with a shrug. "Get cleaned up. We'll talk about your punishment in the morning."

I snort. Feeling the tears on my skin, but not in my heart. I can't feel anything but searing hot anger. I'm not even mad at her. I'm mad at this creature I've become against my own will. I'm mad that it feels like there's nothing I can do about it. I'm drowning, fighting to swim to the surface. But when I look down, it's a smiling Harper gripping my ankle and pulling me into the abyss. There's no one to help. No one to listen. I'm all alone.

CHAPTER FIVE

HARPER

THE TWENTY-FOUR-HOUR TATTOO SHOP'S OPEN SIGN glows and I'm drawn to it like the light at the end of a tunnel. Once I slammed my bedroom door shut for the evening, I changed into sweats and a tank top before calling an Uber and showing up here. I'm still drunk and high and miserable, but there are a few things I have to take care of tonight.

I stumble into the bright lobby, and the girl behind the counter looks up from her magazine. She's pretty, with cropped black hair and purple contacts. Piercings line the curve of her ear and there isn't an inch of skin besides her face not covered in tattoos. I'm envious of her, despite knowing nothing about her life.

"Can I help you?" The pop of her bubblegum ricochets around the empty room, and I can almost taste the cherry flavor.

I tell her what I want, and if she notices I'm inebriated, she doesn't mention it. I could kiss her for that alone. After showing her my ID and filling out a few forms, we walk into the back and she gestures to a chair. A thin layer of paper covers it, and as I take off my bra and press my tits to the surface, a thrill runs through me. Thirty minutes pass as she inks the words into my skin; the burn of the needle rolling down my spine is the sweetest pain.

"Can I use the restroom?" I ask her.

"Sure," she says, covering up her unfinished work and pointing down the hall. "All the way back to your right."

Nodding, I lay an arm over my nipples. There's no one else here and I wouldn't care if there was, but it seems like the courteous thing to do. Pulling out my phone, I note a million missed calls from Cole and Emma. Fuck them.

I step into the bathroom and play the first message, cutting it off when both of their voices come in with apologies. The idea that they're still together makes me want to vomit all over again, but I know I have nothing left to give.

Have you ever felt so empty it hurts? The loss of yourself is a physical pain. Like you're trapped in a body that doesn't belong to you and every time you ask someone for help, they just scoff and turn the other way. I want help. I *need* help. But no one seems to care. To be honest, maybe I'm not screaming loud enough. Maybe this is all my fault ... *maybe* if I was stronger, I could fix it. But I'm not. I'm helpless and hopeless. I just want to close my eyes and never worry about anything ever again. How can I look forward to the future when I can't see myself in the now? I've blurred the lines of who I am too many times and I'm too damn weak to fight myself any longer.

Rifling through my purse, I stare at the bottle of antidepressants in my hands and laugh at how they've failed me. I laugh so hard that big crocodile tears roll down my cheeks, and I have to bend over to catch my breath. I laugh like a fucking maniac as the world crumbles into flakes of dust and ash.

When the giggles subside, I look at the bottle again, unscrew the top, and dump the contents into my mouth, rinsing the tiny failures down my throat with water from the faucet. I can feel the pills rolling together, clashing and clanking off their chalked exteriors as they fall into my gut, and for once I feel in control of something. For once, this train that's running a thousand miles an hour slows and I can get off. It's not freedom, but it'll do.

When I leave the bathroom, I still don't recognize the girl smiling back at me in the mirror. No matter how hard I try, she'll always be a fucking stranger. I throw her a little salute and leave the bathroom.

Bye, bitch.

The nice tattoo artist gets back to work, the needle a buzz in my mind as my head starts to spin. I feel sick and dizzy, but I close my eyes and tell myself it will only be a few more minutes. Just a few more moments and then I can endlessly dream.

"We're done," she says in a chipper voice.

I nod, but I don't move.

"Ma'am?" she asks, gently nudging my shoulder.

I can't feel anything, not even the cold numbness I've become so familiar with. It's fucking bliss.

"Excuse me?" She shakes me a little harder.

I blink my eyes and move to sit up, and then everything turns black.

"COME ON, SWEETIE," A VOICE yells way too fucking loud for my liking.

I lean over and vomit; it's bitter, burning along my throat like a cruel souvenir of my mistakes. Beeping and murmuring fill the void in my head as lights burn my retinas and the room spins.

I'm so done with spinning. I want something solid. An anchor. Nothing comes out of my mouth except a horrible sound indicating my stomach is empty. I spit and heave again.

"Sit up, sweetheart," the voice says again. I want to lunge and choke her, but I don't.

"Jesus fucking Christ." My body stiffens. I'd know my mother's voice anywhere. "What the fuck, Harper?"

"Ma'am, if you could please step outside, we need a little more quiet in this room."

"Like hell, I'll step outside. What did you do?" she sneers. I don't think I've ever heard her sound so mean.

The nurse nudges my focus to her, and the hospital room stops turning. I ignore my mother and look at the nurse, something like dread coiling inside me.

"Hey, honey. I need you to drink this for me." She hands me a paper cup filled to the brim with thick, black liquid. It spills down the edge, trailing the side like some demonic goo.

"What is it?" I croak, my throat sore from everything I've shoved down it and brought back up this evening.

"Charcoal. It's going to help make you feel better." Her voice is so calm that I nod, ease running through my racing heart.

"I asked you a question—"

The nice nurse snaps to my mother. "I will ask you to leave, ma'am. She's of legal age and doesn't need anyone in this room. Now please, be quiet so I can do my job."

I smirk weakly at the nurse. Not having the courage to tell my mother to get the fuck out.

"Unbelievable," she says before storming out.

"Ignore her," the nurse says with a smile.

"I mostly do," I say flatly.

She motions to the cup and I take a sip. It's so horrible, I immediately gag into my lap. The black liquid is sweet and bitter and chalky. Grit slides against my molars. I look up at her with horror and shake my head when she prompts me to drink more.

"Oh, honey. I never said it would be good. But the alternative is me shoving a big ol' tube down your throat and manually pumping your stomach. Trust me, this is better."

"Give me the tube," I demand.

She laughs. "Drink." It's a gentle command. When I take my first gulp I whimper and shake my head again. There's no way I'll be able to drink this and not vomit.

"I'll puke," I threaten.

The nurse gives me another warm smile. She's likely my mother's age, but instead of trying to hide it, she's embraced it. Nice nurse lady is all warm lines and soft eyes. Gray hairs and kind smiles. "Can I tell you a story about the time I got typhus?"

"What?" I stutter in surprise.

"Almost died," she says with a smile, like it's the funniest thing in the world. "Go on, for every sip I'll tell you more details."

For some reason, I'm very intrigued. I'm not even sure I know what typhus is, but I hold on to this woman's kindness like a life raft.

I take another agonizing sip and choke back my gag as she tells me her tale. When I'm done and my stomach has begged whatever God there is to please find it a home in someone else's body, the nurse smiles and congratulates me.

Woo-fucking-hoo. I failed at dying.

"The doctor will be in soon," she says and squeezes my hand.

My mother and the doctor show up before I can even think about what this all means. He's a lanky man with a nose too long for his face, and a mustache that looks like it belongs more to the cast of *Jersey Shore* than *Grey's Anatomy*. I can tell with the first sentence he speaks, he's in a rush. Quickly, he explains what we already know—I overdosed on my antidepressants.

No shit, I was there, dumbass.

My mother is shaking her head in the corner like she can't believe what she's hearing, but the proof is in the goddamn charcoal pudding.

"Was it an accident?" the doctor finally asks me and my mother snorts.

I don't blame her. What kind of question is that? *Yes, sir. I accidentally dumped the entire contents of the pill bottle into my mouth. Whoops, I was really hoping just one would come out.*

"Uh ..." is all I have to say. I'm embarrassed and confused. So fucking confused and even more tired.

My mother turns to me, fury burning a fire in her gaze. "You did this on purpose."

Well, duh.

"What?" I mutter.

"You did this on purpose," she repeats like I'm stupid. "You always want attention. What with the eyeliner and the nail polish and the drinking."

I laugh darkly. "Right, because lots of eyeliner is equivalent to trying to kill yourself. Better alert the media, doctor!" I wave my hands like I'm revealing a title. "Black eyeliner, the new gateway to mental illness."

The doctor looks back and forth at us uncomfortably. "I'll leave you two alone for a few minutes. We can discuss treatment options when I come back." He says options with so much implication I flinch. What kind of *options*?

I'm left alone with the dragon lady, smoke nearly coming from her nostrils. "You're going to get help. You want to play the depressed card so badly, then you're going to rehab."

"What?" I shout.

"I can't even look at you." She storms out of the hospital room, leaving the door wide open for people to peer and get a good look at me.

I want to scream into my pillow or use it to suffocate myself or something. Anything. But I'm too tired to move. So instead, I close my eyes and drift off to sleep.

WHEN I WAKE, THE ROOM is empty. The only light is an illuminated screen measuring my heart rate and rhythm. The sound of beeping machines is a twisted reminder that I'm still here. Still suffering. The consequence of my actions rears its ugly head, and the aftermath is so much worse than I ever anticipated. I feel spent, drained of any sense of joy, and the only solace I have is that I'm no longer drunk out of my mind. My one regret is that I'm still stuck. Those few moments where I thought I might drift into oblivion were some of the sweetest I've ever felt.

My mind is sick. I'm so entirely fucked up. Like whoever made me was just trying to leave early that day and left a bunch of things out.

Perhaps in their rush to complete the half-ass human that I am, they shoved pieces into places that didn't fit. Maybe I really do need to be checked in somewhere.

It's then that something orange in the hallway catches my eye. I turn to see a fox sitting in front of the nurses' station. A fucking fox. Black paws, orange body, big fluffy tail. My jaw drops and I'm ninety percent sure I'm hallucinating. But I've hallucinated before and this ... this feels real. No one else out there seems to notice. So, fifty-fifty chance I've lost it.

Fine, maybe seventy-thirty. I've never been good with statistics.

The fox twitches its little nose and looks me dead in the eye. Like it's daring me to come and get it, and fuck if I don't feel the urge to follow.

"What are you up to, little fox?" I murmur in my half-crazed stupor.

I stare down at my charcoal-stained hospital gown and unclip myself from the wires. Pulling the IV out of my arm with a sting, I watch, mesmerized, as blood drips down my arm for a few moments. When I glance back up, I expect my sanity to have returned and the mirage to have disappeared. Yet, it's still there, quirking its head to the side and pulling me in.

I stand and wobble, weak from everything that's happened in the last few hours. When I walk into the hallway, no one takes notice of me, and the fox hurries off, giving one final glance back as if to make sure I'm following. I am. Sneaking by the empty nurses' station, and grabbing a pair of hospital booties for my feet, I trudge onward, following the invisible paw prints of my new friend. The fox leads me through hallway after hallway and I question my motives several times, but I never stop.

This hospital is a typical hospital. If you've never been in one, the walls are white. In the rooms, they're blue. I read on a poster it's about creating a calming environment. I don't feel calm; I feel fucking insane. The tile floors are the kind that get really dirty in between the cracks, but not here. Here, they must mop them religiously because the crusty white material is barely colored. Beeps fade in and out to a haunted beat, but no one comes to stop me. No one pops out and says, *"Hey you, in the hospital gown, you should probably go back to your room."* So I don't. I follow the fox.

But soon, the fox is nowhere to be seen and instead of sighing with relief that this hallucination has passed, I feel sad. Overwhelming sadness that drowns me like a riptide. I rush down the last hall I saw it in, but nothing. Turning left and right, I note the hospital is empty in a creepy way, a chill running over my skin and sending goosebumps over its surface. I think in my periphery I see a rush of black, so I spin quickly and run in that direction. In this hallway, the walls aren't white. They seem to glow a purple hue, like a nightclub bar.

I should back away, but I don't.

I should start questioning *something*, but I just keep walking.

As I do, the walls seem to close in on me, and that's when I decide to run. When I turn around, I see something at my feet—a hole—and narrowly miss falling into it, stumbling to the side as my knees smack against the floor. My face scrunches in pain as I stare into a black abyss. This seems odd.

The perimeter of the hole isn't normal. It's not carefully carved from the tile. It's crumbling earth and mounds of dirt. The darkness reaches for me, but I don't back away. All I am is darkness.

Caressing the collapsing edges, I gasp as something warm toys with my fingers. I let it pull me in and wrap around me like a blanket. But as I do, it's not soft and comforting—it's the cool metal of chains. Binding and twisting my flesh. I try to scream, but no sound comes out. Air whips past me in a flurry, and I'm falling into nothing.

Part Two

ALL THE THINGS I LEFT TO FIND

CHAPTER SIX

ᴀTLAS

THE ROOM TILTS SLIGHTLY, AND I LAUGH. I'M NOT sure what about, but everyone else is laughing too. Maybe I said something funny? I do that on occasion. The sound in the room is muted as I stare at the wooden table, splintering and stained from Realm knows what. As soon as my vision clears, the noise comes back—loud and blaring. This place is packed as usual and I'm nearly drunk enough to walk over to the female who's been eye-fucking me all night and tell her to get down on her knees when Emery's face drops and I feel nails digging into my bicep.

"Are you kidding me right now?" Pippa leans in and spits the words into my ear. They're only loud enough for me to hear as she schools her face into a smile for everyone else.

I have to give her credit—no one knows how to charm a crowd like Pippa. Unfortunately, my cock is almost hard now from thinking about the brunette in the corner and I sure as shit am not going to stand and speak to my sister with a boner, so I peel each one of her dagger fingertips from my skin and glare back at her.

"So I did say something funny." Turning back around, I look down at the cards in my hand.

Nope. Too drunk to play.

Frowning, I meet Emery's gaze. He doesn't notice, too busy giving my sister puppy dog eyes. Traitorous piece of shit. Officially flaccid, I stand from the bench, not so subtly steadying myself against the table.

Pippa presses her fingers to her forehead and I wonder if that method actually helps her feel better. "You're wasted. That's just ... that's just great."

I feel the casual rise and fall of my shoulders. "I thought so."

"Atlas, we had our meeting this evening with ..." She looks around the room and then decides that a tavern possibly filled with our enemies isn't the best place for this conversation.

I remembered something about a meeting; I simply chose to come here instead. These days, I'm all about doing whatever the fuck I want. Being semi-responsible landed me with two dead parents and a civil war, so you know what? *Fuck it.*

Deeming me a lost cause, Pippa turns to Emery, who is about as pliable as a candy wrapper. I almost feel bad about bailing on her as I take in her attire. It's one of the nicer things I've seen her wear—a collared red top with black pants and all her knives wrapped neatly in a belt around her waist. She's wearing her typical gold earrings, pierced at the pointed tip of her right ear and then cascading down the slope. Her chestnut hair is shiny and curled nicer than it usually is. But it's our mother's emerald ring on her thumb that catches my eye and makes my chest ache.

Fuck this.

Ignoring me entirely, she lays into Emery, "Can you please sober him up and get him back to the house?"

His eyes dart back and forth between us, and if I didn't know him any better, I think he might piss himself having to pick sides. Isn't he used to this shit by now?

I give him the best mean look I have, but in the end his dick guides him, as I watch him take a split second look at her cleavage and then give me an apologetic grin. If I could vomit on command, I'd do it now just to spite him.

He pulls his blond, chin-length hair back into a bun, making the small black horns on his head more prominent, and furrows his brows at me. "Come on, dude, we were going to leave, anyway."

My sister rolls her eyes and walks out.

In all truth, I feel bad for him. He's had a crush on Pippa since we were kids, and she treats him like a little brother. Females and males flock to him like a fucking magnet, but he only has eyes for her. And as much as it makes me cringe, something about it is kind of sweet.

Not that I'd ever fucking say that out loud.

I take another look at corner-brunette—she has big eyes and even bigger tits. Nervously, she lifts her hand and wiggles her fingers at me in a wave. I groan as I indulge in the brief fantasy of having those fingers wrapped around me and then turn back to the task at hand.

Get home. Get sober.

Is it childish to whine and say, I don't want to? To drag my heels kicking and screaming? Probably. I pick up the dregs of ale in my mug and down them. Slip the dagger sitting on the table into its hiding spot on my back and throw my busty, brunette friend a sorrowful glance before following Emery out into the cold evening.

My fingers itch at the magic in my veins, and I look at my best friend. "Let's shift."

He shakes his head. "It's not safe."

"If I can't kill something in my derax form, then I'm dead anyway."

I know what he's concerned about though—whenever we shift *she* can sense it. But it's a big fucking world we live in, and that crazy bitch can't have spies literally everywhere. Or so I wish. The reality is she can, and she probably does.

"Honestly, I could go for a little sentinel snack." I waggle my eyebrows at him in an offer.

Emery chews his lip. I know the animal in him is caged and roaring, but he's fighting the wrath he'll receive from Pippa if she finds out we put ourselves in danger.

"Pippa won't know, Em." I cross my arms and give him my *don't be a little bitch* face. "You can't be whipped by a female who doesn't suck your cock. Them's the rules."

His eyes narrow into slits and he sticks his forked, black tongue out at me. Over a century of knowing each other and it still makes me smile. My heart does a leap of joy as he transforms into the beast he was born to be. Furry paws thud to the ground as his massive frame goes from male to animal—four legs and a feathery long tail. Just seeing him like this turns my fingers into claws and my vision changes to adapt to the night. He howls at me, and when I go to give him my rallying cry back, it's a roar instead.

Emery takes off without me, but the fucker knows I've always been faster. He might be bigger, but I've got the agility. The feeling that runs through me isn't describable. Words just wouldn't do it justice, but shit, I'll give it a go.

The earth beneath my four paws feels like it's molding to my whim. The wind as it blows through my coat is a song I can only listen to with these ears. It licks down my back and flutters under my legs, giving me the true taste of freedom. I can hear everything—the ravens cawing their goodnights, the Varrek working hard under the earth, the Kelpie in the sea hunting their prey. They're all my people, pretending for the evening that this world isn't utter chaos. Dirt buries itself under my talons and I crave more. I want to roll in the grass and sunbathe until my thick, black-spotted fur is hot to the touch. I want to climb and sit in the trees. But most of all, I want to crush something under my feet. To sink my teeth into muscle and bone. As if in response, the poison coating my canines drips onto my tongue. It's sweet and fruity to me, but will melt the flesh off anyone else.

I let out another roar that shakes the trees and sends sleeping birds scattering through the sky. Emery panting next to me gives me a look, his purple eyes gleaming in the moonlight, and I nearly fucking choke up. We haven't done this in months and it's all *wrong*. Before we get too close to home, I tackle him. Reining in the poison, I bite down on his neck playfully and pin him under my weight. His tail wraps around one of my hind limbs and drags me off until he's standing over me.

Emery's derax is the only one bigger than mine—the closest match to my power. He was born to battle me, to help me grow, and teach me manners. He didn't have to be, but he's my brother in every way except the blood that flows through our veins.

I'm about to show him why I'm the best when he whimpers and his ears tuck back behind the horns.

Fucking Pippa.

I can hear her storming out of the house even though it's a mile away. I shift back and nearly pass out at the overgrown monster-dog pinning me to the ground. Emery shoots me a look and whimpers again, moving off me and shifting so that he's kneeling in the dirt.

I look at him, trying to catch my breath. I can't listen to him whine about Pippa getting angry. But this fucker only smiles at me, the tips of his canines shining in the moonlight.

"Fucking worth it." He grins.

And I'm certain that even blood isn't stronger than our bond.

CHAPTER SEVEN

ARPER

I'M STILL FALLING, BUT I STOPPED SCREAMING WHAT SEEMS like hours ago. At some point, the free fall became natural and my panic ebbed. I'm pretty sure that's only because I'm dead and the last few hours in the hospital were just some nightmare segue to the afterlife.

Exit here for: What Could Have Been.

I've never believed in heaven or hell, but fuck, if they're real, it's pretty obvious where I'm headed. Whatever, maybe it's a blessing. Maybe I wouldn't get along with all the sneering little do-gooders up at the pearly gates. Is there somewhere in between? You know, for the people who didn't live life with a stick up their ass but also didn't drown puppies or whatever shit gets you a ticket to ride with the devil?

Who knows how much time passes ... days, weeks, months, years? The thought that maybe *this* is hell crosses my mind, and the panic is back. Am I forever doomed to be caught in a free fall? Never having a place to land. Forever trapped in the fear of what's to come. How fucking poetic would that be? I wanted control and instead I got a dark hole of oblivion. I lean my head back hoping to hit it against the dirt walls that fly past me and snap my neck, but it's as if the hole senses my desire for death and widens so that I can't reach the edges no matter how hard I try.

Yup. This is definitely a punishment. I guess I deserve it. Isn't suicide like the ultimate sin?

"Hey, God, it's me, Harper. I know we don't ever talk, but I just wanted to tell you to go fuck yourself. Thanks." It's not a prayer, but it'll do.

Suddenly, my velocity slows, and I start to float. Something is happening, and my heart flutters wildly in my chest. Like my soul, it's an animal in a cage. Every single part of me is ready to jump ship and I can hardly say I blame it.

It takes for-fucking-ever, but finally I land on a pile of colorful throw pillows. The fabric is silky soft and the colors are so bright it hurts to look at them. Orange and blue and purple and pink. It's like rainbow sherbet down here. I try to stand but it's futile; my legs wobble beneath my weight and I'm so dizzy. It's when I see that little fox that my eyes widen.

He? She? Whatever it is is staring at me like it's been waiting years to see me, excitement racking its tiny, little body in shivers. It gives into its urges and bounds over to me. I'm both horrified and in awe. It's adorable, but however long ago, it was running away from me like its life depended on it and *oh yeah, it's a fucking wild fox.*

But of course I embrace the little kisses and whines.

Wouldn't you? You're a fucking liar if you answered no.

Its furry body wiggles back and forth like a puppy. I realize I'm crying because I don't know what the hell is going on, but what else is new? Finally, I push the creature off of me, certain that it might lick me to death if I let it.

If I'm not already dead.

It gives me these pouty little eyes but obeys and sits down, staring at me. I take a look at my surroundings, noting that I'm in some underground chamber. The walls are dirt. They curve to form a dome and I'm at the center of the room with my pile of pillows. There's a hole at the top where light streams through, and it's actually pretty bright in here.

"Hello?" I call out, feeling like an idiot.

No one responds.

There are holes dispersed randomly within the walls. One is big enough for me to walk through and the others are too small, but seem to go on forever. My fox companion whines next to me like it's bored with waiting.

"What?" I level it with a serious look and then tilt my head to check if it's a boy or a girl. Boy.

He trots around the room, sniffing the ground, black feet bright against his orange fur. A strip of white starting from the bottom half of his muzzle and continuing to his belly makes it look like he laid his head and neck in a puddle of white paint. He's a fucking fox.

I blink and shake my head before pressing it into my hands and start scrubbing my face. And then, for good measure, I slap myself as hard as I can, but I'm not asleep. I'm still here ... in this fucking hole.

"Okay," I breathe, preparing myself to stand and find a way out of here.

I really have no other choice except to go with the flow. I suppose I could sit here forever and wait, but I've never been a patient person.

My second attempt at rising is a little better, but I'm glad no one is around to see me nearly eat shit. I look down and realize I'm still in a hospital gown, my bare ass exposed to the elements.

Great. Just great.

The dirt below my feet is soft. As I walk, I sink into it. It feels like a Tempur-Pedic mattress. I shiver and inspect my options for escape. Like I said, one path is big enough for me to walk through, seemingly the only way out of here.

I take a few steps forward until something gleaming in my periphery catches my eye. I swivel my head and walk to the opposite side of the chamber where there's another hole in the wall. Inside is a glass vial with a corked stopper and a cute little note tied with twine around the neck. The liquid inside is metallic-blue and shimmering. It looks viscous when I tilt and roll the vial around—mesmerizing in a way I can't describe. I turn the note over in my hand and read the elegant cursive writing.

The text is familiar and I reach into the confines of my memory and remember that story, *Alice in Wonderland*. I've never actually read it or seen the movie, but I run through the last few moments and an eerie feeling crawls over me.

What the fuck is happening?

Suddenly I'm frantic, running around and looking in every hole. Some of them contain items with simple commands written in the same beautiful cursive, and others do not. Some are up high and some are ground level. Some are big enough for me to crawl through, but still the only one big enough to stroll down is the same one I saw earlier.

My fox friend thinks this is a game as I pace back and forth and he nips at my heels excitedly. I pick him up—not really thinking that a wild fox will probably bite me—and squeeze hard enough for comfort and gentle enough so that his little eyeballs don't pop out. The contact helps as he nuzzles my neck and licks my cheek, enjoying the salty tears that don't seem to be stopping.

I'm so tired. I slump to the ground, the weird and soft dirt cupping my ass cheeks, and cradle the fox to my chest like a stuffed animal.

My head is light from the overdose and my stomach hurts from the hell I put it through. I don't know what I want, but I'm sick of feeling so helpless and afraid. I'm sick of being weak.

My mind runs in circles, but like a racetrack, the loop has the same scenery over and over again. I don't know if I've completely lost it, if I'm dead, or if I'm in some alternate reality, but it doesn't really matter, does it? I'm here, so I might as well make the most of it.

Sniffling and wiping the disgusting snot from my nose, I look at the vial in my palm. It both scares and thrills me at the same time. I consider my other options—some cake that calls to me from a hole across the room, a jar of jelly beans in one of the holes above my head, and I shit you not what looks like the Turkish delights from fucking *Narnia* on a silver platter staring me down.

"What do you think?" I ask the fox and briefly consider giving him a name, but don't in hopes of avoiding getting too attached.

Who the fuck am I kidding, though? I'm in love.

His plush, orange ears twitch in response, but surprise—he doesn't give me an answer.

"Guess it's up to me to decide," I say.

I look down at the vial again. I feel some sort of weird draw to it and I haven't let go of it this entire time. What if it's poison, though? I cackle at my brief fear of dying.

What a fucking joke.

Shrugging my shoulders and deciding I've never been one to turn down a challenge, I uncork the top and sniff the contents. It smells like the berry-flavored Cap'n Crunch and weirdly enough, my mouth waters. I stand, square my shoulders, and just as I'm about to tip the contents into the back of my throat, the fox whines at me. When I glance down at him, he's sitting perfectly and wiggling his little tail and butt. It's so fucking cute I think my cold, dead heart might actually be beating.

"I can't give you any. What if it's poison and you die too? I won't be a fox murderer," I tell him.

He growls like he's scolding me.

I sigh. "Fine, but don't say I didn't warn you. If you die, it's on your paws, not mine."

I've definitely lost it.

I consider giving it to this little fucker first, but decide that if I have to watch this adorable thing die, there's a one hundred percent chance I'll really lose my mind. So, I tilt the contents into the back of my throat and leave a few drops for him on the floor. It tastes like I took a whole bag of skittles and dropped them into my mouth, except the texture is that of a thin yogurt.

Delightful.

I don't have time to think about anything else as my body reacts to whatever is in this liquid. At first, it feels tingly, like right before you're about to start rolling and every nerve in your body sings in delight. But that feeling fades quickly and in its place is a dull throb that starts in my head and flows in waves down to my toes. It's dizzying, and I drop to my knees, certain I'm going to yak up whatever is in my stomach. And I do. Black, thick charcoal comes up in a puddle and I almost feel better before my head feels like someone is squeezing it with both hands and my vision blurs.

I don't even bother to see what my little fox friend is up to because I can't think of anything but the blinding agony piercing through every inch of my body. It's then I decide *this* is hell and I don't want to be here. I want to be anywhere else. Before I think I'm going to pass out from the pain, it vanishes. I don't have seconds to find relief because I can't breathe.

Everything around me is black, gritty, and viscous. I'm drowning, for real, and it tastes sickly sweet. I try to take in a breath, but there's no air; something heavy weighs me down. Memories of the hospital are coming back and I panic, thrashing around in whatever this is and realize I need to find a way up to the surface.

When I hit oxygen, slick black goo drips from my head as I doggy paddle to safety. The room is different now, it's huge. I don't know if it's the same room or if I've been transported elsewhere because anything is fucking possible at this point. When my feet hit solid ground, I push up and wade through the muck. And when I look around and see that it's the same room, just a giant version, I realize that I've shrunk.

I really am trapped in some weird *Alice in Wonderland* nightmare.

On all fours—naked, because my now giant hospital gown just tried to suffocate me in a river of my own vomit—I heave up the charcoal I've now swallowed twice and begin coughing up a lung. I'm pretty sure that if something else in this crazy fucking place doesn't kill me first, my impending pneumonia will. My long, brown hair is now heavy and black. It covers me like a curtain and drips soundlessly around me. The soft ground feels like it might swallow me whole, and I want to let it.

Instead, I scream. And I scream. And I scream until I'm coughing so hard I collapse. My mind is a blank slate of grief until the rough pad of a tongue pulls me back. When I open my eyes slowly, I see my little companion with his charcoal-coated fur and yellow eyes. Two pieces of my shredded heart seem to fit back together. It's not sanity, but it'll do.

"You didn't die," I manage, but my throat is raw as my voice cracks. He looks like he fared way better than I did.

Wiping the disgusting stomach contents off me to the best of my ability, I stand and try to figure out what's next.

CHAPTER EIGHT

ATLAS

I CAN'T BELIEVE YOU TWO!" PIPPA SCREAMS, SLAMMING the creaky wooden door in our faces.

The humor and bravery Emery had a few moments ago are gone. He's back to having his tail tucked between his legs. Not literally.

"Take care of this," Pippa sneers as I open the door.

She's holding one of her knives out to me and I'm pretty sure it's the dullest fucking one she owns. I have one sheathed to the small of my back, but I take hers instead. Emery sneaks around to my other side as I hold the door open with my foot and make a slice vertically down my arm, letting the blood pool into my cupped hand. I toss him the blade and he does the same, but drips his blood into my palm, too.

I mentioned we have a bond. Well, it goes beyond friendship and blood. It's powerful magic. I whisper three words to the warm fluid and drain nearly all the magic I have in my body to it. It hurts like a fucking bitch and I know that when it's over, I'll feel even worse.

The blood bubbles in my palm, scalding me, but I hold back a wince because I know all Pippa wants is to see me suffer for this. Not that I blame her.

Dipping two fingers in, I paint a symbol above the front door, and like a command, a blue aura bursts from my palm around the house and then disappears. It's a magical barrier effectively making us invisible to anyone who comes snooping around. It will only last twenty-four hours, but that's plenty of time for the queen's sentinels to find somewhere else to fuck off to. The blood is gone from my hand now and it feels like my soul has been chewed up and spit out in pieces.

I nearly fall over, but Emery catches me and lets me lean against him as we walk back to the couch. The magic drain mixed with the impending hangover is unreal. I'm not sure I've ever felt this crappy. At least, not physically.

"I can't even talk to you now, huh?" Pippa stands with her hands on her hips and stares daggers into my chest.

We weren't always like this. We used to be close. She used to be fun and not an uptight bitch, and I used to be ... well, I used to be better.

"I need to sleep," I mumble, my eyelids already drooping.

"Do you even care anymore?" I hear her ask before she slouches in one of the chairs.

I want to stand up and strangle her. All I do is fucking care. How does she not see that that's what's killing me?

It's still dark when I wake, and I wonder how long I've been asleep. You can't trust the sky. Not anymore.

"You're up," Emery says as he walks into the room.

"Up is a loose term," I mumble, not even bothering to lift my head from the couch pillow. This sofa is too small for me to be sleeping on. It barely seats two of us and my height is nearly double its length.

"Here," he says, handing me a glass of water.

I down it in one gulp.

"And here." He offers me his arm. The blue of his veins is faint under lightly tanned skin. "You need it. I've never seen you look like that."

"It was the alcohol," I lie ... sort of.

"It wasn't, and you know it." He shoves his wrist into my face. "Do it before I change my mind."

I'm not a fucking vampire, okay? But there's no faster way to replenish your magic than by taking someone else's. It used to be illegal, done only behind closed doors. But now that the world is on fire, people are murdering in the streets just to feel an ounce of extra magic.

"I'll be gentle," I say with a wink, and he rolls his eyes, looking away as my canines sink into his flesh.

Magic is life. It's what makes our hearts beat and our nerves thrum. We need it to survive and the only way to get it back is by stealing it from someone else or waiting for it to replenish. Replenishing your magic can take days—sure there are foods you can eat and potions you can take to enhance the process, but for someone like me ... that spell on the house wasn't something your average elf could accomplish.

I don't like drinking blood. Honestly, I find it kind of repulsive. Some people are into it, and I've heard that some species' taste better than others, but to me blood is fucking blood—it clots in your teeth and the thick, warm texture is not something I want to sip on. Shredding something to pieces in my derax form is one thing, but using Emery as a juice box is entirely different. Yet despite all that, my body is so deprived of magic that I need this like I need air, and I have to remind myself he's a living, breathing thing that I love, so I don't take it all. He grips my arm as his eyes widen, and I finally snap out of it, retracting my teeth and leaning back against the couch as he hobbles to the chair.

"Sorry," I begin to say, but he dismisses me with a headshake.

"Now we're both at half power," he says with a smile, but it's weak, and I feel like a shitbag for making him run with me last night. But being the good friend he is, he says, "Still worth it, Atlas."

I nod my head. I wholeheartedly agree and I wonder if shifting forms would be the thing Pippa needs to remove the stick from her ass.

My head feels clearer just in time for the onslaught that is my sister as she walks through the front door.

She's back in her typical leather riding attire: it's brown and matches her hair, which is pulled up into a ponytail. She glances at me and I see the relief on her face just seconds before the scowl forms.

"Miss me?"

"You think this is some kind of joke, Atlas, but it's not."

Now I remember. She accused me of not caring, and from her perspective, I can see why she'd think that. I haven't exactly stepped up to the plate since our parents died eighteen months ago. Our people need us more than ever, and I've been deep into either a mug of ale or someone's pussy every night. Often both.

Here's the thing. I know I need to help my sister. I hate seeing her like this and most of all, I'm tired of living in this fucking shack with all my rights stripped from me. Hiding like a fugitive when it's *my* throne that crazy ass bitch has taken over. But I just can't bring myself to do anything, and I'm a piece of shit who makes light of serious situations, so I don't tell her any of that.

Instead, I ask, "Do you think shifting would help you get that stick out of your ass? Because if so, I'd gladly drain myself again to help you."

"Unbelievable," she mutters and storms out.

Emery shoots me a look that sums up what I already know—I'm an asshole.

CHAPTER NINE

HARPER

I SPEND SEVERAL MORE MINUTES SCREAMING. NAKED. IN an underground chamber. Potentially in hell, but most definitely not on planet Earth. What a day.

This may surprise you, but standing here and blowing my vocal cords out doesn't really do much besides make me feel like I've just finished a dick sucking marathon. I'd win that for sure, by the way.

Chest heaving, skin flushed, I pick a tunnel at random and trudge forward. The charcoal drying over my body is causing my thighs to chafe and my skin to feel tight. The hot air makes me feel like I never left LA, but my nipples still harden as a light breeze drifts by, tickling me.

Orange orbs float around me, illuminating the dirt walls and the path forward. They look like fireflies, but this is something different—something magical. I can barely see my four-legged friend trotting beside me, but I know he's there. His presence is like a balm on my cracked and withering soul.

We walk like that for a while—me calming my breathing, my fox friend silently following and occasionally rubbing the tip of his poofy tail against my leg. Almost as if he's reminding me that I'm not alone.

Eventually, the tunnel widens into another massive underground room. This one is much smaller in diameter, but the ceiling is still several stories high. Three massive, closed wooden doors line the left wall. I can barely make out any of their details as I stare up at them. The door handles are far out of reach and I wonder if the normal sized version of me could have opened one.

On the other side of the room is a big, brown leather chest with gilded reinforcements and a shining lock clasp. Painted on the surface of the chest is a mural featuring different creatures. Some have horns, others are half-animal, half-human, mermaid creatures, vampires, and wolves. The paintings are larger than me, but small enough that it feels like I'm in the scene with them. It's not a violent scene, quite the opposite. They bask in the sun and play in a river. Some sleep under thick, branching trees. There's something tranquil about it and I get lost staring at every detail until my fox companion lets out a little yip.

He's dancing next to another hole, this one also containing a small glass vial. I glance around the room and look for another way. Drowning in my own vomit wasn't on my list of things to do before I die, and I certainly don't want to do it twice. Unfortunately, there isn't anything else around, not a single crevice to be seen.

With a sigh, I walk over and pick the vial up. This time it's not filled with liquid but a fine pink powder. The note attached to it is just a winky face and my brow furrows as I unscrew the top and find a small spoon attached to the cap. I think you can guess where this is going. I bark a laugh at the sick twist of fate before scooping a small spoonful and showing it to my fox.

"Can you believe—" I start, not thinking that he's naturally going to sniff it.

After he does, he sneezes violently, and then shoots into the air on a blast of wind. My heart shudders, but mid-jump, he turns into a normal sized fox and dances around happily. I dodge between his giant paws—avoiding death by toe beans—and snort a spoonful of powder.

Unlike shrinking, growing back to a normal size is exhilarating. I feel like I've jumped on the world's bounciest trampoline and I'm never coming down. But gravity exists here and my skin tingles before I thump my ass onto the dirt floor.

Now that I can see the doors, my eyes catch on two words written above them in an arching pattern.

Choose wisely.

I nibble on my lower lip and contemplate what that could possibly mean, but come up short. I check for anything else in the room, but it looks like it's just me, the fox, the doors, and a big leather chest. Walking over to it, I open it cautiously, but when nothing jumps out at me, I let the lid fall back with a thud. Inside, a dozen clear plastic packages are stacked on top of each other.

I zip one open and pull out a faux leather outfit. It's giving me slutty Catwoman vibes, and I'm not surprised when a pair of fuzzy ears fall out as I unfold the clothes. It looks like it would fit me, but the idea of pleather riding me indefinitely has me looking at my other options.

The next one has super ugly khaki pants and a red polo shirt. It comes complete with a train conductor hat and suspenders. No, thank you.

A grin lights my face as I pull out a flowery blue dress from the bag. It has a white doily on the front and long, white socks just like Alice's outfit in *Alice in Wonderland*. What the fuck is this? Some weird sex fantasy fetish chest?

The next bag is thick and heavy. The material inside is purple and I nearly lose my eyes in the back of my head as I pull out a fucking Teletubby costume. It would be funny if ... okay, fine, it's kind of funny.

Catwoman is looking pretty good as the next few bags ultimately disappoint me. My second choice is the one containing pasties, edible underwear, and a long furry tail. Someone has a sick sense of humor, and it's not lost on me that these are all exactly my size. It's as if this nightmare was made for me or maybe ... I was made for *it*.

The next one is the winner though, thank fuck. It's just a nor-mal pair of black leggings, a white crop top, and a gray hoodie. I'm definitely going to get it dirty with the charcoal stained on my body, but oh well. Hopefully washing machines are a thing wherever I'm going. I slip on the underwear, the sports bra, dusting dirt off as I go. I'm not going to win *America's Next Top Model* or anything, but it'll do.

After putting on the rest of my outfit, the other packages literally poof into thin air. I squeal when that happens, for obvious reasons. Peering into the chest, I see a pair of black, lace-up combat boots and soft socks. After slipping those on, I take one more look before closing it, finding a small sheet of lined paper stuck to the bottom. A poem is scrawled in the handwriting of someone who looks like they just learned how to write full sentences:

> A choice of three, a world of dreams
>
> Look closely, all is as it seems
>
> A broken heart, a promise made
>
> A bloodied, poison-coated blade
>
> What you do lack, I can give back through nights that turn to days
>
> But time counts down, around and 'round: don't let it go to waste

Cute poem. Shrugging my shoulders, I crumple the note and toss it back into the chest, but when I do, a pocket watch appears. The gold timepiece is definitely not my style, but I can't help but pick it up. I mean it—I really can't help it. It's like my hand is forced to it by some strange energy. Engraved into the metal is a fox surrounded by flowers and I snort a laugh so hard that pink powder drips down the back of my throat. The clock face inside is navy blue and the silver numbers counting to twelve shimmer, reminding me of stars. I stare at it, but the minute hand never moves. Giving it a good shake—because that always fixes things—I hold it up to my ear. No ticking. I should just drop it back in the chest, but I *can't*. So I hang it around my neck and turn back to the doors.

Choose wisely.

Those words mock me. Today has been filled with choices, hasn't it? Live or die. Fight or give in. Blue glass vial or Turkish delights. Somehow it doesn't feel like I've been in charge of picking a single one, though. I look down at the fox, who has become rather bored by my fashion show, and looks up at me with lazy eyes.

"I guess I should probably name you, shouldn't I?"

Another choice.

"Pants." I'm not sure why I pick it, but maybe it's because I've spent the last few hours wishing I had some.

It's such a simple need that I've taken for granted. As I look down at my goo-covered hands, I realize that maybe I've taken a lot for granted. But fuck if I'm going to have some great epiphany right here in an underground room with a fox.

Pick one, Harper. Just fucking pick.

Reaching out for the middle handle, a feeling of sadness washes over me, and I change my mind about being impulsive. Rocking back and forth on my feet, I try to decide which door to select. I assume I only have one shot at this. Choose wisely, right? What the fuck could be on the other side?

I go for the left door, but when I touch the handle, it burns. I snap my hand back and cradle it against my chest. The feeling fades and I go for the right one instead. Right it is. It's not confidence, but it'll do.

Before I can grab it, I feel something ominous in my chest. It's like when you flip a coin and mid-flight you know what decision you really want. It's a cocktail of disappointment and fear with a cherry of desire on top. I want the left door so badly. Maybe it's because it hurt me and that seems to be an aphrodisiac for me.

Fine, it's the left door for me. There's no other option in my mind. I'll burn my whole body just so I can walk through that door. Seems insane, right?

I've given in to the madness.

This isn't just a door. You know it, I know it, Pants knows it. Alright, maybe Pants doesn't know much about doors or life-altering decisions or *Alice in Wonderland* nightmares.

Bracing myself for the pain, I reach out—closing my eyes like if I can't see it, maybe it won't hurt as bad. My hand reaches for the metal and I don't feel anything except its cool, smooth surface. I turn the knob and step out with Pants on my heels.

CHAPTER TEN

ATLAS

THE DOOR SWINGS SHUT AS EMERY FOLLOWS PIPPA out, and I'm alone in this fucking house. I feel like a half-shelled version of myself, but it's better than when I woke up. My surroundings are bleak. I know we didn't all grow up in a big, fancy castle, but even I know this is beyond squalor. The scaffolding of the building is wood and no one even bothered to paint the inside. So it's just cheap, shitty wood as far as the eye can see. Like we're in some cabin in the forest ... which I guess technically we are. The couch I'm sitting on is tan and worn. Part of me wonders if it was once white. I immediately stand up and walk to the kitchen only a few steps away.

The only demarcation separating the rooms is the furniture in them. Two chairs and a couch around a shitty—you guessed it—wooden tea table. There's a single side-table with a lamp that fills the room with dim, yellow light. It's ugly, with bronze Kelpies swimming around a reef. The artist captured their beautiful faces and sharp teeth well enough, but little, clear plastic crystals hang from the lampshade. It's an attempt to look regal, but all it does is cast the light into cheap rainbow shadows on the walls.

The floor is carpet. It's hideous and brown and I never want to think of what it originally looked like. And it's fucking everywhere except the kitchen—even the bathroom. I swear it's the one thing Pippa hates most about our situation. Personally, I think it makes a nice mat when I step out of the shower.

I pour myself another glass of water from the faucet, sipping from it as I lean forward on my elbows against the L-shaped counter. A bleak, obsidian sky peers at me through the window directly across the kitchen and as I look over, I see a rose sitting on the dining room table. From first glance, it just looks like a regular rose, but it wasn't there yesterday and my heart speeds up as I walk toward it. I approach the table like it might explode if I get too close, noticing a note next to the single flower.

This is not a normal rose. It's white, but appears to have been dipped in a dark red paint. Globs of it are dried where it dripped down slowly. But it's not paint, it's blood. I can tell by the color, by the smell. Immediately, I crush it in my palm, letting the thorny stem poke holes into my flesh before setting it aflame. The rose burns into a deep red, blisters forming on my skin as I melt with it. I don't feel anything. A warning growl rumbles involuntarily in my chest as I read the note.

Time is almost up.

Dread coils inside me like the venomous beast it is. I want to scream and throw the table against the wall, but I know my own strength and the last thing I need is a gaping hole in the house.

This is my fucking fault.

Sinking into the chair in front of me, I cup my face in my hands, which have already healed. A few thoughts cross my mind as I grit my teeth and hold my position in the chair. I don't want to do it. But I have to. It's time to grow up and stop being such a little brat.

When I stand, it's with renewed purpose and, if I'm being honest, a little bit of fear. It's easy to be the party boy who drinks and fucks girls like it's his job. You know what else? It's fun. But now this bitch knows where we are. My sister is in trouble, *Emery* is in trouble, and I'm nothing if I don't protect the only two people in this world who truly care about me. And why they still care about me is beyond even my imagination.

Sifting through the memories of the last few months in my mind makes me wince. All the arguments and rude comments. It's like a montage of Pippa looking sad, flash to golden liquid contents sitting in a mug, flash to some random girl bouncing up and down on my dick, flash to me punching Emery in the arm, flash to passing out on that disgusting couch. Yell, fuck, rinse, repeat.

I hate myself more every day. No one knows what the last eighteen months have been like for me. No one knows what happened the night everyone died. But only a child wallows in their shit for this long and the more I sit here thinking about it, the more ashamed I become. I take another look at the note and light that on fire too, watching it burn to ash in my hand.

When I'm sure not a trace of her is left, I go into my bedroom and stare at the king bed that takes up the entirety of the room. It's got these fucking flowered sheets on it that make me so damn itchy I wish I could sleep in my derax form just to avoid touching them with my skin. In the corner of the room is a grate, and I squeeze through the space between the bed and the wall to get to it.

Kneeling, I gently pull to remove the covering before sticking my hand in and grabbing what I'm looking for. The metal buzzes with magic like an electrical current. It almost hurts to touch it, but I open my palm and stare down at the gold pocket watch. Engraved into the metal is my family's crest, and just looking at it makes me feel like the biggest coward alive. It's beautiful—a crown with a sword through the center and a raven perched on the hilt. The gold gleams like it hasn't been sitting in an air duct for over a year, and I can see my reflection magnified in its image. When I click it open, the face is typical except the numbers are bright red and glowing. I know they don't stand for minutes and hours, but weeks and months. The hour hand sits at the number six, taunting me.

I was only given two years. Do you know how long that is for someone whose lifespan is half a millennium? It's a fucking blink. One wipe of my ass. I got two years to complete this task and save everything I've ever loved, and what have I been doing instead? Hiding here in my vices. You might be asking yourself a few questions:

Two years for what? I'm not going to answer that. That's another story for another time.

Fine. If you had two years, why have you wasted nearly all of it? Well, fucker, there's a simple reason for that. Because I did. Because my parents died and it was all my fault. Because I fucked up ... bad. Because I never claimed to be a hero, but here I am needing to be one anyway.

It's a shame too. I'm probably going to fail, but I might as well give it a shot.

And better late than never, right?

CHAPTER ELEVEN

S A CHILD, I LOVED WATCHING MIYAZAKI FILMS FOR the scenery alone—emerald rolling hills, sunshine you could nearly taste, cottages with flowers growing out of the shingles. That's what I see when I step through a group of soft, parting hedges. It's not what I was expecting, but it'll do.

A huge river glitters in the sun to my right and a dense forest with ominous trees stands proudly, miles away. A couple of mountain ranges pepper the skyline, and one massive tree stands out against the backdrop. It looks like a baobab tree with a thick, light pink trunk that towers to the clouds, and a flat, bare top of branches and shrubby leaves.

Pants runs ahead of me, sniffing the air and grass. Everything is crisp and new, like when you're camping and that first step out of the tent in the morning brings you a rush of joy. My senses are assaulted, but this time, I will not be pressing charges. If only I didn't feel the need to shower as soon as possible, I'd love to explore. I'm debating jumping into the slow-moving river when I spot a lone cottage in the distance. It's surrounded by a small farm, and my chest tightens at the thought of having to interact with people. I don't know where I am or if I'm even alive.

Maybe I did *a lot* of acid. These days, you never know.

I run through my options: stand here and wait for someone to find me or pick my jaw off the floor and continue on. It's not that my heart doesn't feel hollow, it does, but only one choice seems obvious to me.

I head toward the cottage, a small chill running across my arms as wind circles around me. Staring up at the cloudless sky, I note the sun hanging directly overhead probably means it's mid-day. And then, like my thoughts triggered a light switch, it's dark. Pitch black. Nighttime. No dusk, no sunset, nothing. The eeriest thing is that when I look back up at the sky, there are no stars despite the lack of light pollution. The moon perches brightly against the black velvet, but it's all alone.

I knew I wasn't anywhere normal, but this only solidifies the thought, as shivers rack my body from both fear and sudden cold. Pulling the hood of my sweatshirt over my head, I tuck my hands into my sleeves and try to conserve heat.

The moonlight guides me, barely, as I pick up my pace toward the cottage that now glows in the dark. A wolf howls in the distance, and I try to run a tiny bit faster. I can't see Pants, but I hope he's following.

Rushing to the front door, I take in the simple design of the house with its worn, wood porch and the twisting vines that wrap around the structure. I knock on the door, not prepared at all for what awaits me.

Definitely not prepared for what I see as the door swings open a few minutes later. It's not a human. Close, but so very, very different. We both exchange a look of surprise that has silence filling the space. I think this thing is ... part human and part deer. The face of a man with the exception of a nose that turns down at the tip. Cute, floppy deer ears and beautiful antlers sprout out of their head. Everything from the neck down appears to be like a regular guy. Even his clothes are modern. I fight the urge to run away screaming.

"Can I ... Can I help you?" It's definitely English he's speaking, so that's good at least. His voice doesn't sound timid, but confused.

I don't really know what to say. I need so much help, I don't even know where to begin. The list of questions in my head has grown so long it's overwhelming. So I just say, "Where am I?"

The deer-creature furrows his brow and looks around outside like he's waiting for Ashton Kutcher to come yell, "*Punk'd*!" But, I feel confident that this isn't a world Ashton Kutcher exists in. The home behind him is warm; I can see a fire burning and feel the heat seeping out like tendrils of smoke. He catches me eyeing things and smiles.

It's not the kind of smile that puts me at ease. His gleaming white teeth are so bright my breath catches. Canines sharpened into points tell me that evolution has made him a predator.

"You're lost?" he asks.

The voice in the back of my head tells me to lie, but I don't see that getting me very far. "Yes," I reply.

"Who is it?" a voice calls from inside before walking up to join him.

It's the same kind of creature, but this one has long, pretty blonde hair and feminine features. When she smiles, my body has the same sphincter-tightening response. I'm frozen ... a deer in headlights, if you will. Should I run? Who knows when the next civilization will be and I'm so cold and hungry.

Run. Run away, fast.

Instead, I stay put. I've never been known for my sound decision-making skills.

"Come in, dear," the deer-woman says, and normally I'd laugh, but I'm too close to shitting my pants.

The couple steps back, allowing me into their home as I steel my nerves and waltz in with false confidence. Fake it 'til you make it, right? I'll just have a shower and get the fuck out. Eating might be nice too, unless they're having human babies for dinner or something.

"I'm Sora and this is Ren," the deer-woman says, and I start to wonder if maybe I'm overreacting. They seem perfectly nice.

The door clicks closed and unease snakes through me. "Nice to meet you, I'm Harper."

I hold out my hand, but they both look down at it and then back at each other with confusion.

"Just a custom where I'm from," I explain.

"Please, sit," Ren says, motioning at a dining room table. Tufts of white fur sprout from the neckline of his navy blue crewneck.

"Thank you," I murmur, taking a seat.

No one seems to have noticed Pants until now. Sora glances at him trailing behind me. "Who is this?"

"This is Pants."

"Fantastic," Ren replies with an unhinged sort of excitement.

I bite my lower lip, unsure of how much I want to divulge about our situation. When I remove the hood of my sweatshirt, the air thickens.

"What?" I ask immediately as I watch their eyes widen. "Did I do something? I'm not from here so—"

"Clearly." Sora removes her hand from her mouth and reaches out toward my head.

Maybe they're confused because I don't have antlers ... or floppy ears. I take a step back, avoiding her intrusive touch, and that seems to snap her out of it.

"Sorry," she replies with a gentle shake of her head. "You must be hungry from your travels. And ..." She tilts her head, seeming to take me in for the first time. "In need of a bath?"

With my head, I make a slow nod in agreement. "That would be great. I don't have any money, but I'm happy to—"

Happy to what, Harper? You have no skills. Well, that's not entirely true. I'm really good at sucking—

"Nonsense. Repayment for our kindness isn't necessary," the male one says, holding up a hand as if I've offended him.

"This way." Sora gestures down the hall and I follow.

The house is quaint and *feels* human. The walls are lined with photos of the couple at various stages in life, like they've been friends for a long time ... or maybe they're siblings. I try not to stare too long at anything in case it's rude.

"Here we are." Sora stops in front of a small bathroom with white tile in the shape of flowers and pastel-painted walls. There's a claw-foot tub with a wrap around shower curtain in the back of the room. "There's a towel under the sink," she says, motioning to the cupboard to my left.

I nudge Pants into the bathroom, not willing to leave him out here alone, and she takes notice.

"Your friend can stay out here," she says with that creepy smile.

"He needs a bath too," I lie before shutting the door in her face in hopes she won't ask any more questions.

It works.

As I start to lift my shirt, it's not lost on me how vulnerable of a position I'm putting myself in by taking a shower here. Honestly, though, I'm willing to risk death if it means I'll be clean when it happens.

Starting up the shower sets off another million questions in my mind. What if this water is toxic? What if it turns me into one of them? What if my skin melts off? What if the temperature of the water is ten-thousand degrees? Or maybe hot water doesn't even exist here ... all bets are off. I have no clue what kind of place I've found myself in, but we're certainly not in fucking Kansas.

Sniffing the water and running my fingers under it tentatively reveals no concerns, so I drop all pretense, strip, and hop in. It feels *so* good. Not in a magical sort of way, just in an *I've been covered in my own vomit and haven't showered in a day* kind of way.

The water turns black from the charcoal dried in my hair. I look around to see my options for soap and find myself staring at an assortment of glass and plastic bottles. They're filled with colorful contents and the labels nearly make me double over.

One container of soap is called Dr. Faunner. It smells amazing, so I rub it all over my body. The scent of raspberries and something floral mix with the steam as it seeps into my pores. Another black bottle has a label with a shirtless, muscled deer-guy on it and the words, *Buck*

Wild, written in script that appears to drip. It smells like Axe body spray, and I wrinkle my nose as I close the cap.

The containers that appear to be shampoo and conditioner are from a line of products called Rein or Shine. They lather into my hair and soothe my senses. By the time I'm done, I feel infinitely better, trying not to let the strangeness of my predicament freak me out too much.

Being the nosey bitch I am, I towel off and look through the contents of their drawers. It's the usual stuff you'd find in a bathroom—extra toilet paper, loofahs, abnormally long Q-tips, and a bag of makeup. I stop after I find a container of something thick and goopy called *Buck Wax*, dropping it back in the drawer with disgust.

When I open the door, there is calming instrumental music playing, and I feel like maybe this is going to be fine. Sora and Ren can explain to me where I am and what's going on.

I walk back into the combination living-dining room as they look up and smile at me, having been discussing something quietly before I came in. I return the friendly gesture and take a seat.

"Seriously, thank you so much. I really appreciate that," I say.

"Of course," Ren says as he stands from his seat. I watch him wearily, but try to relax. "Can we get you a drink?"

Chill, Harper. He just got up to get a drink. If they wanted you dead, you would be.

What I really want is a shot of tequila and a fucking line, but I'm not sure what my options are, so I just shake my head and smile. "So, I know that this might seem ridiculous, but I'm not from here ... like not even from this planet."

Sora frowns and tilts her head, her floppy ears perking slightly. "Planet?"

I bite my lip. We speak the same language, but how am I supposed to communicate when I know nothing about their world? I try a different tactic. "Where are we?"

"What do you mean?" Ren asks, and I try not to follow him with my gaze as he walks behind me toward the kitchen.

Stay calm. They're not going to kill you.

"Well ... do you live in a town? A province? A country? What is this place?"

Sora laughs, and it's the most bone-chilling sound you can imagine.

Pants whimpers and I turn my head to see where Ren is standing, but it's too late. His massive hands pin me to the chair as he sinks his teeth into my neck. I scream, the pain—sharp and blinding—surging through my body. My eyes flutter as blackness clouds my vision and Sora's eyes light up in a way that twists my gut. The smell of blood coats the room and her teeth elongate before my eyes. I'm trying to fight off Ren, but my body is weak ... it's giving in to whatever power this is, and he's strong. Like freakishly strong.

Pants's barks and yelps start to sound farther away as blood loss grips me in its whirlpool and my body becomes limp. Vampire deer-people? Are you shitting me?

Then suddenly, Ren's hold relaxes as he makes a choking noise. Sora's eyes widen with fear, making me believe things may not be going as planned. I try to turn and gauge the situation, but my neck feels like it's suffering through the most intense whiplash.

"Ren!" she shouts, rushing to his aid as he collapses on the floor.

Move, Harper! Fucking move!

But I can't. I look over at them and watch his body convulse as my blood pools from his mouth and his eyes roll around like scattered marbles in his head. He suddenly becomes very still, pupils fixed and dilated.

"What the fuck did you do to him?" she snarls at me. Like it's my fault he tried to drink my blood and then died from it.

My body finally realizes what's happening, and when I go to move, she lunges at me. Her full weight knocks me down and pins me to the floor as I gasp. I don't have any thoughts in this moment. My body is on fire and my mind is trying desperately to make sense of a world that doesn't fit into anything I've ever known.

Sora sinks her teeth into the other side of my neck as I go rigid. My eyes close, fear flooding through me. I'm going to die here. Isn't that what I wanted, though? Didn't I want it all to stop? Apparently not, because I'm still struggling; my subconscious is fighting for any chance to live. Quickly, her grip loosens, and she topples over, gasping and grabbing for me as I scramble back. She stills within seconds.

My heart has never beat so hard in its useless, little life. I take a second to catch my breath. Pants is laying on the floor, completely still. I crawl over to him, tears running down my cheeks. I suddenly don't care about anything except to make sure my little friend is alive.

When I stroke my hand through his plush fur, his eyes stutter open and I let out a gasp of relief as he rolls over and nuzzles into my hand. I try to stand, but I'm too weak. The daylight flooding through the windows muddles my thoughts even further. I'm not sure how much time has passed. I'm not sure of anything anymore.

Carefully crawling over to my attackers, I check for a pulse in the same place I'd check on a human. I'm ninety-nine percent sure they're dead. Stumbling back against the wall, I bring my knees to my chest. I don't have energy to do anything else as I lie down and press my tear-stained cheeks to the wood floor. I close my eyes, trying to push away the images that are seared to my eyelids as sleep—dark and heavy—pulls me in.

CHAPTER TWELVE

ATLAS

THREE DAYS UNTIL THE PARTY

Moonlight hair clings to her body like tendrils, snaking down her breasts and making her pale skin look even more luminous. My cock is railing her so hard that her head keeps hitting the glass shower walls and I'm mildly concerned her horns might crack it. She doesn't care though, as I drive both of us to the brink of ecstasy.

"Fuck, Atlas," she moans. The sound is amplified in the confines of the shower, making her screams of pleasure slam through my mind and body. It's a fucking dream.

I grip her ankle, straightening her leg so that it's propped up against my chest as her other one barely holds her weight. When I look down to watch my length slide in and out of her as she crumbles beneath my hands, it's enough to finish me.

I brush my thumb over her clit and curses bubble from her lips, her body trembling beneath my touch. She tightens around my dick and we both come together. She's so beautiful like this, and I vow to find a way to make it so that our lives can be overflowing with moments like these.

Letting out a breathy laugh, she closes her eyes as I place her leg back down on the slick shower floor and steady her as she regains her balance. When her emerald pools open up, she looks at me with an adoration I feel like I've been searching for my whole life.

"I love you," I say, and it startles me. I've never said that to anyone before and I guess if I really consider it, it feels right ... I think.

The gleam in her eyes brightens, and she lunges into my arms, kissing my neck, and my cock nearly hardens again. "I love you too," she whispers against my cheek.

A smile so big it nearly hurts spreads across my face. I bite her earlobe and she squeals in delight.

Turning off the shower, I open the door and smack her ass as she leaves. I'm in awe watching as she towels off her hair and hurries back into her servant uniform. It's drab on her like it's meant to be, and I ache to give her everything. To dress her in fine clothes and buy her any jewelry she wants. She deserves it all. She deserves to be treated like a queen.

"The party is in a few days. Are you excited?" I ask, coming up behind her and wrapping her in my arms.

She turns to look at me with hope in her eyes. "Your father will allow it?"

I haven't asked him yet. I've been too much of a coward, but I don't care whether he says yes or no. Soon I'll be the King of Calamity and no one will tell me what the fuck I can and can't do.

"Don't worry about that. I'll make it work," I promise.

She eyes me suspiciously. "He'll never say yes."

"I don't care, Elrora. I love you and once he sees that, he'll just have to learn to accept us."

She runs a finger down my cheek and kisses me gently. "I believe you," she whispers against my lips.

"You better," I reply, tucking a strand of wet hair behind her ear. I let a flurry of power whirl around her, drying her off even though there are fewer things I like more than seeing her wet.

She smiles at my magic. Her nail traces the drawing on my pec, sending a shiver down my spine. "This is new."

"I got it a few days ago," I say, noting the singular crying eye in my reflection in the mirror.

"Are you sad?"

"Not at all, it's just a sketch I made that spoke to me. I figured it should join the collection," I say, stretching out both my arms and glancing at the assortment of tattoos I've collected on my body.

Her hand continues down my arm as if she's imagining me drawing each image. "Maybe one day you'll draw one for me."

"I'd love nothing more," I say, kissing the nose that marks her as half-elf. I don't think it's a coincidence that the two people I love most are half-faun and half-elf.

Grabbing my face, she pushes her tongue into my mouth and I groan with need before she pulls away and says, "One day. I have to go—I know someone has likely noticed I'm missing."

My heart twists as she hurries out the door. When I make her my wife, she'll never have to listen to anyone's orders ever again. "El, wait!" She stops at the door and looks back at me. "Come back tonight?"

She nods. "If I can, I will."

Straightening her plain uniform, she smiles at me and grabs the door handle. "Stay out of trouble," she says with a wink.

I close the distance between us, wanting more than anything to pull her back into my bed and keep her here forever. "No can do. I am trouble."

CHAPTER THIRTEEN

HARPER

WHEN I OPEN MY EYES, IT'S STILL DAYTIME. There are only a few windows, one of which sits above my curled up body, but it's enough to fill the space with an ironic brightness. A fire still burns on one wall, the soothing, crackling noise filling the silence. It's comforting until I try to sit up and my head shouts obscenities at me. It's like the worst hangover in the world. I feel like I'm out of breath just from opening my eyes. When I look around, I see two dead bodies on the floor and my heart stops.

Not a nightmare. At least not one I can wake up from.

Panic overwhelms me. I don't know what the judicial system is like here. Do they have a deer court where they hold trials? Will I be arrested? Will anyone believe that they attacked me first? Maybe here it's legal for them to kill humans. *Fuck.*

I try to get a grip on myself and find Pants snoozing in front of the flames. When I stand, the world leans to the side, but rights itself as blood rushes to the rest of my body. I stumble into the kitchen, my mouth feeling like sandpaper as I open the fridge. There are cans of something called White Tail in here and despite myself, I laugh. It's probably the blood loss.

I reach out and grab a bottle advertised as spring water and sniff it before chugging the entire contents. When I feel a little bit more hydrated, I let go of the vise grip I have on the counter and try to figure out what the fuck to do.

Surely my DNA is everywhere, but I don't know if that will matter. I decide to say fuck it and get the hell out of here instead of wasting my time trying to cover up my non-crime. But not before I eat and not before I snoop around a little to try to learn about my surroundings.

You might be thinking, "Wow, Harper, you're being a little blasé about all of this." Yeah, well, what the fuck do you want me to do? Shrivel up like an old prune until someone shows up and holds my hand? That honestly sounds nice, but would make for a pretty boring fucking story. And there's nothing I fear more than being bored. So I straighten my shoulders, ignore that I can't walk straight, and take another look in their fridge. There's something in here that looks like an apple, but it's orange. I bite into it and a flood of sour flavor coats my tongue. It's the best piece of fruit I've ever had and I devour it in two bites.

Shuffling through more stuff, hoping not to find the blood of their enemies or some shit, I'm disappointed. It's mostly various greens and different types of bread. There's not even eggs in here. I pick up a head of cabbage and take a bite out of it before placing it back, grabbing a few carrots, and leaving the kitchen. My head is filled with crunching sounds as I walk around the rest of their house. Pants has woken up and is following me loyally. I hand him a carrot and he sniffs it, turning up his nose like it's a turd and walking away.

Fine, picky little shit.

On the coffee table is a magazine called **Nice Rack**. It's got a half naked deer-woman on the cover straddling a horse and the titles of the articles being advertised are things like:

Is He Feeling Too Horny?
Six Ways To Get Him Back Into Antlers.
Tail Tucks—Why You Should Avoid One At All Costs.
Your New Favorite Ungulatte Recipe In The Back!

It's the weirdest fucking shit I've ever seen. Shaking my head, I waltz down the hall and into their bedroom. I won't lie to you. Sora has some damn cute clothes and seeing as mine are half covered in dried vomit, I sift through hers to see what might fit me.

I ultimately decide on black jeans that are a little too long, but tuck into a pair of leather brown boots nicely. The shirt I pick is a chunky, loose fitting, cream turtleneck sweater. Noting the bruising on either side of my neck, I decide hiding it is a good idea here.

I grab a pair of big, round black sunglasses and put them on the top of my head. Her closet has scarves of every color, leggings that feel like they're made out of cashmere, and some really cute hats with holes in the top for antlers. It's a shame she's dead and all these clothes will go to waste. I spy a leather backpack in the corner and pull a couple of things into it.

Hey, I never claimed to be a good person and I'm not above stealing.

Still dizzy, I decide to grab a White Tail from the fridge and run a bubble bath. I seriously consider hiding out here, but I don't really feel like burying their dead bodies, and who knows when the next time someone will come around? The last thing I want is Ren's grandmother showing up at the door while I'm living here like a serial killer squatter.

I run a brush through my hair, hoping not to get lice ... or fleas ... or whatever deer get, and curl my hair into long chocolate ringlets. I eat a couple more vegetables, pack some snacks and that delightful body wash into the backpack, and grab a black hooded cloak hanging by the door before wandering outside.

The weather is similar to yesterday—chilly but sunny. I bite my lip, wondering where to go next. I didn't see a single piece of technology in that house or any idea of where I could possibly be, so my guess is as good as any. I decide to head toward the forest since it's the opposite direction I came from. Pants nibbles on the grass and I roll my eyes at him. Carrots aren't good enough, but this dude is okay with munching someone's lawn? *Whatever.*

Oddly, I feel okay. Maybe I'm delirious, but I have some weird high going on. Like I fought for my life and survived. Even though I'm pretty sure I didn't get a single hit in. I don't know what killed them, but it certainly wasn't my will to live or warrior skills. I shouldn't be proud of myself, but I am. I feel kind of like a badass. And the farther I get from that house, the more my fear lessens. I should be terrified. If my first day here involved me nearly dying because someone tried to suck all my blood from me, then I can't imagine what else this place has in store for me.

But here's the kicker. I'm not afraid. I almost feel serene. Invincible. Untouchable. But not in that annoying teenager kind of way, in a magical way. For the first time in a long time, I feel ... alive.

CHAPTER FOURTEEN

ATLAS

I PUSH OPEN THE RICKETY WOODEN DOOR AND IT SQUEAKS in protest, like I've personally offended it by making it do its job. I nearly snap it in half with the way it slams against the wall as I stroll through. Stepping onto the porch, I see Emery in a wooden rocking chair to my right. He's sitting there sipping a beer and staring out at the vast wilderness like he's lifetimes old and just waiting for some kids to run by so he can tell them to get the fuck off his lawn. He doesn't even look at me because even though he's *my* best fucking friend, he still holds me accountable for my shit, and hurting Pippa is at the top of his no-fly list.

"Is she in The Den?" I ask, pretending to stare at the same thing he is even though there's only darkness ahead. It's nighttime ... for now, but who knows when that will change.

"If I say yes, are you going to go apologize?" he murmurs, keeping his gaze away from mine.

I'm staring down at him with so much heat I'm surprised his tiny black horns haven't caught fire, but he doesn't seem to notice and that really fucks me off. I can't blame him though. Someone has to protect Pippa and clearly I'm incapable. He's not dumb enough to not know he answered my question, but I'm too much of an ass to respond, so I stomp down the porch steps and head toward the back of the house.

On the side is a wooden door flush with the ground that leads to a room underneath the foundation. It's one of the reasons why Pippa chose this place as our hideout. We call it The Den because ... you know what? I don't fucking know why and it doesn't really matter, does it?

I throw open the hatch and walk down the stone steps, the air thickening with moisture and heat. I hear a rumbling belly laugh and then a few moments later, Emery's footsteps sound from behind me. When I step onto the ground level, everyone stares at me with narrowed eyes and gaping mouths. I guess I understand why. Every time I'm down here I'm wasted and usually making a mess of things or yelling at someone. My presence isn't exactly welcome.

Pippa is standing by a strategy table, but it's the saddest fucking table you've ever seen in your life. One leg is shorter than the others, propped up with books to stop it from rocking back and forth. The map is frayed at the edges and the strategy pieces are little stone figurines that Torin made with his magic. He's not exactly an artist though, so instead of looking like our enemies, they're mostly just blobs with oval heads and stubby legs. I'm pretty sure the piece that's supposed to represent me is now just a dick that's wider than it is tall. Guess *that* took some fucking creativity. It's not even on the map. It sits on the sidelines, just like I've been doing.

Not anymore, cocksuckers.

"What are we up to?" I ask with a cheery smile on my face.

Emery nearly smacks into me from behind, so I walk in and sit in one of the many fake leather chairs by the fire that takes up the whole back wall. When I sink into it, the fabric reveals rips and cushion stuffing spills out beneath its rubbery surface. Pippa glares at me, but isn't this what she wanted? For me to participate and be something? Fuck, women are so hard to please.

"Hey, Pip. Stop looking at me like that, it's breaking my heart." I frown at her and give her big, kitten eyes. Emery clears his throat, and I sigh heavily. "I'm sorry, Pip. I didn't mean what I said."

Pippa lifts her chin in defiance and pretends not to look at me. You might be forgetting she's a princess. Or at least she was. Like me, she spent the majority of her life getting everything she wanted. She might be some revolution leader now, but to me, she's still the spoiled brat I grew up with. I love her all the same, though; who am I to judge?

Torin stares at me with a smirk from the chair next to me and Ellison is asleep on the cot near the entrance. He hasn't stirred since I entered and I'm not surprised by that in the slightest—dude is stoned literally all the time. I don't know why he gets away with it and I don't. At the table with Pippa are Wilder and Idalia. More on them later.

"It's not just me you need to apologize to, Atlas." Her voice has always reminded me of wind chimes. It's so dainty and musical, but right now it's like a cheese grater to my nerves.

I look around at everyone else. Wilder and Idalia are looking at me like I'm the biggest disappointment in the world. Torin is on the verge of laughter. Fuck me if I ever find myself apologizing to that guy. His dark skin glows as the fire illuminates white teeth. He looks like an evil villain in his study. I'm still not convinced he's not a spy.

I sigh. "Fine. But I'm only saying this once, so everyone listen up!" I take off my shoe and chuck it at Ellison, who startles awake with a snore and peers at me all glossy eyed.

"Atlas," he says with lazy surprise. "What's up, dude?"

"I said listen up. I'm sorry everyone. I haven't been contributing much—"

Idalia interrupts me with a snort of mock amusement, and my palms form into fists.

"I'm sorry I haven't done jack shit this whole time. I just …" I really should tell them. They should know the whole story if we're ever going to win this thing, but at this point, I think they might flay me alive if I tell them the truth, so I don't. Baby fucking steps.

"I don't want to make excuses. I'm a terrible prince and an even worse friend. But I'm here now. I'll do whatever you need, so please, *please* catch me up and put me to good use." I look around at all of them with sincerity in my eyes. I mean the words coming out of my mouth, even though they're some of the most painful ones I've ever had to say. Surprise, surprise, I don't love admitting I'm wrong.

Ellison shrugs, tosses me my shoe back, and goes back to sleep. Wilder, with his long fur and elongated rat-like nose, blinks once at me with black eyes and nods in approval. I can see Torin in my periphery prop one foot onto the opposite knee so that his legs form a triangle. I don't even bother looking at him because my apology was never for him. My eyes are on Pippa, my little sister.

She smiles and runs over to me. I stand and envelop her in a big hug. Her hair smells like baked goods and something about it reminds me of home. It's really a heartwarming moment that I might enjoy if her snide little bitch friend wasn't glaring at me.

"Come on, Idalia. I know you don't hate me that much," I say over my sister's head. Pippa is so tiny compared to me, but I tower over everyone.

"I'll accept your apology when it comes in the form of actions, not words." She's elven like the rest of us, except Wilder, who is var-rek, and Emery, who's half-faun and half-elf—my little mutt. Her long, black hair cascades in braids down her back and she's dressed in leggings and a sweater that seems to swallow her whole. She'd be pretty fucking hot if she didn't live so far up my sister's ass and wasn't such a raging bitch.

I let go of Pippa, and she smiles up at me before releasing me from her hold. She looks so much like our mother that I can't stare at her for too long.

Pippa looks between us and frowns. "Play nice, you two."

"I don't think what I'm asking is too much," Idalia mutters, turning back to the map.

Pippa turns back to me and smiles again like she can't believe I'm here and more of me chips into pieces. "You really need a haircut," she says, ruffling her hand through my hair. "And to shave."

"Do your worst, Pip," I tell her before slipping my shoe back on.

A devious smile appears, and I almost regret my words, but I trust her. She combs my hair with her fingers, her magic working it to be short on the sides and just a little longer on the top. Putting her hands on my cheeks, I can feel my facial hair thinning.

"Don't turn me into a child," I warn.

She pouts her lips, but releases me.

Everyone watches quietly like this is the most interesting thing they've seen in a long time. They all need to get a fucking hobby.

Running my hand over my stubble, I walk with Pippa to the table as she says, "We were just discussing the best strategy to attack the palace."

I stop in my tracks. "You're attacking the palace? When?"

Her eyes narrow at me. "*We* are attacking the palace ... and I don't know yet."

I look around the room at the group of outcasts. "We?" I ask, pointing at all of us.

Pippa rolls her eyes. "We're building an army, Atlas."

I swallow. I guess they've done a lot more work than I've given them credit for, but I don't want Pippa anywhere near that bitch. Torin can fuck right over to the palace for all I care. I'd happily use him as bait.

"The intel I received in my meeting with the Council—"

"Wait," I back up so I don't have to crane my neck to look down at her. "The Council still exists?"

"For fuck's sake," Idalia mutters.

"Perhaps Atlas and I can chat. Catch up on matters to avoid any further ... frustrations," Wilder suggests. His voice is reasonable and calm. It doesn't fit his species, who are usually so busy and frantic they don't even bother to sit still for more than five seconds.

It suddenly dawns on me how big this has become and how much I've missed out on. I really am a jackass. Will anyone even want me to be king when all is said and done? I sure as shit didn't earn it. Pippa should take the crown. I never wanted it anyway.

"That sounds more reasonable. I wouldn't want that vein in Idalia's forehead to burst and have her bleed out all over this nice rug." Everyone looks down at the stained red and blue rug beneath our feet. I'd rather eat off Emery's ass than touch this thing with any part of my body.

"You're such a fucking asshole," Idalia sneers.

"Atlas," my sister chides.

Emery hasn't spoken this whole time. He's sitting by the fire watching the whole interaction like it's the most entertaining thing he's seen. "Come on," he finally chimes in. "We can all go for a walk."

"Wait," I say before we leave.

Everyone turns to me except Ellison, who is still fucking asleep.

"She knows where we are." I don't really know how I'm going to explain this one.

"She ... she ... what?" Pippa stutters.

"The Blood Queen. She knows we're here. My concealment spell didn't work last night, I guess."

"How the fuck do you know this?" Torin asks without moving an inch.

"She left me a note on the table," I say with a shrug. I'm playing off how big of a deal this is in hopes that everyone will stay calm.

"Why are you so relaxed about this?" Pippa's voice raises a thousand octaves. "And how do you know it was for you? Why you?"

Shit. "Probably because I'm the rightful heir; how the fuck should I know? She's insane. And I'm calm because there's nothing we can do about it now. They'd be stupid to come here without an army, which means it will take her time to get here. We have to leave in the next twenty-four hours, but that's why I'm telling you all this now."

"This is your fucking fault, you insolent child!" Idalia screams.

I take it because she's not wrong. I'm the one who shifted and essentially labeled myself **HERE** for the new queen to see.

"This is serious, Atlas," Wilder says in a low voice.

"I fucking know that," I snarl. I walk over to Ellison and slap his little cheeks.

89

"Atlas. What's up, dude?"

"We need to find a new place to stay. Make yourself useful, you lazy shit, and get to work."

"You should be one to talk," Torin mutters.

I'm done being nice. I spin on my heel and prowl over to where he's sitting next to the fire. He stands up like he's going to challenge me, even though that's a fucking joke.

"*You* don't get to talk to me like that. I already admitted I haven't been the most helpful with things, but guess what? You guys need me. No one is more powerful than I am and that power might be wasted on me, but too fucking bad." He's seething and staring up at me with green eyes that almost look orange in the firelight. "It's mine," I growl. "And there's nothing you can do about it. So unless you want to end up with a few less appendages, you'll mind your fucking tone when you speak to your prince."

The room is so silent you could probably hear a snowflake touch the floor. Technically, I'm not a prince, not in any way that matters, but the majority of the citizens on this continent still believe that I am and it's time I start acting like it.

"Yes, Your *Highness*. Forgive me," he grinds out. His jaw looks like it might just snap with how hard he's clenching it.

I show him all my teeth and let a little poison coat my canines, just in case he needs a reminder of who he's dealing with.

The room is still silent except for Torin fuming behind me. I turn to look at them all. I don't want to be their leader, but I won't let them forget who I am.

"Ellison, you'll find us a new hideout, right? In the hour?"

"For sure, dude." He pushes up his glasses and pulls his leather boots on.

"See, Pippa? All will be fine." I'm not sure that's true, but I've always been a liar. Why stop now?

She nods, clearly freaked out by my display of dominance. No one has seen that side of me in a while. I don't like to be him, but for Torin I'll make an exception.

"Wilder, Emery, and I are going for a little walk. Everyone should pack and when we get to the new place, we'll make a plan."

I march forward and up the stairs. It's daytime when I get outside. I couldn't have been down there for more than thirty minutes. This instant day to night shit is a mind-fuck no matter how much I try to get used to it. It's just one of the many things I have to fix and I'm running out of time.

THERE ARE WOODS BEHIND THE house that we walk toward. These trees aren't alive. Well, not in the way some trees are, so our secrets are safe. I inhale the crisp night air and run a hand through my newly cropped hair. Nothing is ever easy.

"When your parents died, so did the Council. They were all at the party after all," Wilder says.

He's referring to the night everything changed. My parents were throwing some extravagant event for something dumb, as usual. I wish I remembered what it was, even though it never fucking mattered. No one survived except Emery and me. The rest of our crew just happened to be out of town that evening.

"But a few months into the Blood Queen's reign, a force banded together under Pippa's guidance. She handpicked a new council. It's still someone from every race and they congregate every few weeks to discuss new information."

I'm filled with pride for my little sister and even more shame for myself.

"There are few who support the new queen's rule. The scum who've always believed that draining magic with vampirism shouldn't be outlawed, of course. Those have been newly appointed to every stronghold. Beyond that, she has some other leverage that none of us fully understand. The Royal Guard is faithful to a fault and getting any information from the palace has been near impossible. It's too difficult to approach with the way she's spelled a barrier around it. The only reason we know she's a *she* is because of the correspondence she signs as queen. In all public events she has someone speaking for her as she paces around in her derax form. And it seems that any who come into her path are dead if she so pleases before they can even draw their sword."

I close my eyes and grit my teeth. "What is her derax?"

Bile rises in my throat as Emery answers. "A lion of sorts."

"Alright, just get to the worst part," I say, dreading what's to come.

Wilder stops and Emery and I follow suit. The air grows heavy in the silence that precedes his words. "The camps she's building to breed and exploit the fendlings are multiplying every month. We have no idea how she's doing it so fast and we can't get any information about where they are or what the conditions are like."

A wolf-like growl emits from Emery. "I think we can guess."

I swallow my horror. Fendlings are a species whose blood is loaded with magic. They can create and do pretty much anything their little minds can conjure up, but they live by a very strict code. One which states that they must never act violently, even in self-defense.

They're powerful, but entirely harmless creatures and they're fucking adorable, too. I could only describe them as small, furry dragons. In their full height, one might come up to my knee. They have these big, wide, saucer eyes that just twist your heart into pieces every time you see one. I'm pretty sure it's an evolutionary thing for them to look that cute—it's their only defense. But leave it to this bitch to literally capture, torture, and breed them. It's fucking disgusting. I'm filled with so much rage toward not only her, but myself. If I had only acted sooner. If I hadn't been such a selfish brat. If I didn't—

"There's no point in beating yourself up, Atlas," Emery says, resting a hand on my shoulder.

"It's my fucking fault," I mutter, pacing back and forth. My derax form wants to explode out of me so badly it hurts.

"It's not your fault," they both say in unison.

But it is, they just don't know it. I'm done feeling sorry for myself, though. I need to own my actions, and as soon as I stop the bitch who stole everything from me, I'm going to find a way to abdicate my throne to Pippa. It's the least I can do for my people.

"So what now?" I ask Wilder when my head has calmed slightly.

"Now we do the only thing we can do. Take her down by force." He shrugs as if it's that fucking simple.

A scoff leaves my throat. "We can't even get past her barrier, let alone take her down. We need to figure out how she's instantly killing people. It must be some kind of dark magic." My brain is working a mile a minute, but I have no idea what skill she could possibly have.

"Autopsy reports of bodies we've been able to look at after she's ..." Wilder trails off, but we all know what he's trying to say. After she's fucking slaughtered them. "Well, they have some disturbing findings."

My breathing stops. "Like what?"

"Their hearts are missing."

Emery's face lines with disgust, but this isn't news to him.

"What the fuck does that mean?" I ask.

"It means exactly what it sounds like. The hearts that were once beating inside their chests are gone," Emery nearly shouts at me and I finally see something I haven't noticed this whole time—Emery is mad at me. Who could blame him? But I can't remember a time my brother was ever truly angry with me.

"She takes them after she kills them?" I still can't wrap my head around this.

"No," Wilder says, like he finds the topic intriguing. "Their bodies are perfectly intact."

"Then how the fuck is she doing that?" I don't mean to yell, but I do it anyway.

Emery punches me so hard in the stomach I double over, gasping. "Nobody fucking knows, idiot. That's the whole point."

I look up at him, half surprised, half impressed, and gritting my teeth from the pain.

Wilder isn't phased at all. I'm sure deep down he's enjoying it. That's fine, let him.

"Some have taken to calling her the Queen of Hearts," Wilder says wistfully.

"I'll never call her the queen of anything," Emery mutters, shaking out his hand. I hope he broke bones.

Catching my breath, I stand up straight. "We need to figure out how she's doing that. We could have the biggest army in the world, but if she's got that power ... who the fuck knows what else she has?"

Daylight suddenly burns my retinas and we all close our eyes at the sudden change. "And has anyone figured that shit out?" I ask, shading my eyes from the burning sun.

"Nope," Emery says, popping the P like the little shit he is.

"Surely it's something *she's* doing," Wilder says.

"If she can change the environment, we're in big trouble," I mumble.

Emery crosses his arms with a triumphant look on his face. "So nice of you to join us, asshat."

My need to dominate him is simmering under my skin, but that heavy coat of shame I have is holding me back from beating his head in.

"I'm going into town," I say, heading out of the forest.

"For what?" Emery calls out.

"Research!" I shout back. And because I don't think I can go back down there and surround myself with all the people I've let down.

CHAPTER FIFTEEN

ℋARPER

THE WOODS ARE DARK AND OMINOUS, BUT THEY CALL to me.

Literally, someone is calling out to me. Not my name, but a plea for me to come closer. The trees remind me of redwoods, their bark the bright orange of rust. My boots pad over the ground covered with leaves, soft from decay. Pants trots in front of me, lifting his leg to pee on a trunk, when a root whips out of the ground and wraps around his tiny body. I scream as he yelps in shock, but it quickly deposits him a little ways away. My body is still. I should stop being surprised by this place, but I'm not.

"I think you should find somewhere else to take a piss, my man," I mutter as he runs to my side.

The whispering has stopped and that voice in the back of my head telling me to run nudges me along, but I keep an easy pace. It's not as though I could outrun anything, anyway. I'm pretty sure an overweight tortoise could catch me.

She's here.

A harmony of melodic murmurs snakes beneath my feet and against my skin. Instinctively, I know it's the trees talking.

She's here.

I spin around, facing none of them in particular. "Something you need?" I ask.

You will save us.

Doubtful. "Save you from what?"

She's here. As day falls to night and winter leads to summer. A version of you will save us.

The words are English, they're even in proper sentences, but they make no sense.

"Are you talking about how it turns to night in the blink of an eye?" I ask, a little more curious.

Sometimes it is years before it's night. Sometimes the dawn stays until spring.

Uhh ...

"I hate to break it to you, but there's only one version of me and you're stuck with her. Also, I'm not from here. I can't save ..."

My words trail off. Why am I even bothering?

A crown that doesn't fit. Blood that covers the sky. Find your selüm-ra. *Bring peace to the earth and transformation to your mind.*

"My what now? I don't want to be transformed, but thanks. Mostly, I'd like to get home. Can you tell me how to get back?"

Valleys and rivers that fill the mountain. Time will change everything before you can.

What. The. Fuck.

Deciding I don't have time to learn how to speak in riddles, I keep walking. They don't seem content to shut up though, as more whispers and garbled sentences fill the air. I shake the urge to plug my ears with my fingers and start walking faster.

I'm not afraid, I'm just annoyed. I need answers and clearly these trees aren't helping me. When a break in the forest appears, I sprint toward it.

My breath catches as I look around and try to process what I'm seeing. A town—with cobblestone streets and nineteenth-century Germanic architecture—is at the edge of the forest. It bustles with the kind of mundane energy a place completely unaware of your existence would have. Life bleeds into the world around me, staining the page with ink blots and smudges. There are *creatures* everywhere. Notice how I didn't say humans? Because they're not human and, guess what, they're not deer-people either ... oh wait, nope—I see one over there.

Okay, *fine*.

Some are deer-people, but others are ... are ... animals and elves? It's a fairy tale come to life and my brain can't fully wrap its head around what's going on here.

I close my eyes and open them one at a time, only to find the same scene. A two-story building to the right of me has a tall, pitched roof that slopes out like a skirt. A porch wraps around the second story and non-humans sit at tables laughing. I assume it's some sort of tavern and smile at the gold, Gothic style windows surrounding it, each one buttressed by teal shutters clipped to the frames.

The road zig-zagging to my right leads into town, and to my left, loses itself in trees and sunshine-soaked rolling hills. A river with an arched, stone bridge sits in front of me. One of the same baobab-like trees and grass as far as the eye can see are beyond that. Leading farther into the distance, colorful, Gothic style cottages line the dirt road. It's so fucking cute my heart grows two sizes before I realize I'm surrounded by aliens.

Elves (I'm theorizing here. I saw half of *Lord of the Rings* like one time) seem to be the predominant species, but there are others. Rat-looking creatures with long noses and beautifully shaggy coats dressed in leather armor. Everyone is wearing either some variation of modern clothing or something from medieval Europe.

No one pays me any attention as Pants and I step onto the street and try to dodge traffic. Keeping the hooded cloak over my head, I peer into the tavern, which seems to be serving rowdy guests despite the fact that it's daylight. The further into town I go, the more I notice cute little shops each seeming to serve one singular purpose—a shoe-maker, a dress shop, a baker. Someone bumps into me, hard, and I excuse myself as a towering elf pushes past me.

"Keep it moving!" he barks.

The harsh tone of his voice causes me to stumble as I scurry out of the way and open up the closest shop door. My brain barely registers the name–Kismet's Chapters and Coincidences. Finding myself inside a bookstore, I let out a sigh of relief. I need something, *anything* ordinary to grasp on to before I collapse into a mental breakdown. But the creature that walks from the back is anything but normal. It's a mixture between a kangaroo and a mountain goat—tall and proud—it has the floppy feet of a kangaroo with hooves on each toe. A tail that's long and smooth floats effortlessly around it. The creature adjusts the gold monocle over its left eye and flips the page of a book it's holding.

A white goatee stands out against the, I kid you not, blue, brown, and white tiger-striped fur. On its goat head is a top hat which accommodates gold ribbed horns sticking straight up, their tips turning into sharp points. I can't help it, I scream and stumble back to run away, but it looks up at me and smiles, keeping me in place.

"Harper," it says.

I slap myself again, but guess what? I don't fucking wake up. If it notices or thinks my behavior is strange, it doesn't comment.

"You ... you know my name?" My voice betrays every ounce of courage I have.

The creature snaps the book shut and I flinch, placing my hand on the doorknob.

"Always startled so easily!" it shouts with a grin.

Always?

"I've been waiting for you, though time is a fickle thing here." It hops back into the tiny corridor of the shop. There's not a lot of space in here. The place is like a store in Diagon Alley—overflowing shelves line the walls, and towers of books pile high on the floor.

"Well, come on now, you know how I hate being late!" it calls after me.

I look down at Pants, who yawns and glances around like this is all a normal day for him. It seems like if I want answers, this weird new stranger may be able to give them to me. I take a few steps and a deep breath. A few more steps and fight the urge to piss myself. A few steps after that, the need to vomit everywhere seems to dissipate.

"Harper!" the creature calls out like we're best friends, and I nearly smack into the huge, furry body as it comes looking for me.

"Ah, there you are. Come, sit." This *thing* has its face shoved in a book and absently points to a chair that's made out of old paperbacks. I reluctantly plop down into it. "As I said, I've been waiting."

"Waiting for what?" Why is everything in this place so dodgy about giving me real answers?

"For you, of course!" The stranger still hasn't looked up from the book it's holding as if it's talking to the pages and not me. "We made this appointment, what ... nearly a year ago now?"

I grit my teeth. My fear is making way to anger and I'm so close to losing it and going full rage black out on this thing. "Impossible," I say slowly and calmly—well, as calm as I can be. "I don't know you, and I've never been here before."

The kangagoat finally looks at me and frowns. "Been where?"

"Here!" I shout, gesturing around the room.

The stranger is unphased, scratching its chin and pondering something. "Well, of course you haven't. I only purchased the store just yesterday."

I can't do this. I get up and begin walking out.

"Do you have another appointment?" Kangagoat asks as it closely follows me out.

I spin, rage burning hot in my cheeks. "No," I sneer. "I don't have another appointment because I don't even know what fucking world I'm in."

"Oh dear," it says, making me pause. My expression becomes hopeful. "I must have my timings off. Oh, for fuck's sake. I keep doing that, don't I?" Kangagoat looks to me for an answer.

I cry out in frustration. "How would I know?! I don't even know you!" Pants scurries behind a stack of books to hide from my anger.

"Well, before you go, I do have something for you," it says, barely missing a beat.

I finally make it to the lobby of the store. "I don't want it!"

"Harper," it says, and the voice is so calm it pins me in place like a spell. I turn and the creature hands me the book it's holding. I look down at the worn cover, blue with a cracked leather spine. It looks ancient, but the title reads, *K&C's Guide: Calamity's Most Popular Hiking Destinations.*

I close my eyes and try to push the blinding rage away as it says, "Now, Harper, you need to go. I have many things to do and customers to tend to."

I look around with wide eyes—there's no one fucking here.

But just as I'm about to tell him that, the jingle of a bell notifies me of someone's arrival, and I quickly pull my hood up before they can see me.

"Welcome! You're just in time," the furry, frustrating creature says.

I give a brief glance to the new customer who is also wearing a hood, towering over me like a giant. "What? You know what—nevermind. I'm looking for something." His voice sends a shiver through me.

"Well, aren't we all?" Kangagoat says. "But, we're closed."

I gape at him. This thing has some fucking nerve.

The creature looks between both of us and smiles, grabbing a book at random from a pile and walking into the back of the store. "Both of you, fuck right along now. And Harper! Next time, do try not to be so late."

I barrel out of the store, not waiting to hear the response of the other customer, and hold back another scream. It's night again in this quaint little town, and I'm more confused than ever. I have no idea where to go, what to do, or what to think before the door opens. I try to move aside to get out of this guy's way, but he must not see me and nearly steps on top of me.

When we collide, he pulls off his hood and glares down. He's so beautiful, I just stand there like an idiot with my mouth open. I'm guessing he's in his twenties. With coffee-colored hair that leaves pointed ears and the strong square of his stubbled jaw completely visible. He's huge—at least a foot taller than me—glowering at me like the ant I am. A light gray hoodie is tight against his broad shoulders and muscled form. Thick, dark eyebrows frame earthy brown eyes as they find mine. The twist of his mouth—so cruel and wicked—is terrifying, but he looks *so* good doing it.

Down, girl.

"Are you going to move or what?"

"Sorry," I mutter, and finally step to the side.

He furrows his brow like he's trying to understand something about me, so I turn and begin walking up the street and away from his scrutiny. I don't need someone else sinking their teeth into my neck. I'm still holding on to this stupid book and I can't for the life of me figure out why. Like the pocket watch around my neck, it feels important, and that only makes me angry because obtaining it was by far one of the more maddening experiences I've ever had. The buildings have become more spaced out as the road turns uphill and the street lamps cast shadows over alleyways.

The wind whistles through a vacuum the buildings create, and I pull the cloak tighter around me before someone pins me up against a stone wall and shoves a knife to my throat.

I hate this place. I hate it so much.

My assailant is elven ... elfish? I don't know. He looks male, but who am I to judge? His dark, greasy hair should make him disgusting, but honestly he pulls it off ... and oh my God, am I really complimenting the guy who's about to slit my throat? I have serious issues. Send help.

"I don't have any money," I say in a whisper, as if talking louder might provoke him.

"I don't want your money," he spits.

It doesn't take me long to figure out that he probably wants my blood, and based on my last few experiences, that didn't end well for those trying to take it.

"I don't think you want what you think you want." I glance down at him in his ratty clothes. "I'm pretty sure it's poisonous or something."

"Nice try, bitch. Now listen, you're going to walk down that alley, and then you'll—" He doesn't finish because his head literally explodes into a fine mist, and I scream at the top of my lungs. It's not like I'm upset about his demise, but come on—that's the third person that's died in front of me in the last twenty-four hours.

His headless body and the knife that was at my throat thump to the ground. Standing before me is the hoodie guy from the bookstore. I can't even appreciate him, though, as I move my eyes to the corpse at my feet and the murderer in front of me. Should I be relieved? I'm not. I'm pretty sure I almost peed my pants. Speaking of which, *my* Pants is sitting next to the hot stranger and staring up at him like he just gave him the biggest steak a fox could ask for. Not really much use for protection, I see.

I swallow, words unable to form or even come from my mouth as blood spatter dries on my face.

"You okay?" he asks, and his voice is gravel in a rainstorm.

I nod slowly.

The stranger cocks his head to the side. "You don't know who I am?"

I shake my head, and as I do my hood falls off. Within a matter of seconds, he's staring at me like *I'm* the confusing creature here. Though I guess it's his world, so I probably am.

Moving quickly to replace my hood, he walks over to me and yanks it down again, staring at my ears.

"Hey!" I whine, pulling it back over my head.

"You're human," he whispers, like he's just discovered something impossible.

Please don't eat me. Please don't eat me. Please don't eat me.

"And?" Apparently even the scared-shitless version of me has an attitude.

"Are there more of you?"

My brows furrow. "Not that I know of."

He frowns and looks me up and down, his eyes catching on the book that's still in my grip. I have a feeling that even if I opened my palm it wouldn't fall out, like it's glued to my skin. His assessment of me must be disappointing because he flips his hood back up and simply turns, walking away in the opposite direction.

"Wait!" I run after him. His strides are six of mine and he walks with an air that tells me he's used to people moving out of his way.

"Wait, why did you save me?"

"Because he was going to kill you," he says matter-of-factly.

"Okay ... well, why do you care?"

"I don't," he mutters and, fuck me, but it really seems like he doesn't.

"But did you follow me? You're going in the opposite direction now."

That gets his attention, and he stops. He's a mountain compared to me as I tilt my chin toward his stupidly beautiful face. His nose looks like it was carved in the image of a Greek god, but never sanded down. He's all perfect angles and rugged features. I'm suddenly very self-conscious.

"Look, human—"

"Harper," I correct.

He shakes his head. "I really don't need this right now. I don't know how or why you're here—"

"Me either!"

"For fuck's sake, just let me finish!" His voice nearly rumbles the earth, and I'm officially terrified of him. He takes my silence as a cue to continue, and when he does his voice is at a frequency low enough to make my toes curl. "Your tiny human brain couldn't even make sense of the pile of shit I have to take care of, so please fuck off and go back to wherever you came from." He looks down at Pants and I can see the tug of a smile that never comes.

"I don't know how I got here or where I am. Please help me," I beg.

Mr. Handsome looks at me like he's considering it, but then says, "No." And begins walking away.

We're nearing the tavern by the edge of town, and he turns around to find me trailing behind. I'm not leaving. He's the first decent person I've met that doesn't talk in circles, even if he explodes heads with his mind.

"Stop following me," he growls. Literally, it's a growl that comes out of him. I couldn't replicate the sound even if I tried.

"No," I say, nearly out of breath.

He turns around and suddenly I'm blasted back by some force. My ass hits the cobblestones and I accidentally bite into my lip. I whimper in pain and Pants finally leaves Mr. Handsome Asshole's side to comfort me. He turns around for a split second and then storms off while I pry my teeth from my flesh.

I couldn't stop the tears from coming even if I wanted to. I don't know what to do and once again I feel utterly hopeless. All I want is to crawl up into a corner and die, the courage I had a few hours ago brushed away along with my pride.

Pants licks the tears on my face, happy to find that they're still salty. I laugh despite myself and gently push him off me. At least this time, I'm not alone.

CHAPTER SIXTEEN

ATLAS

I WRING MY HANDS OUT, BUT IT DOESN'T GET RID OF THE anxiety warring through me. Did that really just happen? Did I really just meet a *human*? I can't deal with this right now. If humans are falling out of the damn sky, I'll quit. I swear to the fucking Realm, I'll just leave. I'm so freaked out that I nearly bump into Emery on my walk back to the Shithole Shack.

"Woah, did your little shopping spree not go as planned?" he asks. I look up at him and something must be written on my face because he pauses. "What happened?"

His voice has an air of protectiveness. I almost laugh that he thinks I need *him* to protect *me*. It's kinda cute, though. Except I don't laugh and I don't really find any of this fucking cute because I just met a fucking human. They're not even supposed to be real.

"I met a human," I say, still in shock.

He laughs because he thinks I'm fucking around and then notes my straight face.

"I said I met a fucking human, Emery."

"You're joking ..." But his voice sounds like he knows I'm not joking at all.

I just stare at him as the world feels like it's melting around me.

"Where? When? How?" He stammers all the questions.

My asshole brain wants to answer, "*Who? What?*" but I don't.

I sigh and close my eyes because I'm either losing my mind or this is really bad. Either way, I'm fucked. "I went to the bookstore, which was a weird experience in and of itself. The whole place was completely redone and—"

"Atlas! Focus, the human."

I shake my head, words rushing out of me like a river. "Right, anyway. The bookstore was closing up, but she was inside of it. At first I didn't know she was a human because she was wearing a hood, but then she was just standing there, blocking the exit. Then *my* hood fell off and when she looked at me, she had no idea who I was. I knew instantly something was wrong."

"First of all, I'm not going to even start to tell you how stupid it is to go into town without a glamour—" He stops at the sight of my scowl and smiles. "What do you mean, you knew something was wrong?"

"She just ... she smelled different." I try to recall it, but when I do, my memories tell me that it actually felt right, but that can't be the case, so I shove *that* fucking feeling aside.

"What did she smell like?"

"Like fucking wrong! I don't know!" I actually think she smelled nice. Like raspberries and daisies and—

"You liked her," he says, reading my thoughts because I can't hide anything from him.

"She's a fucking human. That's what they do ... they're pretty and sneaky and then they stab you in the back the second it suits them."

"I heard their blood is poison," he says with a shrug. "Well, then what happened?"

"I followed her," I mumble. Emery smirks, and I glare at him. "I didn't know she was a human."

"Keep going, stalker."

"Fuck off. Anyway, her dumb ass ended up at the north end of town and naturally, someone cornered her."

"It's like the world has lost their damn minds these days."

"Vampirism isn't illegal anymore and everyone's greedy." The words are true, but they feel terrible coming out. I hate what this place has become. Our home has descended into chaos.

"So I vaporized his skull and then—"

"Atlas, what if someone saw you?"

He's scolding me because no one has the power to do that except me and maybe Pippa if she tried really, really hard. It takes a lot of magic, which I was already in short supply of, but I was being lazy. It was a stupid move and I know it.

"Someone did see me," I point out.

"Yeah, and what if she wasn't human?"

"She *was* fucking human, so it doesn't matter," I snap.

I tell him the rest of the story and how I panicked and left her in the street. I feel kind of guilty about that, but what was I supposed to do, bring her home with me? We're in enough danger as it is.

"So you just left her there?" He folds his arms like he's judging me.

"We don't need that kind of drama. What if she's working for that bitch? She probably is working for her. *Fuck.*" I run both my hands through my hair and let them sit intertwined on my head.

"What if she's not? What if she was telling you the truth and she really doesn't know why or how she got here?"

"Then that sounds like a fucking disaster waiting to happen. I don't fuck with the Realm, and if it put her here for a reason, then I'm staying far away from it."

The Realm is its own entity ... or so they say. No one knows for sure, but legend says it's a sentient being. That it controls our destiny and blah, blah, blah. It doesn't matter because it's not real and even if it is real, that's way above my paygrade.

Emery chews his lip. "If she's not working for the bitch queen and she finds her ... which she probably will ... then she'll use her as a weapon."

I narrow my eyes. "What do you mean use her as a weapon?"

He raises his hands in defense. "I swear, I've heard their blood is a super deadly poison."

"That's ridiculous." But it rings a faint bell.

"So is meeting a human in town," he says. Fucker has a point.

"So, what? You want me to just go back into town and look for her and then what? Bring her home? Fuck no, dude. She's not some lost fendling in search of a warm place to stay. She's a damn human!"

"You wouldn't happen to be talking about me, would you?"

I spoke to her for five seconds, but already I'd know her voice anywhere. It reminds me of big, ancient shrine bells. Isn't that fucking poetic?

Emery looks like he's going to pass out and it's fair, but I turn around and glare at her. She's fucking gorgeous with long hair so brown it's almost black and big soulless eyes to match. There's a furrow in her brow that seems to be a permanent feature from scowling all the time. Her lips form this sexy little pout, like she's just getting started on a long list of demands. And her tits sit tight against a knit sweater, taunting me. The cloak clasp snuggles against her—

Atlas, stop.

"No," I lie, and it's the dumbest fucking answer I could have given.

Emery has composed himself. "I'm Emery," he says slowly and loudly. But she's not a toddler, she's just human.

"I can understand you perfectly fine; you don't need to talk to me like a child," she whips back, and I have to fight my smile.

Emery frowns and looks at me unsure of what to do. Doesn't he understand that I don't know what to do either? But Pippa would, and it really should be her to make this call. I mean she's the one in charge and everything.

"Cute fox," Emery says.

I'm about to ask him what the fuck when I see the literal fox standing next to her. "It *is* fucking cute, huh?" I can't even help but say it as it cocks its head to the side at the sound of my voice, and its tail thumps quietly in the dirt.

The human smiles, but I give her a look that lets her know we're absolutely not talking about her and we're *not* friends. She told me her name earlier, but I don't remember it and I don't want to.

"I'm Harper," she says.

For fuck's sake.

"Well, we can at least take the fox, right?" Emery jokes, but Harper steps protectively in front of it.

"Yeah, I'll take the fox, but not her. Realm, she probably can't even run very fast."

"Excuse me, I'm right fucking here." She's annoying me already.

I turn to him, making a point of ignoring her. "Pippa should decide."

"Good call," he says, relieved.

I sigh and tilt my head up to the sky, just begging the Realm to fucking hit me with a bolt of lightning or something. "Come on," I say motioning for her to follow.

"Me or the fox?" she asks with an obnoxious little smirk.

I turn to her and look between the two of them. "To me, you're exactly the fucking same."

We head back to the house, Emery and I sharing a worried glance. Just when I thought I couldn't fuck us any harder, I had to prove myself wrong.

CHAPTER SEVENTEEN

HARPER

PANTS TROTS BESIDE ME AS WE FOLLOW OUR NEW acquaintances in the dark. The only source of light is a glowing, warm yellow blob that floats over Emery's head. My stranger danger alarm is blaring loudly, but I tune it out. If I'm being totally honest, the view from behind these two isn't half bad ... or bad at all. They're stupid hot. Really, really stupid hot. If this is all a dream, then I've really outdone myself.

The first guy I met—the one who left me crying on my ass in the middle of the street—he's the burlier and bigger of the two, but they're both fairly close in body shape, age, and height. The other one, Emery, has dark, sandy blond hair and a fair complexion. I'm more of a tall, dark, and handsome kind of gal, but Emery has me reconsidering that stance. His hair is pulled into a bun at the base of his neck, with messy little pieces framing his face. The facial hair covering his jaw is longer than Mr. Handsome Asshole's, more like an eight o'clock shadow.

There's one other important feature about him—along with the same pointy ears as his brooding companion, Emery also has two small, black horns peeking from his hairline. They remind me of the sexy devil horns girls wear for Halloween, but I keep that tidbit to myself.

So maybe they're not the nicest people I've ever met, but at least neither of them has tried to rip out my jugular. Low standards are nothing new to me and if one of them or this Pippa person can give me answers, then I'll happily follow them wherever.

I hurry my pace so that I'm side by side with the grumpy dickwad who is so reluctant to help me. "What's *your* name?"

He picks up his pace, intent on losing me. What a fucking gentleman. "It doesn't matter," he grumbles.

"Well, what am I supposed to call you?" I look like an idiot trying to keep up with him—taking big strides like power walking is an actual form of exercise.

"You're not," he says.

Emery shoots me an apologetic look.

"Well ... well, what if I have to pee or something?" Who knows how long this journey is going to go on for?

Nameless asshole stops short, giving me an incredulous look. It dawns on me that maybe whatever creature he is doesn't even need to use the bathroom. I begin to worry that's most definitely the case, as I've obviously rendered him speechless.

"Do you ... do you urinate?" I ask.

Well, there's a question I never saw myself asking someone.

His eyes narrow like he's hoping to shoot laser beams at me. "What the fuck kind of question is that?"

I flinch at his tone, but I've committed. "I don't know! Look, this is all very strange for me!"

"Unbelievable." He shakes his head with disgust and keeps walking.

"He's not much of a talker," Emery says quietly.

"I noticed," I mumble.

After walking for another thirty minutes, we slow as the guys stop by one of the baobab-like trees. Its pink-tinged bark looks ghostly in the dark.

My number one fan taps on the bark rhythmically as I glance around to see if Emery thinks this is weird, but his face is unreadable. When he's finished, the tree seems to take a sigh. Instinctively, I jump backward.

"Is this one of those talking trees?" I whisper, but they both ignore me.

"Ring," the brooding one demands.

"Ring what?" the tree says in a bored, lazy tone.

I muffle a yelp. Definitely a talking tree.

"What the fuck do you mean? I input the number, now *ring*."

"Does no one have *any* manners these days?" the tree asks and I can't help but agree.

Fuck, I'm reasoning with trees now.

"I really don't have time for this," he clips.

"Just say please," Emery says impatiently.

"Please," the other guy commands.

The tree lets out an impatient breath and begins to glow as if it's breathing, and with each inhale, the bark becomes brighter.

"What's happening?" I ask, wishing my voice sounded like I have a little more backbone.

Emery looks at me, puzzled. "What do you mean?"

"Why are you talking to the tree?"

The guys exchange confused looks. "That's how we get a hold of people that are farther away?" Emery explains, like a question.

"So it's like a phone?"

More strange glances. Okay, no phones here. Got it.

"Sorry," the tree drawls. "There's no response." The bark dims again to its original color.

"Are you sure you rang the right number?" Emery asks the tree.

His friend looks like he might explode into a million pieces of rage.

"Of course. But let me leaf through my contacts just in case."

I giggle, covering my mouth quickly. The phone tree laughs with me.

"Don't encourage it," the brooding one snaps.

After a few moments, the tree glows brightly again. "Ah, here it is. The receiver would like me to tell you that until you learn how to ask for things nicely, you can get fucked."

"Atlas," Emery pleads. I see his friend clenching and unclenching his fists.

I close my lips tightly against my building laughter.

"I don't understand why anyone puts up with you," he snaps at the tree.

"Have a wonderful day, sir," it replies.

"Does that normally happen?" I ask as we continue to walk.

"Uhh ... more often than not," Emery says with a smile. "They're finicky creatures, not to be trusted, really, but it's not like we have much choice."

"Sounds pretty *shady* to me," I say with a snicker.

"For fuck's sake," apparently-Atlas moans. "She's worse than I ever imagined."

Emery throws me an actual smile, though, so I feel pretty good about my pun.

After walking for what feels like an eternity, I start to fall behind. My body is just about ready to shut down from lack of food, blood, and sleep. Neither of the guys seems to care much about waiting for me, so I slowly become enveloped by the dark. There isn't a single star in the sky and the thin crescent moon does little to illuminate the path.

"I can't see in the dark!" I shout, but no one responds. I try to run and catch up with them, but I'm blind out here.

Something electric hums underneath my flesh, causing me to shiver. I don't like the dark. Panic bursts into my veins. "Hello! Can you please *stop*!"

The air thickens and I automatically know something is off. I kneel down to find Pants unmoving, like he's frozen in place. My heart rate accelerates. When I pick him up, he's completely stiff in my arms. It's probably not the smartest move, but I just start running. Sprinting, actually, and eventually, I find the orb of light above Emery and Atlas's heads, but they too seem to be stuck. Before I can investigate further, air flows as reality pulses into something new and the atmosphere returns to normal.

Before I can take a breath, Atlas's gaze finds mine and there's nothing in it but pure, unbridled rage. He grabs me so quickly that I drop Pants and his grip on my arms feels as though it'll break my bones. A snarl rips from his throat and two elongated canines are exposed, coated with a thick, black substance.

Nothing I've ever experienced in this world or mine is scarier than the beast in front of me right now.

"Who are you?" he growls, his grip tightening.

"Atlas," Emery says calmly.

"You're hurting me," I whimper.

"Who are you?" he shouts.

I shake my head, unable to process words around the fear and pain that's seizing me. My arms are breaking. We move with super speed as he pins me against something hard. The force of it steals the air from my lungs and something crunches. Ribs, it's definitely my ribs.

Emery is speaking, but I can only make out part of his words. "Atlas, I think you need to stop." He says it like a simple suggestion, ignoring the fact that my skeleton is shattering beneath his friend's hands.

Atlas doesn't stop. He only screams something else at me, but I can't hear the words. My broken body is shutting down, struggling against his hold, but slowly giving in.

"Stop!" I manage to scream.

My voice is so panicked and garbled I don't even recognize it as my own. As soon as I speak the words, I feel a shift again and the pressure from the snarling beast pinning me to the tree lessens. I push out of his grip and a blue shockwave releases from me. It feels like energy or electricity or ... magic. Lighting up the space around us, it propels Atlas and Emery backward. I collapse to the floor, panting and unable to move.

Magic?

Instinctively, I know it's mine. Bred from my blood and soul. Somehow it belongs to me, but I don't know how. Last time I checked, I couldn't freeze time. Tears take their familiar path down my face as

I gasp for air and try desperately to crawl away. Every breath, every moment is agony and then it's too late. Time speeds up and I give in, falling to the dirt and letting the darkness consume me. I'm a quitter. Always have been, always will be.

Sorry, Pants. I can't do it.

I heave, causing the pain to rise to the surface again in sharp, blinding bursts.

"Atlas!" Emery shouts.

It sounds so far away, but then someone is standing over me as I fade in and out of consciousness.

"She's barely breathing. Fuck, Atlas. You killed her! I told—"

"Move," he snaps. In my haze, I wonder if he's ever not angry.

His presence is almost soothing, but that can't be right. He smells like winter, which sounds stupid, but hear me out. My mother burns this candle all of December—cardamom and vetiver. That's what he smells like. A hand covers me, gently dragging along the surface of my skin.

"Please," I beg, but I'm not even sure for what. To save me? To let me die? I still want that long sleep I promised to myself, but now it doesn't seem that simple.

"Don't give up yet, Fox." The words are so quiet I'm pretty sure I've imagined them.

Air fills my lungs and the pain that coated my blood seems to lessen under the consistent and careful strokes against my skin. My vision comes back and I feel painless when I stare up at him. There's something in his eyes that softens, but then it's gone as he stands and turns away.

"I'll get Pippa. Just stay here," he says casually.

Like he didn't just take me to the brink of death and then pull me back. Like I didn't just magically stop him from breaking my spine. It's all good here in Crazyland.

Choosing not to move, I just lay there in the fetal position for a few moments. Enjoying the feeling of air in my lungs and letting my brain play catch-up. Emery crouches over me, and I watch him carefully. His eyes are a violet color that pulls a smile out of me.

"You okay?" he asks.

Reflexively, I wince as I try to sit up, but there's no pain. I feel entirely normal now ... better even. I can taste blood in my mouth, but when I look down, there's not a drop of it on the ground, and the splatters from earlier are gone from my skin. Pants, at my side, does a little down dog yoga stretch like nothing ever happened.

"How ... how did ..." I'm too stunned to finish the thought.

"Healing magic," Emery says with a shrug. "Atlas is really powerful. I probably could have healed some of those injuries, but it would have taken too long." He doesn't say the words, but I can hear them—you would have died first.

Rolling on my back, I stare up at the empty night sky. "Is he always in such a good mood?"

Emery stands over me and smirks. "Only with new people." His smile fades as he contemplates something. "He wasn't always like that, though."

Taking his offered hand, I stand and wipe the dirt off my leggings. The light that floats above his head brightens and he gestures to a tree stump a few feet away. I walk over to it and slump down, letting my head fall into my lap.

"Harper, right?" he asks after a few moments of silence.

I nod, but keep my head down.

"Well, Harper. Our world is complicated right now. Everything we know has been threatened and ..." He seems like he's trying to choose his words carefully. "It's stressful for everyone."

My world turns red. "Oh, okay. Well then, I guess I can just let it slide that he tried to *kill* me!"

Emery scrunches his nose in a way that says, *yeah, what a bummer,* but he doesn't apologize. I wouldn't want it from him anyway. I don't think I want it at all. I'm pretty sure at this point I'm better off wandering around this place alone than with these psychos. Then again, he's the third person who's tried to kill me in the last thirty-ish hours.

"Atlas is actually a really great guy once you get to know him."

"You'll have to excuse me for not making plans to do that anytime soon." I stand up and try to walk away, but Emery gently grabs my arm. He hesitates for a second, hopefully remembering I just knocked him on his ass. Not like I'd have any idea how to replicate that.

"Harper, just wait. If you leave, you'll die. Our world isn't really made for humans."

I bark a laugh. "I can tell. I'm hoping to get out of this place as soon as possible."

His grip tightens slightly, and I look down at our skin touching. "Please, just listen to what we have to say. Maybe we can all help each other."

"Does what you have to say involve breaking any more of my bones?"

He gives me a weak smile. "I promise I won't let him do that again."

As usual, my options are fucking limited. I still don't have any answers and while I'm not keen on the idea of hanging out with the massive temper tantrum throwing child—who is big enough to murder me with a snap of his fingers—I sense honesty in Emery's words. For some reason, I trust him. This will probably be one of those moments where I look back and tell myself, *here was the moment I fucked up*, but what can I say? I'm a glutton for punishment.

I sigh with reluctance and sit back down just as the sky brightens. It's suddenly so sunny it feels like afternoon. We both squint and shade our eyes as heat rolls from the rays, warming my muscles.

"Is that normal here, too?" I ask.

Emery looks up at the sky with concern. "No, it's not. Something ... something is very wrong here."

"Great," I murmur. Just what I need—one hell hole exchanged for another. But if I stop being a whiny brat, I can admit that it's hardly a hell hole. In fact, it's beautiful. There's a sparse forest surrounding us and behind me is a glistening body of water. The dirt road is just up ahead and beyond are the same beautiful hills, and a single mountain in the distance. Trees towering above me resemble aspens with their white trunks and yellow leaves.

Emery straightens his spine, and I look in the distance, noticing Atlas walking back with a stunning creature. Her light bronze skin and pointed ears are adorned with gold jewelry. Acorn-colored hair is plaited in a long braid that drapes over her shoulder. Piercing gold eyes meet mine and automatically, I stand. Even Pants takes notice, his ebony paws placed perfectly in a sitting position.

The sun glints off the belt of knives wrapped over her chestnut riding leathers. I didn't notice until now, but both Emery and Atlas are wielding swords.

Nice, Harper. Way to notice the hot guys had giant slicing weapons before following them into the dark. See? Glutton for punishment.

I'm very self-conscious in the presence of their otherworldly beauty. The woman gives me a slow once over and her features are delicate and soft, but her eyes show no mercy.

When she speaks, the gentle soprano of her voice is almost as beautiful as she is. "Hi, I'm Pippa. You must be Harper?"

CHAPTER EIGHTEEN

ATLAS

I FEEL SORT OF BAD FOR ALMOST KILLING HER, BUT AFTER she pulled that stunt with the time-block, I was certain she was working for the enemy. Pippa basically ignored me when I tried to explain things to her. In fact, everyone in the room looked at me like I'd officially lost it and they were all just waiting for something like this to happen. But when I finally got her to hear me, I saw that same fear in her that I felt. If this is a trap, we're fucked.

"Hi, I'm Pippa. You must be Harper?" My sister is the epitome of calm and collected when she wants to be.

I won't lie. It's reassuring to find this girl still alive. I haven't healed anyone so close to death before ... at least not successfully, and especially not a human. I was half convinced she'd be dead by the time we got back here, but she looks as good as new. Better even. I didn't mean for it to go that far. I didn't realize how fragile she was, but it shouldn't matter. Our lives would be infinitely less complicated if she didn't exist. So why do I feel so relieved seeing her standing there?

I don't smile, though. I stare at her with disinterest because, despite not wanting her to die, I still don't trust her. And whatever magic she has under that human shell of hers is terrifying. Even worse, she doesn't seem to be aware of what it is.

"Hi, Pippa." The words are short and clipped. She's pissed and I can't blame her.

"I'm sorry for my brother's ..." Pippa looks at me with disappointment. "Lack of manners. I assure you that not everyone in Calamity is like that."

Her eyebrows raise in interest. "Calamity?"

Pippa nods. "That's what this continent is called," she says, gesturing around.

The human's gaze goes to a backpack that's sitting on the road. It must have fallen off when I propelled her across the forest.

"How did I get here?" Harper asks.

We all frown. She's either a damn good liar or she genuinely has no idea. My money is on the former.

"I'm not sure," Pippa says. "We were hoping that you could tell us. Humans are somewhat of a myth around here."

Harper laughs and shakes her head. The sound is so agonizingly beautiful my mask of indifference nearly cracks as I look into her eyes. They're deep brown, like burning firewood. What kind of fucking witch is she?

Pippa cocks her head. "Is something funny?"

"It's just that, where I'm from, *you* are a myth. Are you ... are you elves?" She asks it with an innocent curiosity that lights up her face.

My sister smiles. "Yes, Atlas and I are. Emery is part elven and part faun."

"Oh! The deer-people," she says. The three of us look at each other in confusion and she takes note. "Like a deer? The animal ..."

I glare harder at her.

"Nevermind. How can we speak the same language?"

"I don't know," Pippa answers honestly and everyone looks to me.

I don't say anything. Fuck if I know. This whole thing is weird as shit.

Harper bites her lower lip. She looks so fucking cute doing it that I focus on the lake in the distance just so I don't have to stare at her anymore.

"I'm guessing you don't know how I could get home?"

I don't need to look at Pippa to know she's shaking her head. "How did you get between your home and here?"

"I ... I don't know," she says.

I clear my throat and look back at her. "Do you know what you did before? The magic you used when—" When her gaze turns to me, it's filled with so much contempt the words dry up in my mouth.

"When you tried to kill me?" she sneers. Her attitude is like a damn light switch.

"Again, we're very sorry—"

I don't let Pippa finish, because fuck this girl. I did what I thought I had to do to protect my family. "Yeah, when I tried to stop you from hurting everyone."

"Me! Who was the one dying on the ground?"

I scoff. "You started it when you—"

"Enough!" Pippa interrupts, holding her hand up at me like I'm a fucking child.

Emery smirks, and it takes everything in me not to punch him.

Pippa's voice is gentle when she continues. "Harper, you used magic before. Something called a time-block. It stops time and in certain instances uses the energy of the paused movement as a force to be wielded."

Harper closes her eyes and shakes her head like Pippa's explanation is physically hurting her. "I don't understand. You're saying that *I* used magic?"

I'm starting to believe she has no idea what's going on because she looks so damn confused. I don't know how anyone could fake that.

"Yes," Pippa says slowly. "A very powerful and ancient type of magic."

The little human paces, causing us to take a step back. She looks at us, surprised that we're cautious around her. "I don't have any idea how that would be possible ... I'm ... I'm human."

"Yeah, we fucking know that, Captain Obvious," I say.

Six eyes turn to me with anger.

Pippa chews the inside of her lip and turns back to Harper, who looks like she might be sick. "You must be exhausted and hungry."

The human doesn't move. She just keeps looking at the fucking fox at her feet like she might just pick him up and make a run for it. She'd be an idiot if she tried.

"Will you stay with us? We're going to be moving locations soon, but you could come with us," Pippa offers.

Harper glances at me like she'd rather eat the dirt on the ground than be anywhere near me. "I don't know ..."

"Atlas will behave," Emery says, and I growl at him.

"Won't you, Atlas?" Pippa chides.

My jaw ticks as I look at Harper. "Only if Fox does."

The little human scoffs. "You're not seriously calling me that."

I definitely am now.

"Ignore him. You and—" Pippa looks down at the real fox.

"Pants," Harper says like it's something to be proud of. It's the dumbest fucking name I've ever heard.

But Pippa laughs like she genuinely thinks it's funny. "Okay, you and Pants are welcome to stay with us and maybe we can help explain things a little better to you."

The human Fox crosses her arms over her chest like she has any other damn choice. "Why?"

"Why, what?" She's testing my patience. I don't care how hot she is. She's a fucking human. She's dangerous and has the potential to ruin everything. More so than I already have. And she has the audacity to question my sister's kindness?

"Why would you help me? What changed? Last I checked, you knocked me on my ass and left me in that town not too long ago. You know, before you tried to kill me."

Pippa turns and slices me with her glare. I may have left that part out.

My sister sighs as if dealing with me is so exhausting, and maybe it is. "You're right. There may be some benefits for us if we're right about our hunch. But we're not bad people, Harper. I swear to you. Despite my brother's brazen lack of empathy ... we do want to help you."

I snort because I genuinely *don't* want to help her and I'm not going to lie to her face.

Something devilish crosses the human's features as she stares at me. I almost feel like I've underestimated her until I remember I'm double her size and three hundred times as powerful.

"Fine. But only until you explain to me what the fuck is going on and then I'll decide my own fate."

We all smile at each other because no one decides their own fate ... that's the whole point. It's fucking fate.

CHAPTER NINETEEN

HARPER

I RUB MY FACE THROUGH MY HANDS SO HARD I KNOW I'M turning my skin pink. Then, dragging my fingers down, I stop just below my eyelids, exposing my eyeballs to Pippa, Emery, and Atlas. Letting out a deep breath, we watch each other in silence.

"What the fuck are you doing?" Atlas grumbles. He's looking at me like I just took a dump on his dingy ass couch in this gross as fuck hut.

"I'm trying to process what you're telling me," I glower back at him.

"And holding your eyes open for little bugs to fly in is going to help you do that?"

I gasp, releasing my fingers quickly as they all cackle. Crossing my arms, my scowl returns. "I'm just thinking, ass."

"Careful," he growls, but this time I'm only slightly frightened by his tone.

"Sorry, *Prince* Ass," I snap back, using the information I've gathered in the last twenty minutes.

"I like her," Pippa says, and Emery nods.

I beam a little at that, and I hate it. I hate the way I want her to like me. Even more, I hate the way I'm so willing to trust her, despite knowing that everyone I've ever loved has let me down.

Taking another deep breath, I recount what they just told me. "So, you're a prince and a princess whose parents were murdered and now some other queen has taken over the throne and she's terrible?"

"Sure, if you want to sum it up in the most simple fucking way possible."

"*Atlas*, it's a lot to take in," Pippa warns.

It *is* a lot to take in, especially when you're no longer even on planet Earth and you're surrounded by a bunch of mythical creatures. The strangest thing happened to me when they asked how I got here. It was like I knew, but when I tried to speak, the words just slipped from my mind. Every time I try to recount the events that happened after the hospital and before those creatures attacked me my memory becomes muddy and faded.

"I'm sorry ... about your parents," I say. "How long has it been?"

Pippa's eyes soften to mine, and I have the strongest urge to hug her.

"Eighteen months. The queen—"

Emery cuts her off gently, "Don't call her that, Pip."

"Well, what am I supposed to call her? That's what she is, whether we like it or not."

"I don't know, raging bitch? Psycho cunt? Murdering whore? I think those would all do," Atlas says, and I stifle my laugh. I won't give this asshole an ounce of my joy.

Pippa rolls her eyes. "Anyway, the miserable twat—"

"Nice one," Atlas interrupts, a genuine smile passing across his face. When his eyes light up it takes all my self-control to stop staring at him.

"She's got some power we don't fully understand and a spell

around the castle we can't penetrate. Right now she's unstoppable and we need to figure out a way to overpower her," Pippa explains.

"Aren't you guys immortal or something? A year and a half has to be no time at all."

Pippa laughs weakly. "Not quite. Our lifespan is about five hundred years. Atlas and Emery are one hundred and fifty and I'm one hundred and six. A year and a half is certainly a short time for us. I can't even imagine what will happen if we let this go on longer."

Well, they certainly don't look that old. I move on because so many things are more important. "And the shift between day and night?"

They all look down with grave expressions, but Pippa is the one who speaks. "We're not sure what's happening, but it's not just day and night. Sometimes you wake up and it's winter—snow on the ground and everything. The next day it will be one of the hottest of the year."

The sorrow in the room is like a weighted blanket. This is their home and they love it dearly. I can tell how much it's tearing them up, not being able to fix it.

"It's ruining people's lives. Crops can't grow, aquatic species are in upheaval over the constant water changes, nocturnal species can't function normally. It started happening about a week after the ..." Pippa stops herself mid-sentence. Her face turns into a mask of rage and I make a mental note to avoid pissing her off. "Ever since that *witch* took our throne, nothing is the same and everyone is worse because of it."

I still don't understand how I could possibly help them. "So where do I come in?"

They all exchange a look, and my heart feels like it's going to burst. Atlas gives me a feline smile. "Don't be scared, Fox. If we wanted you dead, you would be."

"That nickname needs to stop. And I'm not scared," I say defiantly.

"I can hear that little heart you have pounding a mile a minute, but you're a decent liar ... I'll give you that."

My mouth drops open. He can hear my heart beating?

Emery looks at me with concern. "We don't know a lot about humans, but what I do know is that elves are pretty much superior in every way. We're faster, our senses are much stronger than yours, and we live longer."

"But you have no idea how I got here?" I ask again.

Pippa shakes her head sadly. "Only you know that."

I chew the inside of my lip, Emery's previous words catching my thoughts. "Why would you create a mythical creature that's so beneath you?" I'm thinking of all the magical beings in fairytales and how they're better than humans in every way. That's the point of a fantasy, right? To create something that gets to live without human flaws.

"Well, that's the thing. Humans are—correct me if I'm wrong—cunning, excellent liars, greedy, aesthetically appealing—"

I snort. "Aesthetically appealing?"

Emery blushes, and it's adorable.

"Get to the point, Emery," Atlas says, clearly tired of having to explain anything to me.

"Does he really have to be here?" I ask Pippa, giving Atlas a hitchhiker thumb.

Atlas opens his mouth to say something, but gives me a smirk instead. Somehow, that's worse than his degradation.

"He grows on you." Pippa nudges him with her shoulder.

"Legends also say that human blood is poison," Emery blurts. "Poison like nothing else. It's alluring and sweet and then it will kill anything within seconds."

I swallow and touch the pulse in my neck subconsciously.

"It's true then?" Emery asks, watching the movement.

"I—I don't know ..." I stammer. "I killed some people by accident. Well, they attacked me and tried to drink my blood and then they just ... died." My voice breaks at the end and my fear and shock of this place comes barreling into me at once. I fight the sting in my eyes, refusing to let anyone see how weak I actually am.

"That must have been really scary," Pippa says gently, and it nearly breaks me.

I don't move or speak, sure that my voice will come out shivering if I do.

Atlas lets out a huff I don't understand and then rubs his hand down the back of his neck. "We're hoping that your blood could be the thing to help us have the upper hand. If we could—"

Fear rips through me, and I stand up, shaking my head. "You want my *blood*?"

"We don't want to hurt you, Harper." Pippa takes a slow step toward me in an attempt to calm me down, but Atlas stands and grabs my wrist before I can move.

I try to scramble from his hold, but he only grips tighter. "Let me go!"

"Atlas, stop it!" Pippa shouts, but he doesn't relent.

He leans over and speaks into my ear, "Make me."

Adrenaline pumps through my body and I try futilely to rip my hand away, but he pulls me against him. He's a predator and I'm his prey. My eyes spin around wildly, but Pippa is still glaring at her brother and Emery watches like he's trying to figure something out.

Atlas's voice sends a tingle down my spine as he growls into my ear, "Make me, Fox, or I swear to the Realm I'll rip your throat open on this ugly fucking carpet and drain every ounce you have."

His arm is thick enough to cover most of my stomach as he pins me to his body. My mind is reeling until something electric seems to pulse through me and I feel him smile against my cheek.

"Do it," he whispers, and I'm certain he's going to break my wrist with his hold.

Pain sears through me as I try one last time to break free, the words he wants ripping from my throat in a desperate plea. "Stop!"

It works. Time freezes and a blue glow radiates from my palms as I push him back and he flies through the wall behind us with an otherworldly force. I fall back from the momentum and scramble toward the door before time falls back into place and the crash of the wall bursts into the fabric of space.

Pippa and Emery shield themselves from the debris that rains down as the house shakes and drywall crumbles into pieces through the Atlas-sized hole I've created. I don't know what they're going to do to me now, but I'm not going to stick around to find out. Pants and I make eye contact as I head for the door, but Emery moves with inhuman speed and stops me.

"Wait, we won't hurt you," he says in a huff.

Pippa stands on her toes and looks into the room I threw Atlas in, the separating wall now in shambles. He groans on the other end and I watch her chest heave with relief before she turns and smiles at me.

What the fuck is happening?

The world spins slightly and I'm overcome with a heavy exhaustion. I nearly fall to the floor, but Emery catches me and carries me over to a chair.

"Very impressive," Pippa says to him.

"What the hell was that?" someone shouts. The door bursts open and three more elves pour in, along with one of those human-sized rodents I saw in town.

My mind is a mess of churning waste. I close my eyes for just a few seconds, letting the noise drown out. It feels so nice in the quiet dark that I decide to stay.

MY EYES CREAK OPEN LIKE rusted shutters. When I make sense of the world around me, I find myself tucked into an enormous four-poster bed in the clothes I was wearing before. The pillow beneath my head is like a cloud and the sheets feel like soft canvas against my palms. A fire burns with fervor in a hearth on one wall, the hot glow showcasing the beauty of the room. The blush walls are covered in intricate patterns of washed wood depicting different trees. All the furniture has the same tangled design, like each piece was carved by some forest nymph. In fact, there are actual trees on either side of an arched door, their twisted branches and soft green leaves arc toward one another in an embrace. A plush, plum blanket is draped over a large chair in one corner and an oval, gilded mirror is propped against a dresser next to it.

I push out of bed, my dirty socks sinking into a quilted rug of beautiful shades of pinks and purples. Daylight creeps through the slit under dark curtains drawn over a tall window. Peeking through an open doorway, I find a quaint, but equally beautiful bathroom. I don't know where I am, but what else is new?

Pants lifts his head from his curled position at the foot of the bed, his soft, furred form lost in the squish of the comforter. Laughter filters in through the crack beneath the door and I suddenly feel sick. Spinning around desperately, I look for my bag, finding it hanging on the chair. Relief floods through me as I find everything as it was—the book, some clothes, and the pocket watch are all inside. I don't know why, but this broken clock is important to me. Flipping it open, I note the hands in the same spot as before. I dip my head through the chain and let it fall to my sternum before tucking it under my shirt where no one can easily see it.

My fingers run along the bark of the trees next to the door, a smile crossing my lips. When I open it, I look left and right. The room is in a long hallway and the sound of clinking glasses and friendly chatter come from one end. Pants's paws hit the floor as he follows me. Afternoon light floods into a big space containing a modern kitchen on one side and a living room on the other. The whole house looks like it was carved out of a big oak—the same intricate wood designs everywhere. Plants hang from shelves and sit on table tops. Floor to ceiling windows with gentle, sheer curtains line the entire wall of the living room, showcasing a glittering mound of rock outside. Even though it's enormous, the cottage vibe and lush greenery make it feel cozy. Magical is the only word to describe it.

The talking has stopped as everyone turns to me and stares. Four unfamiliar faces watch me with amusement. They're all elves except the rat, who is giving me the warmest smile of them all and Emery with his neat black horns. Pants walks up to Atlas and curls at his feet. Fucking traitor.

We're all silent until Pippa walks from a hallway hidden across the room. She's talking cheerily and holding two bottles of wine before stopping dead in her tracks and taking in the scene.

We all turn to her for direction, and she smiles broadly. "Harper! You're awake!"

The events of what happened before I passed out are not lost on me. They must have moved me somewhere else because this place is about ten thousand times nicer than their shack in the woods.

They moved me ... without my permission. Though I guess I should be grateful they didn't leave me behind unconscious.

"Let me introduce you to everyone," Pippa says, placing the bottles on a long wooden table next to a fire.

"Where am I?" I choke out.

"We had to move locations—" she begins.

"You're right next to Mt. Fernview. Does that help?" Atlas says with a sickly sweet smile.

Someone else snickers.

I narrow my gaze at him, wishing I could melt him with my new magic, but nothing happens. "How sad to see you survived our last tussle."

Everyone's eyes widen as they stare between us. I guess that's not a very nice way to speak to a prince. But he's not my prince, so he can fuck off if he thinks I'm going to bow at his feet or some shit.

His smile fades, but just barely. "You didn't even come close, Fox, and you never will, unless ..."

Pippa resumes her stride over to the rest of the party. With a movement of her hand, her nails turn to claws and she expertly opens one of the bottles with ease.

"Unless what?" I say, hating myself for taking the bait but also dying to know how to put him in his place.

He doesn't answer. He just stares at me with something akin to hatred.

"Unless you let us train you," Emery says.

My eyes snap to him and my heart lurches into my throat. Train me? For what?

The questions on my face must be evident because he says, "You'll need to learn how to use that power if you want to survive in our world."

Survive in our world. I don't want that. I want to go home. Right? My thoughts fade to my mother's house and I try imagining walking through those halls again. I don't want to. That was the whole point of my little stunt. There's only pain waiting for me there. But to stay here? I don't want that either.

"I want to go home." It comes out so meekly that I clear my throat. "I don't want to stay here," I say more firmly.

Pippa gives me a look laced with pain. "I don't know if we can help you with that. But we'll try everything we can once we have our kingdom back."

I cross my arms. "So you're blackmailing me?"

Atlas is instantly in front of me, using some super speed and blotting out my view of anyone else. He's so close I have to look up at him, his dark brown eyes meeting mine. These pools of fury aren't just brown though, they have swirls of green and blue in them radiating in a starburst pattern around his pupils.

"It's called a trade, Fox. You help us, we help you," he says. His voice rumbles through me like an earthquake.

I now know he could literally crush me with his big toe, but I try my best not to let fear bleed into my voice. "And you want my blood?"

He nods. There's this look in his eye that makes my muscles tighten and heat coil between my thighs. What the hell is wrong with me?

"We'll be gentle," someone coos from the seating area behind him.

Atlas growls like the monster he is and snaps his head to look at whoever spoke, silence descending among them.

When he turns back to me, his eyes are branding. I've been attracted to a lot of assholes in my life. Guys that do terrible things and say worse behind my back. But I've never been attracted to someone who is just straight up mean to me. I still haven't received an apology or even a good explanation for anything he's done and I hate him for it.

I should be thinking over their proposal, but I'm not. I'm trying my hardest not to let my eyes roll over the solid plane of his chest and the tight cords of muscle that make up his arms. Fuck, nope, I'm definitely letting my gaze wander.

He smirks and lifts my chin with his finger. It's gentle enough that I might be able to close my eyes and convince myself he wasn't incredibly malicious.

"Eyes up here, Fox," he says so quietly only I can hear.

A blush crawls up my neck and flushes my cheeks, but I keep my face in a permanent scowl. Just because my body is a traitor doesn't mean I'd actually give in to this elven douche.

His voice is like sleet, burning my skin and making me shiver all at once. "What do you say? Will you bleed for me?"

"Fine," I grumble, pulling out of his hold. "But I'm not doing it for you. I'm doing it for me." I shove past him and find Pippa and Emery smiling. Everyone else is glancing at me warily.

Atlas chuckles quietly as he takes his seat, and I stand awkwardly in front of everyone.

Pippa claps her hands once. "Harper, this is Ellison." She points to an elf who is tall and lanky with wide rimmed circular glasses. He looks up from rolling what looks like a blunt and gives me a Christmas morning smile. "Ellison is our reconnaissance guy, his derax is a—"

"What's a derax?" I interrupt.

"Oh!" Her face scrunches as she tries to think of the words.

"It's our other form," the only other woman says, like it's the most obvious thing in the world. I want to give her a bitchy response back, like *"bite me"*—since the implications of that quip are even more insulting here—but I know I'm outnumbered. Plus, the words that came out of her mouth pique my interest.

"You turn into something else?" I ask, letting a little awe bleed into my voice. "Can I see?"

Atlas's laugh is the only sound as silence descends across the room.

"It's not really proper manners to ask that," Pippa mutters.

Everyone looks at me with something akin to pity or disdain and something in me snaps. "Look, I'm not fucking from here. So I'm going to say things that sound silly and wrong to you. But if I agree to help all of you, then I expect a little respect." All I get are blank looks. "I don't let anyone push me around, and *no one* walks over me, so if that's a problem let me know now." The confidence is false, but it'll do. I refuse to let these elves use me as a blood bag.

"I think she'll be just fine," the black-haired elf says with a smile.

"I told you you'd like her," Pippa says and hands me a cup of wine.

My eyes fall to Atlas, who is giving me an unreadable look from a huge chair by the fireplace that makes him look like a fucking king. He's wearing a short-sleeved shirt that shows off muscular arms, the right one covered in tattooed runes that seem to crawl all the way up the side of his neck like a vine.

"I'm Idalia," the other woman says to me, pulling my attention back to her. She catches my gaze on Atlas and smirks. She's beautiful, they all are. Her long black hair flows in a straight waterfall around her shoulders and her sharp features compliment the ice blue in her eyes.

"Wilder," the rat says. His long gray coat wisps around him and I have the urge to pet him, but I'm guessing that that's not very polite either. "And before you ask, my species is called Varrek. We live primarily underground."

"Don't get him started," another voice drawls. "I'm Torin." I turn to face another guy lounging lazily in a chair opposite of Atlas. His dark skin is contrasted against his buzzed chalk-white hair and his smile is kind.

"How long have I been asleep?" I ask Pippa.

"Two days," she says with a shrug.

"Two days?" I squeak.

"That's what happens when you use up all your magic," Atlas says, picking under his nails like talking to me is a waste of his time.

Before I can reply, Emery pats the seat on the couch next to him. I walk over and plop down.

"Overwhelmed?" he asks as everyone resumes their conversations.

"Hungry, mostly," I say, and my stomach grumbles on cue.

Emery leans back and laughs. "Yeah, you'll definitely fit right in."

CHAPTER TWENTY

ATLAS

I KEEP GLANCING AT THE HUDDLE OUTSIDE THE HUMAN'S room. Emery and Elli press their ears to the door like it's going to announce the way to save our world, and Pippa paces in the hallway.

What the fuck are they doing?

Nope.

No, I don't care.

If it involves her, I'm not interested.

"Just knock," Pippa whispers.

Emery raps lightly on the door. "Hey, Harper. Is everything okay?"

"I'm fine," she shouts, her voice muffled through the layers of wood.

"What if she's doing a weird human thing and she's going to turn into some blood sucking monster with talons?" Ellison asks.

"Then we kill her, obviously, you fool," Torin says.

I'm surprised Torin is with them. Normally he acts too good for any of their shenanigans, but there he is, his back and the sole of one foot leaned up against the wall like he doesn't have a care in the fucking world.

Why am I looking at them? I. Don't. Care.

I turn back to the book in my hands. It's fiction. A story about a talented, but unsuccessful artist who went blind and then reinvented the way they painted. In the process, they became one of the best in the world. It's a story about loss and redemption, about finding yourself. It's absolutely nothing I can fucking relate to, so don't ask me why I'm reading it.

"Atlas!" Pippa whisper-screams and regretfully I turn my head in her direction. "Atlas, come here!"

"No."

She frowns and slouches like a petulant child. Stomping her feet lightly while glaring at me. "Come here!"

I roll my eyes and put the bookmark between the pages, gently placing it down on the tea table and walking over to them.

"What?" I snap.

"Talk to her," Pippa whines.

I shake my head and turn around. "Absolutely not."

Pippa crosses her arms. "She's been in there for *days*."

Emery grabs my wrist, and I turn at the contact. What the fuck is their problem? "Come on, Atlas." His eyes are filled with an emotion I can't place. I'm not sure if he's trying to placate Pippa or what, but I'm fucking confused.

"Why me?"

"You've kept yourself holed up in your room for the better part of eighteen months. Surely you can relate?" Torin drawls from across the hall.

I growl at him. I hate his tone. I hate that he's right. He puts both hands up in surrender, but there's a mock smile on his face.

"You're a female," I say to Pippa. "You go in there. She probably misses her family or her boyfriend or some shit."

Pippa chews on her lip like she's considering the thought. We all wait in silence until a rustle is heard behind the door and it cracks open. Everyone peers their heads in like she's a fucking freak show and I'm sure it makes her feel *really* comfortable.

The human glares her red-rimmed eyes at us...well me, mostly. The skin underneath is puffy from crying and I don't know why, but something twists in my chest. "I don't have a *boyfriend*," she snarls at me, like the suggestion is disgusting. "I'm fine. Do you need something from me?"

"We just wanted to make sure you were adjusting okay," Pippa says with a friendly smile.

"I'm fine." Fox shuts the door in our faces and Pippa squeaks in disappointment.

Emery lets out a breath. "She rivals you in attitude, Atlas."

I don't hear him though, because rage is seeping through my pores like a fine sweat. My friends were just being nice to her and she might as well have fucking spat in their faces.

I reach for the knob, realizing it's locked, and melt the mechanism in the metal contraption. Swinging the door open, I walk into the room and slam the door shut. It's dark in here, the only light coming from the bathroom window, and Fox doesn't even flinch at my arrival. She's buried under the feather-filled comforter like if she doesn't see me, maybe I don't exist.

Tough fucking luck, sweetheart.

"What the fuck is your problem?"

"I said to leave me alone," she groans from beneath the fabric.

"I'd love to ignore your existence, Fox, but everyone here participates. You don't get to sit out and mope about whatever pathetic shit you're going through."

Yes, I hear the irony.

She sits up with a huff, her dark hair in a flurry of directions like she just got fucked, and her nipples peeking through the fabric of her shirt. The sight is doing weird things to me that I pointedly ignore.

"My name is Harper."

"*My name is Harper,*" I mock back for no good reason.

Her eyes narrow into snake-like slits, and I can't help but wonder if her bite is as venomous as her blood.

"Get out," she demands.

"No," I reply, and plop into the armchair in the corner.

She slides out of the covers and saunters over to me, my heart rate picking up at her lithe body. She's skinny. A little too skinny, but she's still stunning. I imagine she's even more beautiful with her legs spread open.

What the fuck is happening to me?

"I know your type," she says, planting her feet in front of me.

"Oh, yeah?" Color me intrigued.

"Yeah." Her voice is sultry and raspy as she leans into me, placing one hand on each armrest. Her shirt tilts so that I have a perfect view of her entire rack, but I don't bite.

Note to self, modesty is not her strong suit.

"Little rich boy." She's rendered me speechless with her boldness. There isn't an ounce of fear in her voice and I can't decide if it's because she's brave or she just doesn't know any better. "You put yourself on a pedestal because you think it's your right to taunt and demean anyone you want. Because you think your cock is *sooo* big that everyone should just get on their knees for you."

I'm nearly fucking hard and she hasn't even touched me.

"But guess what, Atlas?"

I don't give her the pleasure of answering. Instead, I lean in until we're a breath away from each other.

"I've been bullied my whole life by someone much scarier than you. So bring it on, because you can't break me any more than I already am."

Her words catch me off guard as I stare into her black-brown eyes. The darkness I feel washing over me reflects back in her gaze, but there's something else. It fights for control, a flicker of white-hot heat that pushes the darkness back.

"You got me all wrong, Fox," I breathe.

Her eyebrow arches, but I'm so close to her face that I barely see it.

"I'm anything but little and I don't *think* my cock is that big. I know it is."

A smile dances across those pouty little lips, but it doesn't reach her eyes. That darkness in there is almost all-consuming.

"Guess you'll just have to prove it to me."

And fuck do I want to. *Bad, Atlas.*

"In your dreams, human. I wouldn't touch you if my dick was on fire and your pussy was the wettest thing around."

Her glare is back and I feel its heat coil in my gut.

"Fuck you."

I give her a fake smile. "Like I said, pass."

She pushes off the chair and out of my face, walking away as her ass begs to be freed from the confines of her shorts. I beat back the urge to grab her waist and bend her over the bed.

Standing, I brush some non-existent lint off my pants. "You'll start training with Emery soon."

"Training for what?"

"For whatever the fuck I tell him to train you for. You don't get to ask questions, Fox."

I don't know why I'm doing this. I should just let her waste away in here. I *should* kill her. But something in me begs to give her a lifeline, something to hold on to so the darkness doesn't win.

"Whatever, just leave me alone." She crawls back into bed unceremoniously and I sigh.

"One more thing."

Fox groans at the ceiling.

"Apologize to Pippa. She's just trying to help and if there's one thing I won't fucking stand for, it's hurting my sister's feelings. Got it?"

The human lifts her head and looks at me, chewing on her lower lip. "Yeah. Yeah, of course I will. I'm sorry about that."

"I didn't ask you to apologize to me," I snap.

An eyeroll is the only response I get. So fucking rude.

I don't know why I say it, but the words come out before I can stop them. "I know you don't think you can help us, but I have a feeling you're capable of more than you think." The anger in her face melts, but I slam the door shut before she can respond. When I get into the hallway, everyone is gone.

A strange feeling passes over me. Part of me is begging to go back in there. To crawl under the covers and fuck her so hard that the demon lurking below her skin realizes that she's mine and mine alone. But that's actually insane, so instead I go find Emery to spar and hope he's up to challenge the beast raging inside me. He's never let me down before.

I ALMOST FORGOT WHAT A real bed feels like, but even the softness of this mattress doesn't lull me to sleep. I just about lost my shit when Ellison told us this was the place he'd chosen for our new hideout. His Nana lives here, so I told him she wouldn't get caught in the middle of anything and fuck, I really hope I stay true to my word. We're practically *in* the mountain and it's the perfect place to hide.

I sigh and fold my hands behind my head. I've been staring at the same spot on the ceiling for hours. The blackout curtains are pulled tight against the daylight leaking in, but some still trickles through the cracks. I grind my teeth.

I don't know what to make of the human. Her defiance gets so deep under my skin it's unnatural. But being around her gives me this rush I don't understand.

I'm pretty sure her pull on me is a human thing. All the legends talk about how cunning they are and who better to target than the Prince of Calamity. Bitch. Those thoughts don't banish her from mine, though. Instead, she skips around in my head, torturing me. When we get the throne back, she's gone. I don't care how much she's helped us, I'll find a way to send her back to wherever she came from, even if I have to defy the Realm itself.

A soft knock reverberates through the door, and I sit up. "Come in," I answer.

My brow furrows as Idalia steps through the door and shuts it quietly behind her. She's wearing a black silk robe and my eyes immediately drop to the cleavage spilling from the top. When I look back up at her, she's smiling like I've fallen right into her trap.

I push myself up and sit against the headboard. "What are you doing here?"

Her elegant fingers pull the bow tied around her waist, and the robe falls open, revealing her outfit—if strips of clothing can be classified as an outfit. Her tits are nearly bursting from a lacy black bra and long sheer socks cover her legs until they reach buckles sitting over her thighs that attach to skimpy black underwear. My dick takes notice, but I'm not particularly interested in Idalia.

I don't say anything though as she walks over to me, heels clicking lightly on the wood floors. The robe falls as she shrugs out of it. She doesn't hesitate in the slightest, crawling on top of me and straddling my lap. Midnight hair cascades down and covers her breasts, and I want to move it from obstructing my view.

She trails a finger down my naked chest and stops where the blanket covers the rest of me, tugging gently. I grab her hand, forcing her to look at me. "Why are you here?" I ask again, this time with less patience.

Idalia frowns. "Isn't it obvious?" she asks, gesturing to her toned body.

"No, it's not fucking obvious. You've barely blinked at me the last eighteen months and now you're dressed like this in my room in the middle of the night."

"Atlas," she whines, jostling lightly on my lap and ... yup, now I'm fully hard. "You're ruining it."

She's right. I am ruining it. Why do I even care? Lately, I'm the kind of guy that prefers no explanation prior to sex. The less talking, the better.

Idalia notices my hardening cock pressed against her and smiles, rolling her hips against it and moaning lightly. It's enough to sway me as I lean into her and capture her mouth with my own. I close my eyes and unclip her bra, letting her tits bounce against my chest. I roll one of her nipples between my fingers as she moans louder into my mouth and I can't help but wonder what Fox would sound like if I did the same thing to her.

The thought jolts me back, and Idalia gives me a confused look. Her lips are swollen from pressing into mine. Her hands, braced against my shoulders, strain for me to come back.

"What's wrong?"

"Nothing," I say, shaking my head and focusing on the female in my lap and not the one down the hall.

I bite Idalia's lower lip and she giggles, digging her nails into my back and rubbing a hand through my hair.

"Stop teasing me," she whispers against my mouth and instead of her voice, I hear Fox's. It only makes me angry as I flip Idalia down on the bed so that I'm leaning over her, my hands braced on either side of her head. She looks up at me with hungry eyes as I slip my hand down her panties and find them soaking.

"So wet for someone who seems to hate me *so* much."

"I don't have to like you to want to fuck you," she says, lifting her hips as I slide two fingers inside her. Her eyes roll back and she grabs the sheets, whimpering my name over and over as I methodically pump into her.

My thumb finds the soft flesh of her clit, gently rubbing as I watch her lose herself. The octaves of my name are louder on her lips and her breathy sounds fill the room as she comes around my fingers. But my mind keeps wandering to the fucking human, and I growl as I pull out of Idalia and strip off the sweatpants I'm wearing.

"Who would have thought that all along that look in your eyes was really you begging me to fuck you," I whisper, one hand still bracing me above her, the other squeezing her breast so hard she lets out a little yelp. Her hands graze my chest and slowly move toward my cock until I'm sliding in and out of her palm and my head spins with her touch.

"Well, I've missed seeing that alpha in you, but the way you handled Torin the other day ..." I groan as her grip tightens around me and she drags me to her entrance. "I'm not the only one who's noticed," she says, leaning up to grab my mouth.

My body stills. "What the fuck does that mean?"

She pulls back and gives me a simpering smile. "You mean you didn't notice the human giving you 'fuck me' eyes her first night here?"

My heart beats harder. Here's the thing: I know I'm attractive. I'm also a fucking prince, so it's not like females haven't fawned over me my whole life. Yeah, maybe it's made me into a cocky asshole, but if anything that just seems to get me laid more. So, of course, I know that the little Fox would let me tie her up and fuck her until she couldn't breathe if I was anyone else, but I'm not. I'm me. The guy who basically called her disgusting. She hates me—I made sure of that from the second I knew she was human.

"Atlas?" Idalia says from below me, snapping me out of my reverie.

"Don't fucking talk about her," I growl and plunge into her.

She arches her back and falls into a rhythm with my movements, fueled by an emotion I can't name. My grip on her thighs shreds into her skin, but it'll heal by morning. Her tits bouncing with each thrust have me in some kind of trance as pleasure muddles my mind, but her moaning begins to grate on me as I imagine over and over again someone else underneath me.

"Fuck, Atlas ... I'm gonna—"

I cover her mouth, cutting her off, and glare at her. "Can you be silent for me?"

Her eyes widen and then fall in a seductive way that tells me she thinks this is some kind of kink. It's not. In my desperation to orgasm, I've come to terms with the fact that if I want to finish tonight, I'm going to have to imagine a certain brown-haired human, and even though I really hate even admitting that to myself, I'm so hard ... I need a release.

I flip Idalia over because the less I have to look at her face, the easier this will be. I wrap her hair around my fist and line up her ass with my cock as I slowly push into her. She cries out in pleasure and rocks back and forth, begging for me to give her what she wants. But honestly, I don't give a shit if she comes because I'm starting to regret fucking her in the first place.

"Atlas," she moans.

Please shut up, please shut up.

I focus on the way her ass pushes up against me, losing myself in a memory of Fox's umber eyes. I carried her back here when she passed out a few days ago, tucking her into that bed that looked so giant with her small body inside it. She snores, but just lightly, and it's fucking adorable. I feel like a mess. I haven't even known this girl for a week, most of which she's been asleep or locked in her room, and she's already found a way under my skin. She barely speaks to me and when she does, it's always snarky, rude comments.

I fucking love it and I want to punish her for it. I want to know what it feels like to have her full lips wrapped around my cock. I want to shove myself so far down her throat she won't be able to speak without being reminded of how much she likes the taste of me. I want her on her knees, begging for more while I fuck her mouth until tears are streaming down her face.

Fuck.

I groan with relief as I pull out and come all over Idalia's back. Something about that makes me smile as she collapses forward.

"That was amazing," she mumbles into the sheets.

I walk to the bathroom and start the shower. She strolls in a few moments later and I let myself marvel at her beauty for a moment. I wish I could enjoy it more, but instead I block the way of her getting in with me.

She puts her hands on her hips. "What are you doing?"

"Just because I fucked you doesn't mean I like you." I give her a simpering smile as her blue eyes turn to ice and she bares her teeth.

"You're such a fucking prick."

"Night, sweetheart," I call out as she storms through my room. The bedroom door slamming eases the tension inside me. I slink down in the shower and let the water fall over me.

Fucked. I am so fucked.

CHAPTER TWENTY-ONE

HARPER

OMEHOW I FIND SLEEP AGAIN DESPITE THE FUCKING going on loudly down the hall. I don't know who it is, but it doesn't take me very long to imagine a certain prince that thinks he owns the world and when she calls out his name, I roll my eyes hard enough to give myself a headache. I don't know how many hours have gone by when I wake again, but it's night outside. I'm already sick of this weird day-night stuff; I can't imagine what it's like to have lived with this for the last eighteen months.

Even though I've been here for a week, this will be the first time I really leave my room. Last night I did as Atlas asked and apologized to Pippa. How do you explain to someone that your world feels like a perforated piece of paper, just waiting to be torn in half, when *their* life actually has been? Torn in half and then crumpled into a tight little ball, thrown into a trash can, and lit on fire. I don't have any right to be this miserable, but here I am anyway.

Before I went to bed, Pippa lent me some clothes. She even put a spell on them to make them fit me, since she's basically half a foot taller than me. It was really nice of her, like really nice, and it only made me feel more guilty. I made a vow to try to stop being a raging bitch and start acting grateful. It's hard to even open my eyes in the morning, but I'm doing my best, okay?

After a much needed shower, I walk down the hall to the smell of food and a smile begins to form on my face. Everyone is out here except Wilder, but I don't know if he sleeps in the house or underground.

I get a few head nods, but no one really acknowledges my presence except Ellison, who looks up at me as he flips a pancake with a blunt in his mouth. I'm grateful for the silence, though. The last thing I want is to play twenty questions. Ellison smiles at me and takes a puff, handing it over.

"No, thanks," I say, waving him off.

"Let me know if you change your mind," he sings and goes back to cooking.

Soft music plays over the speakers in the walls. Naturally, I don't recognize it. I do my best to ignore Atlas's presence, but it's too big in this room. It feels like it might drown me if I don't greet it.

Instead, I find a seat at the counter next to Emery and wiggle into it anxiously.

"Pancakes?" he asks, leaning over the counter and pulling a few onto a plate.

"Yes, please."

"So polite when she wants something." He smirks.

I stick my tongue out at him and when he returns the gesture, I see that his is forked.

He laughs at my widened eyes. "It's okay. It's a weird feature even in our world."

"He's our little freak," Torin says from his other side, tousling Emery's hair.

"Fuck off, Torin," Emery jokes.

I cave and glance over at Atlas, finding him staring at me. If it bothers him that I caught him looking, he doesn't show it. I quickly turn back to Emery.

"What's on the agenda for today?"

"Meat?" he asks, scooping sausages onto my plate.

"Yes!" I say with a little too much enthusiasm. He arches an amused brow at me and then places the plate in front of me.

I frown as I stare at it. It looks like regular pork sausage, but who knows what the fuck it's made out of. I decide I don't want to know and take a bite. The seasonings explode in my mouth and the meat melts like butter against my tongue.

A little moan escapes me and I'm almost embarrassed, but too preoccupied with the food.

"I think you have a fan, Elli," Emery says.

I nod with my mouth full like a fucking heathen. Ellison winks at me, his eyes glazing over from whatever he's smoking, and goes back to humming to himself and mixing ingredients together.

I haven't really noticed how cute he is. The round glasses give him this sexy Clark Kent vibe. I stop chewing to admire the sleepy, just-got-out-of bed thing he has going on with his white tee and sweatpants. Messy brown hair falls just slightly into his eyes. He looks younger than the rest of them, but I'm pretty sure it's the lack of facial hair and goofy smile that seems to be permanently on his face.

I can feel Atlas standing behind me before he even speaks. "To answer your question, Fox—today we train. I'm guessing your skills with a sword are sorely lacking."

I spin around and face him. "You'd guess correctly, Prince Asshole. Congratulations, you're not as dumb as you look."

Everyone stops what they're doing to look over at us. I keep forgetting that it's probably a big deal to talk back to him. *Whoopsie.*

Atlas gives me that smile that has me fighting the urge to shrink back. He leans in so close I can feel him breathing. Both of his hands brace behind me on the counter so that I'm trapped in an Atlas cage. Emery even backs away.

"Maybe your weak, human mind can't understand that you don't talk to *me* like that. I know you're not from around here, but if you don't cut the bullshit, I *will* punish you."

This conversation might be super hot if he wasn't looking at me like he might slice me open and make a backpack from my skin.

Agree and move on. Don't make more of a scene, Harper.

"You're not even a prince anymore. What gives you the authority to boss people around?"

God dammit, Harper.

Atlas snarls in my face and lifts me from the chair like I'm light as a feather before swinging me over his shoulder and carrying me outside like a sack of potatoes.

"Let me go!" I scream. I'm pounding my fists against his back, but I might as well be punching a brick wall. In fact, I'm definitely hurting myself more than I'm hurting him. The cold air nips at my exposed skin as my shirt follows gravity and falls over my head. "Atlas!"

He tosses me on the ground, the air flooding out of me as I impact the earth. I sit, using my palms flat against the dirt and bending my knees to hold myself up. I reach for the only power I have against him, but find that my lips won't open, as if my jaw is wired shut. Night turns to day faster than a single beat of my racing heart. I squint against the blinding light until a massive shadow comes into view, giving me a brief reprieve before terror sets in.

Atlas stands over me, his canines bared, something black and viscous dripping from them. The sun outlines him in a heavenly aura, yet he's far from angelic. A demon wrapped in the skin of a god.

He snaps his fingers and magic binds my wrists together behind me. I fall backward before I can adjust to catch myself. He snaps again and binds my ankles. I'm tied like a fucking roast pig; all I need is my apple. With anger pulsing through me, I find a way to push up and brace my weight against my hands.

"You think a few friendly remarks from Emery means you have friends here?" he asks as he circles around me. "You don't, Fox. You're a stranger. Barely a guest. Don't fool yourself into thinking that we *need* you. We really don't."

He stops in front of me and squats down so that we're eye level. If I could spit in his face, I would.

"You'll listen to me, Fox, for the same reason everyone else does—because I'm more powerful than you. Because I'm just waiting for any excuse to shatter you into a million tiny pieces. So many it will be impossible to put yourself back together again, even with all the magic in the world."

I breathe heavily, my chest heaving with anger. Somehow, I find it in me to growl at him. It feels right, here in this world, where I constantly have to fight for my place. But it's the wrong thing to do because when I go to take my next breath there's nothing there and a frenzied panic builds in my chest.

"And here I thought you weren't breakable," he says with a grin. "Now, all I want to hear from those pouty little lips is, 'yes, Your Highness.'"

Oxygen fills my lungs and I gasp as the function of my mouth returns to me. "Fuck you," I spit.

The demonic prince continues to smile at me, but the shape of his lips tilts into something more monstrous as one fang peaks out in warning and fire turns his brown eyes golden.

"Atlas, I think she gets it," Pippa comments from behind him and for the first time, I realize they're all standing and watching.

My cheeks betray my steel demeanor, heating to the point of pain.

"I don't think she does." He ruffles a hand over my head, mussing my hair like you would a child. "She'll learn her place, though." Possessively, he trails a few fingers down the side of my face.

Hands still tied, I can't slap him away. All I can do is clench my fists as my stomach twists with his disgusting display of power. When his fingertips reach my mouth, I snap out at him while he dodges my bite and lets out a cruel laugh that has me feeling even more embarrassed.

Everyone watches from the porch with a sick kind of intrigue. Atlas leans into me, invading my space and punishing my senses with the heaviness of his presence and his intoxicating scent. It's then I realize that everything about him is predatory and the self-preserving part of my mind wants me to give in. To be lulled by the strength of his body and the temptation of his lips. By the way he smells and probably tastes.

"Careful, little Fox. I might like it when you use your teeth." The heat of his breath fans against my ear, sending a trail of goosebumps down my neck, hardening my nipples.

Absolutely fucking not. Self-preservation is for chumps anyway.

I move to glare at him, but before I can blink, my bindings disappear and he's walking back into the house.

"Training starts today, Emery," he mutters with a wave of his hand. "Make her at least somewhat useful."

IT'S BEEN A WEEK SINCE my altercation with Prince Bossy Pants and we've been avoiding each other like the plague. I spend most of my time here below the house in the armory training with Emery. It's so boring I could scream.

Emery shakes his head and sighs. He's actually very patient, but I think I could push the Dali Lama's buttons. "Feet wider apart ... no, turn your ankle like I showed you."

I look down at my feet and then over to him—I'm doing exactly what he wants. Flapping my arms in defeat, I tilt my head back and look at the arched stone ceiling.

"I don't want to do this," I whine. "When do I actually get to use a weapon?"

Emery snorts a laugh. "I wouldn't let you within ten feet of a weapon. You can barely hold up your own arms."

I rock my head down to glare at him even though he's one hundred percent right. I'm not an athletic person. I've quit just about every sport or physical exercise team I've ever joined.

He cocks an eyebrow. "If you can't hold a stance, then you'll never last in battle. Forget the weapon—you won't even be able to stand up to a gust of wind."

I sink to the ground in response, propping my elbows on my knees and hanging my head between my legs.

"Let's go running," he offers, like that's supposed to sound enticing.

"What about magic? I thought you guys said you'd teach me magic." I lift my head to plead with him.

He crosses his arms. "That's Atlas's thing. You'll have to ask him."

My lips form a pout. "Why? You all have magic, don't you?"

"Yes, but your magic is old magic. Something none of us are familiar with. Not to mention that in your body it's so volatile, I'm not sure how to control it."

"What do you mean?" I stand and dust the straw that lines the stone floor from my sweaty skin.

"Magic for us is like blood. It weaves through the center of our entire being. We need it to live and function. But you ... it wasn't made for your body. I don't know what it's doing inside you."

I take stock of myself. I feel fine until I focus on that electricity inside me. It does feel like some caged beast thrashing around, waiting to be released.

Groaning like it's going to get me anywhere, I close my eyes and say, "What do I have to do to get him to teach me?"

Emery is silent until I open my eyes and see a look of concern on his face. It fades when he catches me staring.

"What?"

"I'm just thinking about how he isn't usually like this. Something is going on with him and I don't know what it is."

I cock my head. "Like what?"

Emery shakes his own. "Atlas is a little shit, but ... nevermind. I shouldn't be talking to you about it."

I try not to be offended, but I am. Emery and I aren't best friends or anything, but he's the only one that has spent a substantial amount of time with me and I was starting to feel like we were building a connection.

"Tell me what to do. I want to use my magic."

He gives me half a smile. "I'm not sure. We're in uncharted territory here." His eyes widen in mock surprise. "Humans have taken over."

A laugh escapes me. "Human. Not plural, just lil' ol' me." I bat my eyelashes at him for effect. "Come on, you're his best friend. You have to know what would cheer him up."

"You could try apologizing."

My jaw clenches. "*I* need to apologize? He tried to kill me ... twice!"

Emery shrugs. "I mean, the second time you kind of deserved it."

I tug on my braided hair nervously, removing the band around it and separating the pieces. "No one deserves to be humiliated like that."

"You push his buttons."

I run a hand over my scalp and down to the tips of the sweaty strands. "Well, maybe he should stop making them so damn squishy!"

Emery barks out a laugh and his eyes gleam with something I can't quite place.

"What?" I ask with a smile.

He shakes his head. "You just ... you remind me of him."

I gather my hair to one side and begin braiding it again. "He must be really different then, because we couldn't be more opposite."

Emery walks over to the weapons rack and readjusts them mindlessly. "I wouldn't be so sure. You both can give up pretty easily when things get hard—"

"Rude!"

He turns to me and gives me a serious look. "You didn't let me finish. I was going to say that you both fight with all your heart when you really want something. You're two sides of the same coin. It just depends which side you want to be? The kind that gives up or the kind that keeps fighting."

I bite the inside of my cheek and think about his words.

"So, which is it?"

I wish more than anything I had an immediate answer, but I don't. "I don't know," I say in a low voice, pacing the room. "In this world, I'm not entirely myself ... it feels impossible to explain."

"Maybe that's the reason you're here. To figure out which version you're supposed to be."

I let out a big breath.

"Come on, Harper. One run. Just one." He flashes his canines at me with his smile.

I roll my tongue over my front teeth and bite my lip. "I'll puke," I warn.

"I can't wait," Emery deadpans.

Closing my eyes, I nod, relenting. For the first time in a long time, I realize I have something to fight for. Not only that, but I want to.

CHAPTER TWENTY-TWO

ATLAS

LIPPING THE POCKET WATCH OPEN, I STARE AT THE glowing numbers that mock me. The minute hand inches toward seven. I close my eyes and sigh. Despite staying up most nights to strategize and figure out counter spells with Pippa, I feel like I haven't accomplished anything except lying through my teeth every day.

When I stand, Harper is blocking my doorway. I don't know how I didn't hear her and my heart lurches at the idea that she saw me until it dawns on me that she would have literally no idea what she was looking at.

"Hiding your porn stash?" She places a hand on her hip and I roll my eyes up and down her body, enjoying the view a little too much. Every piece of clothing she has on hugs her like a second skin. Her hair lays in gentle waves that fall past her breasts. My gaze finds a tattoo of a snake wrapped around her right forearm. Words follow the curves of its body, but I don't let myself linger long enough to read them.

"It's like the Realm designed you to annoy me," I grumble.

She rubs her chin in fake thought and shrugs. "Mm, no. I think my purpose is bigger than that and annoying you is just an added bonus."

She's been here for almost three weeks and every day it gets harder to be around her. I can't ever tell if I want to rip her apart or fuck her ... maybe both. I've been trying to convince Pippa to let Wilder use her blood for weapons, but she wants her to have time to adjust. What no one realizes—thanks to me—is that we don't have time.

I *should* be teaching her how to use her magic. I get one shot at beating this witch queen and we'll need to use everything we can, but I hate spending more than a few moments alone with her.

"Is there something I can help you with, Fox?" She frowns at the nickname and it fills me with joy.

"I came here to apologize," she says.

I fail to hide my surprise.

"Don't get excited though, because I decided not to." Fox folds her arms over her chest and pouts at me.

"Thrilling," I mutter and try to busy myself to seem disinterested. Really, I can't fucking wait to hear what she says next.

"I questioned your authority in front of everyone and that was rude of me, but you know what?"

I lift an eyebrow at her.

"You're fucking rude."

I have to fight back my laugh, but I fix my features into my typical bored stare. Walking around the bed, I take a few steps toward her so that she's looking up at me. She doesn't back down an inch.

"I don't know who you were before all this happened, but according to everyone else, it's not the guy in front of me. Too bad because this—" She waves her hand up and down in front of me. "This guy is just a spoiled brat who got dealt a shitty hand and instead of doing anything about it, you're taking it out on everyone else. You're giving up."

"You don't know—" I growl as she picks me apart, nailing all of my flaws to the wall.

Fox takes a step toward me. Fearless. "I *do* know you ... unfortunately. Maybe not your favorite fucking color or what your favorite book is, but I know that pathetic part of you. I know it because it's in me, too."

She's right. If I'm being honest with myself, I saw it from the moment I saved her in town. Looking at her is like staring into a shattered mirror.

She leans against one of the columns of my four-poster bed. "I have a proposition for you."

"I'm listening."

"We don't really like each other, that's fine. You've got that whole alpha asshole thing going on and I've got my—"

"Pompous bitch routine?" I suggest.

She laughs, and it takes everything in me not to smile with her. "Sure. Anyway, Emery pointed out that we could both be better. Not just for us, but for everyone else."

"He tends to do that," I mutter. "I still haven't heard any proposition."

Fox chews her lower lip and fiddles with her nails. It's the first sign of nervousness she's revealed since stomping in here. "Train me." It's meant to sound like a demand, but I hear it for what it is—a plea. "Train me and make me *useful*." Cheeky air quotes frame the last word.

"What do I get in return?" I ask.

Fox shrugs. "You get to take all that pent up energy out on me and hopefully turn it into something beneficial for everyone else."

She has no idea the energy I want to take out on her.

"I promise I'll make it a challenge." She smiles and there's nothing but deviance in it. If she had real canines, they'd be sharper than mine.

"I don't think you know what you're asking for."

Fox closes the distance between us. Anticipation glues me to the floor as she leans up on her toes and attempts to whisper into my ear. She's too short, but my hearing is good enough to catch every word.

"I look forward to finding out," she says slowly and then turns on her heel and prances out of my room like the fucking succubus she is.

When she's out of sight, I finally let myself smile. If the little Fox wants me to train her, then I'll make her wish she'd asked for anything else.

It's night, but the clock reads five a.m. I push out of bed, not having slept most of the evening and get dressed. Quietly, I walk down the hall trying not to wake everyone else. Pippa and I were up late last night picking apart the army and figuring out plans of attack. We meet with the Council next week to go over strategy and it feels good to finally be part of something, even if I'm the whole reason we're in this mess.

I put my ear to Fox's door and listen. I'm guessing she's asleep and when no noise comes back, I push it open quietly and slip inside. The human is sprawled out on her stomach in the king bed as if it's a contest to see how much room she can take up and she's going for the gold. Her pajama shorts ride up her ass, revealing perfect cheeks I want to sink my teeth into. A big baggy t-shirt covers her torso.

The actual fox, Pants, lifts his head from the corner of the bed and gives me two thumps of his tail before going back to sleep. Fox's hair covers her face in a waterfall of chocolate. And because I'm weak, I risk my whole plan by gently tucking a piece of it behind her ear. It falls through my fingers like silk, and the urge to wrap it around my hand and pull is overwhelming.

I smile to myself at her furrowed brow. She's pouting even in her dreams and something about that seems so damn right it hurts. At my movement she stirs, rubbing her button nose against the sheet and I step back, afraid I've woken her, but she just goes right back to gently snoring. I'm at peace here in this moment, watching her like a fucking creep, so I decide to ruin it.

With a single thought, I bind her wrists, ankles, and immobilize her jaw so that she can't scream. Her eyes fly open, wide with panic as I sit in the wingback chair in the corner of the room, lazily crossing my legs. When her gaze finds mine, she gives me a look that's meant to rip me to pieces.

I can feel her magic radiating into the room—wild and raw. When we first met, I didn't recognize it for what it was. So foreign, yet familiar. I simply ignored it, but now that I've felt it against my skin, I feel like an idiot for not realizing it earlier. The longer she's in Calamity, the stronger it becomes. It's absolutely terrifying and I nearly shiver with excitement.

The wooden chair legs scrape loudly against the floorboards as I drag it to her side of the bed. The thick quilt covering the floor bunches up against the chair, but I ignore it until I can lean down and look her in the eye.

"First lesson in magic is learning to call on it," I say quietly.

Her eyes are a pit of anger, but she doesn't fight me. What a shame.

I tilt my head to the side and push the hair out of her face, since her hands are bound. She flinches away from me, but I'm much faster than her. "Can you feel it in your blood?"

I know she can't talk, but she doesn't even try to answer me.

"Come on, Fox. Giving up so soon?" I roll my lower lip in a mock frown.

Her eyes turn to molten steel as I lean back and release my hold on her jaw muscles.

"Fuck you," she spits the second she can speak.

I pretend to think about her words. "Maybe after training, if you've been a *very* good girl."

She rolls her eyes and makes a noise of disgust. "I feel it ... the magic."

"What does it feel like?" I ask, genuinely curious.

Fox closes her eyes. "It feels like an electrical current pulsing through my body." Her eyes are still closed as she reaches out to the magic that should never have been hers to possess. "Like a panther pacing up and down in a cage it's too big for."

My heart lodges somewhere in my throat. "Why a panther?"

Her eyes fly open and lock on mine. "I don't know. That's just what I see when I close my eyes. The magic doesn't feel like it's part of me. It feels like a strange beast living beneath my skin."

I briefly wonder if she could shift and then banish the thought from my mind. That would be impossible.

"That's because it doesn't really fit inside you."

She frowns. "What do you mean?"

I lean back in the chair, and she struggles against the restraints. I forgot about them, to be totally honest, and she looks fucking hot all tied up for me, but I guess I've made my point. I rub my fingers together out of habit and the invisible ropes untie and disappear. She shoots me one more glare and then pushes up, adjusting her shorts, much to my dismay, and running a hand through her hair.

"Everyone in this realm has magic. It's as important to our bodies as blood is to you."

"Do you have blood?"

"Of course we fucking have blood." She frowns at me, but I can't stand how often she interrupts. "Let me finish, Fox."

She mimes locking her mouth shut.

"If we don't have magic, we die. Our bodies can't function without it. But you, little human, you don't need magic. It's just additional, and it's trying to find a place to fit amongst all your messy organs and cells." I gesture at her vaguely. "Or so we think."

She's quiet as she considers this. "Will having it hurt me?"

I shrug. "No fucking clue."

"Well, that's reassuring," she says, flopping back onto the bed.

"I'm not here to make you feel better, Fox. Quite the opposite, in fact." I smile at her and she sits back up to sneer at me. "Do you still feel it?"

She nods. "Not as strongly, though. But it's fighting me, like it wants me to react."

"When you're threatened, it begs to be let out, to be wielded. When you're calm, it calms too, but only slightly. We're going to change that because magic doesn't control you; you control it. It's going to learn to be part of you, whether it likes it or not."

I can tell she's not convinced.

"Crawl to me," I command, half hoping she really does it.

Her fury is back. "Excuse me?"

"I said, crawl to me."

She crosses her arms. "No."

"Why not? It could be fun."

"Um, because you're a dick and I'm not going to just do whatever you say."

"Good." She looks surprised as I stand. "Saying no to me is the same as saying no to your magic. Don't let it tell you when to use it or how to use it. Don't let it feel like a stranger in your body. Show it who it belongs to."

She bites her lip, forcing me to imagine what it would be like to sink in with my own.

"What now?" she asks.

"Now, we make it our bitch. Get dressed and meet me outside in five minutes."

I can tell she's fighting the grin that's working its way across her lips, and I wish she wouldn't. I want to see it so I can claim it for myself.

CHAPTER TWENTY-THREE

HARPER

A DECK WRAPS AROUND THE HOUSE SO WHEN YOU sit on the porch swing you can look out at the rolling hills with the mountain at your back. Though right now, as I make my way outside, it's pitch black. Glowing mushrooms light the path down the porch steps and firefly orbs of light float around the deck as I walk onto the grass in front of the house. Earlier, I asked Emery about electricity, but he said everything here is powered with magic.

Blinking into the darkness, I swivel my head, looking for Atlas. He told me five minutes, and I made it here with thirty-six seconds to spare. Now he's going to think I'm late. I don't want to wander into the dark, but I wonder if that's his whole point. Maybe he's just trying to fuck with me.

"Atlas?" I call out, wishing I hadn't. I hate playing into his little games.

Taking a few steps, I let the darkness engulf me. I give my eyes time to adjust, but it's futile, there's no starlight in this sky to illuminate the world—only blackness.

Minutes pass as I lose myself in the darkness, letting my mind finally clear. I hear the door creak open and turn around toward the house as Atlas strolls out. He bites into a purple apple and looks at me like he's surprised to see me. The resounding crunch echoes through the night.

"You said five minutes," I tell him.

"Did I? I'm not really good with time."

I scowl, waiting for him to continue his lesson. I wasn't thrilled to be woken up in a panic, but I'm glad he's at least trying to teach me. Instead of continuing, he stretches his arms above his head and yawns into his shoulder. The porch light orbs surround him like planets orbiting the sun and I too feel some kind of gravitational pull toward him. His body is as perfect as I imagined. Not that I imagined it ... very thoroughly. Black ink covers his left obliques like the runes stretching along his arm. The black v-neck he's wearing hugs his biceps, and maroon jogger sweatpants give him this *I woke up like this* vibe. He's literally a fucking snack. I remind myself that he's despicably mean and hateful while simultaneously deciding if it will be more work learning how to use magic or trying not to stare at him.

Atlas smiles like he can read my mind, and I train my eyes back on his. "Second-guessing your decision to not get on all fours for me?"

I scrunch my nose. "In your fucking dreams."

He walks down the steps, stopping on the last one. "But the question is, are we fucking in *your* dreams?"

Rolling my eyes, I ask, "Are you going to teach me or not?"

He laughs, but it barely holds any sincerity. "I'm waiting on you, Fox. Let's see what you got."

I don't want to scream "Stop!" into the night like a lunatic, but I'm not sure how else to call on it. The only time I've ever used it is to defend myself. "I don't know how."

"I can't help you if you don't try." He looks utterly bored as he leans against the banister and tosses the core of his apple into the darkness.

Rude.

I take a deep breath and close my eyes. Reaching inside myself, I grasp at the magic running in a frantic current, imagining that blue energy illuminating my palms. When I open my eyes, nothing happens. Frustration builds in my chest as I try again, thinking about how I used it before. I was scared, I wanted to escape, I wanted everything to stop. I whisper the word to myself and open my eyes again, but still nothing.

Finally, I look to Atlas, who's watching me with an intensity that makes me feel entirely vulnerable. "Tips would be appreciated at this point."

He walks over to me, and my body stiffens in his presence. I'm not afraid of him ... not entirely, but he's so unpredictable.

"Give me your arm," he demands.

I hesitate for a split second, so he grabs my left one, but he's surprisingly gentle.

"I'm going to use my magic to summon yours. Hopefully, it will help you become more acquainted with it."

He flips my palm up to the sky and draws a line from the sensitive crook of my elbow down to my middle finger. My eyes focus on the black runes painted on his arm; in the dim magic lighting, they glisten like iridescent ink. I shiver at his touch, which feels like someone took an ice cube and followed the same path. Invisible liquid trickles from the area he traced as the magic inside of me lurches to that spot. Involuntarily, my hand grips his arm and holds it against my own. My fingers dig into his flesh until blood wells in the crescent-moon cuts my nails have created. My eyes don't leave his, my mind swirling in colors and shapes I can't quite understand as an all-consuming storm brews inside me. I could say it feels like an out-of-body experience. Or that part of me feels as though it's being freed. Like every cell inside me is warming in anticipation. But none of those descriptions would do this feeling justice.

I don't even notice his nails digging into my skin until trickles of blood drip down my arm and into the dirt. Finally, I tear my eyes from his and watch as our blood forms tiny puddles at our feet. The droplets come alive, swirling and snaking toward each other before sinking into the dirt like they were never there. I can't speak or pull away and I don't want to.

Atlas lets go of my arm first, jolting me back to reality as my attention snaps to his face. He looks at me like I'm trying to explain the theory of general relativity to him in a foreign language.

"What the fuck was that?" I mutter, more to myself than to him.

His eyes drop to my arm that's no longer bleeding. The wounds have healed over, but my body aches to touch his again.

"*Yeren teso veluk syli,*" he whispers. *From our blood comes the earth.*

The words translate instantly in some deep recess of my mind and call to the magic that writhes in my veins.

"*Yeren teso bimav syli,*" I answer quietly. *From our blood comes the light.* I don't even know I'm saying the words until they've already been spoken.

He looks down to where our blood absorbed into the ground and I stumble backward as it changes—first a mound, then a seedling, and within seconds there's a fucking sapling at my feet.

"Atlas, what is happening?" I don't even try to hide the fear in my voice.

The black of night dims as the sun rises slowly in the distance. I've never seen dawn here and from the look on Atlas's face, he hasn't seen it in a while either. It's stunning, the hillsides bathed in shadowy, sherbet light.

"Fucking Realm," he breathes.

The sapling is nearly a tree. Beautiful wouldn't do it justice. It's fire-ant red bark—smooth in some places, knobby in others. The thick trunk makes way to wide, gnarled branches—some low enough to swing from and others soaring far above Atlas's head. Its most stunning feature is the gold leaves that look soft to the touch and glitter despite the low rising sun. As the wood stretches into its full form, the magic inside me opens one eye and surges, filling me until I feel like I can't breathe. Just as I'm about to scream for help, it stops, falling back like the ocean at tide.

I take a deep breath. My body is lighter and more powerful all at once. A sudden panic seizes me as this new feeling overwhelms me, but I find that familiar cloud of darkness and my mind eases.

Atlas steps around the tree and looks at me like I just created the stars. "How do you feel now?" he asks, and a genuine smile graces his face. It's so beautiful my heart skips a beat.

"Scared," I answer truthfully.

"How does your magic feel, though?"

"Free," I say without hesitation.

His smile only widens, and it's impossible to not return it. The sun rises faster than is natural, highlighting the gold in his toffee-brown hair. For a second, I think I see the version of Atlas that Emery sees, and I want to ask him to stay. "Are you going to explain to me what just happened?"

His smile fades into wonder as he looks up at the tree. "I'm not really sure." He strokes the bark. "What I do know is this is a Reign Tree. And I thought they were a myth." He looks from the shimmering leaves to me. "Just like you."

CHAPTER TWENTY-FOUR

ATLAS

I RUN INTO THE HOUSE FEELING GIDDY—WHICH IS FUCKING weird—and storm into Pippa's room.

"Pip!" I shout as I open the door.

"Atlas!" she screams and pulls the covers over her naked body as I wince and close my eyes.

"Sorry ... I just ... I can come back. It's urgent, though."

"Well, fucking spit it out!"

"Can I open my eyes?" I ask, clenching them like my life depends on it.

She huffs. "Yes."

"Fox and I just grew a Reign Tree." My chest heaves from adrenaline as it pumps through my veins. The world feels different, like I'm more connected to everything. Like her power is rushing through my blood and calling to the earth. Fox's magic is different than anything I've ever imagined. I want to taste it, but I also don't want to fucking die, so there's that. There's also something else ... but ... no, that's ridiculous.

Her eyes widen. "You did what? Impossible."

"Look out your window," I say, gesturing with my head toward the closed curtains. She looks down at her covered body and I do the same, frowning. "Just come outside when you're ready."

I shut the door, bolting into Emery's room, and tell him the same thing before running back outside. Fox is resting against the tree—*her* tree ... *our* tree—with Pants curled up at her side. I can't shake the feeling that they both look like they belong there. She doesn't sense me yet, so I take a few minutes to stare at her in wonder before I snap myself out of it. Walking closer, I sit down in front of her with my legs crossed.

"Your magic is ancient," I tell her. She opens her eyes, which are glazed and tired. "I don't know how you got it or why, but it's really powerful. Not all magic is created equal. I'm the most powerful elf in Calamity, and that's because of my blood. I was made to sit on the throne."

She frowns. "Because you're a male?"

"No, because I have these." I bare my canines and let the venom drip from them and onto my tongue. "The venom in my blood is hereditary. If Pippa had it, then she would be heir to the throne, but she doesn't. It's just the way our world works. The heir with *bas raza*, black venom, rules over Calamity and has the most power. Because my DNA is basically enveloped in this venom, it calls to a more ancient form of magic."

She shakes her head. "I don't get it."

I sigh, not sure why I'm bothering explaining this to her. Pippa or Emery would be better at this. "Ancient magic runs through every creature that lives in Calamity, but no one can really use it. It's what the magic we use today evolved from. The venom in my blood—"

"Which only *you* have?" she clarifies.

"Yes. My father had it too." She gestures for me to continue, which is fucking annoying, but whatever. "The venom in my blood is like a key that unlocks the more ancient form of magic. It really just enhances mine, making me stronger than everyone else."

"That's why you're so big?"

I can't even fight the smirk. "No, Fox, that's all me."

Her face turns the same shade as the bark, and my heart rate doubles, but I continue. "Your magic hasn't evolved. It's the oldest, purest form of magic."

"Does that mean I'm more powerful than you?"

I laugh in her fucking face. "No, definitely not." Though I'm not entirely sure that's true. She can't use it for shit, so at least for now she's not more powerful than me. I should be worried, but instead, I'm excited.

"What's the big deal about this tree?" she asks, looking up at it.

"No fucking way," Emery says from behind me.

"How is this possible?" Pippa breathes.

Soon everyone is standing outside, staring at the Reign Tree. It's daylight again. That peek of dawn was so beautiful, but it only lasted a few seconds. It was a hint at how to fix our world. But for a moment, it felt like it was just made for Fox and me.

I can't believe I just thought that.

Fox is standing in her normal pouty stance. "Can someone please explain the fucking tree to me?"

Wilder burrows from the ground and pops up next to her, eliciting a scream that makes me laugh.

"Sorry," she mumbles as her face reddens again.

"How's it looking down there?" I ask him.

"Pristine. It's indeed a Reign Tree—the roots shimmer gold."

I shake my head in disbelief.

"Calamity is split into six geographical areas," he explains to Fox. "Our lore says that the Realm created six Reign Trees as guardians of the world. No one living has ever seen one except those drawn in history books. They became more of a legend than a truth."

"We ... we made one?" Fox looks to me like I'm an anchor. Like I'll give her answers to questions I don't even deserve to hear. I can't explain what it does to me. It feels like her eyes are bludgeoning some wall inside of me. No one has looked at me like that in ... I can't even remember when.

I nod, worried when I speak my voice might betray the bored façade I've forced my face to memorize. "It's the magic in our blood. There's never been two living beings that have access to that raw form of magic. At least not in thousands of years."

"You think *she* found the trees," Pippa says suddenly. "She cut them down and absorbed their power and now the Realm is angry and the world is screwed up."

"Interesting," Wilder says, turning back to Harper. "Legend also says that if you cut down a Reign Tree, you can absorb a special kind of magic. It's not pure like yours is, Harper, but darker—constantly hungry for as much power as it can take. It's more of a tale we tell children, but then again, so is the one about humans."

"Dude," Ellison says. "That's a beautiful tree."

"Fantastic contribution to the conversation," Torin scoffs.

"So Atlas and I can make six new ones and then at least the world will go back to normal?"

"Moving around the continent while she's in power is not that easy," I tell her. "We have to take her out first, then we can fix everything else."

"As of right now, she's more powerful than you, Atlas. We still don't have the strength to beat her," Idalia adds. She's taking a dig at my pride, but too bad, baby, right now, I'm untouchable. I just created a fucking Reign Tree.

"The meeting with the Councilors is next week. We'll bring all this information to them and create a plan," Pippa says. She turns to Harper. "Thank you, Harper. Right now you might not understand how much this means to us, but I hope one day you'll grasp the magnitude of how incredibly grateful we are."

Harper shrugs like it's no big deal, which I guess to her, it isn't. She just wants to get home, and I'm more than happy to grant her that wish once we're done. I'll do everything in my fucking power to get her to leave, if only so that I never have to see her look at me like that again.

CHAPTER TWENTY-FIVE

HARPER

I'M TOO EXHAUSTED TO DO MUCH FOR THE REST OF THE DAY, so I find myself sitting on the porch swing, flipping through this ridiculous hiking book the weird bookstore owner gave me. It's actually very informative. I, of course, know none of these places, but I'm enjoying the pictures (yes, there's fucking pictures) and descriptions. I haven't quite wrapped my head around the fact that I created some mythical tree with Atlas, and now I have to keep making them in order to save their world. Which means that every living creature in Calamity is depending on me.

How fucked is that?

"What's up, little human?" Ellison sits next to me as we both watch Pants hunt in the yard.

"I'm just trying to get a grip on this reality," I say, gesturing around.

He snorts and begins rolling a blunt on his lap. "What is reality?"

Normally I would laugh at his stoner words, but I've honestly been asking myself that question since I got here. Is this fucking real? But more importantly ... does it even matter? I'm here and it doesn't seem like that's changing anytime soon.

I lean back in the swing. "I hope that was a rhetorical question because I don't have the answer."

"You want some?" He offers me his finished product.

I want to say yes, like *really* want to say yes ... what's the worst that could happen?

"What is it?"

Ellison shrugs. "A little bit of this, a little bit of that." He shakes it in my face. "It's gonna be fun."

"But what will it make me feel like?" I'm not really interested in some three-day meth bender, but Ellison seems like a typical stoner, not some cracked out weirdo.

"That is entirely up to you, little human." He takes it back and lights it. Blue smoke curls in the air before disappearing.

"How long does it last?" I say as I watch him.

"So many questions." He tilts his head back and blows smoke at the porch overhang. It smells like lavender and sage and something minty. "You ever just fucking chill?"

"I'm actually very chill." *Liar.* "I just don't want to be high for days on end with a bunch of elves I just met in a mythical world that gave me magic and no way home."

Ellison laughs. "Dude, sounds like you're already tripping."

I sigh. "Yeah, I know."

"But you're wrong," he says. I arch my brow. "We're not all elves. Emery's half-faun and Wilder's here."

I roll my eyes. "Not really the point, Ellison."

He glances over at me through glazed eyes. "I like you," he says, and the words feel genuine. "I'm glad you're here. You've added some much needed light to this place. Everyone's all storm clouds and super bummer vibes." He puts his arm around my shoulders, pulling me into him.

I laugh and lean against him. He smells like soap and lavender. "Thanks, Ellison. That's actually really nice to hear that."

"Even Atlas has been less of a drunk asshole ... well, less drunk."

"Is he really *that* different than he used to be?"

Ellison makes a noncommittal noise. "Dude has always been a little prick. Or a big prick if you want to get technical."

Very technical.

"Emery's not of noble blood, so the other kids always made fun of him. They used to call him basilisk boy because of his forked tongue. Anyway, one night at a dinner party, Atlas turned all of those kids' pasta noodles into snakes." He laughed at the memory. "They screamed and ran to their parents, but by the time they came over to check, he had changed them back. He did it all night, turning their shoelaces into serpents and then flipping them back before anyone could notice."

I giggled, but it was hard imagining Atlas as a child. "You all grew up together?"

"Yeah, my father was the Duke of East Aspendale and Emery is Atlas's üfren."

"His what?"

"His üfren, dude."

"Elli, I'm not from here. I don't know what that word means."

"Oh, right, right, right. An üfren is the heir's ... fuck, it's kind of hard to explain."

I nudge him gently. "Try."

"Atlas is like super fucking powerful, right? Like even as a kid, he could do magic some adults could never do. Well, no one could outmatch him in that except his father, but he wasn't going to spar with his dad all day long ... dude was king so he had, like, shit to do and stuff."

"Okay ..."

"It's like that for every heir. So they came up with a system to find another elf that matches their strength or at least comes close and has good magic potential. It's their job to train with them, challenge them, and protect them. That's what an üfren is. And it's like an honor of the highest degree or whatever. Emery and Atlas are like brothers, but sometimes that kind of relationship breeds competition and animosity. There's been more than one king who ends up killing their üfren at some point."

"So Emery lived in the castle?"

"Yup." He takes another hit.

I frown. "What about his parents?"

"What about them?"

"Well, did he ever get to see them?"

"No way, dude. The üfren is a gift to the prince or princess from the time they're old enough to walk. They don't get to ever really know their birth parents. Him and Atlas are bonded by magic. They literally can't be more than a few miles apart. The king and queen treated him like family, though."

"That seems ... really sad," I mutter. I can relate to having parents that don't really see you as their child.

"Nah, it's just the way it is here, little human. Don't feel too bad for him; Emery grew up in a castle with literally anything he could ever want."

"Sometimes all you want is to be loved," I say without thinking.

Ellison pulls back and stares at me. "Hella deep, dude."

I laugh and roll my eyes. "What about you? Where are your parents? The Duke and Duchess of ..."

"Lilia," he says sadly. "They're dead, little human. Every noble family died at the same party the night the new queen took the throne. We're the only ones left."

My chest feels heavy. "Sorry, Ellison ... I didn't know."

He reaches over and ruffles my hair. "Don't worry about it, little H."

"Does H stand for human or Harper?" I ask.

"Woah. Cool," he answers, eyes turning to saucers.

I lean over and grab the blunt from his hand. He releases it with a smile.

"Can you swim?"

Bringing the blunt to my lips, I suck in. The smoke expands in my mouth as I inhale lightly. It tingles, but in a good way. I release my breath, the blue smoke swirling in front of me.

"Yeah, I can swim."

"Let's fucking do it! I'll get Emery." He's up so fast I barely have time to register what's going on.

My head feels light as I watch Pants pouncing in the grass. A giggle builds inside my chest and I take another puff of whatever this is. The magic in me sings and I close my eyes and drift somewhere else for a few moments. The door slamming open breaks my peaceful trance, and I open my eyes to see Emery and Ellison staring at me.

"What?" My voice sounds so musical. I wonder if it always sounds like that. I wonder if it's magic.

"You sure you want to go swimming?" Emery asks, taking note of the blunt in my hand.

I take another puff to spite him and laugh.

"Hell yes she does," Ellison says.

"Where's Atlas?" I don't know why I'm asking. He's so mean to me I don't even want him to come. I can feel the muscles in my face forming a frown.

"He doesn't want to come," Emery says.

"Don't worry, I'll get him." I stand up and steady myself as the world bends. Emery reaches out for me and I brush him off, handing the joint to Ellison. "If I'm not back in five minutes, he's probably murdered me." I snort and it's such a funny noise that I take a few moments to laugh, marveling at the sound as it echoes around the porch.

I'm at Atlas's door in an instant, and I don't particularly remember getting here, but oh well. I raise my hand to knock and fear slithers through me. I'm not afraid of him, though. He's just a big bully, and I see right through him. The door pattern gives me a friendly smile and I feel much better as I knock. He answers so quickly I nearly fall over from having to look up so fast.

"Why do you hate fun?" Guess that's what I'm going with as an opener.

"I don't hate fun."

"Just me then?"

He gives me one of those evil smiles, and it does weird things to my insides. "I don't hate you, Fox. I just wish you weren't here."

I huff and clench my fists. I don't even know why I bothered. He's only going to make this less fun. "You're really mean—has anyone ever told you that?"

He holds his hand to his heart like I've wounded him, but he's very obviously making a joke and I'm not laughing. "People tend to use more colorful language than that ... wait—" He tilts my head up to look at him. "You're high right now, aren't you?"

"And what?" I put my hands on my hips and stumble a little, but it's fine, I don't think he notices.

I can see him fighting a smile and I don't understand why he doesn't give in. He looks nice when he smiles. I like the way it makes his eyes sparkle. "I'll be out in five minutes."

"Five actual minutes or five Atlas minutes?"

He shakes his head and shuts the door in my face. I stick my tongue out at it and then apologize to the door because it's not its fault Atlas is rude. Letting out a sigh, I walk back outside.

"He says he'll be out in five Atlas minutes," I announce, and Emery smirks at me. "Told you," I tease.

"I never doubted he'd say yes to you. I just didn't think you'd ask." I want to ask him what the heck that means, but I get distracted when he takes the joint from Ellison and breathes out a heavy cloud of smoke.

I wiggle my fingers for him to hand it to me and he does, but as I'm about to take another hit, Atlas is next to me and my magic sings in his presence. *Holy shit*, I have magic. He takes it from me and blows blue smoke into my face.

"Rude," I mutter, waving my hand in the air.

"Someone has to carry little H, she'll slow us down," Ellison says.

They both look to Atlas and he shrugs. Before I can blink, they're gone and it's just me and King of the Dickheads.

"Don't throw me over your shoulder again," I warn.

175

"How would you like me to handle you, Fox?" His predatory gaze is turning my insides into liquid, but I refuse to become a puddle for the Leader of the Asshole Brigade.

"With more care than a sack of potatoes."

Atlas steps closer to me, so I take a step back. "You want me to be gentle?"

I swallow, my mouth suddenly very dry. "I didn't say that."

He steps closer to me again and I back up against the wooden porch post. He's so close, I can feel the heat of his body ... or maybe it's just me getting hot. When was the last time I got laid?

"No," he says and wipes my lower lip with his thumb. "You don't want me to be gentle. Something tells me you like it better when it's rough."

It's too late. My insides are definitely liquid pooling between my legs.

I raise my hand to his face and slowly trace his jawline, which is so perfectly square that I'm pretty sure whatever higher power created him is damn pleased with themselves. The tension between us is a living, breathing thing, so I do the only thing appropriate for this moment—I pat his cheek and give him a big smile.

"I don't think you could handle me if you tried. Let's go, Elf Boy, they're waiting for us."

Before he can react, I dip under his arm, out of the cage he made with his body, and leap onto his back. He chuckles beneath me as I wrap my legs around his waist and breathe in his winter scent. And then we're off in a blur.

THE LAKE THEY TAKE ME to is unreal. But I know it's real because it's so stunning I couldn't make it up even if I tried. We're deep in the mountain, surrounded by enormous slabs of granite or ... fuck, I don't know what mountains are made out of.

Anyway, it's gray and rocky and beautiful. The pretty rocks shimmer in the sun that sits overhead. Teal, clear water reflects the sparkling peaks surrounding us. The pool ends in a rocky grotto with a small waterfall covering the entrance.

Ellison and Emery are already in the water, half their shirtless bodies resting against the black sandy banks as they laugh and share a joint. Emery's lightly tanned skin makes his blond hair seem even brighter. Ellison, paler than Emery, at first glance, appears to be lanky. Let me tell you, he's anything but. He might not be massive like his friends, but muscles cut his abdomen, moving with each burst of laughter.

They're both hotter than any guy I've seen in real life, but my attention immediately draws to the brooding giant next to me as he pulls his shirt over his head and I finally get to see his tattoos.

The runes that start on his right forearm climb all the way up, past his bicep and over his shoulder, ending just below his jaw. There are various other ones on his chest, his sides, but the one that catches my eye is on his back. A giant tree with complex geometrical patterns and gnarled roots starting on his lower back and reaching to curve around his shoulder blade.

Atlas runs a hand through his hair and down his neck, turning to find me staring. He gives me a smile that should be illegal and dives into the water. When he surfaces, it's like watching a fucking Calvin Klein commercial with the way the water drips down his body.

Stop staring, Harper.

"Do you have the courage to back up all that eye-fucking you're doing, Fox?" he taunts.

"You know, it's really a shame that you look like that and then nothing but slime comes out of your mouth," I sneer, trying to hide the blaze of my cheeks at his words.

Suddenly, it dawns on me that I don't have a bathing suit. I look down at my clothes, trying to remember what I'm wearing underneath, definitely a sports bra and a thong. I bite my thumb nail nervously as the boys start wrestling with each other in the water. I spent last summer naked on beaches in the south of France, so I'm not sure why I'm so nervous.

Fuck it.

I pull my shirt over my head and shimmy out of the leggings I'm wearing. The boys don't bother looking over and I let out a sigh of relief as I wade into the water, expecting it to be cool but it's warm like a jacuzzi. My body instantly relaxes as I pull my hair into a bun and sink down to my shoulders. Like everything else in this place, the water feels like it calls to my magic. It's euphoric as my skin tingles like it's feeding off the liquid.

"How does your magic feel in here?" Atlas asks, wading over to me.

"Happy," I say. "Renewed."

"It's healing water," he says. "It's supposed to replenish your magic, but it doesn't really work. For someone like us," he says, gesturing to his friends and him. "It barely makes a dent, but it feels nice."

I stare up at him, wondering why he goes from hot to cold so instantly. I never know which Atlas is the real one.

"What's this?" he says, pulling my right arm toward him. He traces the snake that slithers around my forearm.

I yank my arm back, not enjoying the way his touch lights a firework in my chest. "It says, 'say unto thine heart, I am mine own redeemer'. It's a reminder not to trust anyone but myself."

"Do you?" he asks with curiosity.

"Trust anyone? No. But I don't trust myself either," I mumble, trying to push past him.

What I don't say is that those tattooed words are from the satanic bible. That I read it once to piss off my mother, but the second and third time were just for me. People think that satanism is all about worshiping the devil, but really it's about worshiping yourself. So maybe, in that sense, they're right about me.

"Little H! You want any more? This is the last one." Ellison holds up the blunt on the other side of the lake.

I dodge around Atlas and dunk my head under the water as I swim toward Ellison and Emery. The farther I get from Atlas, the more my magic calls for me to go back to him. I ignore it, remembering his words that *I'm* the one in control, not it. It shuts the hell up, and I'm filled with a sense of pride. As I approach Emery, I notice the tattoo on his chest is the same as the runes on Atlas's arm.

"Aw, did you guys get matching tattoos? That's so sweet." I coo.

Ellison's face drains of color, but Atlas laughs darkly from behind me. "Not really cute, Fox. More like branding."

Emery snorts and whips his hair out of his eyes.

"What do you mean?"

"It's a symbol of their bond," Ellison whispers, but everyone can hear him. The boys exchange a look and Elli shrugs. "What? I told her all about it. Someone had to explain why you guys are so obsessed with each other."

I take the joint from his fingers and puff on it. "It's not something you're proud of?"

"Of course," Emery says quickly.

"Em," Atlas chides. He gives Emery a look that holds so much love I'm nearly speechless. I didn't even know Elf Boy had feelings. He turns his stare to me and it's filled with contempt again. "Neither of us had a choice in the matter. We're just shackled to each other, whether we like it or not."

Emery throws his arm around Atlas's shoulders. "Good thing I wouldn't want to be shackled to any other asshole but you."

"Fuck off," Atlas says, pushing him away, but I see the way he softens toward Emery.

My head spins and I have the urge to hug them both, but I don't because I know it's the drugs and I'm almost completely nude.

"What's yours?" Ellison asks, tracing a finger down my spine and along the words written vertically. I shiver and stiffen at his touch.

Atlas gives him a look that he usually saves for me, and Elli backs away. It's a really weird exchange that I can't understand when my thoughts keep trailing off to ponder how the rocks look so sparkly.

"It says, 'Die young and save yourself.'"

"Fucking dark, dude," Ellison says.

I take another hit of the blunt and hand it back to him. "They're song lyrics."

"Are you sad, little human?" Atlas asks with a taunting laugh. "Do you write poetry, too?"

Anger blazes through me. "I used to," I snap. I don't know why I even respond. He's only trying to get a rise out of me.

But his brow quirks in interest before his face turns into indifference again.

"Poem! Poem!" Ellison chants.

I give them a fake smile. "I said 'used to.' I can't anymore ... it's just—" I stop myself. I don't know why I'm bothering to tell them any of this. "It's none of your fucking business."

"Damn," Emery says under a breath.

Ducking under the water, I swim away.

I force the ever whirling negativity in my mind back and focus on the way the water makes me feel and the sun warming my skin. I can feel them assessing me, trying to understand me from a distance. Good fucking luck. I still haven't figured it out.

CHAPTER TWENTY-SIX

ATLAS

I SNEAK INTO FOX'S ROOM TO FIND HER SLEEPING LIKE A
starfish again. It's early morning and bright out—since the evening never actually turned to night—but she has the blackout
curtains pulled tight so only a small glow emanates from the window. My eyes follow the curve of her ass, on full display as usual
since her tiny shorts barely cover any skin. It's literal agony and I'm
reminded of yesterday when we went swimming. She pretended to be
all shy when she got into the water, but I know full well she knew all of
our attention was on her.

I'm never worried about Emery, his mind is only ever on Pippa,
but I swear to the fucking Realm if Ellison touches her again I'll find
a way to forget every nice thing he's ever done for me. She's a plague,
infecting us all.

The little Fox surprised me with her tattoos. I feel like every day
I learn something new about her. I fucking hate it because every

morning I wake up wondering what it might be and every night I go to sleep thinking about how I'll find out.

Quietly, I call Pants off the bed so he doesn't have to be subjected to today's magic lesson and walk over to her. Before I can stare at her for too long, I summon my magic and dump a torrent of water on her. She shrieks in surprise before I'm thrown against the wall, cracking the drywall in the shape of my head.

By the time I look up, she's standing over me, dripping wet, and there's nothing but hatred in her eyes. "What the fuck?"

"Lesson number two," I say with a smile, sitting up. "Always have your magic prepared for attacks you least expect."

She folds her arms over her chest, deepening her cleavage. A look of pride forms on her face. "I guess I got you back then."

I stand up and look down at her. Her nipples are hardening against the soaking material of her shirt, and it's distracting me. *Fuck*, I didn't really think this plan through. "Don't get too cocky, Fox. If it was a blade I was pushing into you instead of water, you'd be dead."

"I hate you," she huffs.

"Not yet, but don't worry, you will." I head toward the door. "Outside, five minutes."

"Fine, see you in ten," she drawls.

I rain another gallon of water on her for good measure as I leave, the sound of her screaming making my dick hard.

WHEN WE GET OUTSIDE, HER hair is still soaking wet. I lift some air through it to dry it off because I'm a nice fucking guy, but it tugs on some memory I've shoved into the deep dark parts of my mind and bringing it up only angers me.

"Why do you always look at me like that?" she asks. She always has so much fucking attitude and I'm tired of it. Doesn't she realize I'm helping her despite every instinct in me telling me not to?

"Like what?"

"Like I murdered your family or—" She stops herself mid-sentence, eyes wide.

I walk up to her until she's close enough for me to choke to death. "Because I don't trust you. You came out of nowhere with magic that should never have been given to you, and now you've somehow wrapped yourself into our world. I don't want you here."

"Then *why* are you helping me?" she bites back.

"I have to! I'm the only one that can teach you and for some reason fucked beyond all belief, you're the only one that can save us. I'm not helping *you*, Fox. I'm helping my people."

"I don't particularly want to be here either," she mutters.

"Too fucking bad. If we both want our homes back, then we have to deal with each other, but don't think for one fucking second that means I'll pretend to enjoy it."

She looks away from me and mumbles, "I don't really want to be home either."

She thinks I can't hear her, but I can. I don't understand what that could possibly mean, but I don't think about it for more than a few seconds because fuck her problems.

"Just stop asking stupid questions. Stop trying to understand me and we can get through this quickly," I say.

"Fine."

"Tell me what your magic feels like today," I demanded. I'm exhausted already.

She chews the inside of her cheek and closes her eyes. "It feels awake. Like it's weaving its way through every cell and molecule in my body."

"And does it still feel like a stranger?" I ask.

"No, it feels ... it feels like it's part of me."

"Good. Yesterday we must have Ignited it."

She opens her eyes and the look she gives me is filled with curiosity. "What does that mean?"

I sigh and rub a hand through my hair. "Thousands of centuries ago, there used to be a ritual where magic could be shared."

"You mean not everyone had it?" I glare at her for interrupting me yet again, but she only rolls her eyes at me. "Sorry, Your *Highness*. Continue."

"Anyway, the ritual involved someone of royal blood—who carried this higher form of magic—to share it with someone else. They'd bind themselves to it and it would Ignite the ancient magic that lived in them. The royal blood would protect them from the harmful effects of it."

"Why would they do that?"

"If you fucking listen, you might find out."

She narrows her eyes and walks over to the Reign Tree. I swear her skin glows when she's next to it. She slumps against it, sliding to the ground and gives me a lazy wave of her hand to continue. I want to wrap my hand around her throat and fuck her against that tree until she begs me to stop.

"It's lonely," I say. "To have all this power and never meet anyone who rivals it or someone who can share in the way it feels. So people wanted an equal, someone to challenge them."

"Like you and Emery," she adds.

"Sort of. I don't share magic with Emery, though. He's powerful all on his own, but it's not the same. In a world where I didn't have *bas raza*, he might even be stronger than me."

"Why don't they do it anymore?"

"Because magic amongst my people has evolved into something so different, even my blood couldn't protect them from the sheer power of it. That's why the üfren were created."

Fox chews the inside of her cheek in thought. "So, what do you and Emery share? I mean, from the bond. Can you read each other's minds or something?"

I join her on the ground. With my back to the tree, I feel it recharging my magic. Well, that explains the light glow of her skin when she's around it. "No. It's just a link that ties us together so that we can't be apart. When we try, it's physically painful. The farther we are from each other, the more the magic will work to bring us closer together, but it's always worse for Emery than it is for me. When we were kids we'd try to test it, see how far we could push the boundary." I grin, remembering how stupid we were. "One time I went on a trip to the south of the continent. Emery wanted to see how far I would get, even though I warned him not to. We made it fifty miles when he just fucking appeared next to me, panting and gritting his teeth. Tears were nearly forming in his eyes from relief."

"What did it feel like for you?"

I shrug. "Like a piece of me was missing."

"That's kind of sweet in a super fucked up way," she says.

"Sometimes I feel bad that he's tied to me. He's a much better person than I am, and who knows what he'd be doing with his life if he wasn't glued to mine. But really, it's the best thing that's ever happened to me. I think I'd be a monster without him." I frown at the words as they come out of my mouth. I've never admitted that to anyone.

Fox looks me in the eye, and I find something calming in her gaze. "I think you're a monster, even *with* him around," she says and pats my shoulder reassuringly.

I can't help but laugh and it brings a smile to her face. I catch myself before I can get lost in the steadiness of her presence. Fuck this.

"Get up," I say, standing and startling her. "Try to call on your magic and do something with it."

"But all I can do is stop time and I don't feel like I ever have control of it."

"*All I can do is stop time,*" I mock. "Do you realize how fucking powerful that is? You can maneuver around your enemies, you can hit them when they're completely defenseless, and you can buy yourself time to think. But that's just what you've discovered you can do." I poke her in the chest so hard she stumbles back. "Your magic is only weak because of how little you believe in it. Believe in yourself a little more, Fox, and I think you'll find out just how strong you are."

"Careful, someone might think you're being nice to me," she warns.

I scoff. "I'm not being nice. I'm just stating the obvious. I've never met anyone who has so much potential and so little confidence."

"You think I have potential?" she asks hopefully.

"I think your *magic* has potential," I correct. "Don't ever think there's any other part of you that means anything to me."

"Whatever," she replies. The air shifts as her power ripples through the fabric of time, and I hear her squeal as she suddenly appears ten feet away. "I did it!"

I want to smile with her, but it happens again and I'm flat on my back, the air whooshing out of my lungs. "You're right, this *is* fun," she says, leaning casually against the tree.

I push up on my elbows. "I never said we were here to have fun," I wheeze, and magic thrums through the air. I blink and Fox is straddling me, so close to my face I could lick her. She shifts against my cock and stares deeply into my eyes.

"But imagine all the fun we could have," she whispers. And then she's gone as quickly as she appeared, and I turn to find her sitting in our tree. Her legs dangle as she perches on a low, gnarled branch. "What's next?"

Ignoring the growing bulge in my pants, I use my magic to push her out of the tree as she screams and lands with a thud. "Protecting yourself."

I feel her reach out for her power and shield myself with a barrier. Her magic is so powerful it takes almost all of my concentration to block it out. No wonder she got past me the first time we met. Harper appears in front of me, frowning and rubbing her face. "Ow." She tries again, but continues running into my barrier.

With my own speed, I move behind her to pin her arms, but the second I go to grab her, she disappears and reappears behind me. I turn around and fight a smile. "Better."

We go back and forth like that, dancing around each other. She does a pretty decent job, for a human, but her barrier is shit. She's quickly panting and slumps against the tree.

"I'm weak," she announces.

She collapses on herself, and I speed over to catch her before she hits the grass. "You pushed your magic too hard," I say, placing her down. "Didn't it tell you to stop?"

She nods and tries to catch her breath. A slice of worry crawls through me. If she wasn't human, she might be close to dying. I forgot to warn her not to over-extend herself. "I didn't want it telling me what to do though," she pants.

I chuckle despite myself. "Why does that not surprise me?"

She smiles sleepily and leans against the tree. "I guess I'm too predictable."

I shake my head. She's anything but predictable, and that's what scares me the most.

CHAPTER TWENTY-SEVEN

HARPER

THINGS FEEL DIFFERENT SINCE MY MAGIC WAS Ignited, but I'm still just as physically useless. Today, I'm in the armory with Emery, training like we do every morning. He's letting me practice with a wooden sword, despite telling me a hundred times I'm not ready for it. It feels clunky in my hand and when I try to move it in the pattern he shows me, I topple over.

He holds back a laugh as I glare at him. "See, you still need to work on the basics."

"But the basics are boring," I whine.

"The basics are what keep you alive."

When he says shit like that it's still hard for me to wrap my head around—going into battle. I want to laugh just thinking about it.

"Drop the sword and go practice punches on the dummy," he instructs.

Before I can pick myself up off the floor, we both turn at the sound of footsteps.

"I hope Emery isn't working you too hard." Pippa's voice passes through the room as she walks down the stairs.

Emery lights up like a fucking Christmas tree as he looks at her and I wonder, not for the first time, what their deal is. She doesn't seem to notice it, though, and that hurts my heart a little bit. Every time she walks into a room, his attention is on her.

"I think it might be the other way around," he jokes.

Pippa smiles at him before turning to me with the same look. "I think it's time we put something else to the test." I know she's talking about my blood.

No one has mentioned it since the first time I agreed. I was starting to wonder if they didn't need it anymore.

"Just tell me what to do," I offer, and the sincerity in my voice surprises me.

She beckons for me to follow her, and I turn to Emery. "I'll clean everything up," he offers. "Go ahead."

I catch up to Pippa, the elf's pace well outmatching mine. It makes me realize just how considerate Atlas and Emery have been with me. Once we're upstairs, we walk through the open kitchen and living room. It's empty as daylight spans through the large windows. A fire roars in the charcoal, stone fireplace stretching the length of the vaulted ceiling. Our boots click lightly against the wood floor and anticipation coils in my gut. I have no idea what to expect, but I know this will end in me bleeding and I'm not sure how I feel about that.

We walk through the hallway on the other side of the kitchen and pass through a door at the end. I'm not over here very often, but it looks the same as the rest of the house. Light wood paneling on the walls mixed with pale stone. The furniture is earthy, and it reminds me of the winters I used to spend in my parent's cabin but more magical. The door we pass through leads to an office where Wilder sits in a massive green wingback chair and Atlas stares out the window with his arms crossed, not acknowledging our presence. His gray shirt is taught over the muscles in his arms and I turn my focus to the bookshelves that line the walls like a library.

"We've been trying to think about the best way to do this without harming you," Pippa says with a look of concern. "But it's going to hurt a little bit."

"That's okay," I say, even though my anxiety skyrockets.

As soon as my heart starts beating faster, Atlas turns around. "Don't be scared, Fox," he says sweetly, but there's something different about his demeanor.

"Coming from you, that's not the most reassuring," I dryly reply.

"Atlas has a theory that the reason your blood is so poisonous is because of the ancient magic running through it. It makes sense, but I refuse to test the theory."

I cock an eyebrow at her. "What do you mean, test the theory?"

"Do you know the fastest way for us to replenish magic, Fox?" He's behind me instantly and goosebumps pepper my skin as his voice rolls down my spine.

"I can guess," I say, thinking of all the fuckers who tried to suck my blood out of me.

Atlas makes a noise of satisfaction as he gently moves my hair to drape over one shoulder. It feels too personal in this room with his sister and friend. "You are smarter than you look," he murmurs.

I shrug off his hand that begins trailing down my neck and pull on my magic. It feels kind of like singing—sometimes it comes naturally and other times you have to fight to remember the words to the song.

Stop, I whisper in my head. The room pauses and I let out a deep breath as I look around at everyone frozen in time. I still haven't figured out a way to snap it back in place at my will. So for now, I'm on a timer. It usually lasts about thirty seconds before everything begins again.

I've figured out that in this space where only I exist, I have the strength of a freight truck. I could demolish anything, but I have to be careful because if I do too much, I'm so weak after, I feel like a shell of myself.

I walk to the other side of the room, away from the brooding sex idol next to me, and lean casually against the bookshelf. Within a few seconds, everything speeds back up and Pippa whips her head to me in surprise. My eyes are on Atlas as he fights a smirk. One day he'll stop fighting it and just fucking smile at me.

"Looks can be deceiving," I reply back to him.

Pippa's and Wilder's faces light up. "Amazing!" she shouts and claps her hands.

I bask in the attention, but it doesn't feed the need inside me. No, there's only one person in this room capable of that and currently he's staring at me with his usual *I hate you more than anything* face. I think it's the challenge he presents to me. I usually win people over fairly easily, especially those with a cock between their legs. But I'm pretty sure that I could strip right here and Atlas wouldn't even blink.

"Anyway, Atlas thinks he might be immune to your blood, but I refuse to let him try."

I give her brother a mock frown. "I'd happily donate my blood to him if it means I get to watch him choke on it."

"It seems they're getting along well," Wilder says with a smile. "I told you you had nothing to worry about, Princess."

Pippa looks between us and snorts. "I think my brother is just upset because he may have met his match. And she happens to be a girl who actually can and *wants* to run away from him."

She and Wilder share a laugh like it's the funniest thing in the world. I have to force the blood that rushes into my cheeks away at those words, and Atlas actually looks repulsed as he glares at his sister.

The Princess of Calamity claps her hands suddenly and the room goes quiet. "Enough funny business. We need to present the Council with this information in two days. Let's get to work."

The fear is back and I don't care if everyone in this room can sense it or not. But I force myself to face it. This will just be like donating blood. I look around for their medical supplies but come up short.

"So, are you just going to use a needle and collect it in a container or what?" I ask nervously.

Pippa tilts her head in confusion. "A needle? Like a sewing needle?"

I shake my head. "No, like a needle and a syringe ..." But none of them know what I'm talking about. I guess in a world where everyone is healed with magic, they don't need that kind of stuff. "Nevermind," I sigh. "What do I have to do?"

Wilder stands and produces a blade so thin and sharp I can barely see it at the angle he's holding it. My heart rate becomes dangerously fast as Pippa gestures to the chair Wilder was sitting in. She rubs my back reassuringly as I step into the chair.

"It has to be deep enough to bleed, but Atlas thinks he can numb the pain without healing it too quickly," she adds.

As I sit, he kneels down next to me, resting his arm on the chair's, and stares into my eyes. His usual hatred is gone and in its place is something encouraging. No, that's the wrong word ... it's ... it's safe. It relaxes my breathing and slows my racing heart. As his hand gently pulls my arm out and grips my wrist, my pulse quickens again for a totally different reason.

Never looking away, he opens his palm out to Wilder for the blade, and I'm reminded that he and Pippa are in the room. Atlas's presence is so all-consuming that I easily forget they exist again as I hold his gaze.

"Be gentle," I whisper so quietly that even I barely hear the words.

Finally, a real smile shows, but this one is wicked. "With you? Never."

A slice of pain shoots through my arm as he drags the blade across my wrist and blood pools at the site. I look down at the crimson liquid dripping across my skin and into a glass bowl on the floor. My wrist throbs and I start to feel lightheaded.

"Eyes on me, Fox," Atlas says, and I immediately follow orders.

He places a hand on my thigh and electricity shoots through me. My magic claws at the barrier of my skin and the clothes that separate it from him as he rubs his thumb gently against my leggings. A hum of pleasure buzzes around me as he pushes his magic into me and I nearly moan, but thank fucking God I don't, because how embarrassing would that be? The pain in my wrist is gone and just as before, when we made the tree, I can't look away from him even if I tried.

But why would I want to? He's so enchanting, with his walnut eyes that sparkle with different blue hues like gemstones in the walls of a cave. Even the scowl that's permanently etched onto his face seems to ease as he looks back at me. I would think he'd be reveling in the way his magic is making me feel, but he's giving me that same look of admiration that he did the last time our magic ran together like this.

I wonder if he feels it too, this draw to be close. I wonder if his magic aches to be with mine the same way mine wants his. I don't understand it and I refuse to ask him. As if my thoughts reach him, his eyes become hooded and a flood of lust fills his stare. The gentle movement of his thumb turns to a grip that tightens, making me want to whimper.

I fight every urge to lean into him as his painful hold has me wondering what it would feel like to be possessed by him. The air in the room dissipates as my chest heaves and I try to get more of it in. Watching his hand slowly move up my thigh is a torture I've never known. I want ... no, I *need* to know what it would feel like for him to shove his fingers inside me.

"I think that's probably enough," Pippa's voice cuts through my thoughts like a knife, and Atlas's grip lessens. Thank fuck, because I was about point-five seconds from begging.

He heals my wound and the warm feeling passing through me is gone. That was *so* weird.

I feel like a fog has been lifted as I glance at him for some reassurance, but he refuses to look at me. Standing, he walks out of the room, slamming the door on his way out. The ache between my thighs dissipates as I remember all the reasons I hate him.

CHAPTER TWENTY-EIGHT

ATLAS

THE CRACK OF THE DOOR SHUTTING ECHOES IN THE hall as I storm out of the room and speed into my own. I lean against the wall, hanging my head back in defeat as I try to will this erection away, but I'm so fucking hard it hurts.

I knew I shouldn't have done that, but I was so curious to see if I even could. And I hate more than anything that I was right. My magic is volatile fury, dominating and explosive—always has been. Even before all this shit happened and hardened me into the worst kind of asshole. I've worked my whole life to contain it until I realized that there was no fucking point, so I unleashed it, letting it rule my decisions and numb my pain.

Fox's magic is passion and venom, it's unyielding and eternal. It wraps around mine like a python, constricting until I give it what it wants—subordination. It wants me to bend without question and, fuck me, if that isn't the hottest thing in the world. I would have given her anything she wanted in that room. As it turns out, we both wanted the same thing.

My sister was right, I've met my fucking match. In our world, there's an old phrase for that—*selüm-ra*. It means partial soul, and it has never existed for the one who sits on the throne because no one can ever match our power. That's why there used to be rituals to share magic, why the üfren were created. The ruling elves were always seeking a way to be close to something, to not feel so alone. A *selüm-ra* for the ruler of Calamity can't be real. But here she fucking is, and she's a human. What kind of sick joke is this?

Fuck. Fuck. Fuckity. Fuck.

I seal the door and strip out of my pants and boxers. Gripping myself, I groan at the contact my dick has been aching for, except my hand is big and rough. A dull substitution to the dainty, vicious one I wish was touching me. Leaning against the bedpost, I pump my cock with enough force to border on pain. That's what I deserve because wanting her this badly is the second worst thing I could ever do. I don't care how much she wants to help us. She doesn't belong here, and it's not like she's doing it out of the goodness of her heart. She's selfish and manipulative. It's not her I want, though, it's her magic. Magic she was never meant to have. Really, there's no link to *her*.

I try to tell myself that, but my imagination paints very vivid images of her moaning underneath me while I punish her with my cock. Of how she would feel tightening around me, the taste of her on my lips. I can almost see myself pinning her against one of these walls as she throws her head back, exposing her throat and screaming my name until her voice is hoarse and broken. I hear the wood of the bedpost crack under my grip and I have half a mind to find her right now and make her pay for what she's doing to me. Just the fucking idea that she wants me sends me over the edge. I moan, biting into the back of my hand that's nearly snapped the bedpost. Come spills through my fingers and onto the floor as I pant in relief.

I shake my head and take a deep breath. She doesn't want *me* and I don't want *her*. It's just the magic fucking with our heads. I know it's true because my heart is cold and dead. I gave it away once and I've never regretted anything more.

I walk into the connected bathroom and turn on the shower. When I step into the hot water a single thought creeps into my mind: this time it might be different. *She* might be different. I let the thought in and then I take a fucking bat to it, burying it deep into the ground where it belongs.

LATER THAT NIGHT, I PUSH into Emery's room to find him in a very compromising position on his bed. My eyes unfortunately fall to his cock in his hand and I have a deep feeling of sympathy for the guy, considering what happened earlier in my own room.

"Fuck off, Atlas!" he shouts.

I throw my hands up in mock surrender. "Come find me when you're done!"

"Learn to fucking knock!" he screams as I shut his door and walk into the living room to wait.

I really should.

I pass by the front door, which has large rectangular windows on either side, and spot the little Fox sitting against the tree reading that ridiculous book about hiking. What the fuck is with her carrying that thing around? I promptly ignore her existence and find Torin sitting on the couch poring over documents like he's so important. I'm surprised the fucker can even read. Across from him is Idalia, and as soon as she senses my presence she glances up and glowers at me.

"Doesn't have to be like that, baby. I know you enjoyed yourself," I taunt.

Torin looks up, and then his eyes pass between us as a flush colors her cheeks. "You didn't," he says to Idalia, and she looks away.

"She did," I reply for her and sit down next to him. "And she fucking liked it."

"I might be impressed, but pickings are slim for our dear girl, and she can only fuck Elli so many times before she gets bored," Torin says with a chuckle.

I laugh with him as steam nearly comes out of Idalia's ears. "Fuck both of you."

"Just let me know when," I say, even though I'm really not interested in repeating that whole thing.

"You know you're not my type," Torin says at the same time and we both share a laugh at her expense. I'd feel bad if I knew she had a soul in there, but I'm pretty sure it's just a cold, barren wasteland.

We all share survivor's guilt, but I know Idalia doesn't. She was one of the cruelest girls we grew up with—always taunting Emery for his horns and making the staff cry. She'd sell any one of us out to a parent if it meant she'd get praised. When everything first happened, she found me immediately and began sucking up to me. She would have quite literally sucked me if I let her, but I was too hurt at the time to do much of anything. Once she realized she'd aligned herself with the useless sibling, she switched all her attention to Pippa. Now they're best friends or some shit, but I don't believe it for a second.

Some say people can change, but I don't think that's true. We all have darkness and light inside us; it's just about which side you show to the world. It doesn't change who you are deep down, though. Emery walks into the room and saves me from having to converse with Torin any further.

"You fucking ready, dude?" I ask, leaping to my feet. I've been waiting for this for days. Ever since Pippa decided we could do it.

"Born ready," he says with a conspiratorial wink.

I turn to Torin. "Last chance, you want in?"

He stares at me like he's considering it, and I regret asking. I was hoping this could be time for just Emery and me. I've been feeling like I haven't had enough time with him to myself. I don't fucking care how that sounds.

"No, but thank you, Prince. I think it's best I stay behind and save up my energy for the real battle."

He's such a pompous prick. I snort and walk out the door with Emery. "You got it?" he asks.

I draw the sword from the holder on my side and let it gleam in the moonlight. There's a hint of Fox's dark blood glittering on the blade and I have the strongest urge to taste it, but I put it back in its holster and clear my thoughts.

"Race you," he says quickly before speeding off.

Fox looks up from her reading and opens her mouth to ask me something, but I run as fast as I fucking can away from her. Partially because I want to beat Emery and partially because seeing her against that tree is doing things to me that I don't want to feel.

I catch up to him quickly and we sprint far away from the house and mountain. We pass through town and ignore the whispering trees that make me want to punch something, and I skid to a halt in a big open field. There's a little rusty cottage in the distance, but otherwise it's just fields and rolling hills for miles.

In order to showcase our new poisonous weapons, we need a volunteer, and who better to use than one of the bitch queen's guards? And there's no easier way to catch one than by shifting into our derax form. That vile cunt always knows when we switch, so moving as far away from the house as we can is necessary. How does she know, you ask? Well, it's your lucky fucking day because I'm in such a good mood I'll take the time to explain it to you.

Derax magic is different from all other magic, and it belongs solely to the high elves. We're the only ones that can switch forms, and every elf has a different one. What you turn into isn't decided by heritage or anything—it's just who you are, how the Realm intended you to be. Your derax is sacred, whether you shift into a dope fucking black panther like me or a sneaky little snake like Ellison.

The blast of magic instantly refuels your own reserves, but it also puts a giant fucking target on your back for, say, an evil witch who somehow has the power to sense the magic of others. Not being able to shift at will is like wearing tight jeans you're never allowed to take off. My balls are fucking ready to be free. It doesn't seem to be the case that she can find us once we've already shifted, so I plan to use this time to my full advantage with my best friend. It's a shame it's night out because I really want to bask in the sun.

"Seems as good a place as any," I say to Emery when he catches up about ten seconds later.

His smile is infectious as we both let the magic ripple through our bodies. I feel refreshed as my four massive paws hit the grass and I dig my nails into the dirt. With a stretch of my arms, I open my mouth to yawn and a roar comes out. We can't communicate with each other like this, but it doesn't matter—we're so in tune with one another I know exactly what he's thinking. One of us has to switch in order to use the blade, and I nuzzle against his furry head to let him know I'll do it. I can always shift back. But for now, I want to play. He grins as much as a wolf can, opening his mouth to pant happily, his forked black tongue bobbing back and forth.

I tackle him to the ground and let out the energy that's been building up in me on him, he can take it. And he must be harboring some pretty dark feelings, because he gives it back to me in full force. I feel the magic in the air change and jump off of him, both of us taking a defensive stance back to back. Growling shakes the earth as the guards appear out of thin air. I just hope *she* doesn't show up. If she does, we're all fucked.

Six of her sentinels surround us. They're in their typical black armor that appears thin, but I've bitten into that shit before and it's pure metal. I don't know what species they are because they wear masks over their heads that look like cats with a creepy ass grin on their face. The masks are impossible to take off—trust me, I've tried. I know the cat masks are a dig at me, but no one else has seemed to notice. The venomous witch is taunting me, just in case I forget. Like I ever could.

I'm giddy as I pounce on the first one and rip into his throat. My canines, coated in venom, sink into his flesh as his skin begins to slough around my jaw. To his credit, he doesn't scream. Actually, now that I think about it, they never make any noise except the occasional grunt.

Anyway, my venom is different than Fox's: it doesn't kill instantly, but slowly, painfully. Unfortunately for me, that's not exactly the perfect weapon when you're fighting a bunch of enemies at once.

When I have one of them down, I switch back to my elf form and whip out the sword just in time to block an attack from my next victim. I just need to try this once to make sure it works and then I can shift back. I dodge his blows as we dance around each other before catching him off guard by flipping the sword in my hand and jamming the hilt into his head. I slice into his arm, a wound that should heal if this was just a regular blade. But Fox's blood calls to me in the moonlight and I grip the handle tighter, like maybe she can feel it.

The sentinel grabs their arm, cocking their head in surprise that I have such terrible aim, and then drops dead on the ground.

Fuck, that's so cool!

Pride swells in me as I think of Harper before switching back into my derax form and taking out the rest of these fucks with ease. I look over at Emery, who has one pinned beneath him and switch back to my elf form. As I grab them, the sentinel writhes in my grip, so I bind their arms and legs with my magic. It's not nearly as fun as when I do it with my little Fox—

Wait. Not *mine*. Never mine.

I growl at the thought and clench my fist before slamming it into the sentinel's face. The creepy smile that's painted on their mask is laughing at me. I do it again. And again. And again. Emery whines and nuzzles my other hand, reminding me not to kill this fucker. I reach down and pet my brother lovingly.

"I'm fine. I just ... I hate this situation," I tell him. It's not a lie. I've conditioned myself not to feel these feelings and so far it's worked very well for me. I look around at the dead bodies. "Though if her army fights like this, taking over should be no problem."

Emery lets out a howl in agreement.

I strap the sentinel onto Emery's back and shift, relishing the way my body feels. I'm always powerful, but like this I feel unstoppable. The noise that's normally in my head fades away as my body instead focuses on what's around me, my senses heightened to the fucking sky.

Inevitably, my thoughts shift to Fox and an overwhelming need to be around her washes through me. For some reason, in this form, the urge to be close to her and make sure she's safe is almost unbearable. I shake out my body and roar as loudly as I can. How the fuck does she manage to ruin literally everything? My bellow tells the birds in nearby trees to fuck off and I fight the feline need to chase and hunt them as Emery and I take off toward town to stow our prisoner for the meeting tomorrow. When we're done, we can head home.

As much as I hate it, the closer I get to her, the more the beast in me calms. It's not just that though, there's some other emotion pumping through my veins. For once, I think we might be able to save our kingdom, and it's all thanks to her.

CHAPTER TWENTY-NINE

HARPER

TLAS AND EMERY TOOK OFF LIKE MANIACS THIRTY minutes ago. I tried to focus on reading, but my mind keeps falling back to where they went. They looked so excited, and if they're having fun without me, I'll be pissed. Pants settles in next to me, sleepy from hours of playing in the yard. Sometimes I wish I could be him and not have a care in the world. Must be fucking nice.

I nudge him awake and head into the house, for once enjoying the starless night sky. Every day here brings something new, and this place is growing on me. When I enter the house, Torin and Idalia are sitting in the living room reading.

"Where is everyone?" I ask, taking a seat.

I'm still not used to having people around all the time. At home, I was almost always alone and even though I've partied more than anyone my age should, I feel like my social skills are lacking. It's for that reason that I haven't talked much to these two and I see their own surprise in the creases of the foreheads.

Idalia looks up from reading a book titled, *It's Not You It's Them,* which seems fitting.

"Atlas and Emery are off killing sentinels—"

"They're what?" I don't know what a sentinel is, but I don't like the idea of them killing anything. What if one of them gets hurt?

Wait ... why the fuck do I care?

Caught in my own thoughts, I miss Torin's explanation and only catch the tail end of what he's saying as I stare blankly at his gold-rimmed glasses and cropped hair the color of clouds. "—so naturally they're all excited about it."

"Heathens," Idalia mutters, turning back to her book.

"Almost joined them myself," he says haughtily.

"Don't fucking kid yourself. The day I see you jumping in with those two is the day I surrender myself to that slimy, bitch queen," Idalia replies.

Torin rolls his eyes, and I'm so lost, but I'm also too fucking polite to let them know I was barely listening ... I'm the one who asked the question, after all.

Torin continues, "Pippa is in the study with Wilder planning for tomorrow's meeting with the Council, and Ellison is on a reconnaissance mission."

I don't miss the quick furrow of Idalia's brow.

"Is that dangerous?" I ask, trying to get a read on her.

"Of course it's fucking dangerous. He's going into the lion's den," she spits at me.

"Good one," Torin laughs, his long fingers flipping the pages of his book.

I'm still lost, but at this point I'm glad if I understand fifty percent of what people here are saying.

"Hopefully they're all okay," I mutter.

"Don't pretend like you care, we all know you're only doing this so you can get back home," she sneers.

Alright, bitch. I tried to be nice, but if you want to fuck around then I'm happy to help you find out what happens next.

"And you'd be doing something different?" She only stares at me. "Oh, so you can be a bitch to me for no reason, but you can't back it up." I realize that this is really petty of me, but what can I say? I'm a petty bitch.

Idalia stands up, and I go to meet her. She's infinitely taller than me and probably one thousand times stronger and faster. She also looks like a fucking supermodel even though she's wearing sweatpants and a cropped sweatshirt. My magic pulses in my veins. It has no mercy.

"Oh, sit the hell down," Torin interrupts. With some unseen force, we both plop down in our seats. "Don't be offended, Harper. Idalia is only jealous because the prince is paying so much attention to you. And Idalia, of course she's only doing this to get home ... why else would she do it?"

I huff with vindication, but then I remember the other part of what he said. "Ew, this is over Atlas? Please, take him. I have no interest in the brooding asshole, thank you very much."

Idalia puts her book down, and then she's standing over me in the blink of an eye. "This isn't about Atlas," she says slowly. "This is about you trying to fit into a place where you don't belong."

My magic is nearly bouncing off the walls of its confines, so I let it out slowly and time stops. The crazy elf girl has caged me in, so I climb over the back of the chair and run to her seat as time speeds back up.

"If you want to scare me, Idalia, you'll have to catch me first."

Torin bursts into laughter and I wish so badly I could've seen her face when she realized I wasn't there. She turns around and glares at me. The look is legitimately horrifying, and I worry I've made the wrong kind of enemy. *Too late now.*

As soon as she's about to say something the door bursts open and, I'm not fucking kidding you, a massive black panther and a wolf stroll in. I scream so loudly it totally ruins my whole bad bitch act. Idalia and Torin start laughing and the panther growls at her before bounding over to me and knocking over the chair I'm in, smashing the wood into tiny pieces.

"Hey! No breaking the furniture!" Idalia shouts.

I barely make out her scolding because there's a five-hundred-pound panther on top of me. Well, to be fair, it's not on top of me, really it's standing over me. When I finally remember to breathe, I realize I haven't used my magic to escape and that's fucking stupid of me. Atlas would be so dissap—

I look into the giant cat's eyes and see flecks of blue and green against a brown background. My magic hums happily in his presence and I feel silly for not realizing who it was before. To say I'm speechless is really an understatement. He might even be more beautiful as a giant panther than a man ... male?

His coat is raven-black, but every now and then I can make out little spots mixed in with his fur. He's really like a black jaguar ... but is that the same as a panther ... or maybe it's a puma? Fuck, who cares. It's amazing. I reach out to touch his furry face and he snarls at me, lifting one lip to expose his venomous canine, but I'm not afraid of him anymore. Not even slightly.

"Oh, you're just a big, fluffy kitty," I coo.

Torin laughs, reminding me once again that we have an audience. An audience I just told I had no interest in Atlas, yet here I am marveling at him like a fucking groupie. But his fur is *really* soft as it slides through my fingers. I want to wrap my arms around him like a teddy bear, but I also want to keep my arms and legs, so I decide not to do that.

Wiggling my way out from underneath him—because for whatever reason, he doesn't seem to want to move—I pat his head lightly. Emery is curling up next to the fire and the size of him is ridiculous. He's an even bigger animal with charcoal fur. He opens one beautiful purple eye and lifts his lip into a wolfy grin before coming over to me and licking my face with his serpent-like tongue.

"Ew!" I squeal, but secretly I love this. They turn into fucking animals—how cool is that! "You know, I'm more of a dog person," I whisper, knowing they can all hear me.

Atlas barrels into him, and their snarling has me backing away. Pants barks at both of them and I scoop him up. I don't think either of them would hurt him, but I'm not taking any chances. A glass vase breaks and Pippa comes out of the room at the end of the hall.

"Not in the house! For the love of the Realm, can you two act like adults!" she shouts and the door slams shut.

Emery whimpers and curls back up in front of the fire. Atlas goes to move next to him, nuzzling his face in what seems to be an apology, before the giant wolf scoots over to make room. Curling up behind him, Atlas rests his massive blocky head over Emery's back. It's literally insane—there's an enormous wolf and a panther cuddling in front of the fire.

"See, Idalia, that's who you really have to compete with," I say as I stride out and head for my room.

I startle awake, the bed groaning in response to some massive shadow coming toward me. I reach for my magic in a panic, but it recognizes him before I do, and a soothing calm slides over my beating heart.

Atlas, still a giant fucking panther, curls up next to me on my bed. He nearly suffocates me trying to maneuver himself around because apparently even king-sized beds aren't made for asshole elf panthers. Something snaps under the weight of him and I slice a glare in his direction.

"I swear to your damn Realm if you break my bed trying to cuddle with me as a big, fluffy cat, I'll never forgive you."

Something akin to a chuckle rumbles from him and I laugh, too. I'm not sure what the hell is going on, but honestly, it feels right and I'm not going to ruin it by asking or letting myself think that this could mean anything.

"This is my preferred form of yours. You're so soft and quiet," I say, snuggling into him. A vibrating growl emanates from him, but it's not threatening. He sniffs my head and I shiver as a tickle trails over me. Satisfied with something, he huffs and rests his massive head next to mine. Every time he breathes, air washes over me.

"Can you not? I can't sleep with you blow-drying my hair."

His big cat eyes blink at me once. The bed finally snaps, but only underneath him and he falls to the ground as I scramble to not fall too. He lets out a breathy roar and then nudges me down with him. Before I can smack him for ruining a perfectly good bed, he takes his massive paw and breaks the other side so that the whole thing has collapsed evenly. Pulling the sheet over me with his teeth, he rests his blocky head on my chest—a command to sleep.

I laugh and rub my face in my hands. "How did I get here?" I ask rhetorically.

He opens one eye and stares at me. I know he's asking himself the same thing.

Lucky for him, I'm too tired to talk anymore, and I quickly fall asleep to the gentle rumble of him purring. It's fucking weird, but it's also kind of perfect.

The next morning when I wake up, he's gone and my bed is fixed. I shake my head, wondering if it was all a dream. My eye catches on a book sitting on my dresser. I walk over to it and read the note written in perfect cursive inside its cover:

> This is one of Calamity's most famous poets. I hope you love it as much as I do. If not, you can get fucked.

I can't help the laugh that bursts out of my mouth or the fuzzy feeling that's squeezing my heart like a vise.

CHAPTER THIRTY

ᴀ̆TLAS

THREE DAYS BEFORE THE PARTY

MY FATHER ASSESSES ME FROM ACROSS HIS DESK. *I just told him I loved a girl, a servant girl, and I have no clue what he's going to say. Instead of responding, he reaches into his desk and pulls out a crystal decanter filled halfway with gold liquid. Removing two glasses, he places one in front of me before filling both. Something in my gut tells me this isn't a celebratory drink and I slump farther into my seat.*

"Kings don't slouch," he says.

I straighten, but I also say, "Good thing I'm not a king."

He takes a sip of his liquor and sucks his teeth like he's savoring every last drop. "Yes, good thing."

"What's that supposed to mean?"

My father is a ruler worthy of his title. He's even bigger than me and stands proudly, like the weight of the world is something he was born to carry. *A night-blue cloak trails behind him as he walks around the desk and perches on the edge in front of me.*

"It means that your charades are getting a bit ... tiresome."

"What cha—"

He holds up a hand to silence me. "Atlas, you know that I love you and your sister more than anything."

I don't speak.

"You do, don't you?" *His brow creases in worry.*

"Of course, Father."

Letting out a sigh of relief, he nods. "I've stood by while you've had things all young males should—females, adventure, partying. I want you to have everything, Atlas. Every experience. But there comes a time when you have to grow out of that and into the role you were born to take."

"I'm not being childish," *I argue.* "I love her, Father. And I don't see why I can't be king and marry who I want."

He stares at the wall of his study, lined with tall, brown bookshelves, the sage wallpaper in between the wood brightens the gold accents coating the room. "Do you want to be king?"

I stare at him, opening and closing my mouth, but nothing comes out. He's never asked me that question before.

He looks at me with amusement. "Answer honestly, son. It's just you and me in here."

I bite my lip and look into my lap. I'm wearing a navy blue, long-sleeved button up that I'd love to tear off. The black leather shoes I have on feel so tight I have to actively ignore the pain. "I'm not sure," *I answer honestly.*

I've never desired to be king—the responsibility or the title. I'm not interested in power or politics. I like to read and travel and more than anything, I like to draw. But a prince becoming an artist is about as un-realistic as growing Emery's cute little horns out of my head. And more importantly, I want to make my family proud.

"That's okay. We're not all born wanting this position," *he says.* "But those who aren't born with the desire have to learn it. It's time you start figuring out how to do just that."

"So, what? You want to force me out of marrying someone I love because it doesn't look good to you?" I snap. "How does making me miserable for the sake of appearances help me rule a nation?"

He frowns. "Because half of being king is keeping up appearances. Presenting a strong and unified front when houses are divided. Carrying confidence and bravery in the face of war. Marrying into a family, who has for centuries or even longer, provided this continent with stability. That *is* what being a king is about."

My heart sinks because I know that there's no winning this argument. "And if I wanted to marry someone who was faun?"

He seems to think about that for a second. Interspecies marrying isn't entirely frowned upon, but as far as I'm concerned, Emery is the first mixed child to run these halls. "There are plenty of noble faun houses who I would deem appropriate candidates if that is what you so choose."

"Unbelievable," I mutter.

My father stands from his perch and walks toward the bookshelf, taking a few history books off the shelves. "Maybe some examples of elves who have sacrificed for their nation will give you some perspective."

I cross my arms. "I doubt it."

He snaps back around, his patience thinning. He sees this conversation as trivial. I'm just a child in his eyes. I always have been and I always will be. "You haven't ever had to sacrifice anything, Atlas. Your mother and I have made sure of that, but you will learn how to do so and if this has to be your first lesson, then so be it. Life isn't about bending the rules to your whim. And I certainly won't stand here and teach you that being a king or being in love exempts you from that rule."

I stand up and face him. He's taller than me, but just barely. I've grown in the last ten years and I'm almost certain that one day I'll be bigger than him. "What can I do to make you see how much this means to me?"

A look of pity washes over his face, and I clench my jaw. "I want you to be able to follow your heart. I want you to feel love, but just because you can't marry the serving staff doesn't mean that you won't ever know what that's like."

Rage builds in me so loudly I can barely hear anything he's saying. "You want me to just find someone else then, is that it?"

"That's not what I'm saying—"

"If I died, would you just have another child to replace me? Maybe fuck a younger wife that could produce another bas raza heir?"

"You're being dramatic and petulant," he growls.

"Why?" I spit at him. "You'd do it, wouldn't you? For the sake of this continent and its people. You'd turn your back on everyone you love for honor and what you think is right."

People often say we look like each other. The chiseled square of our jaw, the thick, brown eyebrows that furrow easily with emotion, the broad frame of our shoulders. But right now, I can't find a single part of myself in him.

"Teach me about being a king all you like, but forgive me if I chose learning how to be a male from someone else."

Even as I speak the words, I regret them, but I don't care. He needs to know how important this is to me, and I refuse to back down. I leave his study before he can respond and storm back to my rooms.

CHAPTER THIRTY-ONE

HARPER

UMPING OUT OF THE SHOWER, I RUN A COMB THROUGH my hair and think about last night. I'm trying to decide if it's weird I'm attracted to a guy who turns into a panther. At that thought alone, a slimy feeling cozies up to the smile I had on seconds ago. I recognize it as betrayal and heartache, slipping around my insides as I imagine being pressed against Cole. I swallow it all back, ultimately deciding there are about ten million reasons why nothing good will ever come of thinking about Atlas that way.

Pulling on black leggings and a cream-colored sweater, I split my hair into two braids and run some mascara I stole from the faun I accidentally killed over my lashes. Jeez, that seems like ages ago. The mascara is called Doe-Eyed and I snort a laugh before I remember that I should probably feel bad about that set of events. For fuck's sake, I *killed* someone. No matter how hard I try, though, I don't feel anything. Maybe I was made for this world after all.

I grab the pocket watch I left out on my bed and move to tuck it into my shirt. Flipping it open, I note that the hour hand has finally moved to the one and chew my lip, wondering what it could possibly mean. It's been one month since I arrived ... is it keeping track?

A knock sounds at my door and despite my better judgment, I smile because I think it's Atlas. But then caution and nervousness bleed in. Do I bring up last night?

I decide to play it cool, like it meant nothing to me, because it's definitely not all I've been thinking about this morning.

"If you wanted to get into my bed so badly, you could have just asked, you didn't need to break—" I trail off because Pippa is smiling at me and her face is filled with obvious confusion. I'm so embarrassed, I can only stare at her while I try to remember every single word I said to spin it into something else.

She's merciful as she smiles and says, "I was wondering if you wanted to come into town with me? We have our meeting tonight with the Council and I think you should attend. They're somewhat formal events, and I figured you don't have anything to wear."

I nervously play with the end of one of my braids. "You think it's a good idea for me to come?"

She nods eagerly. Pippa has been nothing but welcoming to me over the last few weeks and I want to shoot myself in the foot for even considering flirting with her brother ... even though *he* started it. "I think it would be good if we showed everyone proof of why the weapons work so well."

"Okay," I agree. I find that every day I spend here, the more I want to stay. I know I can't ... it's temporary, but I'm happy to help them for the time being.

"Yay! Shopping trip!" she says while clapping her hands.

You know those girls who are just perfect in every way? They're beautiful and nice and strong. You want so badly to be their friend just in case some of their energy rubs off on you. Pippa is one of those girls.

Her hair is always curled into perfect waves that fall around her angular face. Her gold eyes are straight out of *Twilight* and her presence is so calming. She doesn't take shit from anyone, but she wouldn't hurt a fly ... unless said fly attacked her or someone she loved first, then she'd squash it easily. Not to mention she's the leader of a rebellion. How much more badass could she get?

I want more than anything to throw caution to the wind and fully invest in my friendship with her, but there's so many reasons not to. The first is that everything in this world is temporary and the second is the niggling feeling in the back of my mind that screams at me to never again let my guard down. That tells me even her perfect smile is probably hiding some hideous lie.

Doing my best to push the negativity aside, I frown as I remember something. "Pippa ... I don't have any money." I refuse to let them spend whatever hard earned money they've worked to collect over the last year.

She shakes her head and turns on her heel. "Don't worry about it."

I grab her wrist gently, turning her to look at me. "I do worry, though, Pippa," I say with a half-smile.

"The shop owner is part of the rebellion. I've promised to make her the seamstress for the Royal Family when we take the throne back and she's happily provided us with necessary items. I made sure her family was well taken care of before I ever accepted her help."

I chew on my lip, still not really liking the sound of this.

"If it makes you feel better, I think you're vastly underestimating the advantage you've given us. Think of this as a small payment for a debt we'll never be able to repay."

"You haven't won yet," I add. It's entirely rude of me to say and I have to remember to filter my thoughts better (not like that's ever worked for me).

Pippa only smiles. "Not with that attitude," she chimes and boops the tip of my nose before rushing down the hall. "Come on, Harper! I refuse to let you borrow anymore of my clothes and I don't think you want to be naked in front of all of these males."

I follow her closely, agreeing with her on one thing at least.

"I don't mind." Ellison laughs to himself in the living room.

"Shut the fuck up, Elli," Atlas grumbles.

Emery snorts, but they don't look up from whatever card game they're playing.

When we make it outside, Pippa looks at me and frowns, her hair glowing caramel in the sunlight. "It's about a two-hour walk at your pace."

"I'm happy if you want to pick something out for me," I offer.

She ignores me, looking off into the distance and tapping her chin. "Is it weird if I carry you?"

I shake my head. "I won't be too heavy?"

Pippa laughs hysterically before realizing I'm serious. "Oh, no ... of course not."

"You guys are a lot like vampires," I murmur as I walk over to jump on her back.

She turns around so fast I nearly fall backward. "Don't ever say that again." Her words aren't meant to sting, but my heart sinks to my stomach all the same.

"Sorry ... I—"

Pippa shakes her head as if reprimanding herself. "I should explain. Do you understand why that's offensive?"

"No," I whisper, feeling like a child being scolded. "I didn't mean—"

"I know, Harper," she says gently. She goes on to explain everything else the queen is doing with the fendlings and the heart stealing—things that no one cared to explain to me before. I didn't fathom the depths of her evil behavior or just how cruel she was. I knew it was bad. She killed hundreds of people after all, but I didn't know she was continuing to go all Dracula-Hitler style on innocent creatures.

"Is that why those faun tried to kill me when I got here?" I ask. "For her?"

"Not *for* her, no." She chews on her lip. "When my family was in power, there were laws against vampirism, but when she took over she did away with that. Now, the monsters have come out of hiding and everyone is greedy to get more magic as quickly as possible."

"That's awful," I say with disgust. I have about a million other derogatory words to use, but Pippa continues.

"It's worse than just that. Other species, besides the fendlings, are starting to go missing too. We don't know what she's doing with them, but she has to be stopped."

"Where did she come from?" It's something that has been bothering me ever since I heard about her. "Was she a noble?"

"No. That's the disturbing thing. No one knows who she was or where she lived before all of this. She's never been seen outside her derax form. No one even knows how she got into that party."

"Going somewhere?" We both turn around to see Idalia standing on the porch steps.

"D! I couldn't find you, but I'm taking Harper to Lana's shop. Want to come?" From the surprised look on her face, I can tell Pippa's words are genuine, though I'm less than enthused about the prospect of spending the day with Idalia.

I have a feeling Idalia would rather let me stab her before allowing me to go on a shopping date with *her* best friend. They're very possessive, these elves.

She feigns disinterest and shrugs. "Sure."

"Great, we were just leaving." Pippa turns to me and touches my forehead before touching her own, and Idalia does the same.

I'm about to ask what she's doing when she answers for me. "It's a glamour. You can see us and we can see you, but to anyone else, you're just a normal faun. Same for us," she says, pointing between her and Idalia.

"Why?" I ask.

"It wouldn't be great to let the queen know the princess she's hunting is running around town on a shopping spree, now would it?" Idalia jeers.

"Got it," I say, biting my tongue. I give them both a tight-lipped smile. My mom always says to kill them with kindness. So that's what I'll do with Idalia. She has no reason to not like me and surely there's at least one thing we have in common ... me and the supermodel elf.

It still takes us quite a bit of time to get into town, but we're moving too fast for me to ask Pippa if she wants a break. I have to trust that if she does, she'll say something. My eyes light up when we finally get there and I take in the town for a second time. I'm less distracted by the different types of people walking around and can focus on the buildings, which are all similar and entirely different.

Everything is smushed together like in San Francisco, but these buildings have tall, peaked gable roofs and timber-crossings on the outside, reminiscent of medieval Europe. Some have bay windows popping out of the frames and they're all painted different bright colors. The store fronts have well-crafted displays and cute hanging wooden signs with symbols identifying what they sell.

The store we're going to is called Blue Jeans and when we walk through the white wooden door, a female faun peers over the counter on the left side of the room and gives a friendly wave before going back to reading. The store is split into two levels, with the ground floor only a few steps below the top floor. I'm slightly overwhelmed by the floral smell in here and the *clothes*. They're everywhere—on circular racks, on the walls, on cute wooden tables displayed between mannequins.

"Hi, Lana! What beautiful weather for sipping on danjula tea," Pippa says in greeting.

I furrow my brow in confusion. What a random thing to say.

"It's code for who we are," Idalia says under her breath.

"Oh! My favorite customers!" Lana says, coming around the counter and greeting Idalia and Pippa with a kiss on the cheek. The shop owner's cream antlers twist like ram horns against her bubblegum hair. She looks to be in her thirties, but here I never know how old anyone is. When she spots me, she smiles and then confusion passes over her face. "Who ... who is this?"

"Don't worry, Lana," Pippa says, patting her arm. "This is Harper. She's a *friend*."

Lana's anxiety doesn't ease, so I say something to clear the air, "I love your antlers." I gesture to them and my gut tells me I should have picked literally anything else to compliment her on.

Lana gives me an awkward smile before walking away with Pippa and discussing things in whispers.

I turn to Idalia, who is snickering. "Wrong thing to say?" I ask.

"Just a weird thing to say. It's unique to you, but not to us. It's like if I said I like your lips."

I shrug. "Is that weird?"

"It is if they're the very first words I've ever spoken to you." She walks away to look amongst the clothes and I have to agree with her.

The selection in the store is so diverse my head spins. The styles range from boho chic to business casual to coronation Barbie. Everything is cute though, and each item of clothing has a tag with an area for a thumbprint.

"What is this?" I ask Idalia as she flips through a rack of jeans.

She looks at the tag and rolls her eyes. "What size are you?"

I tell her and she presses her thumb to the tag, whispering some words I don't quite catch. The jeans shift into my size and I stare at them, awestruck. "That's amazing," I whisper, but Idalia's moved on and I'm only talking to myself.

I put the jeans back and focus on finding a dress to wear tonight. Because the store doesn't stock various sizes, every piece of clothing is something different and the options feel endless.

We've already gone over this—I'm not good with decisions. Nine times out of ten, I make the wrong one. So instead of picking out something to wear, I aimlessly sift through dresses and marvel at the way they all feel like silk between my fingers, even though they're made of varied fabrics.

"Find anything good?" Pippa asks.

I smile sheepishly at her. "I'm a little overwhelmed," I answer honestly.

She looks around the room like she's seeing it for the first time. "Is this different than what you're used to at home? If you don't like the style, I'm sure—"

"No, no, it's not that. Everything is wonderful. I'm just ... indecisive," I say.

"Ah, got it. Well, Lana can help." She calls the shop owner over and explains my predicament, which really isn't a predicament at all. I should just pick a damn dress and call it good.

"Do you need something with a tail slit?" Lana asks.

I have to fight back a laugh because it's one hundred percent a serious question here. "No," I answer.

"Right, then. I have the perfect thing!" Lana rushes off to somewhere in the back of the shop and I bite my lip nervously. What if she picks out something I hate and then I either have to lie or tell her I don't like it. Fuck, brutal honesty is kind of my go-to.

She comes back and stands on the steps separating the two levels— holding the dress out for me like she's Vanna White. It *is* perfect. It's a two-piece outfit. The top is a cropped black tank with a heart-shaped cut and straps that tie into bows on the shoulder. The bottom is a mauve chiffon maxi skirt that flows gently with *zero* poof. If there is one thing I want you to take away from this story, it's that I don't do poofy.

I give her a wide smile. "I love it. Do you have a changing room?" The three of them look at each other, confused. "You know, somewhere I can try it on?"

"Why would you do that?" Idalia asks as if it's the most absurd question in the world.

Heat creeps up my cheeks. I shouldn't be embarrassed; this is all new to me, but my face decides to be a fucking tomato anyway.

Pippa's face pales slightly as she looks to Lana. "Harper is from out of town."

"Far away," Idalia drawls.

"I'll show her," the princess adds, hurrying over to take the dress and dragging me with her.

"It's been a long day," I tell Lana for dramatic effect.

Pippa leads me to a gold oval-shaped full-length mirror and holds the tag to the glass. I'm watching her with such interest I don't even notice my reflection has changed and suddenly I'm wearing the dress Lana picked out. I try to act like I've done this a thousand times, but it's so fucking cool I can't avoid the smile that's plastered to my face.

"You love it then?" Lana asks, misreading my giddiness.

The dress does look good on me, though, and I nod eagerly. "It really is perfect."

Lana beams from behind me in the mirror's reflection.

"Atlas will like it," Idalia says with a sneer.

"D," Pippa scolds.

She shrugs with that bitchy smile on her face, the one that says *what I'm about to say may sound nice, but I mean it in the rudest way possible*. "What? I see the way he looks at you."

"I *hear* the way he fucks you," I snap back. So much for kindness. Maybe I can just kill her instead.

Kidding!

Idalia glares at me and clenches her fists at her sides. She's about to open her mouth when Pippa interrupts, "We should get going." She snaps her fingers and I'm back in my regular clothes. I grin at her and Lana before turning to Idalia and giving her an even bigger smile.

"Should we get ice cream?" Pippa asks as we walk out of the shop and onto the town's cobblestone streets.

My patience for Idalia is thinning, but the way she's gritting her teeth makes me think going for ice cream is the last thing she wants. "Sure!" I say. See? Petty bitch.

Pippa squeezes Idalia's shoulder. "Oh, come on, D. You don't even like my brother." She strolls farther into town. The sidewalks are too narrow for all three of us to walk side by side, so I let them in front of me and follow closely behind.

"And I don't even like Atlas," I add.

Pippa spins around and looks at me, surprised. "You don't?"

"No!" I say, a little too defensively. But honestly, why in the world would she think that?

"Because he's an elf?" Idalia asks.

"No, because he's an asshole," I explain.

"Well, he's not *always* an asshole," Pippa says protectively.

"Yes he is," Idalia and I reply at the same time. She gives me a little smile and then puts her resting bitch face back on.

Pippa pouts, genuinely saddened by the fact that I don't want to fuck her brother. But what am I supposed to say? *Hey, Pippa, your brother is totally hot and I* would *hate fuck him, but that's about it because he seems intent on making my life here miserable.*

Actually, now that I think about it, he seems just my type.

"Why do you *want* me to like him?" I ask instead.

She shrugs and turns back around. "Let's not talk about him anymore."

Thank their fucking Realm.

We get to the ice cream shop and I'm surprised to see they have normal flavors and not something weird like Fairy Berry Blast. There are circular metal tables with floral designs carved into them and we pick a seat at one of them outside. The sun beats down, but the shade of the buildings is a welcome reprieve. Like everything here, the ice cream is to die for.

"Can I ask you a question about magic?"

"Of course," Pippa answers.

"How does it work? Do you just think of what you want and it appears?"

Idalia snorts and I fight the urge to bash her head into the table.

"Not really. I'm sure you've learned that everyone in Calamity has magic in their body to help with normal functions like making your heart beat or helping your blood flow, but we tend to refer to that magic as *ezren*, or essence. It's not really magic in the same way that we think of typical magic. So, everyone has *ezren* and others have even more magic on top of that.

"For most, the ability to use magic comes down to only things they could normally do with their hands. For example, I may *want* a pile of gold to appear on this table, but unless there's gold in my pocket or somewhere else within reasonable reach, I can't just create it from nothing. But, let's say there's gold in that guy's pocket." She points to an elf across the street. "Some may be able to move it from his pocket to this table, but some may not. Certain creatures in Calamity only have *ezren* and nothing more, making them essentially magicless in your eyes, but that's not how we see them."

"And they're just born that way?" I ask.

Pippa nods. "Magic is passed through the bloodline, so the stronger your parents are, the more likely you are to wield higher abilities. Then, there are darker ways to obtain magic, like stealing it from someone else. The body can only harbor so much magic, though, and it's something that takes time for it to adjust. If someone with only *ezren* tried to drink my blood, then they'd likely die quickly. That's why when your blood comes into contact with anyone, it kills them instantly. It's such a potent form of magic that it overwhelms their body. Or so we think."

"Why would anyone risk vampirism if it has the potential to kill them?"

Making a face like she understands my logic, Pippa says, "Powerful magic is very rare. You've just happened to surround yourself with some of the most powerful individuals in Calamity. Our level of magic is not the norm."

"So that's why only Atlas could heal me when he attacked me and not Emery?"

Pippa's eyes light up at my understanding, totally glossing over the fact that her brother almost killed me a few weeks ago. "Exactly! Emery's magic is very powerful so he can heal wounds, but fixing things like bones and nerves is not easily done."

"And what about back in the shop, with the different clothing sizes?"

"There are spells you can apply to certain things—spells to make plants grow faster, or to heal things, or to switch the size of jeans. They're all temporary though. One use only. The clothing shop is spelled to allow that kind of thing to happen, but it won't work when you get home ... well, for normal people. I just so happen to be strong enough to use spells like that on a more permanent basis. That's how you've been fitting into my clothes." She waves her hand vaguely and takes a spoonful of ice cream. "There are, of course, laws and things ... or there used to be."

"And manipulating time?" I ask.

Idalia shifts uncomfortably while Pippa smiles warmly. "That is something only *you* can do."

CHAPTER THIRTY-TWO

ATLAS

I'M SITTING IN THE STUDY WITH PIPPA AS SHE GOES OVER the plans for the meeting with the Council later tonight. The meeting is in the usual spot—underneath the main tavern in town, Stella's Faux Paw.

The owner of the tavern, Stella, is on the Council and the place is so crowded that no one expects it's where a bunch of revolutionaries are hiding out. It's the perfect spot because after we're done discussing the end of the world and how unlikely we are to save it, I can get drunk enough to black out and not have to think about Fox for a single fucking second. The only downside is that these meetings are kind of formal, a nod to the old days where we all dressed up like uptight douchebags while the rest of the continent wore normal clothes. I think it's ridiculous, but Pippa thinks it appeases the older members of the Council.

Just as I settle in for a night away from the human siren, Fox waltzes into the room looking like the princess of my dreams. Her outfit is in two pieces, with a strip of skin between the top and the bottom, taunting me. Her cleavage spills over the center of the top, teasing me. Her legs are lengthened in heels, mocking me. I want to rip it all down the center and find out what she's wearing underneath.

"Why the fuck is she here?" I growl.

Fox ignores my question and looks at the rest of the room—Wilder, Pippa, Emery and me. "You all look very nice, except for the scowling sourpuss in the corner." Her eyes find mine and she's all fight. For the fucking Realm.

"Pippa ..." I say, trying to keep my cool.

My sister, perched on the edge of the desk, crosses her arms. "Atlas, she has to come. Don't be such a buzzkill. You look lovely, Harper."

"But why?" I ask again and for the last fucking time because if someone doesn't give me some answers, I'm going to lose it.

"We need to show them proof of why the weapon works so well," she says, like I'm stupid.

"We don't need more proof than the dead sentinel display," I grind out.

"If we go in there saying we have a cool new weapon, they're going to wonder how we got it. They're going to ask questions, Atlas. Instead of hiding things from them, don't you think honesty is the best policy?"

No. I never fucking think that. Whoever does is an absolute fool and if Pippa hasn't learned that lesson by now, then I've really failed her.

"No, I don't." I cross my arms.

"Well, it's not up to you, it's up to me."

If we bring her there, she won't be a secret anymore. If anyone beyond our inner circle finds out what kind of weapon she is and it gets back to that raving psycho queen, then she's in danger. And I won't fucking have it.

"It's only going to cause problems, Pippa. A human saving our world? People won't like it." It's an absolute lie, and she sees right through it. Her brow furrows as she tries to figure out what's going on in my head.

"Can everyone give us a second?" she asks the room.

I don't take my eyes off of her as the others scurry out. Mostly because I can't bear to look at Fox looking like a sexy ballerina.

When everyone's gone, she leans against the desk. "What the hell was that about? I know you don't like the idea of her being here, but you're seriously being an ass."

I give her a smug look. "That's hardly new for me, sis."

"Atlas," she warns.

I rub a hand down my face. "If Her Royal Whoreness finds out we have Harper, she'll make sure she does everything in her power to take her from us."

"How would she find out?"

"I don't know, Pippa. The more people we tell, the more risky it becomes."

She chews her lip in thought. "If someone goes to the queen about things discussed at this meeting, we have bigger problems."

I hate when she's right. I *could* tell her what I'm really feeling. And what is that exactly, Atlas? That I have some unnatural desire to protect the human girl living under our roof. It won't change anything. We're all in danger.

"Our people deserve to know, Atlas. They deserve to feel the hope I feel right now. Don't you feel it too?"

I close my eyes and breathe out slowly. "Fine, but she gets glamoured like the rest of us."

When I open them, Pippa is smirking at me. "This wouldn't be for any other reason, would it?"

"If you have something to say, don't be fucking cryptic about it."

She looks at me innocently. "You wouldn't happen to be worried about Harper? Maybe because you like her?"

I snort and it's probably a little too obvious. The thing is, I don't like her. I like her magic. Right? "I'm trying to protect all of us, Pip."

"I just see how you are around her ..."

I raise a brow. "An absolute tool?"

My sister rolls her eyes. "You're always a tool. I mean, the way you look at her. Like your broken pieces aren't as sharp when she's around." She says it all wistful and shit because Pippa is a romantic at heart. Well, I'm about to burst her bubble.

I sigh. "Her magic feels like it was made for mine, but it's nothing more than that."

"That doesn't sound like nothing."

"It is," I snap. "It has nothing to do with her as a person. She's just a vessel for something that should never have existed. Why are you pushing this?"

Pippa shrugs. "I just want you to be happy. We all deserve some happiness after everything that's happened and ... I don't know. I like her, she's different."

Everyone *does* deserve some happiness. Everyone except me. I deserve every terrible thing that's happened since that night.

Before I can respond, she starts talking again, a nervous lilt to her voice. "I know you were in love. Emery told me and I assume she died when everything happened. I don't know who she was and you never talk about it, but—"

My heart breaks into a million pieces, but not for the reasons she thinks. "Pippa, stop." Silence consumes the air around us. Finally, I walk over to her and grab her head in my hands, tilting her face to look at mine. "I love you, you know that?"

She nods.

"You know I'd do anything to make sure you and Emery are safe?"

"Yes," she whispers.

"I'm sorry if I ever made you believe that wasn't true." I kiss the top of her forehead and step back.

"You didn't. We all handle grief differently." A mischievous smile lights up her face. "I just happen to be better at it than you."

I give her the best smile I can muster. "Yeah. You're just better than me, Pip."

"Then listen to me when I say she needs to come to the meeting. We can glamour her when she's out in public, but they need to see her."

I nod, relenting. She's organized this whole rebellion without me. Who am I to get in the way of her plans now?

CHAPTER THIRTY-THREE
HARPER

WHEN I WAS YOUNGER, I USED TO WANT TO be carried *everywhere*. My sister would joke that my dates would have to carry me. I can with one hundred percent certainty say that if another elf never lifted me off the ground again, I'd be happy.

Emery places my feet on the dirt in front of the bridge that leads into town and I adjust my skirt and the underwear that's been eaten by my ass as subtly as possible. When I finish and look around, everyone is staring at me. *Great.*

We walk over the bridge and toward the tavern, which has a big sign hanging outward from the siding stating the name: Stella's Faux Paw. I giggle and everyone looks at me.

"It's a play on Stella Artois, right?" I ask.

I only get silent and confused stares in response.

Emery clears his throat. "The owner, Stella, actually has a fake paw. It's a hook she uses to open the kegs."

"*Alrighty*, then," I mutter as we walk into the tavern. It's times like these I know I've lost it.

The tavern is noisy and loud, like any bar would and should be. My feet peel off the floor with each step on the sticky wood. When I look up, I note two stories. The second one is a loft with a balcony overlooking the first floor. It leads to the outdoor patio I saw when I first got to Calamity. Somehow that already feels like a lifetime ago. Stone and wood walls make up the scaffolding and a giant iron chandelier hangs from the ceiling, illuminating the center of the tavern and dimming the lighting in the corners.

"Come on," Pippa says, dragging my arm to the back of the tavern.

Everyone follows and Atlas might as well carry me with how close he's trailing behind.

I stop and turn around fast enough that he almost falls on top of me. "Cling much?" I joke.

He looks down at me with a stern face and pushes me forward. "Move, Fox."

Prince Asshat is wearing perfectly pressed, black pants, a matching silk vest, and a navy fucking tailcoat. The black cravat around his neck *might* be making my panties wet. Dude looks like an actual prince straight out of some historical drama and it's unearthing a kink I didn't know I had.

Pushing the slew of dirty thoughts from my mind, I give him a mock salute, which earns me a look of confusion, and turn to catch up with Pippa. The hall is long and winding, the farther we go, the more the walls seem to press in on us. It's not an illusion as I reach out with my hand to touch the wall a palm's distance away. When I make contact, there's something that calls to my magic and I eagerly want to run my fingers down the wood. As I'm about to, Atlas swats my hand away with force.

"Ow!" I murmur, and Pippa whips around to give us a scolding look.

"Hands to yourself," he whispers into my ear. The hair on the back of my neck stands to attention.

We finally arrive at the end of the hall. It's so dark I nearly can't see the floorboards in front of me, but I can make out a small, red door that comes up to my breast. There's no fucking way the giant elf boy behind me is fitting through that thing.

"Why—"

"Shh!"

I'm interrupted by everyone around me and I purse my lips, heat crawling up my cheeks, as Pippa does something in front of me that I can't see. Maybe that's the point. This is obviously some secret door in a passageway that was made to deter people from continuing forward. The claustrophobic walls and suffocating rush of magic make me want to run and hide. I'm clearly not made of the same stuff as my companions.

Pippa chants something unintelligible. I can't make out the words because she's whispering, but also because at the same moment Atlas runs a finger down the length of my arm and my skin lights with a buzz so strong I nearly gasp. I don't, though, because believe it or not, I have some semblance of self-control and I'm not going to melt in the presence of any affection this asswipe gives to me. Well, at least not yet.

He continues the path down my arm, to the edge of my palm, lingering near my pinky. My whole consciousness zeros in on the feeling of his skin on mine. Involuntarily, my fingers reach out to wrap around his. I expect him to laugh at me or pull away, but he doesn't. Instead, he laces his through mine and squeezes. His palm burns against my flesh before he pulls me into him so swiftly and with so much power, I don't stumble as my back fits perfectly against his torso.

Well, fuck. Now I'm so close to melting it's hard to think of all the reasons I was against it mere seconds ago. But lucky ... or unlucky for me, something far more interesting happens ahead of me. The red door grows in size and expands before popping open, and Atlas lets go of me so effortlessly, I again wonder if it was the magic of this place fucking with my head. It's dark beyond the doorway and I can't make anything out, but Pippa walks easily into it and I lose her as I take tentative steps. Atlas nudges me to hurry and my heart rate quickens.

"I can't see," I whisper, because the magic of this place is kind of freaking me out.

He makes a snarl of disapproval that does nothing to ease my fears.

I'm about to ask him how the hell he expects me to move forward when magic washes over me. How do I know it's magic? Because it tells me. Not with words or sounds, but with intention. It intertwines with whatever is in my blood and caresses my mind. Part of me wants to run away screaming, while the other part of me tingles in anticipation. It's that reckless version of Harper. The one that plays Roofie Roulette and takes drugs from strangers. It's the version of me that jumps down random fox holes because what else do I have to lose?

Curiosity wins out as I accept the magic and breathe it in. When I do, my eyesight enhances and my hearing sharpens. It feels like all of my senses are on ecstasy. This time, I let out a sound of wonderment as euphoria consumes me.

I see a vinyl, black-and-white checkered path in front of me. To the left are vintage style lamp posts that emit an eerily dim light, and a wrought-iron fence with spires that could rip into flesh. Looming, rectangular hedges stand like guards to my right; their forest green color makes them seem even more menacing in this spectral hall. Goosebumps run up my arms, effectively extinguishing the fire burning under my skin.

"Scared, Fox?" Atlas taunts from behind me. His voice holds none of its usual playfulness. In fact, I'm not even sure it's him.

"Yes," I say honestly. No point in lying—my pounding heart is surely audible to all of them. "Are we still in the tavern?"

He doesn't answer and I turn around to glare at him, but when I do, he's not there. No one is, and I realize I'm alone in this creepy hallway. I don't know if my heart is beating so fast that I can't feel it anymore or if it's stopped entirely. Panic consumes me as I fight the urge to collapse to the ground. I can't explain it, but I'm scared. Truly frightened to be here in this place that's cold and dark. There's that voice again in my head, telling me to run, to get away as fast as possible.

ALL THE JAGGED EDGES

It's screaming. I make a move to escape, fighting the urge to fall to the floor and vomit, but my feet are stuck.

"Fox." Atlas's voice reaches out to me, but it's only an echo in my mind as my body is consumed with terror.

I don't understand where I am. Who I am. How did I get here in this world that is so different from my own and makes no sense? I was supposed to die. I should have died. The one thing I could control and I fucking failed. How am I supposed to help save an entire world when I couldn't bother to save myself?

"Fox!"

I can't see him. My vision has tunneled into an abyss as my mind collapses in on itself. But suddenly I'm not as cold anymore. The darkness starts to melt away as a soft glow replaces the shadows. My eyes flit to the ones staring at me with concern as I find myself back inside the dim tavern hallway, the magic thrumming in it before, gone.

"Fox," he repeats. When I look into the depth of his gaze, it reminds me of home. Not the Spanish style mansion that sits behind an iron gate, but a real home. The kind people always talk about, but I never believed existed.

I look between the worried faces of his friends as unease begins to fill me again.

"Don't look at them, Fox. Just look at me." He wraps my fingers through his.

I do as he says, looking down as he makes a motion to them with his hands before he takes my chin and tilts it back up to meet his gaze. He wipes tears I didn't even know I had from my cheeks.

"Deep breath," he says calmly, his voice filling me with reassurance.

I do as he instructs and let the air fill my lungs. I feel it expand my chest and clear my mind. He nods, an instruction for me to do it once more. I do and my heart slows as oxygen coats my blood.

"Is she okay?" Pippa asks from beyond us. I don't follow her voice, instead I keep looking at the brown eyes that bind me to this world.

"She's fine. Start the meeting, we'll catch up," he says, keeping his focus locked on me.

I'm fine. I repeat his words in my head.

I don't feel fine, but I trust him. Fuck knows why, but I do and if he thinks I'll be okay then I believe him. I can faintly hear the others shuffle away and the close of a door.

"What happened?" I ask, my voice cracking around the fear that's starting to subside.

"I told you to keep your hands to yourself," he chuckles.

I look at him with confusion.

"You touched the wall, despite my warning, I might add. I guess your magic reacted with it. I'm not sure what happened from there."

I bite my quivering lip and Atlas murmurs something as he lets go of my hands.

"Wait!" I say, reaching back for his absent touch. It's pathetic, really, but I need him closer to me.

"Harper," he says in a low tone—not a warning, but a request. It's the first time he's ever said my name and my heart decides it wants a shot at being an acrobat.

I ignore his request, every part of my body wanting to be in his arms, and lunge into him. I wrap my arms around his neck and stretch onto the tips of my toes until I can rest my head just below his shoulder. I can still feel the cold hall constricting my chest, but with him holding me, I know his magic will protect me. His grip around me tightens and I sigh in relief. The stubble around his jaw brushes against my ear and makes me shiver as he leans down, enveloping me.

"Do you want to talk about it?" he asks. His voice is unmistakably Atlas, but softer. A version I've only caught glimpses of. It's terrifying in a way I'm not ready to acknowledge.

"I went somewhere else ... I don't know ... I—" I shake my head. I can't relive the way the darkness felt wrapping around my soul. When I make the movement, I nuzzle into his chest, letting the heat of his cardamom and vetiver scent ease the knot in my chest. But as I do, my heart starts to beat heavily for a different reason. A sound of impatience rumbles through him and ignites a desire that races through my veins.

Before I can breathe him in again, I'm slammed against the wall of the tavern hallway. Fear and pleasure roil in my gut as I look at him towering over me, pinning my arms at my sides, and staring at me like he wants to devour every inch of my soul. The warm and soft Atlas is gone. The male looking down at me is all monster, coated in the flesh of something crafted from my deepest desires.

"Stop looking at me like that," he demands.

"Like what?" I snap, the sorrow and panic feeling like a distant memory.

"Like you're daring me to kiss you."

I swallow as my heart tries desperately to crawl up my throat. "Maybe I am."

"Maybe I will." His grip on my wrists tightens to the point of pain.

"Do it," I command, baiting the demon in front of me.

His gaze drops to my mouth and my lips part.

"Sorry to interrupt, but we're ready," Emery says with a nervous cough.

I flinch, but Atlas never removes his gaze from my mouth. The rise and fall of his chest is heavy.

"Be right there," he grumbles. His eyes linger for just a moment and then he lets go so suddenly my knees nearly buckle. In a blink, he's gone.

Taking a deep breath, I smooth out my outfit and hair, wiping away any residual moisture from beneath my eyes and hoping my makeup isn't ruined. What a bizarre fucking turn of events. My stomach tightens from the whirlwind of emotions. I decide to try and wrap my head around those when I'm alone. Best not to examine them when I'm about to walk into a meeting filled with a bunch of strange alien creatures regarding a magic that maybe shouldn't belong to me, but might save their world from an evil tyrant.

I walk down the rest of the hallway, surprised when I see Emery waiting for me by the door. He gives me a half smile and I return it with a look that says *if you fucking say anything about whatever you interrupted I'll find a way to gut you.*

He gives me a nod of understanding before saying, "They're already expecting a human. Pippa gave them the whole spiel, but don't take your glamour off until you get in there."

I raise an eyebrow at him. "I don't know how to remove the glamour."

Emery smiles shyly at me. "Right. Well, you ready?"

I shrug. "I don't think I have a choice."

CHAPTER THIRTY-FOUR

ATLAS

HER MAGIC IS POISONING ME. I FEEL IT THICK IN THE air of every room she enters. It wraps around my mind and suffocates me like some gaseous fog. When she's not near me, I need to touch her. When she leaves, I can still smell her—raspberries and daisies and fucking rainbow clouds. But it's so much worse than the desire to be around her, because it's the desire to protect her that replays in my mind. Taunting me and calling out to me until the only way I can think of anything else is to have her by my side, knowing she's safe.

I briefly wonder if this is how Emery feels about me, but shake it off. I know it's not. This bond is different. Ever since that day we created the Reign Tree, her magic has intertwined itself into mine. It makes my heart beat and my soul flicker impatiently from the darkness I shoved it into however long ago.

Every bit of me wants to claim her. To make her mine, this part of my soul that's been missing. I bite the inside of my cheek until I taste blood. This situation is so fucked. It can't be her. She's *human*. She doesn't belong here, and that magic shouldn't be hers. She's reckless and defiant and so fucking rude.

I don't want it. I don't want her.

I have this ridiculous notion that if I say it often enough, it will be true. The thing is, I won't be convinced that it's *her* I want. I know it's her magic and the more I remind myself of that, the easier this will all be. So I let the blood in my mouth coat my resolve and swallow my craving for her until all there is is a faint buzz from her presence in the room.

For the fucking Realm, I haven't even been paying attention to this meeting that's nearly over. The Council was ecstatic about the weapons, as they should be. They were less than enthusiastic about Fox, which makes perfect sense and also makes me want to rip all of their fucking throats out.

I hate her. She's perfect.

It's a never-ending war inside my head. I quickly glance at her over-whelmed expression in the seat next to me. I need her to be gone. She's a distraction of the worst degree.

"Any news on the camps?" Stella asks.

My sister bites her inner cheek. "Ellison got back from the castle recently. With the new weapons we were able to make, I felt more comfortable sending him over there, but there's no new information. We only know what we've always known—her derax form is a lioness, and no one has seen her as anything but. She must be high-elf, but who knows what she truly is."

Stella nods and then looks to Fox with hesitation.

"We can trust her," Pippa repeats, for the fourth time tonight.

Stella drums her furless fingers on the table, each one covered with a thin sharp nail. "We had some bucks traveling underground from South Ashberg, arrive two days ago. Nothing along those routes, though the trail to Spruce Hollow is still barred by magic."

"She has to be hiding them there," Emery growls.

"Easy," Deena, one of the faun councilors, adds.

I snarl at her in response. Fuck her telling Emery to take it easy.

Deena arches a brow at me with smug deviance. "Something to add, Prince? It's so lovely seeing you here ... at last."

I bite back every retort I have at the look Pippa gives me. She needs me to be calm. "The same magical barrier is built into the roads that cross over into Willowby."

Everyone in the room—except Fox, who knows fuck-all what we're talking about—gasps.

"How do you know this?" Wilder asks.

"And why didn't you say something sooner?" Pippa adds.

"I'm saying something now. There's nothing anyone can do about it anyway."

Stella's voice is calm, but stern. "But why didn't you inform anyone?"

I shrug. "I just found out."

"Atlas," Pippa warns.

I don't want to tell them the truth, but secrets are piling up in my mind like a fucking house of cards. It's all going to come crashing down sooner or later. *Fuck.*

"First, tell them about the Reign Tree," I say to Pippa.

Everyone looks around, startled. "Your Highness," says Ileene, one of the Kelpies in the room. Physically, Kelpies appear to be part elf and part fish, but they're their own species. Their fish-like features vary from the different types they surround themselves with. Some have dolphin fins, while others may have koi scales. When they're out of the water, they take a purely elven form with scales that climb up their skin and gills that pucker angrily at the dry air. "This is a Council meeting, not a show and tell of your brother's unwillingness to cooperate." She crosses her arms, tucking in the manta ray fins that protrude from her back like wings. Green and blue iridescent spots glitter in the incandescent lighting.

"Watch it," I snap.

"Atlas," Wilder chides.

I take a deep breath and clench my fists under the table. Fox's small hand reaches out, wiggling her fingers into my grip. I keep my fist tight so she can't, but she persistently pries my fingers loose. I almost laugh as I eventually relax and let her in. Her warm hand traces patterns on my palm before letting go, a smile pulling at the corner of her lips.

"I think it's best if you explain it, brother. You're the one that did it."

I sigh and delve into the story about how Fox and I created the Reign Tree. I barrel through all the ooo's and ah's and the singular "no way" that comes from Duskan, the other faun councilor. During the whole thing, Fox's hand hovers close to mine below the table, not touching but enough for me to feel her presence.

"Impossible," Deena murmurs.

"It's not impossible. It's actually quite visible for everyone to fucking see," Fox says casually and we all turn to her in surprise.

The councilors look like she just jumped on the table and shit a magic brick for each of them. Fox just shrugs and leans back in her seat, gesturing for me to continue. I fight the smile that my body is begging to give her; it's easy because I'm dreading the next part of what I'm going to tell them.

"Since then, my magic seems to be amplified. I'm able to sense all sorts of things I wasn't before. It's hard to discern what is what. Right now it's just a clusterfuck, but it's there. Somehow I'm more connected to the earth and the pieces of magic that make up the topography of the continent. When you mentioned Spruce Hollow, it tugged on something in my mind and I just instantly knew. *That's* why I didn't say anything until now."

I'm hoping no one else knows the thing I'm not saying. That the real reason it's amplified is because now it's linked to Fox's magic, because we're *selüm-ra*. I'm basically wielding both of our powers even if I can't access the same abilities she can. If she was skilled enough, she'd be able to do the same thing, but right now she has the skill level of a blind toad.

Pippa's eyes widen and then she frowns, but no one else makes a move. With the information I admitted before the meeting, there's no way she hasn't connected the dots. They're all just staring at me with wide eyes and looks of awe on their faces. I hate it. Yes, I'm this powerful. I'm also still a giant asshole.

"Happy, now?" I throw in just to remind them I'm not the king they want or deserve.

Everyone keeps staring until Fox starts giggling and all their attention goes to her.

"What?" I demand.

"You're just such a fucking tool. It's great. Sorry, please continue."

She's back. The fire in her eyes that flickered out in the hallway when her magic collided with the concealment spell around the meeting room is burning brighter than ever. I let out the laugh I've been smothering and the tension in the room rises as the others try to understand the dynamic between us. Good fucking luck.

Wilder clears his throat. "So there are several places she could be hiding her nefarious plots."

Everyone nods in agreement.

"What kind of magic does the human possess if she can help to create a Reign Tree and where did she get it?" Deena asks, a cruel curiosity gleaming in her eyes. I fight the urge to pluck each one of her eyeballs out so she can never look at Fox that way again.

Instead, I turn to Fox so she can explain because I'd really love to know the answer.

"I'm not sure." The steadiness in her voice cracks.

"How did you get here?" Duskan questions.

She looks to me for reassurance, and it breaks my fucking heart. I don't let her see it, though; I stare at her with cold indifference as she seems to be searching her memory.

"I don't know," she repeats. "I can't remember."

Deena scoffs. "How convenient."

I'm about to tell her to choke on her own saliva when Harper beats me to it. "Yes," she sneers. "It's *so* convenient that I was taken away from my home and everything I know. Given a power that sometimes feels like it might consume me, and land in this fucking fantasy world with the moodiest dude to ever exist." She points her thumb at me. "With nothing I love, nothing that's familiar, and nothing to guide me back home. I'm having a great fucking time, *Deena*."

"I'm surprised you two don't get along better," Deena says, pointing between us.

I open my mouth to say ... I don't know what, but once again the little Fox can hold her own. "With all due respect, fuck off. I'm here to help you people. If you don't want it, I'll happily go sell myself to the next highest bidder." She pushes out of her seat as we all stare at her in surprise. I'm not sure anyone has ever had the audacity to talk to a councilor like that. I've never been more turned on.

Fox stops behind my chair and places her hands on my shoulders in a possessive way that brands my skin. "Also," she adds, moving her cataclysmic stare across the room. "Atlas might be the biggest tool I've ever met, but it's painfully obvious that he loves Calamity and everything that inhabits it. Maybe if you paid more attention to who he's trying to be instead of who he was, you'd see that too." She lets go and walks toward the door.

Nope, I'm officially more turned on.

"Where are you going?" I ask her. I quickly place a glamour over her before she bolts.

"To dance," she says airily and shuts the door.

"She's a liability," Deena says immediately.

"She's the best option we have," Emery argues.

I'm still stuck looking at the fucking door she just walked out of. Did she just defend me?

"I have to go," I murmur as I stand to follow her. She can't just wander around by herself., What is she thinking?

"Atlas," a voice says that makes me pause. I turn around to see Malor, the only fendling councilor in attendance, motioning for me to sit down. Dude is old as shit, clear by the white beard that travels down his tiny dragon body. He was probably there when the first Reign Tree was created. I'm not about to disrespect my elders, even though the thought of her out there by herself is ripping me in two.

I take a seat and wait for him to continue.

"There's a fendling in the Blackbone Mountains, a druid of sorts."

"The Blood Collector," Emery says quietly.

Malor nods. "She knows many things ... for a price. But human blood may be worth a lot to her. Find her and see if she can help us understand the appearance of our new friend. I do not think it's a coincidence. And, perhaps if Harper can be explained, we may help return her home when the time comes."

"Thank you," I say and mean it.

I sprint out of the room, leaving Pippa to deal with the rest of the meeting's logistics, and go in search of Fox. She's standing at the end of the hallway, staring at the red door. When I approach she doesn't move at all.

"Have you been taught *any* manners?" I joke, but she doesn't turn around. "Fox?"

She spins slowly, fear lighting her gaze and that need to hold her opens a chasm inside me.

"Hey, what's wrong?"

"I'm scared," she whispers, turning back to the door.

"You? Scared? I'm pretty sure everyone else should be afraid of *you*."

Fox turns back to me and gives me a weak smile. It's not good enough. I want the one that lights up her face, the one she gives me right before she's about to cut me down to size.

"If I walk through the door, will I go back to that place?" she asks.

I'm not sure what she's talking about. Her magic must have done something really weird with that concealment spell. "What place? Nothing like that should have happened."

She shakes her head quietly.

I place my hand on the door and push it open. "Come on, Fox." I gesture for her to follow, but she's glued to the floor. "Fox," I say, dragging out the vowel. I hold my hand out to her and she looks at it, but doesn't take it. "You'll never get to dance if you stay there all night."

She looks up at me through long, black eyelashes, her deep brown eyes a reflection of my own. "Fine," she says with a smile, taking my hand.

We walk through the door with no problem and she seems surprised, glancing between me and it as it closes and I seal it with my magic. "The spell conceals it so that people turn away when they approach. When we walked in, it was stronger than when we walked out, but it shouldn't have messed with your head."

"I'm fine." End of conversation, apparently.

I stare at her hand in mine and she pulls it away quickly, crossing her arms and looking away. I want to pull her back to me, but I don't. "You didn't need to say all that in there."

Fox rolls her eyes. "Please, that bitch needed someone to hand it to her. I knew none of you could do it because you're all royalty. So, you're welcome."

"I meant the part about defending me." I don't know why I'm bringing it up. As soon as I say the words, I regret them.

Her gaze meets mine, and for a brief moment, I feel like she sees me. Not the cocky asshole I've been, but all the dark pieces and maybe some of the light ones, too. The ones that are sharp and broken. "Don't get used to it," she says before sauntering off down the hall.

Being around her is like flipping a coin. I never know which side I'm going to land on—sunshine or darkness, honey or salt. At this point, I'm starting to feel like I win either way.

I SIP MY ALE AND stare into the contents of the mug, golden and hazy with white bubbles that fade as seconds tick by. Emery nudges me from the thoughts that swirl around in my head like a tornado.

"Are we going to talk about it?" he asks, leveling me with that all-knowing stare.

"What?" I play innocent, even though I knew this was coming.

Emery snorts. "Harper. What you said about your magic being amplified with her around."

I peer over my mug at him and take a gulp, finishing my beer and wishing more than anything there was more, so I could buy more time. He knows. Of course he knows.

"Were you going to tell me?" A shadow of hurt flashes over him lightning-quick. There and gone before I can fully process it.

"Eventually," I say.

He smirks and takes a sip from his own glass, looking way too fucking smug.

I grip the mug almost hard enough to break it. "How long have you known?" Bastard.

He chuckles. "Probably before you did. Well, I had a hunch."

"Emery," I growl. "Explain."

"Her magic feels like yours. So much so that I almost feel the same need to protect her. At the very least, to help her out since you seem so inclined not to."

My eyes widen. "Is that a thing? Could you be bonded to her, too?"

He takes another sip and finishes his ale, slamming down the mug on the table. Still holding that smug as shit look on his face. "I doubt it; it's not that strong. But it's not like any üfren has ever experienced this before. A ruler hasn't ever had a *selüm-ra*. At least, not that I know of."

I spin my empty mug on the table and find Fox in the room. She's at the bar with Pippa laughing about Realm knows what.

"I know you like her," Emery says, nudging me again.

I punch him in the arm, hard, and he snarls at me. "I'm conditioned to like her. Nothing about this is natural and it's not *her* I like, it's her magic. She's a fucking human, Emery. She's not my mate." It's the first time I've said the words out loud and they feel wrong on my tongue, like all the promises I've turned to ash.

Emery knows me better than anyone. I need his confirmation that what I'm thinking is right, but I don't get it because Ellison and Idalia sit down at the table.

"She said it herself, all she wants is to go home," I mutter. Even if something did come of this ... no, I won't even let myself think that far.

Emery chews his lip, brow furrowed in thought. I wait for his words like a lifeline. "Have you ever noticed that for someone who truly wants to go home, she doesn't talk about it very often?"

I have noticed. I assumed she was just being private, but Fox is about the least private person you could meet. Last week she worked out in the yard in her bra and those skimpy sleep shorts. A few days ago she played truth or dare with everyone and picked truth every time. She's not shy about anything, so why is she keeping this a secret? And it's not like she hasn't said anything about where she came from. I know she has a sister and friends. That she got into plenty of trouble long before she found herself in Calamity.

"How'd the meeting go?" Ellison asks.

"Later," I murmur.

"Always in such a wonderful mood," Idalia drones, looking around the room. "Where's Pip?"

"At the bar," Emery and I say in unison.

"Oh, with *her*," Idalia says, distaste coating the air around her words.

"You don't like her?" Ellison asks with genuine curiosity. It's kind of cute how much he misses.

"You do?" Idalia implores.

Elli nods eagerly, and I restrain myself from questioning his motives. "She's super chill."

"Atlas likes her too," Idalia sneers.

"Jealous already, baby?" My tone is sweet, just how she hates it.

Ellison snorts a laugh. He and Idalia fuck fairly regularly, so after it was too late, I apologized to him privately. He couldn't have cared less, which almost made me feel bad for her, but I guess their relationship is purely physical.

"Don't flatter yourself," she mutters.

I never break my smile. "I don't need to, you do it all for me."

Pippa and Fox approach the table with a pitcher of ale and a few more mugs. They're still laughing about something I only catch the tail end of, hearing my name and Emery's. What could they possibly have in common? I scowl at my sister and she throws me a warm smile in return.

Fox looks between Ellison and Idalia. "Where's Torin?"

"Asleep on the couch with Pants," Elli says.

Fox smiles, and it's like all the light in the room dims in her presence. The song playing over the speakers switches to something with a funky beat, and Fox jumps up and down with excitement. "Come on! You promised!" she squeals to my sister.

Pippa rolls her eyes, but she looks happy. Carefree. I haven't seen her look like that in months and it thaws some hardened part of my heart. "Fine," she relents.

My sister starts to drag Fox to the dance floor, but something interesting happens. The little human glances over at Idalia, who is scowling at the two of them with the ferocity of a wild animal. Fox holds her hand out to Idalia, who looks at it like it's going to fall off and grab her.

"You can hate me all you want, but I know you want to dance," she says, wiggling the tips of her fingers enticingly. A smile tugs at Idalia's lips.

I'm fucking enamored. I have to actively remove my eyes from the creature in front of me because I'm worried if I don't do it now, I'll never be able to stop staring at her. Idalia caves and takes her hand, the three of them taking off and giggling like they don't have a care in the world.

Emery has the biggest fucking smile on his face watching them. Obviously seeing the same happiness in Pippa that I saw, but feeling an entirely different set of emotions about it.

"She fits in well, huh?" Ellison says with a grin, his gaze on the girls.

"She's different," Emery replies.

My eyes flash back to Ellison, still trying to determine what his motives with Fox are.

He must feel me staring because he turns to me and his eyes widen. "What?" He takes a gulp of his ale, giving us a nervous look.

"She's Atlas's *selüm-ra*," Emery announces casually, sipping his refilled mug.

Elli spits the liquid in his mouth out across the table with enough force to aerosolize it, and the mist fades into the atmosphere.

I'm too stunned to even speak as I turn to Emery. He's just sitting there smirking and avoiding eye contact.

"What did you just say?" Elli looks from Emery to me for confirmation, beer mist coating his round glasses.

I don't bother looking his way. I'm hoping that my stare is hot enough to turn this horned fucker into ashes.

"I think if I repeat it, Atlas might eat me," Emery gives me a wary look.

"How is that possible?" Ellison asks.

"I don't know," I snap. Grabbing the pitcher, I fill my cup and chug its contents in one go. I'm hoping to feel something that isn't this mind numbing, all-consuming desire. It doesn't do shit, so I repeat it once more. Twice more. The edges of the room blur slightly after my fourth cup.

"Why are you acting like this is a bad thing? Harper is funny and ..." He looks her over and I growl, daring him to speak the words I know he's about to say. "Fuck off, dude. She's beautiful. You can't get mad at me for saying that."

"She's also a terrible dancer," Emery notes.

I steal a glance at her that turns into a stare. She really is *horrible* at dancing, but it's cute. As with most things, she doesn't seem to give a fuck what anyone else thinks as she sways her hips in an untimely rhythm. Occasionally she'll just jump up and down in excitement and there's something entirely free about it. The song ends, and she pants happily to my sister and Idalia. Her smile is a window into something good, something I don't deserve, something I stopped believing in a long time ago.

"She doesn't belong here," I answer.

Emery gets up to refill the pitcher. As he passes by, he pats me on the shoulder and leans down to speak quietly in my ear. "Doesn't look that way to me."

CHAPTER THIRTY-FIVE

HARPER

SLIPPING INTO THIS ROOM HAS ME FEELING SOME kind of way. It's mostly fear until I see him sleeping in his bed—his head shoved under a pillow like he's trying to drown out the world even in his dreams. Sun creeps into the room under the blackout curtains illuminating his summer-kissed skin. The thick muscle in his back forms ridges in the planes of his shoulders as his arms flex over the pillow. I didn't notice it before, but the tattooed tree on his back looks suspiciously like a Reign Tree. Staring at him like a stalker introduces a whole set of new emotions, but that's Atlas for you—scary hot. As much as I'm enjoying the view and wondering what that sheet is covering up, it's not why I'm here.

I throw the rubber ball in my hand into the air and catch it before using all my strength to hit him in the back of the head. The ball melts before it can even touch him, hitting his barrier, and I frown before I'm tossed into the wall.

My jaw clenches as my head smacks the surface and I can't even be mad since it was me who snuck up on him sleeping. I expect him to be angry, but as he turns over—not even startled—he laughs.

"I was wondering when you'd try to get revenge." Even laced with sleep, his voice is rough and sexy.

I squint against the pain. "Teach me how to shield," I groan.

He tilts his head as I grab onto the dresser next to me for support. His room is just as enchanting as mine, but slightly bigger, with slate blue walls and matching textiles.

Now that he's awake, he's turned over, his abs rippling with every breath, tattoos dispersed along his torso. The white sheet lays just below the carved V in his pelvis, drawing my attention like a lighthouse.

"Why should I?" he taunts.

Rubbing my head, I steady myself. "Isn't that like your job or something?"

Another laugh. "Taking care of you is not my job, Fox."

"Good thing," I murmur. "Come on, *please*! You said you'd help me."

In the last few weeks we've had a few moments where I feel like we're getting along, but then he'll give me a look of pure hatred and I'm convinced he'd still kill me if Pippa was on board with it. It's kind of confusing, but it's making my attempts at ignoring the way my heart flutters whenever our eyes lock much easier.

Atlas closes his eyes and yawns, stretching his arms over his head as the sheet falls slightly. Every cell inside me tenses as I watch all of his muscles flex, something sinful sending tingles down my body and tightening between my thighs.

His eyes open lazily as he runs a hand through his silky brown hair. "Fine, but I need to get dressed, so unless you plan on coming over here to show me what you've been imagining this whole time, you should get the fuck out."

My jaw nearly drops to the floor.

"You'll have to open it *a lot* wider than that, Fox," he says smugly and I snap my mouth closed so fast my teeth clack together.

248

"You're a pig," I sneer and storm out before I can think twice about his offer.

When he shows up in black sweats and a gray v-neck, my ovaries nearly explode, but I give him my best scowl and tap my foot impatiently.

He's just a hot asshole, Harper. Stay away.

"Sorry I'm late. After you left, I thought of a few ways you could make this session up to me." The gleam in his eye has my insides starting a civil war.

"Make what up to you?" I hiss.

"This," he says, gesturing between us. "Me helping you. It's not really benefiting me."

"I'm not sleeping with you," I say, but there's not as much bite to the words as I hoped. "Besides, what happened to never touching me?"

Atlas's laugh is so cruel I want to run back inside and forget I ever asked him for help. But I suck it up and stand my ground because like hell if I'm going to let this guy belittle me. "What is your obsession with fucking me? I never said it was something sexual. Jeez, Fox. Get it together."

"I hate you," I growl.

"That's it baby, show me how much."

Stop, I whisper in my mind, and time slows. I close the gap between us and stare at his stupid fucking face that haunts every dream and nightmare I have these days. I can feel the energy wavering around me, but I siphon a little more magic from the well inside me and steady it out like we've been practicing.

This is my domain.

Reaching my arm back, I punch him as hard as I possibly can, but nothing happens—his barrier shoves against me like a trampoline. I reach out for it a second time, and instead of trying to break through it, I examine it. Closing my eyes and imagining it as a physical thing. I try to copy it with my own magic and speed time back up.

"I can't show you if you don't let me," I say with a saccharine smile.

A force of wind knocks me back and I try to recreate the magic barrier I felt around him, but it's too late and I fall flat on my ass.

"Come on, Fox. Is that all you got?" He throws another gust of wind at me and it pushes me back farther.

I'm gritting my teeth trying to mimic the way his magic felt when I pushed against it, but it's not working and when he dumps a river of water over me I'm screaming.

"I don't think shouting is going to help!" he yells with his finger in his ears.

"Fuck you," I spit. Why do I ever bother asking him for help?

Calmly, he walks over to me, sopping wet on the floor as I try to stand, but some other magical weight pushes me back down. "You see why hopping out of bed to help you isn't the number one thing I want to do in the morning?" Atlas crosses his arms like humiliating me is *so* inconvenient for him.

"Just go away then," I seethe.

"Not until you show me what you're made of, Fox. I know the power that's in you. You can do better than this."

I don't even want to sort through his words to find the compliment that's sandwiched in there with my anger this hot. I push against his magic, but it's too strong. "Has anyone ever told you that you're a terrible teacher?"

The shadow of him blocks out the sun, casting him in a dark glow. "You're my one and only student. Now hurry up before I give you detention." He smirks and I can't help but return it.

Atlas only pushes his magic down harder until I'm flat on my back and he's looking down at me. "You're so focused on your anger that you're forgetting how powerful you are."

"Stop making me so angry then," I gasp.

"No can do. Haven't you noticed? Your emotions, specifically the malicious kind, are the channel between you and your magic. But you need to harness one in order to control the other."

My heart slows at his words as I try to find the emotions within myself and warp them into something new. The pressure lessens and I can sit up. As I do, his smile grows.

"Harder," he commands.

I take the heat building inside myself and push it out. It's the same burning feeling that makes me feel weak. It's the flood drowning me and making me lose control. I imagine the worst parts of Harper Elliott as a bubble tightly wrapped around my body. I use *it* instead of letting it use me and it feels ... good. I feel powerful. Before I realize it, I'm standing in front of him, physically pushing him away from me.

His smile fades into something else. If I didn't know him better, I'd guess it was pride. "You'll never drown if you're strong enough to swim," he tells me.

My magic stutters out as I exhaust myself. A delicate wind wraps around me and dries my clothes and hair. I've never met anyone who pushes me so hard, only to be the soft padding to catch me when I fall.

"Thank you," I mumble.

"Recharge and we do it again in an hour," he states, his mask of indifference back on as he walks away, leaving me breathless.

CHAPTER THIRTY-SIX

ATLAS

TWO DAYS BEFORE THE PARTY

I didn't sleep well. I'm feeling anxious and guilty from my confrontation with my father, but also furious at how stubborn he's being. I have half a mind to talk to him about it again, but I lack the emotional energy it would take. With the state I'm in, I know I'll just say more things I'll likely regret.

I stare at the drawing I've been working on for the last few weeks. It's of Emery and I in our derax forms running through Dogwood Dell four summers ago. It's a memory I keep close, but can never perfect on paper. I shut the sketchbook in frustration and drop it onto my desk, the sound reverberating through the room.

What I really want is Elrora. To wrap my arms around her and hold her close. I want to promise her the world. I swear to myself that eventually I will be a male who can make that kind of promise. But she's not here, and she didn't show up to my rooms last night.

Sighing, I push the window open and look out at the perfect sunny day, beckoning me to come and enjoy it. The castle grounds glow in the spring light, flowers of every color blooming in the gardens that surround the stone walls. I should train with Emery today and try to take my mind off things.

I leave my room and walk out into the common area of my quarters. As I stroll across it, I see the door is cracked open and Emery's room is empty. I call out his name for good measure, but I get no reply.

I walk down the castle hallways, crowded with everyone bustling around for the party tomorrow. It's the start of the spring festival and what better way to celebrate it than to hold a party? It's actually a lot of fun. All of the nobles will show up and I'll get to see friends I haven't spoken with in months. But everything will feel colorless without Elrora on my arm.

Emery is nowhere to be found, so I stop one of the guards occasionally posted outside our rooms. "Have you seen Em?"

He shakes his head.

When we were younger, we'd go down to the kitchens before every festival party and steal bites of all the sweets being made. The cooks spend days preparing, and it's easy to sneak under their noses while they hustle through their workday. I doubt Emery is feeling nostalgic, but I decide to check it out before going to the training grounds.

The smell of butter and sugar wafts around me in a delightful air as I walk down the steps to the lower levels of the castle. There's not much down here except storage, the kitchens, and—

"El?"

I pass by the treasury and pause. Elrora is strolling through aisles of wooden crates filled with weapons from thousands of years ago. On the back walls are glass showcases, with more jewelry than I could ever dream of using.

She turns and my heart races as her face lights up in my presence.

"My Prince," she says with a curtsy.

I step into the treasury and shut the massive gold door. I find my-self by her side and breathe in her lilac scent before squeezing her tight. El squeals in mock fear and then giggles, kissing me passionately and rolling her tongue across my lips. There's always something a little wild in her gaze and I long for a day where we can get into trouble together.

"What are you doing in here?" I say, arms still wrapped tightly around her.

"Oh, your mother requested a necklace for the party and I just got caught up looking at all the beautiful things."

I didn't realize she spent much time on my mother's service, but I don't really know the servant schedules. "Oh, yeah? See anything you like?"

A blush covers her porcelain cheeks. "It's all beautiful." She walks over to a case covered in gold jewelry. Stones as big as my fists on long elegant chains, diamonds and rubies in delicate rings. It all means nothing to me. Everything in this castle, power—it's worthless if you have no one to share it with.

I come up behind her, pulling her back to my chest and leaning down to kiss the side of her head. "Pick something," I say, whispering into her hair.

She stiffens. "Atlas, no."

I spin her to look at me. Her beautiful jade eyes lined with concern. "One day, El, I'll give you the whole world. Let me start with this." I kiss her gently and spin her around. "I'm not letting you go until you pick something."

Elrora laughs nervously, but nods her head. Her slender fingers sift through the items, trying some on and marveling at their beauty. I'm sure there's someone who keeps inventory of this shit, but I highly doubt anyone will notice something missing anytime soon. She points to a necklace with a thin gold chain and a five carat heart-shaped ruby. It's locked in a case that looks different from the others. She turns around and looks at me for permission. I nod, unlocking it with my magic. I don't give a fuck what she picks.

"Let me put it on you," I offer.

"Oh, I can't wear it now!"

"Yes, but don't you want to see what it looks like on?"

"I know it will be beautiful, Atlas," she says.

I frown a little, but concede. "Okay, just promise me next time we're alone together it will be all you're wearing."

A wicked smile spreads across her face. "Such a naughty prince."

I lean in and kiss her slowly. "Always, for you."

"Will you ever stay out of trouble?" she asks, somehow our tradition for goodbyes.

"Never," I promise before tearing away.

CHAPTER THIRTY-SEVEN

HARPER

VER A WEEK HAS PASSED SINCE THE COUNCIL meeting. Everyone has been searching for ways to find this so-called Blood Collector on whatever mountain. It all sounds creeeeepy as fuck, but I'm hardly surprised anymore.

Despite his earlier protest, Atlas continues to train me in the mornings. I'm getting better at mastering my magic and pushing the limits on how long I can freeze time. I don't even have to use the word *stop* anymore, but I still do it out of habit. Even my barrier is stronger. Other than that, I haven't gained any new skills and while I know I should be happy with the magic I have, I can't help but wonder what else I could do. Sometimes I sit in my room and try to will things to me like Matilda, but it's pretty futile. My head ends up hurting like I spent an hour crossing my eyes and eventually I fall asleep next to Pants.

The only thing is, other than those training sessions, Atlas just ignores me. I mean, it wasn't like we were the best of friends before, but at least before he acknowledged my existence. Now unless we're training together, he barely speaks to me. I never thought I'd miss him taunting me, but I do.

Currently, he's reading a book in the chair by the fireplace, Pippa sitting just opposite him. There's something utterly divine about a guy who likes to read, and Atlas is no exception. I steal glances at him out of the corner of my eye as I eat my breakfast. Idalia is curled up on the couch next to the window and Torin is digging through a stack of papers with Pants at his feet. The heat of someone's stare prickles the top of my head, and I look up to find Elli staring at me.

"What?" I ask, trying to fight the blush that's creeping up. Did he see me staring at Atlas?

Ellison shrugs. "Nothing."

Phew.

"You could go talk to him, though," he says quietly.

Fuck.

"I have to meet Emery in the armory," I lie. We're meeting in an hour, but I could always use the practice.

As if he fucking heard me, Emery pops his head out of his room down the hall. "Harper, don't forget we're meeting in an hour." His door shuts immediately and Ellison laughs against closed lips.

"What? I forgot. It's a very human trait," I mutter.

He nods his head in Atlas's direction.

I glare at him and shake my head.

He rolls his eyes at me. A silent argument passes between us before I stick my tongue out at him and go back to eating.

"I'll stop making the bacon extra crispy," he whispers from across the counter.

"What?" I say a little too loudly.

Everyone else in the room looks at us for a few seconds. We both smile like guilty maniacs, earning a few weird looks from Idalia before everyone resumes what they were doing. Atlas never reacts at all, obviously engrossed in whatever he's reading.

"You're blackmailing me into talking to your friend?" I whisper.

"No, I'm bribing you with cured meats. There's a difference."

I snort. "Why?"

"Because I can tell you want to."

I bite my lip and think about his words. Do I want to? I glance at Atlas again and wonder why he's been so standoffish lately. Part of me worries it was the moment in the hallway last week when I dared him to kiss me. Was that a totally weird and creepy thing to do? The answer is definitely yes.

He seemed into it, especially when he made that comment while I was in his room last week. But maybe he really is just fucking with me. *Fuck*, am I imagining him flirting with me?

"Do you think I'm hot?" I ask Ellison as quietly as I can. In my periphery, I see Atlas's head turn in our direction, but I ignore it.

Ellison glances at him nervously before turning back to me. "Huh?"

"Do you," I say slowly, "think I'm hot?"

He gulps. Am I making him nervous or is he trying not to insult me?

Oh my God, they really all think I'm hideous. I don't know why that surprises me though ... they're these beautiful creatures that look like they're carved from different shades of marble and kissed by the Son of Odin or some shit. Wait ... who is the goddess of beauty? I digress.

"I don't know how to answer that," he says awkwardly.

My eyes widen. "Sorry I asked." I stand up from my chair, trying not to be offended. "You can keep the crispy bacon," I murmur before I sprint down the hall and into the armory. I'll just do extra practice today.

I tie my hair into a braid that falls over my shoulder and spend a few minutes warming up. I'm hoping it will clear my head, but I can't shake this feeling of disappointment, which is *so* weird. I mean, what did I think was going to happen? I know I'm attractive, but clearly that hasn't kept anyone around long. Staring at the rack of weapons, I grab the wooden sword, letting the feel of it coat my palm.

Why would I ever think that anyone would ever like me as more than a piece of ass? No one ever has before. I'm bossy and stubborn and I obviously annoy the shit out of him. With one hand, I squeeze the bridge of my nose.

No.

It's not me. It's not my fault. Cole and Emma fucked up. I didn't do anything wrong and I'm worthy of more than that.

With a shuddering breath, I pick up the wood sword I've been practicing with and start weaving through the obstacles Emery built for me. Duck, spin, hit. Duck, spin, hit. I hear footsteps coming down the stairs and turn, expecting to find Emery.

"I started early—"

Atlas stares at me from across the room as he leans against the arched doorway. His arms are crossed, the sleeves of his blue v-neck tight around his biceps.

"Sorry, I thought you were Emery," I say.

He smirks, and my breathing becomes heavy. "How disappointed you must be."

I walk over to the wall and lean the sword against it. Turning back to him, I cock one eyebrow. "That depends. Sometimes you make things entertaining."

He chuckles darkly. "Sometimes?"

I don't meet his gaze. "Yeah, lately you've been ..." I bite my lower lip, searching for the right word. My focus bends slightly as he starts walking closer to me. "Tame."

Atlas gives me a look of genuine surprise with a hint of insulted. "Tame?"

"Yes. Polite, decorous." I purse my lips and fold my arms over my chest. "Boring." I can't help but poke the bear. My previous thoughts couldn't be farther from my mind because despite what my traitorous brain likes to think, Atlas looks at me like I'm the most interesting thing in the world and it fills me with the knowledge that maybe I am.

He's close enough now that I have to crane my neck to look up at him. His cardamom and vetiver scent wraps around my mind like a haze. How does he *always* smell good? "Well, Fox. We can't have you thinking I'm *tame*."

"I dare you to prove me wrong." Being around him lights something inside me that was always there, but I forgot existed.

A slow and wicked smile flashes at me before his gaze drops to the sword against the wall. "A sword?"

I nod. "I believe the words you said were, 'make her useful.'"

His brown eyes catch mine again. "And are you? Useful?"

I frown before steeling my nerves. "Of course I am." I find that with the magic running through my veins and the surety of my stance, I actually believe those words.

Yeah, fuck you, self-loathing Harper.

Atlas picks up the sword with ease and runs the fake blade through his fingers. "A sword," he mutters to the weapon. When he looks back at me, there's a child-like curiosity in his gaze. "Are you stabby, little Fox? Or are you more blunt force trauma?"

He strides past me and over to the wall of weapons I've marveled at since my first days down here. He picks up a weapon that looks like a metal spiked bat and hands it to me. "It's called a mace."

The leather wrapped grip is soft, but sturdy. I swing it, surprised to find how easy it is, and smile. "Do I need two, though?"

"Two?" he asks with a laugh. "I think you'll be plenty deadly with one."

I step over to the wooden dummies lined against one wall and smack the bat into it, watching as the spikes pierce through the wood and get stuck.

Atlas is behind me in an instant. "Tear up *through* your opponent. Hit, dig deeper, and rip up."

I push the mace into the wood slightly and pull upward with all my strength. The wooden dummy splinters in half and fissures form as chunks fall off and it crumbles into pieces.

I squeal in excitement and spin around to look at him, not really watching where my spiked mace is swinging. He dodges out of the way quickly. Cursing something about the Realm as I step backward to avoid hitting him.

"See? Deadly with just one. It's quality not quantity, Fox."

I tuck a stray piece of hair behind my ear. "Thank you," I say.

260

He stares at me like he's trying to decipher something and then turns away toward the exit. "Emery should be down here soon. I'll make sure to tell him he's doing a good job making you *useful*."

"You're such a benevolent leader!" I call out to his retreating form. I make sure my words are loaded with as much sarcasm as they can manage.

I'M SITTING UNDER THE TREE, flipping through the hiking book, when the sun disappears and a starless night sky fills its place. Cursing the immediate darkness, I gently push Pants off my lap and walk into the house where Emery is in an animated discussion with Idalia.

"What I'm saying is, that year I was the one who should have won." Emery holds his chin up, the firelight in the furnace glowing off his golden hair and highlighting his ebony horns.

"He would have, too, if you hadn't ratted out Atlas," Ellison adds.

"I was six years old!" Idalia whines in defense.

"Six years old and already a bitch," Atlas mutters.

"Oh, fuck you. You're so much better? Don't you remember the time you turned my dress into a swarm of beetles?"

Emery chuckles. "That was pretty messed up."

"I'm sure she deserved it." Atlas laughs, looking up from the book he's reading.

Idalia lets out a huff of impatience, blowing a lock of onyx hair from her face. "Hardly. You three were just as much bullies as me."

"Can you all just shut up for one second? I feel like I'm so close to figuring out how to get through the mountain." Pippa's flipping through a bunch of books laid out on the dining room table, a big map of Calamity spread out across the wood surface.

"What's the problem?" I ask, approaching her as the others continue to mutter insults quietly at each other.

"The problem is we've been forced into being a dysfunctional family when some of us never got along to begin with," Torin mutters from his seat at the table.

I laugh, looking at the group. "I think you guys are doing pretty good, considering. No one's killed each other yet."

Emery nods in agreement like I was being serious. I guess to them it's not that far from the truth.

"I was referring to the mountain though," I say closer to Pippa. She looks up from the map, shadows forming around her eyes from lack of sleep. "I probably can't help, but I could try?" I offer.

She smiles sadly at me. "Blackbone Mountain is a full day's journey to the east. With you in tow, it will take us two or three days to get there." I purse my lips guiltily. Pippa notes this and lovingly squeezes my arm. "Don't feel bad. We wouldn't even have this lead if it wasn't for you."

"It's hardly a lead." After the meeting, Pippa filled me in on what happened after I left.

"It's something," Torin says, looking up from his task. "Something we didn't have before and we need every advantage we can get."

"So fill me in on the problems," I say to Pippa. "You know, if it's not too much."

"It's not. Maybe a fresh set of eyes will help me see things differently." She spreads her hands over the already flattened map of Calamity. It's almost cartoon-like in its design, but elegant with shimmering foils over the river running across the continent and areas to indicate Varrek burrows and Kelpie territory. It looks as magical as the world it's depicting, but missing the air of danger that coats the atmosphere.

"This is us, here in North Birchshire near Mt. Fernview. When you met up with us, we were here in West Aspendale." She points to an area northeast of where we are now. It's south of a place called Oakland where there is a symbol of a castle.

"Is that where *she* lives?" I ask.

Pippa nods. "It was dangerous to be so close to her, but when we fled we didn't have many options. We were hoping that by being near we'd be able to infiltrate easier, but we were wrong. She has an impressive magical barrier around Oakland. Blackbone Mountain is on the complete opposite side of the continent, here." She points to a spot near the eastern edge in a region called East Aspendale. I remember

Elli telling me this is where he's from. "Easy enough to get to if we go through town and follow the Sticks River."

"Why is it called that?" I ask, with a little humor.

"Sticks River?" She shrugs. "I imagine it has to do with the level of driftwood that flows into it about halfway, thanks to the forest on its southern border."

"Got it," I say, keeping the joke to myself.

"Anyway, the problem is, surrounding Blackbone Mountain is a trench. It would take days to cross it and the only other way up the mountain is on the northern side, which is covered in snow and at an almost perfect ninety-degree incline."

Something tugs at my memory when she says the word *trench*. Subconsciously, I put the book I'm still holding down on the table, opening it up to a section called Hidden Features that I'd skimmed a few days ago. My finger traces the page like the wooden indicator on a Ouji board until it lands on a hike titled Trench Conqueror. Pippa gasps, her sound of shock drawing the attention of the room.

I can feel Atlas at my back in the span of a breath. "What is it?"

Pippa doesn't speak as she flips the pages of the book, worn like its cover, though depicting images clearly taken on a modern camera. When she gets to the correct page, she nervously chews on a nail while reading the blurb out loud:

> *"There are fewer things more pesky than the Blackbone Trench. If you're trying to get some altitude without becoming a trench wench, this is the hike for you! Explore the wonders of Blackbone Mountain without wetting your britches or scaling that northern back crack."*

A detailed description on an elusive trail is described underneath it.

Pippa turns to me with a look on her face like I've just gifted her the throne back. "Harper! If this is real, then it's the answer!" She squeals and lifts me up, squeezing me in a bear hug so tight I lose my breath.

"Where the fuck did you get this?" Atlas asks once she puts me down.

"The bookstore owner in town," I answer breathlessly.

"I've never seen a book like this before," he notes.

I'm glad the world's most annoying interaction was worth something in the end. Everyone else comes over to read the inscription in the book and I can't help but chuckle at that weird kangaroo thing. Not that he could have predicted this book would have something I needed in it.

"Good work, LH," Ellison says from the couch, patting the spot next to him as he rolls a blunt.

"I'll pass," I say with a smile.

"Yes, we have a lot to plan!" Pippa says triumphantly. "We'll need hiking supplies and snacks."

"Definitely lots of snacks," Emery agrees.

"Don't forget those little sour candies Atty likes," Ellison coos.

"Atty?" I laugh.

Atlas scowls at Elli. "Stop trying to make that a thing. It won't stick."

"I think it's cute," Torin says with a gleam in his eyes. "Atta boy."

Laughter fills the room as a smile goes to war with the permanent frown that occupies Atlas's features.

"Realm be damned, is he going to smile?" Emery teases.

I lean against the arm of the couch as Atlas turns away. "Fuck off."

"What is it that you call him?" Elli asks me.

"Prince Ass," Pippa chirps.

"Prince Bossy Pants," Idalia giggles.

"My personal favorite is Leader of the Asshole Brigade," Emery snickers. I cover my mouth as a fit of laughter escapes me.

Atlas turns around to look at us and his smile is hiding, like it's too shy to come out and play. It's innocent and devilish at the same time, twisting my insides until it feels like my organs are one heap sinking to the bottom of my being.

"Don't forget Elf Boy," he says.

Walking over to him, I stand on my tiptoes and ruffle my hand through his hair. Stretching my body fully, I'm just barely tall enough, and I know I'm purposefully toying with the beast inside him. "I think I like Big Fluffy Kitty best."

His smile grows as he looks at me, and for a minute, the whole room is Atlas. The air I'm breathing and the ground I'm standing on. The gravity holding me up and the beating heart in my chest. Every particle is laced with him.

The moment fades and I'm suddenly aware of everyone's eyes on us, but only a small part of me cares because whether I can truly admit or not, I'm comfortable with these people. They've made me feel like I'm part of something—a cause, a family. I'm not sure I deserve any of it, but I'm getting tired of questioning everything that feels good.

Ignoring the choking feeling building in my chest, I turn around and look to Pippa. "Let's plan a trip!"

Part Three

ALL THE THINGS I LEFT WITH YOU

CHAPTER THIRTY-EIGHT

ATLAS

"HERE," PIPPA SAYS, HANDING ME A LIST OF ITEMS I need to get before we leave for our trip.

"And why can't you go?" I ask for the third time.

She doesn't meet my gaze. "Because I have things to do."

I hope she can feel my impatience building. "What kind of things?"

"Things! You don't get to be privy to every piece of my life."

I raise my hands in surrender. "Jeez, got it."

She calls out to me before I leave. "We'll need to bleed Harper before you leave for Blackbone. Take her with you into town. Make her feel included."

"Absolutely not," I say without hesitation.

My sister wrinkles her nose at me. "Yes."

"No. You're just trying to get me to spend time with her alone. Stop forcing something that isn't there."

"Maybe you should stop fighting something that is!" Pippa crosses her arms and turns away from me.

"What happens when she goes home, Pip? Did you ever think about that?" I sigh and run a hand through my hair. It's getting too long, the front pieces falling over my forehead.

Pippa turns around and her eyes convey a sadness I really don't want to see. I don't need her pity. "Maybe she won't leave," she says quietly.

I make a snort of amusement. "Pippa, she's her own person. She has a life, family, friends. From the beginning, all she's wanted is to go home."

"That was before, though," she whines, climbing into one of the large wingback chairs. She's holding on to the side and peering at me from behind it like she's hoping if I don't see her entirely I'll continue to engage in this ridiculous conversation. But she doesn't need to tiptoe around me. We'll have it out once and for all so she can see how obtuse she's being. The world isn't a fucking romance novel. Not everyone has a happy ending.

I lean my back against the door, and slide down, resting my elbows on bent knees. "Before what?"

"Before she got to know you or us."

"You hear yourself, right? It's absurd. She's not going to pick a group of strangers in a different realm over everything she's ever known and loved."

"But she feels it too! I know it and you know it! She just doesn't understand why yet. Tell her why, show her who you really are!"

I tilt my head back, letting it hit the door and groan. "Pippa, this *is* who I really am. I don't know what idealistic image you and Emery have painted of me, but that male is gone. Things change. *I've* changed."

My little sister whimpers against the wood of the chair. Tears lining her eyes.

"Pip," I beg, standing and walking over to her. "Pip, don't cry. What is this really about?"

270

"I know she's your *selüm-ra*. A ruler of Calamity hasn't ever had a *selüm-ra*. Don't you understand how lucky you are? Some of us never even find ours. Haven't you felt the connection ... don't you want to love her?"

Love her? Fuck. I can barely wrap my head around liking her.

I mean ... I do like her. As much as I hate to admit it, she's funny and beautiful. I like how she doesn't take shit from anyone, me included. Sometimes the rudest and weirdest shit comes out of her mouth, but she never shies away from it. She is authentically and unapologetically Fox. There's something liberating about that.

I don't answer my sister because I don't even know what to say. Do I want to love someone who was made by the Realm *for* me? Of course. But we're not living in a fucking fantasy world.

Pippa shifts in her seat and grabs my hand. "Let's try something else. Pretend she's gone. We finish what we need to and get the throne back. Don't worry about the politics or fighting, just look to the future. We find a way for Harper to go home, and she does. Do you regret not telling her how you feel?"

I try to imagine the world she's created, but I don't need to work very hard. Just facing the idea of Fox going home makes my chest feel like Emery's derax form is sitting on top of it. I squeeze my sister's hand and let go. "I don't even know how I feel, Pip."

"That's because you won't let yourself." Pippa lets out a groan of impatience. "Atlas, just *try*. I know if you don't, you'll regret it."

There's a million things stopping me from doing that. Most of them are things I hope she never has to find out about. "I can't, Pippa," I whisper. "Please stop asking me to." Even if I did give into these feelings, it doesn't change the fact that Fox is very clearly not my biggest fan. We don't even know if the bond affects her in the same way it affects me.

Pippa frowns, but nods. "Take her with you into town, though. I'm not taking no for an answer."

"Fine, but I'm taking Emery too," I relent, needing more than anything to get out of this room.

I think Pippa smirks, but it's gone so quickly I can't tell. "Fine. See you later."

"Emery," I plead. "Please come with us."

He shakes his head. "No can do, brother. Ellison and I have to help Wilder with the weapons."

I narrow my eyes at him. "Since when?"

"Since he asked, fucker. Stop being a bitch and just go with her." Emery gives me a cruel smile. "Or you could take Idalia and Torin if you need a buffer that badly."

"Fuck off," I say, shutting his door. The only thing I want to do less than spend one-on-one time with Fox is add those two to the mix. I cross the hall to her room hoping she won't be there or that she'll just flat out reject my proposal. *It's fine.* We spend time alone together almost every day when we train.

I raise my fist and rap against her ornate door, but she doesn't answer. Where could she be? It's dark out, so I know she's not sitting outside. I guess she could be in the armory, but I know she and Emery trained earlier today, so I doubt it. I knock again and she still doesn't answer.

I should just turn away. This was the out I was looking for, but I don't fucking do that, do I? No. I wiggle her doorknob to find that it's unlocked, cautiously cracking open the door. Heat and steam from her bathroom hit me as I walk in, calling out her name quietly, but I get no response. It smells so good in here. Like a sauna where the aromatherapy is Fox scented. Floral and fruity and—

Her voice rings out in an echo from the bathroom as she sings in the shower. I don't think she should take up a career in singing or anything, but it's not bad either. In fact, the more I listen, the harder it is to leave this space that's so warm. Where every breath is tainted with her presence. Finding myself drawn to them, I stare at the collection of things on her dresser. Little mementos of her short time here—

pink lip gloss, training gloves, a dried Reign Tree leaf, and a hairbrush. There's a picture here too, from last week at the tavern. Pippa must have developed it to see through the glamour. I don't even remember taking this, but Fox is smiling happily, squished between Emery and Elli. She *does* look like she belongs with us.

The water turns off, startling me. If I leave now she'll hear the door close, so I might as well make the most of this. Taking a seat on her bed just opposite the bathroom door, I wait. She's humming and singing the same tune. Big fucking shock, it's a song I've never heard before. Another reminder that her life was filled with experiences and things I'll likely never understand.

Fox continues to hum and sing, the sound getting louder and louder as she approaches the connected room where I sit. The melody is cut off by a punctuated scream as she finds me smirking on her bed.

"What the fuck, Atlas?"

"Don't stop on my account. You have a lovely voice."

"Fuck off. Why are you in my room?"

She's wrapped in a towel. Her hair is black from the moisture and dripping down her body, flushed from the heat and embarrassment. It takes everything in me to fight against the urge to rip the cloth from her grasp and lay her on this bed.

"I'm going into town, and I wondered if you'd like to join me." Not for the first time, I'm grateful for her weak human senses. She'll never know how fast my heart is beating.

"Fine. Get out, though, I need to change." She points to the door in demand.

I give her a mock frown. "You mean you won't be wearing that?"

"No, perv. Do you need help finding the exit, or is your tiny male brain capable of doing that on its own?"

I chuckle to myself and leave her room. For a moment, I glimpse a world in which she lets me stay. Where she drops her towel and sits on my lap, her wet skin pressing into my clothes so that they weigh heavily on my body. I lick the water droplets off her neck and run my hands through her soaking wet locks. And when I'm done with her, she stands naked in front of the mirror and brushes out her hair, smiling at my reflection. She's breathtaking in that simple moment. Everything is easy, and the world isn't falling apart around us.

Sighing, I sit on the couch in the living room and wait. I don't know where anyone is, and I have the sneaking suspicion that Pippa planned this all out. A way for me to spend alone time with the little Fox. I should be annoyed, but I'm not. Maybe I'll just give myself this one day to enjoy her company. It couldn't possibly hurt—one day.

I hear her bedroom door shut and lean up to stand. When she walks out of the hallway I stop breathing, frozen in motion as I wonder if she's stopped time. But she smiles at me, so I know that's not the case. It's not even like what she's wearing is that special, but paired with my previous fantasy, I have the urge to adjust my cock. Tight, light blue jeans hug her ass and accentuate her hourglass frame. Her white cropped shirt has thick straps and a low cut, showing off the swell of her breasts and the sculpted skin of her abdomen. A long, black knit sweater hangs loosely around her arms.

"Ready?" she asks, tucking a hand in her back pocket. The movement pulls her jeans down a little further and I nearly groan in longing.

"Sure," I mumble. I'm definitely at half mast and the last thing I need is her knowing the effect she has on me. "I'll meet you outside. I need to grab something."

She nods and heads out the door. I make some pathetic movement to look like I'm standing. The second she's gone, I reach into my pants and readjust myself.

This whole situation is deplorable. It's everything I deserve from life and while I'd love to shout fuck you to the so-called omnipotent Realm, I know I got myself here *all* on my own.

I walk outside and see Fox by the Reign Tree. I'll never get used to the sight. The magic from the tree makes her skin glow just slightly, like she's some ethereal being. Before she has a chance to protest, I scoop her up and head to town. She whines for a few seconds, but surrenders quickly, wrapping her arms around my neck and tucking her head against my shoulder. I swear she's inhaling my scent.

"You smelling me, Fox?" Running and talking isn't hard, but it isn't ideal. My tenor is strained as oxygen floods my lungs.

Her voice is muffled against my skin. Her breath, the perfect warmth in cool weather. "Maybe," she murmurs. "Has anyone ever told you that you smell like winter?"

"Like the season?"

She makes a quiet noise of agreement. "And citrus. My mom burns this candle in the winter—cardamom and vetiver. That's what you smell like."

"Is that a good thing?" I ask, finding myself needing to know the answer like I need air in my lungs.

"No more talking. I'm nauseous."

I laugh silently; the only indication is the juddering rise and fall of my chest. "Okay," I say, tightening her body against mine.

When we arrive, I slow my pace so she knows it's time to let go. She lifts her head to look around as I stop before the bridge leading into town. I set her down gently and hold my hand out to steady her—she's always dizzy afterward.

Her top has bunched up so that her entire stomach is exposed and she quickly pushes it back down, wiggling her pants up and then looking up at me. "I hate that," she mutters.

"Being carried? Or me carrying you?" I pass a glamour over both of us.

She rolls her eyes. "Surprisingly, not just you. It's just so dizzying and weird. I can't imagine doing it for a full day."

"Poor little Fox," I taunt.

She ignores the jab. "Where are we going, Elf Boy?"

I smirk at the nickname. I don't know why. It's fucking annoying that she calls me that. I'm the Prince of Calamity, for fuck's sake. "The market," I answer. "It's about four stores down from the tavern on the—"

She skips off in front of me and I curse, catching up to her quickly.

"This place is so cute," she says, looking around.

I shove my hand into the pocket of my sweats. "Does your home look different?"

She nods, keeping her eyes on the road. "Very different. This is how my world looked hundreds of years ago. Now it's all skyscrapers and parking lots."

There's a lot to unpack in that sentence. "What's a parking lot?"

She turns up to me and smiles. "Long story. Just be happy you don't have them. They're ugly and a waste of space."

I furrow my brow. "Okay, I'll take your word for it."

Fox stops and takes a deep breath, closing her eyes like she's savoring the moment. "This is ... simple. In the best way. Beautiful and charming." I watch her closely as she does a little twirl on the sidewalk, the glowing street lamps lighting her up in hues of yellow and casting shadows that dance in the dark. Fox stops and looks up. "Our skies have stars, but you can't see them with all the lights."

I let go of my gaze on her and look up at the starless sky. "I miss the stars."

"Me too," she says.

When I find her again, she's watching me. "Do you miss home?" I ask.

She shrugs and continues our walk. "Sometimes."

It's not the answer I was expecting. Part of me is disappointed—she clearly doesn't want to continue the conversation. The other part of me, the one I chose to ignore, is relieved. If she doesn't miss it, then she won't be in a hurry to leave. But she *will* leave. Eventually.

Fox sees the market sign and turns in, a bell ringing as she walks through the doorway. The store owner greets us briefly, but with our glamour nobody pays much attention. We scour the shelves and gather supplies. I'm glad she's here, she knows way more about camping than I ever would.

"My dad, sister, and I used to go camping when we were younger. I have really fond memories of it." I stay quiet, hoping she'll share more. "We stopped doing that though when my sister went off to university." Fox looks up at me. "Do you have university here?"

"Yes, there's one in Ashberg," I answer and then clarify, "South of here. There's a bigger town there, too."

"Did you go?"

I shake my head. "No, I had private tutors in the castle."

She dances around with her hands in the air like she's in a ball-room. "Private tutors in the castle," she mocks in a weird accent.

I can't help but laugh. "You making fun of me, Fox?"

She giggles, her eyes sparkling with that beautiful laughter, and my chest feels like it's filled with helium. "No, you're probably way smarter than me. I still haven't gone to university."

Cocking a shoulder, I let a smile tug at the corner of my lips. "Probably."

She makes an exaggerated gasping noise and hits me on the arm. It feels like a butterfly fluttering against my skin.

"Try again. I'm about four times your size."

I feel her magic ripple through the air and my heart stops. She taps me from behind on the shoulder and gives me a beautiful smile. It turns into an immediate frown as she takes in the look on my face.

"For the fucking Realm. You can't do that in public." I grab her and the things she's carrying and drag her to the cashier. Taking a look around, I make sure no one but me noticed. Nothing seems suspicious, but I can't be sure.

"Ow, you're hurting me!" Fox whines.

I pay for everything as quickly as possible and pull her out of the shop.

"Atlas! Tell me what's going on."

She doesn't understand how much danger she's in. If the wrong person sensed that ... if there was a spy around. No one can know she exists.

I move to grab her and she swats me off. "Tell me what the fuck is going on, Atlas."

She's not a match for me, though. I throw her and the bags over my shoulder and race from town as fast as possible. Halfway back I feel confident that no one is following us, but just to be safe, I rush past the road to the house and go to the lake we visited a few weeks ago. When we arrive, she pushes off of me hard and stumbles away.

"Fox," I groan, following her steps. Why won't she just stay still?

She holds a hand up to stop me from coming closer and vomits all over the floor. It's pretty fucking gross, but instead of wanting to be as far from her as elvenly possible, I need to be close to her. I speed to her side and hold her hair as she continues to puke up the contents of her stomach.

"I'm sorry, Fox," I say, rubbing her back.

She heaves once more and falls to the dirt, but before she can land, I catch her and set her far away from the vomit.

Fox glares up at me. "Explain," she demands in a low voice.

I pull my shirt off, and her pupils dilate. It boosts my ego slightly before I speed to the lake's edge. Dipping the shirt into the water, I head back to her side. A feeble attempt at wiping her mouth earns me a swat as she grabs the shirt from my grasp and wipes her own mouth. I've surprised her and myself with the gesture, but her scowl is permanent.

"Explain," she repeats.

"Your magical signature is unique. You can't just set it off wherever you want. Most others won't notice, but that ruling bitch has spies everywhere. I can't—" I stop myself from finishing the sentence.

She cocks an eyebrow up.

"She can't find out about you."

"Because then she could use me as a weapon against you?"

Because I think losing you would fucking shatter me and I'm nearly too broken to keep going as it is.

"Yes," I say instead.

Fox stares into my eyes like she's daring me to say those words. To say something that might indicate what this is between us, but I won't. I'm a fucking coward and I've already lost too much.

She pushes off the ground. "Well, we wouldn't want that, now would we? Can't have your newest weapon be used against you."

"Fox," I plead, but even I don't know what the fuck I'm begging for.

She looks around dramatically. "Well, no one followed us, so don't worry. The weapon is secure."

"That's not what I meant."

"Take me back."

"Please, Fox. I didn't mean—"

She laughs, but there's no humor to it. It's dark and lifeless, like the sky. "I actually had fun with you tonight. I thought maybe we could ..."

I take a step closer to her. "Maybe we could what?"

"Take me back," she demands. "Now."

I nod, picking her and our things up and running us back to the house. When we get inside, she gives a half wave to everyone sitting by the fire and goes to her room.

I walk in and look at my friends. My companions. The people I've already sworn to protect and have failed miserably. I don't want to talk to them, so I go to my room, hating myself even more than I did before we left. Sitting on my bed, I realize how entirely wrong I was—even one day of giving in to her is complete agony.

CHAPTER THIRTY-NINE

HARPER

TRIED NOT TO CRY. I TRIED REALLY FUCKING HARD, BUT I guess not much has changed in the weeks I've been here. I'm still the same sad girl that falls apart at the whim of a boy. He doesn't even have to be human, as it turns out.

Mostly I feel stupid. How is it that despite my best efforts, I still believed he saw me as something other than a tool to be used? It's just sometimes we have these moments where I think he sees me. Past the walls I've built and the armor I wear. And when he looks at me like that, I see something in him too. It's just as lost and broken. I thought we could heal each other.

Okay, fuck. Even *I* know how pathetic that sounds.

A gentle knock comes from my door, and I quickly wipe my eyes, sitting up in bed. "Come in," I manage.

Pippa peeps her head in and takes a few steps forward. "I don't know what happened tonight, but I'm sorry. Sometimes my brother is just ... he's a male. Males are," she punctuates the sentence with an eye roll and I laugh ... or try to. "Is there anything I can do?"

I shake my head. "No, I'll be fine. I'm just exhausted."

"Okay." She comes to sit on the edge of my bed as I hug a pillow against my chest. Her face grimaces before her next statement. "This might be terrible timing, but I need your blood so Wilder can make weapons when you guys are gone."

I figured I wouldn't get off with a one-time thing and last time wasn't terrible ... with Atlas there. "Sure," I say, dreading having to go through that experience with him again.

"Tomorrow?"

"Yeah," I agree.

"Okay," she says gently. "I'll leave you alone."

"Thanks, Pippa."

She walks to the door and pauses. "Harper?"

"Yes?"

"I know I've said it a lot, but in case it helps to hear it one more time—thank you. You saved us."

It's an awfully optimistic statement considering nothing has even happened yet, but I guess that's the kind of thinking a revolution needs to survive.

"I hope so," I say. I've never been great with optimism.

I SPENT LAST NIGHT THINKING a lot. Which admittedly is always a dangerous game for me. I never know which way it will go—mature and responsible or dark and suicidal. It's a fucking flip of a coin. Fun, right?

Lucky for me, I think this time I came to some pretty good conclusions and later that night I snuck out to sit underneath the Reign Tree and I wrote. For the first time in months, I found a piece of me within the pen and paper in my hands. It felt like waking up. It felt like living.

Pippa asked me to meet them in the office today, so I head out of my room and walk through the living space, finding Atlas reading by the fire in his usual spot. My heart skips a beat, but I approach him, knowing I owe him this.

"Fox," he says as I get closer.

"Hey." I'm nervous and I shouldn't be, this whole thing is silly. But I shove my hands deeper into the pockets of my cardigan like I might find some bravery in there. "I wanted to apologize."

"You have nothing to apologize for. I should be the one—"

"Just hear me out," I interrupt. "I overreacted. I'm embarrassed by my behavior and ..." I practiced this, but I can't get the words to come out properly. "We made a deal and you're only holding up your end of it. So, I'm grateful. I shouldn't have been offended by what you said."

"I shouldn't have freaked out in town. I'm sorry." He's giving me this look like he wants to say more, but it's probably just my fucked up heart wishing that was the case. And I'm grateful he doesn't. Truly. We both stare at each other awkwardly before he stands up and gestures toward the office. "Should we go?"

"I don't need you to come." The words come out in a rush, more rude than I intend them. "What I mean is, you don't have to help in there. I can handle the pain and Pippa can heal me after." I really just can't deal with the idea of bleeding in front of him again. It's like every part of my soul lights up like a fucking police siren.

"I don't mind," he says, something akin to hurt in his eyes. I refuse to examine that too closely. Nope, I need to walk away.

"I'm good," I repeat. "Really," I add, but for whose reassurance I'm not sure.

Atlas sits back down and frowns. "Alright, then." He picks up his book and resumes reading. I walk toward the office, fighting the urge to turn around and see if it's his gaze drilling holes into my heart.

AFTER PIPPA HEALS ME, I stand, feeling a bit dizzy. Her magic just isn't the same as Atlas's. Last time, it was like he replaced mine instead of just healing me. Kind of how every time I stand next to the tree, I feel rejuvenated. I avoid looking at the bowl filled with my blood that's sitting on the floor.

"Are you okay?" she asks with a worried look.

I rub my forehead. "I just need to grab something to snack on."

Pippa gives me a half smile. "This should be all we need for a while, maybe ever."

"There's something I need to say," I confess before I change my mind.

Wilder picks up the bowl and carefully carries it outside, leaving me alone in the room with Pippa.

"I'm hoping to find more answers after this trip. When I do, I think our business together is complete." Her face turns to stone. "I'm really grateful for your help, but you don't need me here anymore. I'm happy to donate more before I go."

"What about Atlas?" she blurts out.

I'm lightheaded from the blood loss and having a hard time piecing her words together. She must mean how Atlas needs me for the Reign Trees. "You have my blood. That should work for creating more trees. I'm happy to wait and test the theory first if need be."

"But where will you go?"

"Home, hopefully." The words feel hollow.

Her eyes dart around the room like she's looking for something. "Did you tell Atlas?"

Why is she so concerned about him? He'll be the happiest to see me go. "Not yet," I say with confusion. "I'll let you give him the good news for me."

"You don't have to, you know," she says before I can reach the door. "You could stay. Help us fight the queen and plant the Reign Trees yourself."

Part of me wants to. I'm not even sure what home will be like when I get back. Has time frozen while I've been gone? Does everyone think

I just vanished? In reality, they probably think I ran away and offed myself. *That* should be awkward.

The other part of me can't stay here any longer, in this house, with these people. It feels like every second I'm here my soul is healing and shattering at the same time. Like I'm caught in a limbo of emotion with nothing to anchor myself to. Inadvertently, I ran from my problems and I think it's catching up to me now. The truth is, being here has brought to light so many things I shoved down for so long—loneliness, emptiness, the idea that I'd never be good enough. The time I've spent here hasn't solved all of those things, not even close, but it's made me realize I'm not helpless in all of this. I can change the way my future looks ... and maybe that's a good enough start for now. It has to be.

Suddenly, the air feels too thick in here, so I just shake my head sadly and say, "I can't."

CHAPTER FORTY

ATLAS

WE LEAVE FOR **BLACKBONE MOUNTAIN** TODAY and I have a surprise for Fox. I left Ellison and Emery as they readied things out front to set it up. Pippa needed to stay in case one of us was needed by the Council and Idalia said she'd rather eat raw meat for a week than go camping. Naturally, I informed her I could easily arrange those stipulations while we were gone. I didn't even invite Torin, though he's been less of a pain in my ass lately and Wilder is busy making weapons for the armies.

The Realm has blessed us with daylight today, which makes my surprise even better. Walking around to the front of the house, I find the group waiting for me on the porch. Emery and Ellison's eyes widen at the black stallion I'm leading.

"Did you make a new friend, Atlas?" Emery asks.

I ignore his jab and walk closer to Fox, who is standing with her back to me on the porch kissing Pants.

"I'll be back," she tells him, putting him down. They stare at each other for a few minutes as if communicating in a silent language. She picks him up again, nuzzling and kissing him a few more times before letting him sit on the wooden steps. "Be good."

When she turns around, she seems more confused than impressed by the horse.

"Have you ridden one before?" I ask her.

She nods, brows furrowing in speculation.

"I figure you'd rather ride than get carried the whole way."

"This is for me?" She takes her eyes off of me and looks at the horse for the first time.

"If you want. Otherwise I'm sure you can ride any of us." It's a joke obviously, but she looks like she might burst into tears. "You don't have to if you don't want to." What the fuck? This was supposed to be a nice gesture.

She shakes her head and smiles. "No, I would love to ride. I just ... it's very kind of you. I'm just surprised."

"Yeah, you going soft on us, Elf Boy?" Elli asks with a grin. I want to smack it right off his face, but it makes Fox giggle, so I settle for flipping him off.

"Well, I'm all about having someone else carry our shit." Emery fills the stallion's saddlebags with supplies and I offer my hand to help her onto the horse.

Fox looks at my outstretched palm like taking it might lock her into an irreversible decision. My body aches to be closer to her, to find a way to touch her, but she seems like she feels the opposite. Fuck, I can't blame her, I'd hate me too.

Pippa told me last night about her leaving after this trip. I know she was hoping it would sway me into doing some grand romantic gesture, but I'm just not that guy. Not anymore at least. Fox leaving is for the best, at least that's what I keep telling myself. Maybe one day I'll fucking listen.

Eventually, she takes my hand, and I lift her onto the horse with ease. Her shirt rides up causing my fingers to graze her hips and my mind tunnels to the feeling of her skin against mine.

"You can let go now," she whispers from the saddle.

I don't blush ... ever, but I swear to the fucking Realm I feel my cheeks turn a nice rosy fucking pink.

"I hope you got a fast horse," Emery says. He looks up at Fox. "I hope you can ride."

She smiles so wide, I can't help but hate him for the thirty seconds it lasts.

"Let's see if you can keep up with me," she taunts and then takes off, the horse galloping like the wind.

"Fucking Realm," I mutter as we all speed off to follow her.

She lets out a howl of excitement and I let myself smile. She'll be gone soon anyway. I might as well enjoy her company while it lasts.

CHAPTER FORTY-ONE

HARPER

THANKS TO ATLAS GETTING ME THE HORSE, IT ONLY takes us a day and a half to get to the head of the trail that leads up Blackbone Mountain. My legs are sore from riding, but I'm not a stranger to long horseback rides.

The boys definitely overpacked. Some of the things they brought were so excessive that I had to laugh. I thought I was a spoiled brat, but Atlas didn't even know how to use a can opener.

Blackbone Mountain lives up to its name—black granite rocks covered in bone-white snow. The trench that surrounds most of the mountain is a matching charcoal due to the terrain's run-off. The whole scene is rather ominous, and to say I'm not excited about going on a multiple day hike is the understatement of my life. Luckily, I have good hiking boots that Pippa let me borrow and the sweater I'm wearing is almost too warm, despite the overcast sky. How there's so much snow in this climate is beyond me. As we slow to a walk, I realize it's not snow ... it's trees. Hundreds of evergreens with white leaves. Everwhites?

"What kind of trees are those?" I ask with wonder.

"Frost Trees," Ellison says from my left side.

"Did you come here often when you lived here?" I ask him, hoping I'm not prying.

To my relief, Elli gives me his goofy smile. "Yeah, all the time, but we never hiked the mountain. I didn't even know about this hidden back way."

"Remember the time Atlas bet you a hundred gold you couldn't swim half the trench?" Emery asks, pointing to a lone island in the black water.

Ellison snorts. "Dumb bet. I might as well be Kelpie."

"Hey, no one knew your derax form was a water snake," Atlas says.

"That's pretty cool," I add.

Elli gives me a wicked grin. "The coolest."

Emery snorts. "I'm obviously the coolest and the biggest."

"No remark?" I ask Atlas.

"I don't need to. This competition is stupid, since everyone knows being a panther wins every time."

"Guess you'll have to be the jury, Fox," Emery says from ahead of me.

I think of Atlas's massive body snuggled up to mine. How one of his paws was the size of my torso, but his fur was softer than anything I've ever felt.

"What do you think mine would be?" I ask instead.

"Something spiky," Atlas remarks.

"Definitely something spiky," Emery agrees.

"Sharp teeth, too," Ellison adds.

I'm about to make a guess when we see a wooden hut pressed against the mountain.

"That's weird, I don't remember that being there," Ellison says.

Atlas stops my horse and helps me get off. My legs are gelatin, but I try not to show it.

We walk closer to the hut, which looks like a child painted it. Pink and blue and yellow paint splatter the dark wood in uneven coats and patterns. On the side of the hut is a flip-out window and counter where postcards dangle from the edge over the opening. The surface is covered in different brochures depicting various parts of Calamity.

"Hello?" Emery calls out.

I frown as I notice a sign on the outside of a hut that says *Information Booth*. There's a sign below that reads, **Hours: Now or Never**. Something about the whole thing seems like déjà vu.

"Anyone there?" I call out.

The tiny hut shakes as someone begins rustling around from inside beyond our view. "One moment!" they shout, and the blood in my veins turns to ice. Somehow I'd know that voice anywhere, so I'm not surprised when the large half-goat, half-kangaroo creature peers its head out of the red doorway.

"Oh! You're here!" his gruff voice cheers, hopping over to me and shaking all of our hands.

"Elijah, pleased to meet you," he says to each of us with a firm handshake.

"Harper. We've met," I say when he gets to me, purposefully keeping my hands away from him.

He tilts his head to the side, his gold monocle chain and top hat shifting with the movement. "I don't think we have."

"When would you have met him?" Atlas asks as he shakes the creature's hand.

I look up at Atlas. "At the bookstore in town. You were there too."

"Bookstore?" Elijah asks with confusion. "I don't think so."

Atlas shakes his head. "It was probably someone else. Wasn't that your first day here? I'm sure you were overwhelmed."

"No," I say, closing my eyes and trying to calm myself. "You owned the bookstore, and you gave me the book on hiking."

The creature bursts out in a laugh that rockets through the trees. "Can you imagine," he says through his chuckles. "Me in a bookstore?"

"Not really, my friend," Ellison says, patting him on the back. "What do you have here?"

"No, it was you! I wouldn't forget someone like this!" I argue, but everyone's shifted over to look at the storefront.

Elijah stays back with me. "You're not fooling me," I growl.

"You must be Harper," he says with a roguish wink.

"Of course I am, I just said that!" I shriek. The boys turn around and give me a strange look, like *I'm* the one acting weird.

"Pardon the big fucking mess," Elijah says, hopping over to them. "I just *hop*ened up a few months ago." He winks at us again. I wish he'd get his fucking eye muscles under control.

Wait, a few *months* ago?

"You sell this stuff?" Atlas asks suspiciously.

"No, silly. It's information! I give it away. Hey, can I ask you something?" Elijah takes off the monocle and cleans it with a blood-red handkerchief he pulls out of Realm knows where.

We all turn to him, but his attention is on Atlas. Thank fuck.

"Sure?" Atlas says, narrowing his eyes.

"I had a necklace on the counter. Must have misplaced it. You wouldn't happen to know where it is, would you?"

Atlas looks at him with the same look I've been giving him, and I let out a yelp of frustration. "What!"

Elijah shrugs and places the monocle back on. "Never hurts to ask," he mutters.

By the cart, Ellison reaches for a brochure and Elijah quickly hops over and slaps his hand. "Please don't touch."

We all exchange a confused look.

"Well, I've got work to do and I'm running late. Fuck right along now!" Elijah says.

"Riiiiight, nice to meet you." Emery waves at us to follow down the trail.

I lead my horse around the hut when Elijah grabs me with his furry hand and I yelp with surprise.

"Oh, didn't mean to startle you. This is for you, Harper. You might find it useful."

"Fuck off," I growl, eyeing where he's touching my arm.

"Please," he says eagerly.

"I don't want your gifts," I say, trying to pull away.

Atlas comes over and grabs it from his hand. "Just take it, Fox. Stop being so uptight." He smirks and moves to catch up with his friends.

I narrow my eyes at Elijah once they've all gone. "I know you're fucking with me."

"Wouldn't dream of it. He sure is handsome, mate," he says with a wink and a terrible Australian accent. I shake my head and walk away. Does anyone here even have an Australian accent?

"Harper!" Elijah calls out and I groan at the sky.

"What?"

"Don't forget the saying: An eye for a guy and the whole girl's blind."

"What the fuck does that even mean!" I scream before stomping off. I swear I hear him chuckling behind me.

I catch up to the boys who have moved on from the bizarre encounter.

"Here," Atlas says, handing me the brochure.

I look down at the title: **Kismet & Coincidence presents the 69th edition of: A Minor's Guide to Gemuinely Interesting History.**

What. The. Fuck.

There are pictures of various gems and where you can find them all across Calamity. Why would I ever need this? And why is miner spelled minor? If I was a cartoon character, steam would be whistling out of my ears.

I want to shred it into pieces, but it's actually rather sturdy so I shove the brochure deep in my saddlebag, hoping I'll forget about it by the time this trip is over.

"Not a big fan of gems?" Atlas teases.

"I swear I've met him before," I whine.

"Sure, whatever you say, Fox." He rubs his hand over the top of my head, tousling my hair. "Whatever you say."

I can't decide what's more weird. Meeting Elijah for a second time or Atlas being so nice to me.

CHAPTER FORTY-TWO

ATLAS

ONE DAY BEFORE THE PARTY

THEN SHE GRABBED MY HAND BEFORE *I* COULD *get in the shower and told me she prefers her meat dirty."*

"Fucking gross," I choke out through my laughter.

"I basically told her to get the fuck out ... nicely."
Emery smiles, and I know he truly did find the nicest way to say it. *"That's what I get for taking a random tavern girl home."*

"So you still haven't been laid. How long has it been now?" I raise an eyebrow, ready to taunt him mercilessly.

Tomorrow is the party and just when I thought the staff couldn't be any more frantic, they're sprinting through the halls with hurried apologies and polite smiles as we walk back to our rooms. Rays of warmth break through the tall windows that line the castle halls, glinting off Emery's blond hair and creating a glare against his black horns.

"Do you ever think about anything other than pussy?"

"No," I say back without hesitation.

Emery rolls his eyes and punches me lightly on the shoulder. Even though we've just come back from sparring, the beast in me stirs, ready for the challenge.

He takes note as his eyes widen. "Ready for more already?"

"Oh, I'm always ready, baby," I coo.

"Well, I might be having a dry spell, but I'm not desperate enough to fuck you ... yet," he jokes.

I give him a wink as glimmering blonde hair catches my eye. Turning quickly, I see Elrora hurrying down a hall to my right. Worry churns in my gut and I glance back at Emery, who has stopped to see what I'm looking at.

"I'll catch up with you later, I need to ... ask my mother about something."

"Alright," he says, not entirely believing me.

I feel bad lying to him about Elrora, but he's the one who won't admit he's in love with Pippa so he can fuck off trying to learn my secrets.

With a wave, I sprint after the beauty rushing down the hall, grabbing her wrist when I catch up to her and spinning her around.

"Hey, where are you—" my voice catches in my throat at the sight of her tears. Red rimmed and puffy green eyes look up at me as she tries to wiggle away.

"What the fuck happened?" I growl, my panther simmering at the surface of my skin. I will murder anyone who hurt her.

"Atlas, it's nothing," she murmurs, still trying to get away.

Worried we'll gather an audience, I pull her into an alcove off the hall, the thick walls barricading any sound.

"Like fuck it's nothing. Tell me," I demand, wiping the tears from her cheeks.

She wipes under both eyes at the same time and takes a breath. "Just one of the court ladies scolded me today for not cleaning the room properly. She told me she'd report me to your mother."

A growl builds in my chest and echoes off the stone walls. "No one is going to do anything to you. Tell me who she was."

She shakes her head. "I don't know. A visiting noble."

"She's just trying to scare you," I say, not sure how true the words are. I needed to speak to my mother about Elrora anyway. I still hadn't had the chance to discuss it with her ... or maybe there was a small part of me that was avoiding it.

My heart starts to crack at the sad smile she's trying to paint on her features. "I'm sure you're right. I just ... after our moment a few days ago, I dare to let myself hope for a different life ... one by your side." Elrora laughs nervously. "It's so silly."

Grabbing her chin and tilting it so that she's staring into my eyes, I try to convey to her just how serious my promise was. "I love you. I will make you my queen. Don't be afraid to hope."

She nods silently.

"I have your dress from the ball in my room. I'll have it delivered the day of." I meant to show her as a surprise tomorrow, but I hope telling her now will cheer her up. "Come to my room tomorrow at six and we'll go to the party together. Once I have you on my arm, no one will question who or what you are to me."

"Atlas," she whispers.

"I'm serious. Do you hear me? Everything is going to change."

She leans up and presses her lips to mine, the electricity of our kiss going straight to my cock as I wind my fingers through her hair. "I love you."

"I love you too," I tell her. "Tell me you understand your worth. Tell me you believe me when I say that everything will be okay."

"I believe you," she says against my lips, kissing me once more. "Stay out of trouble."

I pull away from her mouth and lean into her ear, biting her lobe and licking all the way up its edge to the point of her ear. "Never," I whisper.

CHAPTER FORTY-THREE

ARPER

OUR FIRST DAY HIKING WASN'T TOO BAD. WE HAD to leave the horse and most of our gear behind, which meant days of sharing a tent. Whoop-dee-fucking-do. No one knows exactly where this druid is, but Atlas has been using his magic to sense any changes in the earth that might indicate one direction or the other. We could be out here indefinitely if we're heading in the wrong direction.

Moisture hangs heavy in the air, slicking my legs and turning the dirt to mud beneath my boots. I lift a shoe as it squelches from a particularly mushy area. Atlas turns around to look at me. Look, not glare.

"Maybe we should stop for the night?" he asks the group.

There's not much level ground, but there hasn't been the whole hike. A small ledge juts out and Atlas declares it our spot for the evening.

I help set up camp, thankful that Atlas's ability to wield fire means not having to collect any wood or find flint. As usual, Elli takes on the role of chef while Atlas and Emery wander around the camp deciding what direction to go tomorrow. It turned dark the second we started hiking, and I am eternally grateful I packed a flashlight.

Now, I'm chopping up meat from a Fernlope Emery shot with a bow earlier. As far as I can tell, it's a deer without antlers. At the time, I wanted to ask if anyone thought it was weird they kind of looked like the faun, but I held back any remarks. I can't imagine a comment like that will make me very popular. Ellison stirs the stew, heated with magic, and hums while we work.

"Does it feel nice to be home?" I ask.

"You mean back in this part of Calamity?"

"Yeah. Do you miss it? It's foggier over here and just seems different."

He takes a sip of the stew with his wooden spoon and wrinkles his nose, shuffling through a bag to get more spices. "It's the coast that we're close to. The beaches there are always cold because they get the downwind from Willowby up north. But to answer your question ..." He pops his head up and looks at me. "Yes, I do miss it."

I open my mouth to speak again, but he cuts me off with his own question. "What about you? You barely talk about home."

My eyes dart away. "I didn't leave much behind," I mumble.

Elli is silent for a few moments and when I gaze back up at him to gauge his reaction, his timid eyes brighten with a smile. "So what you're saying is you like us better?"

I roll my eyes and nudge him with my shoulder, realizing that there's so much truth to what he's saying. Without noticing, Elli and Emery have become real friends. Even Pippa. When I leave, where will Pants go? How is it that in the last few months I've accumulated the kind of relationships I always dreamed I'd have? And how am I supposed to leave it all behind? Am I just running again?

I can't bear to think about it anymore, so I clear my throat and ask, "Will you come back? When Atlas and Pippa take the throne?" I finish cutting the meat and rinse my hands.

"I haven't thought much about it, to be honest. It feels ... too hopeful."

His words surprise me. Elli is always so optimistic.

"I wasn't supposed to take my father's place; my brother was. He died that night, too."

"I'm sorry," I say quietly.

"Thanks, LH. It's a bummer, but nothing we can do about it now. Anyway, he was the one made for politics, not me. I don't know jack shit about being a landowner or a diplomat."

"Does your grandma? I mean, she seems to be doing well for herself." I never see the woman, but I know she's around ... I think.

Ellison chuckles, but it lacks any genuine humor. "She's got a few screws loose, but I suppose."

"Is she your mother's mother?"

He nods. "Never liked her much, but she's all I have left. I guess I'm lucky I even have that."

"Maybe we should talk about something else," I offer, feeling guilty I brought up the topic in the first place.

"Like you and Atlas?"

I hope he sees me glaring at him in the dark. "Next topic," I grumble.

"Come on, we all see it."

"Well, then, you're all just as delusional as me. He told me himself he doesn't see me as anything more than a pawn for this war."

Emery stops stirring and frowns. "He said that?"

I shrug, pretending like it doesn't feel like a bulldozer to my chest. "More or less."

"It's not how he really feels." He gestures for me to add the meat into the stew. "You should talk to him about it," he says quickly.

"I tried."

"Did you try though, or did you do the same thing he does where the conversation doesn't go exactly as planned so you just give up?"

I push his shoulder. "What is with people telling me I'm such a quitter?"

Ellison puts the spoon in the pot and wraps his arm around me, pulling me into his side. I turn to look up at him and smile at his half steamed glasses. His brown, messy hair is just barely emerging from a gray beanie. "Let me tell you a little something about life, LH. I'm, what, more than a hundred years older than you?"

"Ew, when you say it like that it's creepy," I mutter.

"Well, anyway. I know more than you do. That's just facts, so listen here. Life will give you many windows of opportunity. Sometimes the blinds are shut or the window just straight up looks like a door, but they're there ... everywhere you look."

"Is there a point to this weird analogy?" I tease.

"Once, when you were drunk, you told me that you're good at sneaking into people's houses. Climbing through windows cause you're all small and shit."

My cheeks heat. "I said that to you?" Wow. I really need to drink less.

"Yeah, I told you I did recon for the group and you said, 'I've probably broken into more houses than you.'" His imitation of my voice is all girly and slurred words.

I'm happy it's dark so he can't see how red I am. "What are we even talking about anymore?"

"My point, LH, is that sometimes you have to push boundaries. Sneak in through the windows that look like they're locked, but are really just stuck shut. Don't pass by ones that seem closed and assume it's not the right time or place."

"So, you're suggesting I ignore what the world is telling me and do whatever I want anyway? That doesn't sound like good advice. That just sounds selfish ... and kind of insane."

He shakes his head. "You're missing the point."

"Which is?"

"If the opportunity is there, grab it. If there's a window, there's a way. The Realm won't show you a path you can't take."

I chew on my lip. "That's actually very insightful of you ... in a backward kind of way."

"I'm a genius. But don't tell the others, I have a reputation to uphold." He mimes smoking a joint and I giggle.

What I don't say is that some windows really are sealed and locked from the inside. You could be the best burglar in the world, but unless you shatter the glass, there's no way in. And who wants to make that big of a fucking mess?

MY LIGHT SLEEP IS INTERRUPTED by Atlas leaving the tent, and my mind wanders to what he's doing. An inordinate amount of time passes while I stare at the nylon ceiling, sleep evading me. Would you believe me if I told you that there's some part of me that just can't stay away from him, no matter how hard I try? I swear it's not just the fact that he's really nice to look at—there's something else.

I cave and follow the brooding panther outside. His hulking form is sitting on a rock overlooking the trench. It's basically impossible for me to see, but my dumb ass decides to crawl out of the warm blankets and go sit next to him anyway. I'm almost there when I trip and catch myself on his back.

"What the—"

"Sorry," I say, clutching to his shoulder and finding the spot beside him.

"What are you doing out here, Fox?" His voice is like a gravel hillside I can't help but fall down.

"I couldn't sleep."

"Me either, obviously."

We sit in comfortable silence, overlooking the water. I can't see it or anything else for that matter—because it's night, there are no stars, and the moonlight is obscured by the dense forest—but I can hear it lapping against the side of the mountain.

"Penny for your thoughts?" I ask.

I hear him turn to me. "What's a penny?"

I snort a laugh. "It's a human form of currency."

"Is it, like, the highest form of currency?"

"No, it's the lowest." I giggle through my hand, trying to be quiet.

"Why would I tell you my thoughts for a singular piece of your lowest currency?"

"It's an idiom, Atlas. I'm not actually going to give you a penny."

"Good, I don't want one." I can hear the smile in his tone, and it warms me against the cool night air.

"I'll give you my thoughts if you tell me something," he offers.

"What do you want to know?" I'm not sure I'll agree to this, but I wonder what his one burning question is.

He pauses, and for a minute I think he's not going to ask. "What do you miss most about home?"

I chew my lip and truly think about his question. The things I miss about home are things that no longer exist. Childhood memories that have grown up and moved out. In fact, I haven't thought about anyone from home much since coming here. Does that make me a bad person? I don't know. I'm sure you've already formed your own opinion.

"Hot Cheeto fries," I finally answer.

"Excuse me?"

I nod eagerly. "Hot Cheeto fries. They're these poofy, rectangular chips with red spicy seasoning."

"*That's* what you miss most about home?"

"I think you're underestimating how good they are."

"I think you're a liar."

I sigh. "Okay, fine. Music."

"Music," he repeats the word like he's tasting it. "We have music."

"I know you do, but it's not the same. You asked me what I miss, and that's my answer."

"Hot Cheeto fries and music, got it."

"Now tell me what you were thinking before I got here," I demand.

Atlas sighs. "I've made a lot of mistakes, Fox. Big ones." His voice lowers to a whisper. "Most of them are things Emery doesn't even know about." I stay completely silent, afraid if I take a breath, he'll stop talking. "I just ... have you ever felt like your life is on a collision course, but there's nothing you can do about it? Everything is already so fucked that now you just have to sit back and watch it all turn to ash."

"Yes," I whisper immediately.

"Really?"

"Yeah. You feel helpless and useless and alone. And then there's that super fucked up part that wants to keep stoking the fire, so everything just burns faster."

Atlas chuckles, a dark sound that echoes off the rocks. "Yeah, exactly."

"And that nagging little voice in your head that says you could *try* to fix it. If you really wanted, you could do it, but the idea of that seems more impossible than anything else." I realize I haven't said these words to anyone. I've only let them fester inside me. Eating away at my existence and feeding on anything good that tries to take residence.

"Yeah, that's it," he says breathlessly.

More silence passes, but I've never felt less alone.

"When I was younger, my mom used to read me this book. The main character is on a quest to save a princess and he gets stuck in a forest called the Forever Forest. It's a maze of trees that no one ever escapes from. Doomed to spend their days amongst others who have gotten lost, but everyone is miserable or going mad trying to find a way home. Sometimes I feel like that, like I'm stuck in a gloomy forest and I'll never find my way out."

"Does he get out? The prince."

I nod into the blackness. "He finds his way by walking backwards. He just keeps going until one day he's somewhere else entirely."

Atlas lets out a little laugh.

"I'll tell you what this vacay to Calamity has taught me, though. Life is full of surprises. There's always something new and I'm not sure where I'm going—if it's forward or backward—but I know it's not over yet."

"I just feel lost," Atlas says in a low voice. I have to actively keep my jaw from dropping at his confession. "Like pieces of me went missing that night and I'll never get them back."

I consider his words for a few moments.

"I think that's okay," I finally say. "Maybe you had to break in order to be forged into something that can save this world. And maybe it's not so much about losing pieces but making room for new ones. Things you've collected along the way."

"What if those things make me a monster?" he asks. I can barely see him in the dark, and maybe that's the point. This vulnerability he's giving me is cruel and beautiful.

Scooting into him, I don't think, instead I put my hand over the steadfast rhythm in his chest. He sucks in a breath at my touch. "'He ran from the fear and the beasts and the darkness.'" He places his hand over mine. "'He ran until they swallowed him inside and out. And in the pit of empty night …'"

"'He found his bravery like a beacon of light,'" we say in unison.

The air feels as though all the oxygen has evaporated as he stares at me.

"You read the book I gave you," he whispers.

"Of course I did. I loved it," I tell him. "Atlas, you'll never become the thing you fear most because with fear and darkness, there's always bravery and light. I know it because I've seen both in you. The male who fears for his family and friends is the same one who would protect them at all costs. He's the one who—maybe reluctantly—let me into his world and showed me how to be someone new." I give him a gentle smile, hoping he can see it. We're close enough that I can feel his breath. Nearly taste him on my lips.

"That's a lot of wisdom for someone so small," he muses.

"Wisdom? I don't think so. Mostly my thoughts just run in circles, but every now and then they end up somewhere useful."

In the silence that follows, I find myself exactly where I need to be.

"You're different than I thought," he murmurs eventually. "Better than I ever gave you credit for. I'm sorry, Harper. Truly."

My heart explodes into exactly four thousand pieces and then I die before my magic somehow drags it all back together and forces it to continue beating. Or at least that's what it feels like.

"I'll tell you how you can make it up to me," I say as I stand, pulling from his hold before he takes all of me.

"How?"

"Don't ever call me Harper again." I squeeze his shoulder before I leave. "Goodnight, Atlas."

"Fox," he says, pausing me in my tracks. "I know you'll find your way out of the forest."

That makes me smile because I think maybe I already have.

CHAPTER FORTY-FOUR

ATLAS

I T'S BEEN TWO DAYS OF HIKING AND I'M READY TO GIVE up. With the exception of the occasional wildlife, the mountain is still. Silent. I look over to the little Fox who is repeatedly blowing a sweaty piece of hair out of her face and getting nowhere with it. The same dark brown strand is determined to fall back every time as she adjusts a backpack on her shoulders. I told her to just let us carry everything, but her stubborn attitude insisted she carry her own weight. By the looks of the backpack, she meant literally.

I chuckle, looking at her face as it reddens.

"What are you looking at, dickwad?" she snaps, but there's a humor in her eyes that feels new to me.

I zip to her side and lean in to whisper in her ear so the others can't hear me. "You're awfully cute when you're frustrated. Has anyone ever told you that?"

She stops walking and stares at me with surprise before narrowing her eyes like my words are a trap.

I smile smugly at her.

"You're certifiably insane. Has anyone ever told you that?" she sneers back.

"I like to call it creatively enthusiastic," I tell her.

She snorts. "That's generous."

"It might surprise you to know that I can be *very* generous when I want to be, Fox." My words taunt her. I know they do. I honestly expect her to turn around and blast me back with whatever power she has.

She looks me up and down with distaste, and it almost injures my pride. Too bad for her, my ego could devour the fucking world. "Interesting. I'd definitely peg you as the kind of guy who puts his *needs* first," she hints.

I hold back a growl in response. She has no fucking idea the things I could do to her. Would do to her.

"Nothing," Emery says, coming back from scouting ahead.

Fox tilts her head back and groans. "Are they hiding, or do they just not exist?"

Something clicks in my mind and I feel like an idiot for not thinking of it sooner. Despite this mountain being extremely remote, of course they wouldn't want anyone finding them. They obviously came here for peace and quiet. I close my eyes and exhale deeply.

"A concealment spell," I say.

Elli perks up. "You think?"

"I know." I pull on the magic living within me and will it into the environment. This time I'm not looking for something physical. I'm looking for something magical. As soon as I find it, I grasp onto it. It's hidden—covered by the breeze and dense forest—but it's there. "This way," I motion behind us and we move backward.

It's not far off, but the closer I approach, the stronger the magic becomes. It goes from zero to one hundred like a fucking lightning bolt and I nearly wheeze from its immensity. Like I said before, fendlings are some of the most magically powerful creatures. Creating a barrier like this isn't even something I considered they could do, and my heart sinks at the idea that they're not currently using them before being captured by the bitch queen. What does she have that could overcome their passive defensive magic?

"Everything okay, Atlas?" Emery asks, sensing I'm pushed up against something stronger than me.

"You can't feel it?" I ask, nearly out of breath.

Fox looks around with concern.

Ellison shakes his head.

I know why. This magic would likely overwhelm either of them if they tried to sense it. It's the same reason why no one can truly sense Fox's magic except me. There's just something about the ancient thrum in my veins that runs on a different frequency.

I take a deep breath and kneel in front of Fox, looking into her depthless black-brown eyes. "I'm going to need your help," I say to her.

Her eyes widen at me on my knees before her. "What?"

The air smells like electricity—burning and urgent. I know that if I reach out my hand, the force of the barrier would overwhelm me. "I need your magic to help get us through this barrier. Just you and me, though. I don't think I can get the other two through." My stare stays hooked on hers even though I feel Emery shift his weight uncomfortably behind me.

Fox looks at Emery and Elli standing behind me. I'm not sure what she finds in their gaze, but her attention turns back to me and she nods.

"You're not seriously considering absorbing her magic," Emery asks. He knows damn well that's what I'm about to do.

I stand and face my friends, letting my silence do the talking.

"You could die," he growls. "Use mine."

I shake my head. "It won't work. It's too strong."

"Isn't it worth trying, though?" Ellison asks, his gaze darting between everyone.

"I won't drain you of your magic and then leave you defenseless," I tell Emery.

Fox is quiet behind me.

"It's not going to kill me."

"How do you know?" Her tone is laced with something that sounds an awful lot like concern.

I turn to her and try to give her a reassuring smile, but coming from me, it probably looks murderous. "I just do, Fox."

She chews the inside of her cheek, but shrugs. "I'll do whatever you need."

My dick twitches at her words, but this is hardly the time. Reigning myself in, I look back to Emery. "I'll try not to go far," I say. "If it's enough magic to draw the evil witch's attention, then shift and run."

Ellison scoffs. "Like hell we're running."

I hate the idea of them fighting an enemy without me. I stay silent though, never giving them a direct command, and turn back to Fox. She's watching the interaction with unyielding focus.

"What do I need to do?" she asks innocently.

"Just hold on to me. Don't let go and try to keep your clothes on," I say with a wink.

She rolls her eyes, but they quickly drop to my crotch, and her cheeks turn pink when she sees me notice.

I hold my hand out for hers, and she tentatively places it in mine. Pulling her wrist to my mouth, I try not to think about how I'm nearly salivating to bite her. I give her one last chance to refuse, but she only watches me with heavy-lidded eyes.

Before I can think on it further, I sink my teeth into her quickening pulse, letting the taste of her wash over my tongue and fill my mouth. Her eyes flutter closed with the euphoria that has us both in its grip, threatening to send me to my knees again.

A new feeling consumes me when her blood mixes with mine, melting into my bloodstream. It's a monsoon of power, of lust, of everything *Fox*. My senses are overwhelmed until she's all I can see or think or taste and the heat of her magic rubs against mine like a purring cat. My chest cracks open and it feels like my blood begins to freeze. It slows and turns to sludge in my veins, darkening in color and sending a sharp, explosive pain through my body. I pull her wrist from my mouth, keeping her hand in my grip.

Shit. Maybe I am going to die.

But just as suddenly as it appears, the pain is gone. Her warm hand clutches my shirt and she presses her body against me. My vision, clouded by only thoughts of her, begins to clear as I find her in my arms, hand still gripping mine. She lets out a breathy moan and bites her lower lip as she looks up at me. Her pupils dilate, swallowing up the brown in her irises and turning them wholly black. I take my other hand and trail it down the outline of her face. My soul is unraveling, picking up pieces of her before weaving itself back together.

"You're so beautiful," I whisper to her. Only her. "My little Fox."

A montage of us runs through my head and I catch glimpses of I don't know what. Things that haven't happened ... things that may never be? In every image of her, whether she's laughing or serious or screaming at me, there's one constant—I'm happy. Deep in my soul and my heart, there's a happiness I know I couldn't possibly deserve, but fuck do I want it. She's strong and beautiful and brave and she's so much better than me. But these memories that seem painfully unreal make me feel like there's a world where I could be good for her too.

"What's happening?" she asks me quietly. Her voice is a lighthouse against the raging storm inside me. She presses her body closer to mine, nearly grinding against my cock, which is at full attention, begging to be used. I want all of her. I need to claim her soul as thoroughly as she's claimed mine.

I shake my head slowly, as I lose myself in this heady feeling. "I don't know."

Someone clears their throat and the sound shatters the world we've built around ourselves. "Barrier," Emery reminds me.

Fox blinks a few times, her pupils constricting down to a normal size, and looks at our bodies pressed together. She lets out a little laugh. "You weren't kidding about keeping my clothes on," she murmurs before pulling away from me.

I keep her hand gripped in mine while my heart, the one that beats just for her, sinks. I want to know if she saw it too, but the words don't come out. Instead, I focus on the task of taking down the barrier. Our magic surges through me, powerful and explosive.

"Put your other hand here," I demand as I place mine against the invisible surface.

I grit my teeth as the shock of the barrier's magic pushes against me. When she lifts her hand out, I pump my own magic back into her so that it numbs the pain of the barrier. She smiles at me again, and I want to bottle it and wear it around my neck like some sort of crazed Fox cult leader.

As soon as her skin makes contact, we begin falling through something and I catch her as she collapses to the ground. Taking a look around, I see we're still on the mountain, but the air is warmer, the sun shining. Instead of dead, moist foliage on the ground, it's soft, green grass as far as the eye can see. It takes me a few seconds to realize she's limp in my arms and when I look down at her, a panic I haven't felt in a long time races through me.

"Fox," I say, shaking her lightly.

Feeling her fluttering human pulse only brings me mild relief. Her eyes are closed and her face is contorted into one of anguish.

"Fox!" I shout.

Fuck. Was the magic too much for her? Is this some weird human thing?

This overwhelming feeling that I'll never properly be able to take care of her crashes into me and sends my heart careening down the side of a cliff. What if she gets sick? What if she needs human things she doesn't even realize she's missing? What if she disappears as silently as she arrived? What if she never feels the same way I do?

"Please, Fox." I shake her again, but the sight of her head freely rolling around makes me sick.

"She'll be fine, Prince," a voice impatiently says to me.

CHAPTER FORTY-FIVE
HARPER

I'M HERE AGAIN. THAT PLACE I NEVER WANTED TO BE. IN a darkness that threatens to devour me. It's a reminder that even though I feel like I've grown since being here, I'm still the same weak girl that tried to end her life. The shadows press in on me and I turn around, trying to find Atlas. He's nowhere to be seen. All that's around me are shadow-light lamp posts lining a black-and-white checkered path beneath my feet. Impenetrable wrought iron fencing and hedges spanning the length of the path to my right. The sound of a grandfather clock rings empty and loud in the background like the drums of war. It fills me with a dread that tells me time is running out.

I hold on to the warm feeling I had in his arms when our magic collided. It was white hot and a deep, calming blue. It was the feeling that no matter what happened, everything would be alright. This place is the opposite of that. Cold and empty and terrifying. It threatens to take everything I am and suffocate it until I can no longer remember who Harper Elliott is anymore. But did I ever really know?

I try to be brave. I've always tried to be brave, but I always fail. The sum of my life is that … failing. Failing to be a good daughter, failing to be a good friend, failing to try to figure out who or what I am so that I could, for one single second, feel like I belonged somewhere.

But I felt that once, in Calamity. A feeling of belonging. Despite not being born in their world or familiar with its strangeness. It felt more like home than anywhere I've ever lived. I felt strong and courageous and useful there. I hold on to those thoughts and walk down the path, my shoes making a clicking against the tiled floor as I look down. I'm wearing a short-sleeved, a-line, light blue dress with a big black bow wrapping around my middle and tying in the back. Black peep-toe heels are the origin of the clicking sounds my feet are making. My hair is in loose gentle curls and my hands find a black headband with a silk bow sitting on my head.

"Hello?" I try to make my voice steady, but it still comes out trembling.

The sound echoes off the tile floor. I shiver, wishing I had a coat.

"Hello?" I try again, but no one responds.

I do the only thing there is to do: I keep walking forward. I hear Atlas scolding me in my head. He'd want me to stay still until he could find me. Always so weirdly protective, despite his cruel demeanor. But Atlas isn't here; it's just Harper, so I hold on to that warm feeling and I keep going … because I'm stronger than I ever gave myself credit for. I keep going because I *can*.

CHAPTER FORTY-SIX

ATLAS

"SHOW YOURSELF," I DEMAND, HOLDING A LIMP Fox in my arms.

I push off the ground, gripping behind her knees with one arm and cradling her head against my chest with another. Her scent, raspberries and daisies, and that otherworldly thing constrict my heart. I scan the environment, sweat beading at my temples.

"I'm right here! Hello!" a little voice says from up ahead. When I squint, I see a small creature dressed in a long robe the same lush green as the grass, blending in with the environment. Onyx locks fall from the fendling's head to the ground, picking up debris at the ends.

"Are you the Blood Collector?" I ask. It sounds so silly saying it as I approach the smiling druid. Their wide eyes against black-scaled skin look at me with adoration and I might have smiled back, if Fox wasn't unconscious in my arms.

The fendling waves at me dismissively. "I've always despised that nickname. Please call me Clover."

"Clover?" I ask in disbelief.

She nods eagerly. "Yes. I haven't had a visitor in, say ... a thousand years?"

Fendlings live extraordinarily long lives, at least when they're not being hunted and farmed. They only breed once every hundred years, which makes the idea of the queen forcing them to breed all the more gut-churning. I have so many questions, but only one that matters.

"What's wrong with her?"

Another dismissive wave and she heads into the forest. The sun defies nature, bleeding in despite the dense treeline, and causing the leaves to glow with radiance.

"Clover," I warn.

"Yes, yes, I know. You love her. She's everything to you and you just feel *so* terrible that you've spent all this time hating her when you could be ..." She gives me a seductive wink that makes me shudder.

"Tell me how to fix her," I plead. Her words voicing the truth of my feelings weakens me.

"If I tell you that she'll wake up soon enough, will you relax and tell me what you really came here for?"

"No," I growl. I want Fox back, whole, and spitting venom at me for any reason she wants.

Clover leads me to a small camp with a tent made from sticks and leather. A small fire lays unlit in the center and a wooden workbench is built into the massive tree that throws shade over the entire camp.

"Shame," she says. "The spell I created for this place will only allow you to stay for a few minutes."

"Minutes?" I shout impatiently.

She doesn't even flinch. I must be fifty times her size, and she blinks once at me. "Yes, unfortunately."

"She'll wake up?" I confirm, my voice quivering.

She nods and points to a blanket laid out in the shade. I walk over and place Fox on top of it, tucking her hair behind her ear. I place my hand over her heart to triple check it's beating, despite being able to hear it.

"I'll fix this," I mumble to her. "Is she in pain?" I ask Clover. Fox's full lips, forming a frown, worry me.

Clover sighs like she's losing patience. "She's in the Backwood."

"What?" I snarl, turning on her.

The Backwood is a different realm ... well, kind of ... realm adjacent, I guess you could say. I've only heard of it. It's supposed to be a dark replica of our world where nothing lives and everything good is sucked out of anyone who dares to enter. Legends say it is only accessible with a dark magic no one has used in a millennium.

"How?"

Clover shrugs. "You'd have to ask her."

"Well, it doesn't seem that I can fucking do that, can I?"

"So it seems," Clover confirms with a smug look. "You're wasting time, Prince."

I sigh, trying to collect my thoughts, but my mind is wrapped in so much fear it's hard to concentrate. I hear her voice in my head, "*Be brave.*"

"She's a human," I manage to say.

"I can see that."

I glare at the fendling. "How? How is she here in our world?"

Clover shrugs again. I grit my teeth and she laughs. "Okay, alright, I'll tell you what I do know ... for a price."

I raise my brows at her. "Which is?"

"Well, blood of course. I'm the Blood Collector after all. Yours and hers. That will be the perfect addition to my collection."

"I thought you didn't like that nickname?"

She gives me a demonic smile that startles me. "There are many truths we don't like to see. Unfortunately, that doesn't mean they aren't accurate."

I look at Fox laying on the blanket. I don't want to hurt her more than I already have. "Mine first, hers if she wakes up before we leave."

Clover looks to her and frowns. "Fine," she says, and whips out a blade faster than I can blink.

CHAPTER FORTY-SEVEN

HARPER

MY FEET SHUFFLE SLOWER AND SLOWER THE LONGER I walk. I can feel the sharp burn of blisters forming against my heel and the forced curl of my toes. I'm certain the temperature is dropping with every step. I stop and look around, panic rising and falling as a red door twinkles in my periphery. It's hidden in the hedges and I have to wonder how many doors like this I may have passed along the way.

The door, with its arched frame and golden handle, reminds me of something from the past. A dirt tunnel flashes in my memory, but not long enough for me to hold on to it. I press my hand against the door and turn the knob, falling into a warm room with bay windows overlooking an overcast sea. Rich greenery rolls over the coastline like carpet before turning to sand. Fog rolls steadily along the beach. It doesn't look like home, but it doesn't look quite like Calamity either.

The room, dark with blackberry drapes and red velvet furniture, reminds me of a castle. Black marble stands line up against the right and left walls like a firing squad. A low, pink glow emits around each one, illuminating six beating hearts—one on each stand. They appear to be made of light wood, but that doesn't stop the rigid flesh from squeezing and expanding, pumping a thick substance through purple-blue vessels that jut from the top and wrap pathways around the hearts. Hot, red liquid spurts from each one in a mess of crimson, splashing along the floor before being sucked up by the dark tile and repeatedly forced through. My stomach churns at the sight as terror stakes its claim on my mind.

A sound shatters the silence of the room as the door creaks open and my own heart feels like it might fall out and succumb to this same bizarre fate. I turn to see a woman walk in. She's gorgeous, in a red, flowing gown that hugs her hips and adds a pink blush to her pale skin. Her lips are painted in matching cherry lipstick and her smile is purely feline. Long, milky hair cascades down her back in perfect curls. A golden tiara crowns her head, circling the base of two black horns that twist like cyclones a foot in the air.

"What has the Realm brought me today?" she purrs.

I stumble back toward the window. I don't know who she is, but she's bad. I feel it in every part of my being, from my toes to the split ends in my fucking hair.

"Pretty thing, aren't you?"

"Who are you?" I ask.

She frowns deeply, and it almost makes her look innocent, but I grew up around fake bitches and I'm not falling for it.

"No manners, I see," she remarks as she walks closer to me. "You're in my home and yet you think it wise to ask *me* questions?"

"I don't know how I got here," I mumble.

"Interesting."

I must have been caught in the shadows because the closer I get to the windows, the more her face lights up, her eyes dragging to my ears and I know that she's surprised to find I'm human.

"Very interesting." The joy that lights her face should make her more beautiful, but something vile pours into her eyes. "Tell me, human. Where did you come from?"

317

I don't want to tell her shit. I need to find a way out of here.

"Not very talkative, I see," she continues, her steps getting closer and closer to me. "And I was *so* looking for a friend. I'm quite lonely, you see." She's close enough now that I can see that she must be half-elf and half-faun, like Emery. Her canines seem to be longer than others, painting her features in a demonic hue.

"I didn't mean to come here," I say vaguely.

Her eyes widen, and her nostrils flare, inhaling the air around me and my scent. Her devilish smiles turns to rage and her beautiful face becomes ugly. "Where did you come from?" This time, her question is an icy demand.

"Fuck you," I snarl. I can't explain it, but I'd rather die than tell her anything about Calamity.

"Get out," she snaps.

The room shakes, and my body feels like it's being torn apart.

"Get out!" Her scream is shrill and piercing, cutting through my mind like a serrated knife.

I want to tell her that I don't want to be here. I'd love to leave if she could point me in the direction of the fucking exit, but I can't move. My brain feels like it's melting into a molten wax that oozes from my ears.

"Tell Atlas his time is up. I'm coming and he's in a lot of trouble."

My attention snaps to her at his name and something primal in me clicks before I lunge at her and fall into darkness.

CHAPTER FORTY-EIGHT

ATLAS

"IT MAY SURPRISE YOU TO KNOW THAT HARPER HAS A purpose that has nothing to do with warming your bed," Clover says. "She didn't fall into our realm by accident." The fendling looks up at the sky. "The Realm has a reason for all things."

"You think the Realm brought her here?"

"Well, what else?"

I stay silent because I don't know. That's why I fucking asked.

"Are you aware of what's been happening in Calamity?" I ask her.

She frowns. "Unfortunately, yes. It seems as though you made quite the blunder."

My heart drops and I stare at her in disbelief. "How ... what ..."

"I don't know everything, but I know many things. I'm also teasing, though I suppose it's not as funny of a joke to *you*." Clover ponders her words thoughtfully and fury builds inside me.

"Are you going to tell me anything useful?"

She gestures at Fox. "You'll need the human girl to defeat *her*. Well, there might be a way around it, but in order to bring order to the world, Harper needs to finish what she started."

"But we can do it?" I ask.

"Oh, nothing is what it seems, my young elf. And everything is as you remember. If you embrace your past instead of shoving it into the deep recesses of your mind, you'll find the way." I go to speak, but she continues, her eyes somewhere else. "But not alone. No, definitely not. Your worst fears will have to become your truth in order to save what you love."

"The queen ... she's so powerful," I mutter.

"Indeed," Clover says. "A worthy opponent. One you will face and die against or live and tales will be told for eons."

"I don't care about fame," I growl.

Clover shakes her head. "I suppose you don't. Such a noble prince."

I roll my eyes as Clover looks at her wrist as if checking a watch. Nothing but bangles adorn her scaly arm. "Time is running out."

"How does Fox get back home?" I can admit that I don't really want to know the answer, but I know she wants to leave and at this point, I'd do anything for her.

Clover smiles, but it's the smile of a blood collector, not a dainty fendling. "With her magic and a gift from the Realm. Do you know how powerful time is?" I give her a confused look. "It can be moved forward or back. No one knows what the future will hold, but the past is an already finished puzzle. It has fixed points and places to return to."

"You're saying she can travel back in time?"

Clover holds up a single finger. "Just once," she says quietly. "It is her time to do with as she wishes. Someday you may learn that, like you, she too has a past that darkens her future."

Fox stirs, and I'm next to her before I can even take a breath. "Fox?"

She groans quietly. "Atlas?" Her eyes find mind and relief fills her vision before they shutter closed once more.

"Fox, stay with me," I say.

Clover is standing over her body. "She'll need rest." The fendling whips her knife out again and I growl.

She raises one eyebrow at me, but there's no fear in the look she gives me. I don't move as she cuts into Fox's flesh and uses her magic to bring the blood into a vial. Fox flinches slightly and I push my magic into her so she doesn't feel the pain.

"Time to go, Prince," Clover says when she's finished.

"But she has questions for you too," I argue.

"And you have the answers." Clover winks and then the world turns black.

I fall to my knees, the air feeling like it's been punched out of my lungs. Emery and Ellison rush over to me.

"What happened?" Emery demands, looking down at Fox, who is asleep again against my chest.

I close my eyes, suddenly more exhausted than I have been in a long time. "We both need to rest and then I'll tell you."

"Is she okay?" Ellison asks.

I realize then that it's not just me that cares about this girl. It's all of us. She's snuck her way into our lives and none of us would have it any other way. My sly little Fox.

"She'll be fine," I say, needing more than anything for those words to be true.

Fox sleeps the entire journey home, only stirring every few hours to use the restroom and eat whatever I shove into her view. My heart beats to a rhythm of worry, but I try not to show it. No one else needs to know how soft I've become for this girl.

When we get home everyone is waiting, pale faced and eager, like they've done nothing but pace in circles since we left. I haven't spoken much. I don't feel like I gained a lot from that stupid, cryptic-as-shit conversation I had, but one thing is clear to me. I have to tell them what happened that night. The whole truth ... I just don't know how or when.

I place Fox in her bed, the window closed tight, even though it's night and has been for days. It's like the world is trying to match the darkness that has descended upon my fucking mind. I kiss the top of her head, her brown strands rubbing against my stubble. I realize that it's a thousand more times intimate than I have been with her, but she's fucking asleep so she'll never know.

When I go to pull away, she clutches my shirt in her fist. Eyes closed, I'm not sure she's aware of where she is or what is going on, but the desire to lie in the sheets and hold her burns through me. We haven't been more than a few feet apart in days and something about that feels right.

"Stay," she murmurs.

"I can't," I mutter back. The weight of the words is almost too much to bear. I lift her tiny fingers from the fabric of my shirt as she frowns in a dreamy state. I never want to be the source of her suffering ever again, but I know that's a wish that will never come true.

When I leave her room, I'm empty and weighted at the same time. A sick feeling boils in my gut and all I want is to turn around and wrap myself in her scent. But Pippa is waiting for me at the end of the hallway, so I walk over to her. I don't deserve the comfort Fox can provide me, and as soon as she's lucid, she'll be the first one to tell me to fuck off.

"What happened?" Pippa demands, hands on hips.

I shake my head. "Would you believe me if I said not much?"

"No."

"Can I shower first?" I plead.

"Fine," she mumbles and heads toward the kitchen.

I turn back to Fox's room and stare at the door. Hoping for ... I'm not really sure. In the end, I go into mine and start the water. Steam fills the room and hides my reflection in the mirror. Good, I can't stand to look at myself.

CHAPTER FORTY-NINE

HARPER

THE NEAR SILENT CLICK OF THE DOOR WAKES ME from a sleep that feels like it's lasted forever and will never be enough. My head is heavy and foggy. Like some sort of thick soup or chili or ... a clam chowder bread bowl. Yeah, that's definitely the analogy I'm going with.

As my eyes open and my mind tries to sift through the clams and bits of sourdough that make up my thoughts, I hear Atlas and Pippa in the hallway. Their voices are hushed, so I can't make out their exchange of words. I don't remember much for the last three days and a panic runs through me. My memories aren't quite my own and I have to sort out fact from fiction. All I know is I have this manic urge to be close to Atlas. To tell him something important that I can't quite put into words. In my soul, I know that certain things changed between us, but I don't know what they were or how it happened.

I scrub my face and kick off the sheets, frowning at my mud-covered clothes and overall dirty appearance. Who in their right mind thought it was acceptable to put me in my bed like this? Shuffling across the room, I peer out into the hallway. It's mostly quiet, so I sneak out and head to Atlas's room. I have no idea what time or what day it is since it's still night out, so I hope he's not asleep. A gentle knock on his door has me looking around, waiting for someone to come up and ask me what I'm doing, but no one does. I turn the knob when there's no answer and step into his empty room. It smells so much like him that I nearly sigh in relief like a fucking weirdo before noticing the steam rolling through the cracks in the closed bathroom door. Finally, I tune my hearing to the noise of the shower that plays off the walls like white noise.

I'll never be able to explain why the fuck I open his bathroom door and waltz in like it's the most natural thing in the world, but that's what I do. The heated fog envelops me like a blanket as I pad with dirty socks into the massive space. I don't think he hears me since the shower is running and instead of sneaking up on him like a truly crazy person, I call out his name.

The glass shower door opens, and he sticks his head out.

"Fox?" Confusion laces through the name and I can't blame him. I don't even know what I'm doing.

The steamy glass door hides everything below his neck. Water drips from his hair to the overgrown stubble around his jaw, and covers the ink that slides down his skin like oil. His eyes widen as I pull my filthy, travel worn clothes over my head and shimmy out of my pants. My throat feels like all my insides are trying to come out of it, but I don't stop. Everything about this feels like the right thing to do. Not to mention that I'm literally dirty as fuck and could use a shower.

I'm waiting for him to stop me. To let out some sound of disgust and tell me to get the hell out of his bathroom, but he doesn't. He watches me with the stressed attention of someone who has been waiting for something their entire life. It makes me feel entirely vulnerable and utterly whole. Atlas's eyes drink me in and every single thought I've ever had about my body being flawed is banished by his hungry gaze and the lust that drips from his body.

He holds the shower door open as I walk to the entrance and I can finally see him in the way I've thought and daydreamed and wished for against all better judgment, and holy fuck, is he even more beautiful than I could have ever imagined. His body is like a marble sculpture of some long-dead Greek god. Except Atlas is even better than that because he's here, touchable, in all his tattooed glory. My eyes trace the images inked into his skin and catch on the water droplets that fall down pathways of strength and power. They lead my eyes all over his body, drifting toward the massive cock that sits between his legs, seemingly throbbing and begging for my attention.

"Should I ask what you're doing?" he rasps out, the broken sound of his voice sending heat through my shivering body.

I shake my head in silence. He holds his hand out to me as I step into the delicious heat of the shower, the origin of his winter scent spinning me into a cocoon of Atlas.

The hot water burns just the way I like and I close my eyes as it runs down my body, running my hands over my head to make sure every part of me is drenched. When I open them again, I find Atlas watching me. I swallow and look up at him, the consequences of my actions heavy in the air.

He grabs a container filled with swirling blue body wash and squirts it onto my chest. The bottle makes a farting sound that echoes off the shower walls. We both burst into laughter, and I'm grateful for the mood shift.

"I figure you're into that," he says with a smug grin.

"Fuck off," I laugh, lathering the soap on my body.

He does the same, but his eyes always drift back to me as bubbles foam over my breasts. Just how my eyes drift over the muscular v at his hips, drawing attention to his dick. Still hard. I'm pretty sure that thing would destroy me, but I'm willing to test the theory.

"I want to touch you," I say between heavy breaths, our eyes locked.

His throat bobs as he drinks in my lust-filled gaze. When Atlas grabs my hand and places it on his chest, it's like everything happens in slow motion. The way he grips my wrist—tightly, but with trepidation. The feel of his skin—hot and slippery against my palm. I swear I can hear the slow thud of our tandem heartbeats as the sound bounces off the glass and pebbles my skin. Part of me wants to close my eyes and soak in the feeling of being wrapped up in him, but I can't. I won't. I don't want to miss a single moment of whatever happens next.

Just as slowly, my eyes follow the trail of my palm down his chest until I'm grazing the soft skin around the base of his cock. It twitches in my grasp, sending a flutter straight to my clit. With a gentle motion, I rub up and down the length of him as a moan leaves his lips and seeps into my bones. He pushes me up against the shower wall, the freezing tile lighting up the skin of my back and ass. I move my eyes from the sight of him fucking my hand to his parted mouth as he leans his forearms above me.

"Fox," he grinds out.

We're close enough that my thumb brushes against my own abdomen with every stroke of my hand.

He grips my jaw and runs the pad of his thumb over my lower lip, letting it part. My grip on him tightens as he hisses through his teeth. His thumb is still tauntingly close to my mouth, so I reach out and nip it. A wicked smile passes over his lips. I want him to bite me again—my neck, my breasts, literally anywhere. His sharp canines, the ones that sometimes drip poison, gleam with promises of just that as heat pools between my thighs.

In fractured seconds, I see where this leads—the feel of his cock stretching me open, the taste of his tongue as I swallow every bit of him he's willing to give me. I don't want it to end, but I'm a masochist. A pathological over-thinker. The road my thoughts lead me down has the movements of my hand pausing, questions on my lips, memories brewing in the recesses of my mind.

At my slowed movements, his own expression changes. His body stills and we're touching a thousand miles apart. I swallow heavily, unsure if it's me or him that pulls away first. Before I know it, I'm watching him with profound disappointment as he rinses in the water one more time and steps out of the shower without a word. I want to stop him, to ask him the questions only he has the answers to, but my tongue is thick and heavy in my mouth.

Stupid. Stupid. Stupid.

I finish up, washing my hair and hoping he'll come back and fuck me against this wall, but he doesn't. It's probably for the best. Sleeping with him would have only made things messy. Still, I can't help but wonder why I'm so easy to walk away from? That maybe if I wasn't leaving ... if this wasn't temporary ... if maybe, for once, I could be the kind of girl that makes him stay.

With that thought, tears well up in my eyes, but I refuse to cry in his shower. How pathetic would that be if he came back and I was just bawling in here? I turn off the tap and step out to find a towel waiting on the counter for me. When I go into his room, it's empty, mirroring the feeling I have in my chest.

I tiptoe back into my room. The ache between my legs has dulled, but the image of him pressing up against me is seared into my brain. Getting dressed, I walk into the living room where everyone seems to be waiting for me. Pants runs between my legs, dragging a smile from my lips as I greet him and face the others.

"Good, she's here." Pippa says, leaning against one of the chairs by the fire. I can tell she's been pacing, waiting for the news.

Atlas gives me an unreadable look and begins telling everyone what happened, what I missed when I passed out, and where I went. When he asks me about my trip to the Backwood, I pause, searching through my foggy memories for something and coming up blank. I remember walking down a creepy path, but everything else is a blur. In fact, when I try to conjure up what happened, pain ricochets through my skull, and I collapse onto the couch next to Ellison.

"You okay, LH?"

"Yes," I mumble, pulling an eager Pants onto my lap and letting his plush fur slide through my fingers.

Everyone looks at me for a few seconds and then turns back to Atlas.

"The Blood Collector was cryptic and useless. There's a way to beat the queen, but she wouldn't tell me how ... only that it's possible."

"And did she say anything about how I could get back home?" I ask.

He looks at me for a while, a range of emotions passing in his gaze like he can't decide how to feel. "No, she wasn't sure," he says.

"Fuck," I mutter under my breath. I don't know if it's relief or anguish that washes over me. Maybe a little bit of both. A voice in my head tells me that I'm strong enough to face whatever awaits me here or at home. But that little bitch has lied to me before.

CHAPTER FIFTY

ATLAS

EVERYONE'S LOOKS OF DISAPPOINTMENT FEEL LIKE tiny daggers wedged into my heart. Especially Fox, because I'm lying to her. I'm lying to all of them and right now would be a really good fucking time to tell them everything, but I can't. I open my mouth and only silence seeps out.

"Anything else?" Pippa asks hopefully.

I shake my head. I need time to sort through this. Everyone gets up and begins chatting about the days spent apart. Ellison is launching into a detailed account of all the meals he made and which ones were his favorite to Idalia, who looks like she'd like very much to cut off her own ears, yet she stays and listens.

Emery scoots over to me on the couch. "Atlas, we tried. Don't beat yourself up over it."

I grunt in acknowledgment.

He looks at me like he knows there's more I'm not saying. Like he knows I'm a liar and a terrible brother.

"We'll figure something out," he says half-heartedly.

"Like what?"

"I mean, there's always running in there with an army and taking her out. She can't possibly stand against hundreds of us."

"There were a hundred people at that party, not including the staff." All dead.

Emery lets out a long sigh. "I'll never understand why we were the only ones to survive."

My jaw tightens.

Emery takes another thoughtful glance at me and then stands, patting me on the shoulder. "I love you, Atlas. We'll make things right ... or die trying."

I snort a laugh. "Love you, too."

When Emery leaves me alone, I head out of the house wanting to clear my head. It's been night for days. Endless shadows and cold winds. It seems fitting for the end of the world. I slump against the side of the Reign Tree that doesn't face the porch, hoping that it hides my silhouette so I can fucking think in peace.

Everyone will hate me when I tell them the truth, but that's probably for the best. I've never done a single thing to earn their trust or love. I've never been worthy of ruling over these people.

Loud as fuck footsteps that can only be Fox's crunch through the icy night air. Images of her naked flash through my mind. Of her hand around my cock and the feel of her magic in my veins. Pulling away from her was the hardest thing I've ever done (no pun intended). But even though I don't deserve it, I don't want the little pieces of herself she's willing to give away. I want all of her.

She sits next to me, close but not touching. "Hey."

I don't respond. Those visions I saw of us when our magic mixed together ... they can't be real. They were made to taunt me or be some kind of punishment because there's no world where I could ever be enough for her.

"I can go if you'd rather be alone," she murmurs.

"Please," I beg. "I can't be around you right now." The words cut through the air like a knife, and she recoils.

"Well, excuse me for giving a shit."

"Why do you?"

She stands, but hesitates. "Why do I what?"

"Why do you give a shit? After everything I've done to you. Why would you even bother trying to make me feel better?"

"I don't know."

"Yes you do," I taunt.

"No, I don't!"

"Think about it, Fox!" I stand to tower over her and she flinches away from me. "Haven't you wondered why you can't stay away from me? Why in the silence of a room your mind always wanders to me? Why seeing me hurt or in pain is nearly unbearable?" I don't know if any of that is true for her, but it's what she does to me.

Her eyes widen with horror. It's all the confirmation I need. "I've never had the best judgment. Chalk it up to horrible taste," she spits.

"Well, that might be true." The idea of her with someone else makes me want to rip this fucking tree from the ground. "But this time there's more to it than that."

"What the fuck is that supposed to mean?"

This should be a conversation to savor. A moment between us that's magical and good. Yet here I am yelling at her, proving to myself more and more that I should just walk away.

"Are you going to leave?" I ask instead of answering her question.

"Well, with all your *helpful* information, I wasn't planning on it anymore. Where the hell would I go, anyway?" She throws up her arms and replaces them on her hips, like she could rule the world with that motion alone.

"Anywhere but here!"

Fox's eyes narrow. "You'd like that, wouldn't you? For me to wander off and get killed by whatever the fuck roams around here."

The thought makes me sick, so I don't respond.

"I have half a mind to stay here just to fucking spite you. But unlucky for you, Atlas, I have nowhere to go." Her voice climbs a few octaves. "I can't go home, so you're stuck with me. You want me gone so badly? Find me a way back."

I reach out and grab her, pulling her close and pressing my lips against hers. She instantly melts into my arms, opening up for me to let my tongue wrap around hers. Her mouth on mine is like lava in my soul and I need to fucking burn. She tastes like every sinful thing I've ever done.

A soft moan escapes her as she leans farther into me and I grip the back of her head, letting the soft strands of her hair weave through my fingers. Fox runs my lower lip through her teeth and I nearly lose my fucking mind. The feeling of her magic hums in the air and then the wind is knocked out of my chest as I find myself on the ground with her standing over me. The anger pouring from her as she looks down on me makes me feel so small.

"What the actual fuck, Atlas?"

"You're my soulmate," I blurt. It's probably the worst way I could have possibly said it, and she blinks at me a few times.

"What!?" she screams.

I panic, scrambling for an explanation. Still too stunned by how well she's mastered her magic and how I ended up on the fucking floor. "In our world, there's one single individual that you're supposed to be with. Someone whose magic is cut from the same cloth as yours. Your equal in every way. Not everyone ends up meeting theirs, but they're out there, and you're mine."

Fox shakes her head in confusion. "Isn't that what Emery is?"

"Emery is a poor substitute for the real thing." I can hear him laughing in my head so I don't feel bad saying the words. "Üfren were created because whoever sits on the throne could never have a *selüm-ra* ... because no one else has the same level of magic."

"The ancient magic," she whispers.

"Yes, Fox, please. I can explain better, just ... that's why we're so drawn to each other."

She's quiet in her thoughts until she asks, "How long have you known?"

"A while. Since we made the tree ... I suspected it."

"And you still continued to treat me like garbage?" Her words carry so much hurt I can't even stand back up.

"I was scared," I say honestly. "I didn't want it to be true."

She scoffs at me. "How can it be? I'm human."

"I don't know," I tell her. "But it is. I feel it in every part of me. Don't you?"

"You're fucking insane." She turns to leave, and I stand in front of her before she can take a few steps.

"Fox, please. I'm *sorry*."

"Why are you telling me now?" Tears line her eyes and my heart cracks.

"Because every day I spend with you makes imagining days without you even harder. I could try with all my might to push you away, but the part of me that wants you will always win. I'm a coward and an asshole and I don't deserve you, but I need you to know the truth."

My little Fox sucks on her lower lip as a tear falls and I wipe it from her cheek. "Well, thanks for finally bringing me up to speed. I'm *so* sorry that you failed to fight your desire to be with me. That must have been really hard for you."

"Fox," I beg.

"How could I ever want to be with someone who never really wanted to be with me?"

"That's not it!"

She pushes past me and toward the house as I reach out and grab her wrist. "Let go of me," she snarls.

"Please, just let me explain," I say, releasing her.

"I really don't want to hear it, Atlas."

I might regret this, but I think I'll regret it more if I don't do it. Before she can take another step, I scoop her up and speed off to the lake. She's flailing and screaming the whole time, but she hasn't used her magic to fight me off, and that's all the encouragement I need.

When we reach the lake, I put her down and she pushes both of her hands against my chest, but it genuinely feels like she threw a pillow at me.

"Fuck you," she seethes.

"I'd love nothing more, Fox, but I think I owe you an explanation first."

Her glare almost makes me cower. "Why did you bring me out here?"

"Because sometimes you're too stubborn for your own good," I say with a smile. She doesn't return it. I grab her hand and take her to the water's edge before summoning my magic.

I fight my smile at her gasp as the water parts, allowing us to walk along the sandy lake bottom as the water turns to rising columns. I clear a path and then a circular spot in the middle of the lake. I add a few orbs of light in the water to create a glowing cave of liquid surrounding us.

"Atlas," she breathes, but I'm not fucking done yet.

The path disappears because I can't have my little Fox running off before she's heard everything I have to say. I place my hand in the sand until it grows and forms around my imagination—a throne made of soft silt. As I'm standing and offering her my hand in the seat before me, she snorts.

"I could make you a crown, but I don't think you'd appreciate the sand in your hair."

"I'm not a queen," she grumbles, but sits on the throne all the same.

"You are to me."

Fox rolls her eyes, but her anger has mostly faded.

"This is beautiful, but I'm still livid."

"But will you let me explain?"

The water roars around us.

"It doesn't appear I have much of a choice," she says, gesturing around. I swear a smile tugs at her lips as she says, "Let's hear it, Elf Boy."

I swallow my fear and kneel at her feet, taking her hands in mine as I look into her eyes. "When my parents died, I lost myself. It's such a long story, one I promise I will tell you if you want to hear it, but for now you'll just have to take my word for it when I say that everything bad that's happened since that night, I've earned.

"I pushed away the people who care about me the most and gave up the only real responsibility I ever had so that I could fuck around and drown in the darkness that consumed me. Before you came here, I was just pulling myself up from that place ... but I was doing a shit job. I've tried to be the male I want to be and I'm failing."

Her mouth parts, but she stays silent.

"But when you showed up, I think part of me knew I needed you even before we made the tree. That's why I followed you into town. I was always drawn to you. At first I saw you as a threat to everything we had built. At least, that's what I told myself. When I realized with certainty what you were to me, I was so scared I'd ruin you just like I've ruined everything else, so I tried to keep you away. Make you hate me so that I wouldn't drag you into whatever fucked up shit I've created. I told myself it was only the magic, it had nothing to do with you, but that was always a lie. You've had me from day one. With your smart-ass mouth and your ferocity. You were never afraid of me and saw the good even when I was pretty sure there wasn't any left. More importantly, you accepted all the bad with it.

"That's not magic, Fox, that's just *you*. You're strong and brave and funny. But even more than that, you've helped us. You've been selfless and caring. You've laughed at all of Elli's terrible jokes and put up with Idalia's snarky fucking comments. I wasn't sure you'd ever see me as anything but a monster."

Tears stream down her face, making her brown eyes sparkle in the light of the glowing orbs.

"I'm so sorry, Fox. I'm sorry for how much I fucked things up and for who I am. I want to tell you I'll be better, but I don't know how long that's going to take. What I can tell you is that I'm so fucking in love with you. With every flaw just as much as every beautiful thing about you."

Her voice is a whisper. "Atlas, you don't know me. You know nothing about my life before I came here."

"But I *do* know you. If our past is what defines us, then I'm fucked. But I don't think it does. I think it's who we are now that matters most. There's nothing you could tell me about your past that would make me love the person with me now any less."

"But I don't know *you*."

335

"I know," I say, breaking eye contact with her for the first time. "I'm not asking you to marry me or stay forever or anything like that. I'm just asking for the chance to let you get to know me. Just let me try … for whatever time we have left."

In her silence, I can hear both of our hearts beating the same broken rhythm.

"You can say no," I offer, my voice nearly breaking at the thought. "Tell me to fuck off and I will. Tell me that there's no way you could ever love me and I'll leave you alone. But if not, if there's any chance, then I swear to the fucking Realm I'll spend every day of my life proving to you that we're made for each other."

Her eyes never leave mine, but it feels like days, weeks, months, fucking years go by in a silence that rips me to pieces.

I squeeze her hand in a plea to say something … anything. "Tell me what to do, Fox. I'm not above begging."

She swallows as her lip quivers. "I think begging would be unbecoming on you, Elf Boy." And then she smiles. A smile I'll never forget. It's tattooed in my fucking memory bank as the most beautiful thing in the world.

Interlacing her fingers with mine, I lean in to wipe the tears from her eyes. "I don't care. I'd do it for you."

She leans forward and presses her forehead to mine. Our breath mingles, heating what little space there is between us. "I want to be happy with you, but I'm not sure I know how to do that anymore."

Whatever happened before she met me broke her. I knew it from the first time I looked in her eyes, but even the sharpest shard of her soul is more than I deserve.

"Me either," I admit. "But I think, maybe, we could learn how to do it together."

She nods her head against me, the tracks of her tears soaking into my flesh. "Together," she whispers as I pull her mouth to mine.

CHAPTER FIFTY-ONE

HARPER

TLAS'S MOUTH CLAIMS ME WITH TEETH AND TONGUE.
With heat and passion, taking everything I have, everything I am, and giving me himself in return. I happily
oblige, rolling my tongue in his mouth and biting his lip
until the tang of blood explodes through my tastebuds.
It's fucking ecstasy, and I need him more than I've ever needed anything in my life. As our magic mixes, his grip on me tightens until he
pulls me out of the sand throne and I wrap my legs around his waist.

Moaning into his mouth, my hands run up the corded muscle
of his neck and tug at the soft strands of his chocolate hair. I grind
against him, too high up on his waist to feel his cock and it's fucking
torture.

"Fox," he groans. "As much as I'd love to fuck you right here, I
think your first memory of me inside you should not include any
sand."

My laugh falls into his mouth, and I nod my head in agreement. But the thought of him doing just that has every muscle in my body tensing in anticipation.

"Let's go home," he says, running his tongue up the side of my neck and then speeding off into the night.

When we get to the front porch, I slam my mouth into his again as he leans me against the side of the house and rips my shirt open.

"Atlas!" I squeal as he pulls away from my lips to look at what he's uncovered. His devilish smile sends a shockwave through my whole body.

"Fuck me right here," I beg.

He almost looks like he's going to agree before Pippa snorts from the porch swing. "Please don't."

We both turn to look at her sitting with Pants and a book. I can feel my cheeks turn cherry.

"Ignore her," he mutters, but carries me inside the house.

"I love to say I told you so!" Pippa shouts, the end of her sentence being cut off by Atlas kicking through the front door.

"What the fuck—" Emery stutters as we burst into the house, both laughing.

I'm pretty sure my skin is still brick-red as I turn to him and open my mouth to apologize, very aware that I'm shirtless, but caring less and less by the minute.

Before I can get a single word out, Atlas grabs my face and turns it toward his. Lust, sticky and swirling, is the only thing glaring back at me in his earthy-brown eyes. It turns my insides to liquid. My heart beats at a rapid pace as it tries to avoid turning to mush with every-thing else.

"Don't look at him," he growls, continuing the walk to his bedroom.

I want to laugh, but he's dead serious. "Atlas, I'm not interested in—"

"I don't care," he interrupts. There's nothing kind in his voice. It's guttural and needy and it makes my head spin. "Until I have fully claimed every inch of your body, you're not going to so much as breathe in the direction of another male."

I swallow at the command in his voice. It's kind of ridiculous, but that doesn't stop electricity from rushing through me at the raw possessiveness exuding from him.

He turns the doorknob, and I nearly sigh in relief. The need to feel him inside me is building into something explosive. I'm like a feral animal as I tug at his shirt, but he only pins me to his chest tighter, chuckling against the shell of my ear.

"I'm gonna need to hear you say it, Fox." He nips my earlobe and slams me against the wall, kicking the door closed.

Air whooshes out of my lungs as I stare at the beast I've wrapped myself around. "Say what?" I ask on a breath.

He grips my jaw tightly. "Tell me who you belong to."

Part of me roars in defiance—I don't belong to anyone. But there's another part of me, one that craves him so deeply I'm nearly blinded by it. She's begging me to bow to him. To get on my knees and give him anything he wants.

"Fox," he warns. "I'm going to fuck you so hard against this wall that the only thing keeping you in place will be my cock shoved deep inside you, and my hand, wrapped tight enough around your throat that death will always be seconds away. But don't worry, baby. From now on, if you bleed, I bleed."

I'm a puddle. A fucking puddle of need as I whimper for him.

"Do you want that, Fox?"

I nod eagerly.

"Then tell me who you belong to."

"You," I whisper without missing a beat.

"Good girl," he growls. He tucks a strand of hair behind my ear and the adoration in his gaze has me fighting back tears. "Because I've been yours since the first time I looked into those pretty, brown eyes."

His mouth captures mine in a swirl of heat and desire, and I lose myself in the taste of him. Like a winter I've never experienced and a home I've never known. It's finding myself and the pieces I always thought were missing. But here it feels like there was never anything wrong with me; my soul was just waiting to find his.

Atlas places me down on the ground gently and looks me over. "Get naked," he commands.

I blink up at him.

"Fox, I swear to the fucking Realm if you don't do as I say, your clothes will be shreds you don't even recognize by the time I'm done with them."

I smile up at him and slowly shimmy out of my leggings. Taking my time pulling each article of clothing off as I watch him simmering with desire. When I'm finally naked, a sound of approval rumbles through him.

"Your turn," I say, gesturing at his fully clothed body.

He shakes his head as I frown.

Before I can blink, he has me pinned against the wooden bedpost, my hands high above my head as he carefully ties my wrists to the long piece of wood. The ropes aren't magic this time, they're dry twine that burns when I pull against them.

"Where the fuck did you even get that?" I wriggle against his grip.

"Such a demanding little Fox," he says, shaking his head with a feline smile.

My eyes widen as he lifts my body up until my pussy is level with his mouth. Magically, he tightens the rope around my hands so that I'm hanging from the bedpost like a carcass of meat. He wraps my legs around his neck and steps back slightly to get a full view of me.

"Fucking beautiful," he whispers as he spreads me open.

I can't even speak before his mouth is covering my clit and all of the need I felt explodes like a symphony of light in my mind as he rubs his wet tongue over the most sensitive parts of me, over and over. Sucking and biting and growling in pleasure as I writhe against the binds that keep me from touching him.

"You taste fucking divine, little Fox," he says into my flesh as I cry out. "You're so ready, aren't you?"

I let out a moan of desire as his tongue flicks artfully against me.

"Come for me, Fox. I want to taste every bit of you."

I want to savor this heady feeling, but I can't. I'm a slave to the desire that courses through me and when he sticks one finger inside me, I'm coming all over his tongue as he eagerly laps it up.

"Fuck," he groans, plunging a second finger in me and working me past my orgasm.

"Atlas," I beg.

He pulls away and gathers me in his arms, untying the rope. "What do you need, baby?"

"You," I murmur, fighting to remove his shirt.

He places me on the bed and pulls his shirt over his head, exposing bricks of muscle that fucking glow in the dim light of the bedroom. I fidget, trying to grab his pants, but he backs up and chuckles at me. "Don't worry, Fox, I'm going to give you what you want."

"Hurry," I grumble.

Just like I tortured him, he takes his time undoing his pants before pulling his boxers down and revealing the thing I so desperately crave. I saw him in the shower, felt him in the shower, but the size of him still surprises me. I bite my lip in need as he lines himself up with my center. Pushing in inch by agonizing inch, as my teeth sink into my flesh.

I cry out in pleasure and pain as he spreads me open. "Atlas," I groan.

"Fuck, your pussy looks so good wrapped around me," he murmurs as we both watch him plunge all of himself into me.

The full length of him takes my breath away, as my eyes roll back. Keeping his word, he scoops me up and presses my back against the wall, the cool surface bleeding into my hot flesh and making me even more sensitive to his touch. Wrapping his hand around my throat, he sets a slow and steady pace that has me tilting my head up and giving thanks to some unknown God for the pleasure that radiates through me. His palm tightens around my neck as he leans in and fucks me harder, muttering light obscenities into my ear as I fade from this world and into the next, before pulling me back and reminding me that I'm still alive.

341

Our mouths melt together again as Atlas pulls away from the wall, placing me back down on the bed. His cock pushing in and out of me is the sweetest punishment, and with every thrust, my eyes roll farther back into my skull. He pulls me close, opening my hips and seating himself even deeper inside me as I scream out in ecstasy.

"I'm gonna make this even better for you, little Fox."

"Not possible," I gasp.

He pulls away and looks me in the eyes. "Do you trust me?"

"Yes," I answer immediately. Without pretense, unconditionally, blindly, implicitly.

Atlas smiles, and it's not smug or devious. It's pure unbridled joy and my heart sings at the sight of it. He brings his palm to his mouth and slices into it with the sharp points of his teeth until blood drips freely over our bodies pressed tightly together. My mouth salivates at the sight of it, like I can see his magic glittering through it. He brings his bloodied palm to my mouth and I roll my tongue over his skin, coating my mouth in the tang of it, and pleasure shoots through me in fireworks of color. Bright and faded, clouded and sharp. He pumps in and out of me, growling in approval at the purely animalistic noises that come from me as I suck the blood from his wound, and his magic wraps itself around me. When some semblance of my consciousness comes back, I let go and tilt my neck in an offering to him.

"Fox," he whispers. My name on his lips is so filled with gratitude that I wrap my legs around him even tighter.

"You bleed, I bleed, right?" I say never breaking his gaze.

He nods silently and leans in, kissing the spot over my pulse before shoving his canines into my skin. The pain is sharp and blissful. A necessity for the pleasure that follows. We both moan in tandem as he fucks me harder and harder, taking my magic and filling me with himself. I can almost feel our bond like a tether, tightening and pulling us closer together. I'm whole and free and dying all at once.

"Atlas."

He lets up and licks over the bite wound on my neck, sending a shiver down my spine.

"Fuck," he mutters, barely getting the word out. "You taste like rain clouds and daisies, and it's fucking nirvana."

My breathing acceleratesas air evades me. An orgasm building in me like a monsoon. "Please," I murmur.

He laughs and the sound is so cruel it feeds the deep void inside me. "Begging already?"

I nod, unable to form words.

"I don't think so, beautiful. I'm not done with you yet."

He pulls himself out of me and I yelp in alarm, so close to the precipice of release. Atlas lifts my body so that I'm half sitting up against the bedframe, and sticks his thumb between my lips, prying my mouth open and shoving himself so far down my throat I don't even have time to process it. One hand bracing himself against the wall, the other squeezing my breast and rolling my nipple through his fingers. I suck on him greedily as he moves his hand from my chest and rolls his thumb over my clit. Slowly, he pumps two fingers into me. Moaning around him, digging my nails into the perfect sculpt of his ass, I look up at him, our eyes locking as he fucks my mouth.

"Tell me how we taste, baby."

My cries are muffled as he shoves himself deeper and deeper down my throat. Tears form at the corners of my eyes and fall down my cheeks before he groans and gags me with his length.

When he pulls out, I grip him. "So fucking good," I answer, eyelashes fluttering through tears as I look up at him.

He bites his fist and groans. "Fuck, I need to come inside you."

"Who's begging, now?" I tease.

He grins at me, eyes lidded and full of emotion. "Shut your beautiful, fucking mouth." In a precise movement, he flips me onto my stomach and lines my ass up with his dick before plunging into me again without warning. I cry out from the force of it, as my body molds around him.

Chest against my back, he leans in and wraps a hand around my throat, tightening just slightly as he brings my ear to his lips. "You should know that I'll always be fucking begging for you, Fox. That tight pussy and those pouty, little lips."

Pressure builds inside me, drowning out his filthy words with emotions I didn't even know I had. The world explodes into shades of red and black. I'm dragged through a dream of sound and color, each hue and harmony reminding me of how whole my soul feels intertwined with his. The orgasm tears through me, a sucker-punch to every cell, as I lose myself in everything that is Atlas and me.

My nails dig into his thighs as I ride through the aftershocks of pleasure. I'm vaguely aware that I'm screaming his name as he finishes inside me and the feeling of him coating my insides sends me over the edge again.

"That's it, baby. I want to feel you squeeze every last drop from me."

At his final thrust, I collapse into a heap of flesh on his bed as he strokes my hair, my back, cupping my ass and pulling himself out of me. I can't move. I'm a glistening puddle of lust that needs to soak into his skin and live inside him forever.

Atlas turns me over so that I'm panting up at him as he smiles and kisses me deeply. "Whoever you were before you met me doesn't matter anymore, because I'm going to ruin you, Fox. I'm going to take any piece of you that thought you didn't deserve every fucking star in the sky and force it to believe in the queen you truly are. And when you deem me worthy, I'll embed myself so deeply into your soul that your heart won't remember how to beat without mine."

Every sweet promise is laced with pain. His words are already doing what he intends: cracking the plastic facade I've placed around myself and sucking out bits of me that usually crumble at the slightest touch. He's helping me forge myself into something greater, not for his own benefit, but for mine. I'll happily take the misaligned pieces of him and melt them into my own. It might not be perfect, but it'll do.

CHAPTER FIFTY-TWO

ATLAS

FOX SNORES QUIETLY NEXT TO ME, THE STEADY RHYTHM of her breaths matching the beat of my heart. I run my fingers through her hair, savoring the memory of the many times this evening I pulled it as she screamed my name. I told her that I'd ruin her, but the truth is my little Fox has ruined me so thoroughly I hardly recognize myself.

Thank fuck for that. I'd happily trade all of me in for someone worthy of her, but I know it's not that simple. I know I'll have to work to become a male she can be proud to link herself to and I'm ready to do it, grateful for the opportunity she's giving me.

I kiss her head lightly and trail my fingers down her back for what feels like the first time tonight. I'll never get sick of the feeling of her skin beneath mine. The words *"Die Young and Save Yourself"* are written in thin vertical letters down her spine. My gut clenches at the idea, wondering if she's some kind of wraith that left her world to play in mine. I don't care what she is, I'll keep her here forever if that's what she wants.

Fox stirs beneath my strokes and I trail kisses down her cheek, along her neck, pulling her into me and breathing in the scent of her, now mixed with mine to make something I might always have a hard-on for.

"Go back to sleep," I murmur against the planes of her body.

Ignoring my request, she turns around and nuzzles into my chest. "What are you doing?"

"Thinking about you," I answer honestly.

She likes that response, sitting up on one elbow and cocking her eyebrow at me. "Oh?"

"What does your tattoo mean?" I ask, tracing the curve of her lips, pink and plump and so fuckable.

"I told you, they're song lyrics." She runs a hand down my chest, waking up every inch of my body. I know she's deflecting.

"But what do they mean to you?" I press.

She sucks her lower lip in that innocent way that drives me wild. She's anything but harmless. "Before I came here, I tried to commit suicide," she confirms and my gut flips, turning and twisting, like it's a towel I'm trying to squeeze the agony out of.

"Why?" I growl. I'm ready to find a way back to where she came from just so I can tear through every person who ever hurt her.

She backs away from me. "What do you mean, why?"

Her anger only causes mine to boil harder. "I mean, why would you ever do that ... what would make you feel like that was your only option?"

She stares at me in disbelief, and it catches me off guard.

"No one hurt me, Atlas. I'm just fucked up. My mind is sick and wrong and broken." She shakes her head and slinks out of the sheets, pacing in front of the bed. "That's the thing. My life was good. Nothing truly bad has ever happened to me and I just gave up when things got hard. It's pathetic and weak." She pauses her movements and looks at me, tears streaming down her face. She couldn't be more wrong.

I reach for her, pulling her into my lap. "Hey, hey, hey," I chant, as if my words can soak up her sadness. "Listen to me." Grabbing her chin between my thumb and forefinger, I tilt her gaze to meet mine. "No matter what happens in life, the darkness we battle inside ourselves may always be our strongest opponent. But that never makes you weak, beautiful.

"It makes you a fighter. Maybe right now you're broken, but so what? That's okay, remember? It just means you're building yourself into something better, something stronger." I repeat the words she told me not too long ago. "And all those sharp pieces, all the jagged edges, they're what I love most about you. Every time I touch you, I bleed."

Her eyes, glistening with moisture, widen, and her brow furrows. "And that's a good thing?"

I smile at her and rest my forehead against hers, nodding my head. "It's the best thing," I breathe. "It reminds me that I'm still alive."

A sob escapes her as she wraps her arms around my neck, and I pull her close. I know I can't take away her pain, but I'll weather through it by her side. Kissing the top of her head, I trail my mouth down the side of her face, whispering my love for her against her skin.

Her crying ebbs and she pulls away to sit on the sheets next to me. "Do you think it will ever stop? The battle against the darkness?"

Fuck. I want to tell her yes. I want to tell her I'll protect her from anything, but there are some things even I'm incapable of rescuing her from. "Maybe, but maybe not. It might leave and come back. It might always be present. But you taught me something important about that Fox."

She raises an eyebrow in question.

Slipping my finger beneath a tear-soaked strand of hair, I tuck it behind her ear. "That life isn't about battling that darkness. Even though some days it may be all you can do to push through to the next sunrise. Life is about finding those pieces of light, the ones that surprise you, and enjoying them while they last. Keeping that warmth going to fuel your fight. If you forget those moments are there, that's when you've lost."

She smiles at me and I'm not sure I'll ever get used to the beauty of it. "That's very profound of you," she says in a mocking tone, but I know she's being sincere. "Is this the part where you tell me I'm the light?"

Leaning back on my elbows, I grin at her. "Baby, you're the fucking fire that fuels my soul."

Fox squeals as I pull her on top of me so that she's straddling my torso with her knees. When she leans down to capture my mouth in hers, the dark strands of her hair create a curtain around us.

I cup her face between my palms. "You may think you're too familiar with darkness," I tell her. "But I'm grateful for that. Without you, who would have guided me out of it?"

"You're a better male than you give yourself credit for," she says, leveling me with a stare that nearly stops my fucking heart.

"You haven't heard my secrets yet," I tell her.

Fox rolls her hips against me again, a groan leaving my lips at the lust pooling beneath her gaze. "They won't change my mind. I'll still believe in you enough for both of us."

"Don't say that until you've heard them." I try desperately to focus on her words instead of the image of her coming all over my cock, but it's too much. I pin her under me and press my hand against her throat, squeezing until her eyes roll back as I rock my hips against the wetness between her thighs. "I'll make you a deal, little Fox."

She lets out a whimper of agreement.

"I'll tell you all my secrets, but in return I want your tight, little cunt weeping for me."

"It is," she rasps. She's not wrong, but that's not what I'm talking about.

"No, Fox," I say, leaning into her ear, giving her just enough air and then clamping back down on her windpipe. "When I'm done, I want to be flooded with your desire."

"I don't ... I've never done that before," she whines, catching on quickly to what I'm asking for.

"You will, baby. Maybe then you'll see just how much we were made for each other."

"Deal," she chokes, and I drive myself inside her.

Even after a night of being inside her, it still takes my breath away—the way she molds around me like she really was made for me, hot and needy. I don't know where she came from or how she got here, but if I have any say in it, I'm never letting go.

Her breathy moans fill the space as the bed smacks rhythmically against the wall. If I was a nicer friend, I'd feel guilty for keeping everyone in the house awake with our fucking, but I'm not nice. I'm a fucking asshole and somehow I'll have to find a way to make my little Fox love me anyway.

We're both spent from going at it over and over, but I'm going to keep her in this bed until neither one of us can move or starvation takes us both, whichever comes first. Her overstimulated pussy pulses around the length of me already, but I'm not even close to being done with her. In this moment, her body is mine to command.

Slowing my pace and spreading her open, I nearly lose myself in the sight of us coming together. My cock has never been harder as it drives into her and becomes coated with her, the wetness an echo to our lovemaking.

"Yes, yes, please," she cries beneath me.

"Please what, baby?"

"Please let me come," she begs.

I flip her over, kneeling on the bed and seat her back on my cock. Pressing her back against my chest, I grip her throat again. I love the feel of it, so fragile and breakable in my grasp. I move her legs so that each one of hers is on the side of mine; she's spread so wide I can tell it's painful. Good.

My dick arches into her and hits that spot I now know she likes. Bouncing her up and down on me lightly, she pants heavily, and whimpers helplessly as I bring her to the precipice, but hold back assaulting her enough to make her erupt.

"Atlas," she growls, frustrated by my teasing.

"We have a deal, Fox. You can come, but you better do it right. I want you to shower me with it."

"I can't," she breathes.

"You can," I encourage. "I'm gonna help you." With those words I take two fingers and shove them into her mouth, and she sucks them eagerly as I groan against her ear. "Such a good fucking girl."

She moves to rub her clit and I grab both her wrists with one hand, pinning them behind my neck, her back arching against my chest like a bow.

"No touching," I snarl.

Removing my fingers from her mouth, I plunge them into her pussy, pressing them against my cock. She cries out at the pressure and I can barely move them.

"*Fuck*, Fox. You're so fucking tight."

I wrap my other arm around her waist and use it as leverage to drive myself into her, fucking her with my fingers and my dick. She's shaking, convulsing against me, curses and moans leaving her filthy little mouth. Her arms, bent over my shoulders, are digging into my back and I can smell the blood her nails are drawing.

I close my eyes against the urge to paint her in my come and rub her clit with my thumb instead. "Do you want to please me, beautiful?" I whisper into her ear. I can barely contain the need in my voice. Her body is like a harp and every string I pluck makes a sound that will bring me to my fucking knees.

"Yes, yes, yes," she chants between gasps.

"Show me how much, little Fox."

I'm gonna lose my fucking mind, but her body must take notice. It wants me to know it now submits to me, because when she cries out and tightens against everything I have inside her, a flood of desire pours into my lap, soaking into the sheets, and the feeling of it breaks my will. I pull my fingers out of her and lean back on my knees so that her spine falls flat against my chest. Removing my cock, I flip her on her back as I come all over the planes of her stomach and breasts. Streams of me coat my hand as I pump whatever's left of me onto her, the surge of her arousal mixing in. Fox pants against me, both of us staring at the canopy of the bed. I slap my cock against her pussy and she laughs.

"I knew if I asked nicely you'd find a way to do it," I tell her.

She rolls over and pins me beneath her, come dripping down her stomach. "You never ask nicely, but I like it anyway," she giggles and kisses me. The sound of her laughter is like a river in my soul, rushing through and smoothing out the barbed crags.

I grab her mouth and savor the taste of her, hoping she'll still feel that way when I give her my whole truth.

CHAPTER FIFTY-THREE

HARPER

I STRETCH MY ARMS AND FEEL THE EMPTINESS OF THE BED. Panic settles into my cobwebbed breathing. I can't help but wonder if everything that happened last night was a dream, but then I catch the sound of the faucet running and notice the bathroom door is shut. Atlas walks out a few seconds later and catches my worried stare. He's a ridiculous creation. So much so that the image of him with his disheveled hair and five o'clock shadow, the ridges of muscle that ripple over his body, his square jawline that's in a perpetual state of tightness, adds to the part of me that questions my sanity.

We stay frozen like that for a few minutes as reality bleeds into the bubble we created last night. Today's a new day and with the information he armed me with, I know we have a lot of fucking work to do.

"You're upset," he finally says, breaking the silence.

I shake my head. "Not at all."

I can see that he's scared. Afraid just like I am that our declarations from last night might look different in the light of a new day. "What I told you ..." he starts.

But I peel the covers off, taking steps toward him and press my body into his. My nipples harden as our flesh meets, and he wraps his arms around me. "I meant what I said last night, and I hope you did, too."

It's true. So fucking true it hurts. After he shared the shadows of his past with me, I curled into his lap and sat there for what seemed like hours. No half-assed "it will be alright" or easy placations. Neither one of us is that type of person. We know that the world is dark, that happy endings are possible but never promised, that our time together could be limited. I sat with him like that until his breathing eased, until his grip tightened around me and our bodies felt like they had become one.

I'm here, I told him. That's all I can really give him anyway.

He squeezes me tight and kisses the top of my head. "There's one more thing."

My body goes rigid in his arms.

"I lied when I said the Blood Collector didn't tell me how you could get home."

I pull away immediately and frown, confusion and anger warring inside me like old friends. They're pushing back the feelings of comfort he had wrapped around me and laughing in their faces. *I told you so*, my subconscious screams.

"Fox, stop. Just listen."

My flight mode kicks in and I glance around the room for my clothes. It feels like the walls are closing in and I nearly cry out in frustration when I remember he tore my shirt into pieces.

"What are you doing?" he asks, gripping my arm.

"Leaving," I murmur. I wish I could come up with something more witty, but my mind is too busy sifting through the surge of emotions.

"You're not even going to listen to what I have to say? What the fuck happened to everything you just told me?" His voice raises with each word.

"That was before you lied to me. You said you'd tell me everything," I bite back.

"I'm trying! I'd do it if you just fucking stopped for one second." He picks me up and pins me to the wall. "Stop running from me." His gaze is so searing I feel stripped down to the basest parts of me—blood vessels and connective tissue, a beating heart and a broken soul.

I was wrong. I'm not made for this. I don't think I'm strong enough to even defend myself. How could I ever promise him that I'd be someone he could rely on?

Give up, give up, give up, my mind screams, drawing me into its familiar hold.

I wiggle in his grasp, even though it's futile. He's an immovable force. The perfect anchor.

"I've had time to come to terms with how much my feelings toward you scare me. I'm terrified, Fox. I'm so worried I'm going to fuck it all up. That I'll fail to protect you, or you'll take off your rose-tinted glasses and finally see me for the monster I am, but I don't care. I'll risk every bit of my pride for the chance to be with you. I realize you might need the time to process it too, but I'm not going anywhere." He smiles down at me with his perfect fucking teeth and his perfect fucking lips and his poisonous sincerity.

"You lied," I manage to choke out.

He stares at the wall next to my head. "It's more complicated than that."

"Well, I'm fucking waiting."

"If I let you go, are you going to sprint out of here?"

"You'd catch me anyway," I say with an eye roll.

He grins again, backing away. "Damn fucking right I would."

My shoulders drop as the fight begins to burn out of me. I still want to run, my mind urging to take any excuse to get the fuck out of this situation. It feels permanent and permanence means I'm stuck.

"The druid told me that you possess the ability to turn back time."

"How?" I think back to all of our training. I'm getting better at controlling just how much time I pause, but I've never been able to do anything remotely close to that.

"She said with a gift from the Realm, but who knows what the fuck that means."

Memories come rushing back to me in torrents and waves. I nearly collapse under the weight of them. A tunnel and drink and chest of silly clothes. Choices I was forced to make and the feeling of being lost. I gasp, covering my mouth as my mind remembers.

"What?" he asks in a panic.

I ignore him, rushing over to my pants and pulling out the pocket watch I always carry with me. "This," I say, handing it to him.

His face drops and my anxiety builds. "Where did you get this?" he says in a low voice.

"You know what it is?"

"Where did you get this?" he repeats, trying to open it and meeting my gaze.

"When I arrived ... I ... I found it."

I tell him about the underground tunnels. About the hospital and Pants and all of the pieces I can remember. It's not everything, but it'll do. At the end of it, he sits back on the bed, a look of disbelief painting his features as he stares at me standing before him.

"The Realm really did bring you here."

I chew on my lip. I don't like the way he's looking at me like I'm imaginary. Like I'm something magical. I'm not ... I'm just Harper and I made no real decision to come here.

"Can you open it for me?" He hands me back the pocket watch, failing to open it himself.

I easily flip the cover, furrowing my brow as I hand it to him.

"It's spelled just for you to look at," he says, staring down at it. "It's just a plain watch face to me. What does it look like to you?"

I explain its appearance, the navy blue face and the glimmering numbers that count to twelve. The hour hand now sits in between the one and the two. "What is it counting?"

"Months," he whispers.

"Months until what?"

"I don't know, but I have one too." He moves below the bed and pulls out a box, handing me the pocket watch from inside and sitting back down. I turn the cool metal surface over in my hand and try to open it, but it stays closed. "In this world, true promises are bound by magic. When the contract is created, a time limit is often put on them. It could be until the day you die, or hours from that moment. Some people report clock faces changing with fate ... never knowing if the numbers represent months or years or centuries. They're promises only made with serious intent and an agreement that must be carried out."

"But I never agreed to anything," I tell him.

"Maybe not with words. Maybe not in a way you recognized, but you did."

I don't like a single thing he's saying, it's making my stomach twist. "How do I know what it is?"

He shrugs. "I don't know. I don't know how you could use it to reverse time, either. I've never heard of that being a possibility. Then again, everything surrounding you is a mystery to me."

"Why did you keep this from me?"

Atlas pulls me into him, hands on my hips so that I'm standing between his legs. "If you go home by turning back time, I don't know what that means for us. Does it change time here? Does it erase everything you've done to help us? Will you ... will you even remember ..."

He doesn't finish the sentence, but I already know what he was going to say. Will I remember Calamity? Will I remember him?

"I don't want to keep you from going home, Fox. If that's what you really want. I just ... I needed time to process it. It's a decision that affects everyone I love and one you can only make once ... or so I was told."

If I can find a way to turn back time, maybe I can go back home before everything went to shit. Before the hospital and the drugs and the bad decisions. Atlas looks up at me, waiting for an answer.

"I understand why you hid this from me," I admit. Even I'm not sure what to do with this information.

"Do you ... do you want me to help you figure out how to do it?"

The breath leaves my lungs all at once and feels like it won't ever return. How could I go home and leave this all behind? How could I possibly stay here? It all feels impossible. The decision is too big for me to carry. I lean forward and press my forehead to Atlas's.

"I don't know," I say honestly.

He kisses me. First gently and then with fervor, wrapping his hand in my hair and pulling me close. "When you decide, I'll support whatever decisions you make," he whispers against my lips. A single tear drops down my cheek and his mouth is covering it instantly, tasting the salt of my sadness. "I need every bit of you, but I'll do everything in my power to never make you feel trapped again."

My arms wrapped around his neck hold on tighter, like I might disappear right now before I'm ready.

"Do you understand, Fox? As long as I'm breathing, you'll never have to worry about being stuck in that forest ever again. I'll always find you. And then I'll burn it down and take you home."

"I'm holding you to that, Atlas ..." I pause.

"What?" he asks, puzzled.

"I don't even know your last name."

"Does it matter?"

I push away from him. "Uh, yeah dude. It kind of matters. You're promising me forever, and I don't even know your last name." I run my fingers through my hair, trying not to freak out. Again.

Atlas's laugh brings me back to him. "I didn't realize it's so important. It's also such common knowledge I just didn't think to tell you."

Glancing around the room, I return my gaze to him. "Well, what is it?"

"Ravenwood."

"Ravenwood," I repeat, rolling the word around in my mouth. And then, like the stage-five clinger that I am, I think, *Harper Ravenwood*. I'm preparing to write it down in every journal I own.

He raises an eyebrow. "Is that good enough for you?"

"I suppose," I say haughtily. Running my hands through the dark strands of hair that feel so good against my skin, I'm overwhelmed with an unfamiliar feeling.

"I'm glad I don't have to change it," he says jokingly. "Anything else you want to know? Favorite color, shape, animal? What foods I like?"

"Favorite animal is obviously a fox," I say with an exaggerated eye roll. "And I'm guessing you'll eat almost anything."

Atlas grins. "You'd guess right."

"And these," I say, tracing my finger over his tattoos. "I want to know what they all mean."

"I drew most of them," he murmurs.

"You draw?" I don't know why I'm surprised, but I am.

He nods nervously, and it's so unlike him I can't help but smile. "I used to."

"There's a lot to learn about you." I press my lips to his. "I want to know everything, Atlas."

"I want to know everything, too," he says, kissing me back. "Good thing we have some time."

"You need to tell Pippa what happened that night. What really happened. She loves you so much, it will be okay."

"I know," he says, but there's so much fear in his voice. I know I'm catching glimpses of who he used to be, this person Emery and Pippa always talk about. I also know that version of Atlas is gone, he's been molded into someone different. Someone who is a little less polished and a lot more fractured. Someone whose soul is made to match my own.

"I'll be there with you, no matter what."

There I go again, making promises. I can't even help myself. All I want is for him to be happy, to be less burdened, and feel whole again. Something tells me I'd sacrifice anything to make that happen. It's not bravery, but it'll do.

CHAPTER FIFTY-FOUR

ATLAS

THE NIGHT BEFORE THE PARTY

Readying myself for bed, I gaze into the mirror at my reflection, seeing more than just the physical parts of me, and trying with all my might to see the male I want to become. The tattoo running down my right arm brings back a memory that makes me smile. The panther that stretches with a lazy roar across my side is a reminder to never take things too seriously. I run a hand through my hair, ruffling it messily, and head into my room just as a knock sounds.

"Come in," I call out, hoping for Elrora. She hasn't been here in days.

My mother strolls into the room like the queen she is as I prepare for the opposite of what I was hoping.

"Atlas," she says with a warmth that still has a way of worming into my heart.

I pull a shirt over my chest and walk over to hug her. She's dressed in a deep blue gown with a sheer cloak. Her light brown hair reminds me of Pippa's as it rolls down her back. I'm always astonished by her beauty. She looks my age even though she's about a hundred years older than me.

"Mother," I answer, gently kissing her cheek.

She walks over to the couch on the opposite side of the room and sits on the edge, patting for me to join her. "I wanted to speak with you about something."

"What kind of something?" I ask, joining her. I sink into the plush cushion and lean back.

Turning to me, she smiles. "About matters of the heart."

My pulse quickens as my eyes widen.

"I spoke to your father, gently reminding him that his mother wasn't of noble blood."

"She wasn't?" I'm genuinely surprised.

My mother shakes her head, her hazel eyes boring into me and seeing me for who and what I am. "She was the daughter of a merchant. Her family came here during a supply drop. The ship had to dock for several days due to a storm and since her father was one of the more wealthy merchants, he was invited to an event being held at the castle that evening. Your grandfather saw her and the rest is history."

A smile crosses my face.

"Bring the girl tomorrow. I'm dying to know the female who has won my son's heart. If you love her, we will too."

I nod. "I know you will."

My mother leans forward and kisses my forehead. My heart is too full to be embarrassed as I embrace her tightly and she laughs softly.

"You are going to be a wonderful king someday, Atlas." She pulls back and looks at me. Really looks at me. "You have the warmest heart and the kindest soul. Never let anyone tell you to be something different, including yourself."

She places a gentle hand to my chest. "I love you, My Prince." Somehow she makes the title seem anything but political.

"I love you too," I tell her. Looking down at my hands, I frown. "I said horrible things to Father."

She ruffles my hair. "Apologize after the party tomorrow. He loves you more than you know."

"I was thinking about what you told us. About breaking down the Blood Collector's barrier with Harper and your magic," Torin says, staring at me across the table as we wait for Ellison to serve breakfast.

I don't want to hear the next words that are going to come out of his mouth. I already know them. I should have thought of them myself.

"What if you tried to do that with the spells she has blocking the castle," he suggests.

It's too dangerous, I want to say. Or perhaps, *fuck no*, would be a more appropriate response.

Harper hears it and her head perks up. My little Fox is impulsive. It's one of the many things I love about her, but right now I want to pick her up, take her back into my room, and seal her away from the rest of the world. The thing is, I promised her she'd never feel trapped, so I keep my fucking mouth shut.

"Atlas?" she asks me with excitement in her eyes. You'd think she was asking permission to go on a shopping spree. For the Realm, does she have a fucking death wish? Don't answer that.

"It's worth a shot," Pippa says before I can even agree.

"She's not ready, she can't fight." I know she'll hate me for saying the words, but it's true.

"Excuse me?" she snaps, but I'm ready for it.

"Baby, you can run circles around most people with your magic, but you still can't dodge a hit for shit. No more lies, remember?" I give her a shit-eating grin and she glares at me.

"So she'll use her magic to escape immediately after the barrier has been knocked down," Pippa argues.

"She can't escape with her magic if it's all drained from taking the barrier out." Not to mention this weird affliction she has with disappearing into the Backwood. I shake my head. "She needs more training."

"I don't think you get to make that decision," Fox states.

"As the elf training you, I think I'm exactly who gets to make that decision. You're not ready, Fox." I know this is a losing battle, but I have to try.

She stands from her seat and comes to the side of my chair, wrapping her arms around my neck and enveloping me in her scent. Resting her chin on my shoulder she says, loud enough for the room to hear, "I hope you're as quick a learner as you are pretty because I'm going to tell you something I need you to remember—no one tells me what to do. The more you try, the more I'll push."

If this weren't her life on the line, I'd bend her over this table and punish her for being so damn defiant. "Two weeks," I mutter. "Two weeks of training all day—magic and fighting. No fucking around." I crane my neck away from her to look in her face. She's smiling at me with that devious glint.

"Starting now?" she asks eagerly.

"Yes, after breakfast." I pull her onto my lap as she squeals. The happiness in her tone makes my chest feel tight.

"I'm not sure what's worse," Torin says to Pippa. "When they were pretending *not* to make googly eyes at each other or this." He gestures to me and Fox, and Pippa smiles. My happiness is hers. I want to freeze this moment and live in it forever. I'd even tolerate fucking Torin being here.

"You knew?" Fox looks between us all for reassurance.

"Honey, everyone knew," Torin drawls.

Pippa purses her lips. "We thought it would be best if Atlas was the one who told you ..."

I'm not sure how Fox will feel, but I instinctively tighten my hold on her.

She rubs her lips together like she's trying to moisturize them. "I guess I can't blame you for Atlas's shortcomings."

"That's good because he has quite a few of those," Torin says. His reading glasses fall down to the bridge of his nose, and it makes him look like such a pretentious asshole. I'm pretty sure his eyesight is just fine.

Fox laughs loudly and a little forced.

"Be nice," Pippa chides.

"The fact that he's not fighting the urge to strangle me is new," he remarks. He's wrong. The image of me snapping his neck replays over and over in my vision.

I don't catch Pippa's response because Fox leans in and whispers in my ear, quiet enough that the words are just between us. "No fucking around?" She pulls away and frowns, batting her eyelashes at me in a comical way.

"No fucking around," I murmur to her. "I'm serious, Fox."

She leans back in, pressing her tits against my chest. I can feel her nipples harden at the touch and she wraps her arms around my neck. "But what about fucking?" Dirty little minx.

I peel her arms off my neck and flip her so that her back is pressed against my chest. Pulling her close, I speak slowly into her ear. "You need to behave."

No one seems to notice our little interaction as they discuss plans, or maybe they're just choosing to ignore us. Either is fine by me.

Fox not-so-subtly wiggles her ass over my hardening cock. With one arm, I grip around her stomach, pinning her to me. My other hand grips her thigh, hard enough to bruise and hopefully enough to remind her what I'm capable of.

"Behave, little Fox, or I'm going to punish you and I promise it won't be in the way you want."

I can see the frown forming on her face, puzzlement furrowing her brow as her mind works through my threat. She places both hands on my thighs and backs into me slowly, rolling her body over my dick.

I chuckle quietly. "You asked for it."

"When do I get it?" she asks, chewing her bottom lip. I want to pull it through my teeth until her blood is dripping down both our mouths.

"When I decide to fucking give it to you." She's a brat and I'm already wrapped around her perfect finger.

"Ready!" Elli shouts from behind the counter.

Fox rubs her ass over my crotch one more time and lets out a breathy moan. This time it's loud enough for the others to pick up and Pippa rolls her eyes.

She hops out of my lap and waltzes over to get food. Naturally, I can't stand because my dick is fucking hard and the sweats I'm wearing might as well be a stage with the spotlight focused on my erection. Sighing, I run my fingers through my hair. She's so going to regret this.

CHAPTER FIFTY-FIVE

HARPER

I BREATHE IN AND RUN, LIFTING MY KNEES HIGH TO MY chest to avoid every obstacle laid out before me in the armory. Third times the charm, right? *Wrong.* I trip on the next rung and fall flat on my face. The last pole I had to dodge hits me in the gut. I'm pretty sure my spleen has ruptured. Wheezing on the floor, I'm relieved that no one was here to see that.

"Ouch," Idalia says.

Wrong again.

I open my eyes, squinting against the pain, and stare at her. I hope I look scary, but curled up on the floor with straw matted to the sweaty parts of my body, I somehow doubt that's the vibe I'm giving off.

"Can I fucking help you?" I say between searing bouts of pain.

She gives me a tight-lipped smile. "Sorry, I'm not here to argue."

"How refreshing."

Her eyes gloss over the obstacle course. "You're much better than me, believe it or not."

Guess which option I choose.

Idalia takes my silence as her cue to keep talking and I'm still too weak to stand or protest. "I haven't trained to fight since I was younger, and my magic isn't even very strong."

I put an arm under my chest and try to push myself up. I might be shocked by her words if I wasn't focusing on breathing. Pushing up, I latch onto a practice dummy because this elf bitch is still just standing there, staring at me. She's not even smirking. There's not an ounce of satisfaction on her face like I'd expect.

"By all means, don't help," I say, gripping the dummy's wooden arm.

"Oh!" Her surprise seems genuine as she reaches out to help me, but it's too late. I'm standing. So instead, she just awkwardly puts a hand on my arm and pulls up.

Nope, that's as fucking high as I go.

I wiggle out of her grip, and we look at each other. Silence consuming the room like a poisonous fog. I hate awkward silences.

Breaking eye contact, I pluck the hay off my body. "Do you need me for something?"

"I wanted to ... I haven't ... I didn't know."

My eyes shoot up to her at her stuttering words. I've never seen her as anything but a calm and collected bitch. "Didn't know what?"

"About you and Atlas ... when we slept together ... I didn't know."

I'd love to say I'm not petty enough to remember that little fact, but I'm tired of being anyone but me, so here's the real truth—I think about it every time I look at her. Petty bitch.

"Good to know."

I believe her. And I'm grateful for the admission.

"So you forgive me?" Her eyes light up with hope and I'm thrown for a fucking loop.

"Why does it matter to you? You haven't exactly been the friendliest elf to me."

Idalia sucks on her lower lip. "Because even if I didn't know that you two were *selüm-ra,* I wasn't blind to how much attention he was paying you and it just feels wrong, okay?" Her hands meet her hips and her expression turns back into indifferent shrew.

"Fine. You're forgiven." I walk away from her, fiddling with the weapons. "It's not like we were together at the time and I know what it's like to sleep with someone just because you need to feel seen."

Was that nice, or did I just insult her? I peak over my shoulder to see which way she's choosing to interpret it, but her face is unreadable.

"Well, it didn't really work. He hates me and I can't say I feel much better about it."

I turn around and face her, leaning against the weapons table. "Pretty sure that kind of thing never really works in anyone's favor."

Idalia smiles. Actually smiles at me. It's genuine and warm and it makes her look even more beautiful.

"You'd think I'd learn by now that sex isn't going to fix all my problems, but here we are," she says shrugging her shoulders like we're talking about the weather, not her fucking my ... my ... whatever he is.

I can't help but laugh and she joins me.

"Really, I'm just *sorry*. I shouldn't have been so territorial," she says.

I can't even blame her. I like to think I'm better than that, but who fucking knows.

"You're forgiven," I repeat, this time really meaning it.

"Great, well, maybe I could come down here and train with you sometime? I could use the practice."

I sip from my water bottle to buy me time to think about my answer. The bottle is pink with a cartoon creature that looks similar to a porcupine, but its head is much more like a frog. Apparently it's called a pudgy.

Emery got it for me a few weeks ago. When I stared at it and then back at him, I said, *Thank you?* like I wasn't really sure what else to say, because I wasn't. Ellison ran over and grabbed it out of my hand, cackling at the image, and I frowned as they both laughed at something I didn't understand. "It's your derax," Emery said through a fit of giggles. So offensive for so many reasons, but I couldn't help smiling at the gesture.

"Sure," I end up saying to Idalia.

"Great. I was—"

"It's time, Fox." Atlas sing-songs the words as he walks down the stairs, stopping in his tracks when he sees Idalia.

The room's weirdness level shoots off the graph as the three of us all exchange looks.

I. Hate. Awkward. Silences.

"Let's just point out the elephant in the room," I say casually.

"What's an elephant?" they both ask.

I wave my hand dismissively. I'll never get used to the inconsistencies of our worlds. "Doesn't matter. The point is that you two have fucked," I say, pointing between them. "And we have fucked." I gesture at Atlas and I. "It doesn't have to be weird if we don't want it to be."

"You're being weird right now," Atlas points out.

I smile sheepishly.

"Are you being mean to her?" he asks Idalia. His protectiveness might be cute if it wasn't so poorly misplaced.

"Fuck off," Idalia spits.

"Idalia is being very nice, actually," I say calmly. Since when am I the most composed person in a room? These two make me look like a fucking saint. "We were just saying it would be nice to train together, which should make you happy," I tell Atlas.

He grunts. What it means, I don't know.

Idalia glowers at him, arms crossed. It's hard to imagine them ever being intimate.

"What is it time for?" I say, breaking the silence, *again*.

A cruel smile forms on Atlas's face and all his attention is on me. My body tingles and pressure builds between my legs. "Your punishment."

"Gross," Idalia says, making a fake gagging noise. "See you later, Harper."

Her steps barely make any noise as she climbs up the stairs. Atlas never takes his eyes off me.

"Making peace, Fox?"

"Something like that. I'm fucking Gandhi, haven't you realized?" I catch myself before he can ask who that is. "Nevermind."

He steps toward me and my skin flushes in his proximity. The magic in my veins is nearly bursting from me as it seeks out his. "Does the little Fox actually know how to play nice?"

Atlas gets even closer and I feel my throat closing, but I manage to say, "Not for you."

He laughs and tucks a piece of hair behind my ear. "I would hope not. I like it when you're mean."

"Oh, yeah?" I say, tilting my chin up to look at him.

"Do your worst, beautiful."

"Well then, I definitely don't want you to lay me on that table and make me come so hard I forget everything but your name. That would be so gross."

Atlas arches a brow and grabs my hand, placing it on his erection. Heat pools between my thighs. "What about this?" He tenses his jaw as I let him force my hand up and down his shaft. "Do you want this?"

"Absolutely not," I choke out.

"Are you lying, little Fox?" He takes steps forward, pushing my back against the wall.

"No," I lie.

"So if I stick my hand inside your panties, I won't find your pretty little pussy wet and ready for me."

I shake my head no, egging him on.

"Get on your knees, Fox."

Against my better judgment, I comply, dropping to the ground so fast that my knees smack against the concrete floor. But all I feel is his presence and how it roars through me like a wildfire.

"What if someone comes in?" I ask.

Atlas grins down at me. It shows off his canines and if I didn't know any better, I'd say there's nothing good inside him. Maybe it's all darkness and danger. But now that I've seen him, I know it's both, and it feels like home. "I hope they do. Then they'll get the pleasure of watching me fuck your throat until you cry."

His voice is dark and it should scare me, but it only makes me want to reach in between my legs and satisfy the need that's engulfing me.

"Would you like that?"

"No," I whisper.

"Good. I hope you fucking hate it." With a surprisingly gentle touch, he pries my mouth open with one hand and unbuttons his pants with the other. I fight the urge to watch him unleash himself, instead keeping my eyes on the pools of lust looking down at me. "Open up wider for me, baby."

I do as he asks and find my hands magically bound behind my back. Dude has a serious thing for restraint and I'm more than happy to play along.

"So pretty with my cock in your mouth," he murmurs as he pushes himself past my lips and over my tongue. He doesn't stop, moving back and down my throat as my lips stretch over the massive size of him and I choke. "Good girl, just like that."

I moan around him, and he smiles, fisting my hair for leverage.

"Swallow, Fox," he commands.

I stick my tongue out, inviting him further in, and flex it so that I stroke the side of his dick, never moving my gaze from his. A deep growl of approval emanates from him and I feel it spread through my body. Breathing out through my nose, I swallow as much of him as I can.

Atlas tilts his head back and groans. Watching him come undone by me is my fucking crowning achievement. His dark hair, tousled and sticking up half messy on the top, the ridge of his biceps nearly bursting from his t-shirt, the muscle in his jaw tightening underneath a thin layer of facial hair. He speaks the words I'm thinking. "Fuck. You're so fucking perfect." As he praises, he looks back down at me, his eyes hooded and drunk with need.

His pleasure is a drug. It swims through my arteries and pumps desire into every inch of my soul. It's never enough. I'll always want more.

As if reading my mind, he weaves my hair tighter through his fingers and pulls himself out of me before pushing back in with full force.

I wrap my lips around him like a suction, licking at any opportunity and letting him fuck my throat raw. Atlas is relentless, a storm of brutality and longing. He's so unhinged and I'm literally insane over it. We should never have been brought together, but here we are, and I'll hold on until my last fucking breath.

His wish is my command as tears form in the corners of my eyes and roll down my cheeks. At the sight of them, something like a whimper comes out of him and the sound is nearly enough to make me come. I blink against them, making them run faster. The magic restraints around my wrists disappear and through gritted teeth, he tells me to pull down my leggings. The movement of cloth against my throbbing clit makes me moan. The cool air passing through my legs makes the slick wetness between my thighs more pronounced.

Atlas's gaze falls to my naked waist. "How badly do you want to come, Fox?"

I can't respond with his dick in my mouth, so I just look up at him, pleading. My hands itch to rub against my center, but I know I need permission. This is the only time I'll happily bow to his whim.

He slows his pace, gently pumping himself through my lips. I let my teeth just barely graze against his skin and his jaw clenches, pupils dilating. "Show me what you do when you're all alone and thinking of me."

Without hesitation, I run my fingers over myself, rubbing my clit and moaning at the shot of pleasure that runs like lightening up my body. I close my eyes and dip my middle finger inside myself, soaking my hand in the process.

"Open those pretty brown eyes, Fox. I want to watch them roll back."

As I do, he pulls out of my mouth, letting go of my hair, and pumps himself through his hand. My jaw hurts from the work, but I can barely focus on anything except the movement of my fingers urging my orgasm forward.

"Tell me how wet you are," he rasps, watching me with deep satisfaction.

I bite my lip and cry out in response, leaning back on my knees and resting my head against the wall. I'm on full display for him, the dark look in his eyes pushing me toward that thing I want so badly as my fingers work faster and faster.

"Should I fuck you and find out?"

I shake my head, watching him grip his cock. He's so beautiful and there's only one thing I want more than to feel him inside me.

His eyebrows quirk up at my response.

"I want you to come in my mouth." The words come out strangled. "I need to taste you."

"*Fuck,* Fox." Atlas grips my hair again and I open my lips automatically, rubbing my tongue over him. The world blackens and my jaw goes slack, heat building and exploding inside me like an atom bomb. I cry out, the sound muffled by his flesh filling my mouth. He lets out a string of curses that would normally make me laugh but I'm not here anymore. I'm in a realm of fucking bliss as his hot come pours into me and down my throat, coating it like paint.

His grip on my hair lessens, and he pulls out of my mouth, letting me rest against the wall again as we both pant with exhaustion. Atlas places his hand on the wall above me and leans into it, dropping his head down to look at me.

"How am I supposed to get anything done with you around?"

A tired smirk is my only answer. "Wasn't that my punishment?"

A laugh rolls through him. "Not even close. Get up, we have work to do."

CHAPTER FIFTY-SIX

ATLAS

I HOPE YOU BELIEVE ME WHEN I SAY I HAD NO INTENTION of fucking her in the armory. But my will—which I once thought was iron—is like rubber around her. It's the only flaccid thing about me in her presence.

I told her I'd punish her for that little stunt yesterday. But it wasn't me fucking her into the early hours of the morning later that day or strangling her with my cock just now. No, it's a real punishment. One I don't want to hear a single fucking complaint about.

"You want me to do what?" She comes to a halt as we walk toward the peaks behind the house.

"I said, we're running to the top of the mountain."

"No," she whines.

Wishful fucking thinking.

"Fox, you're going to run that tight little ass up that fucking mountain or so help the Realm, I will ..." I'm at a loss for a threat. *Well, that's a first.*

She smirks, thinking she's won, and cocks her hip. "You'll what?"

Switching tactics, I fall to my knees in front of her. "I want you to help us in battle, Harper ..." She frowns at me using her actual name, but I don't care. "I'm serious right now. Listen to me. If your life is on the line, then I'm going to do everything in my power to make sure you're ready. I won't stop you from helping, but I'll lose my fucking mind if anything happens to you. If you won't do it for yourself, then do it for me."

Fox chews the inside of her lip.

"Please."

"Fine," she huffs. "But I'm going to puke."

I stand, shaking off the dirt from my shorts. It's daylight right now, and the sun is burning my skin. "Wouldn't be the first time."

She punches me in the arm, and this time my body actually tenses from the hit. I'll have to thank Emery later for training her. I owe that guy my life or a blow job or something.

Two hours later, we've made it a quarter of the way and her feet are literally dragging while Pants runs happily ahead.

"You're so fucking slow," I grumble as I try to pace next to her.

She stops, bending over and putting her hands on her knees. "Get fucked," she wheezes. "Don't be mean."

I pull her arm to drag her forward. "Baby, all I am is mean."

Fox looks up at me with a face that strips me of every facade I've ever tried to pass as something real. "Liar."

My heart does that thing in my chest whenever she's around. "Come on. Halfway and then we can stop. Don't give up."

I watch the words have their effect as that fiery determination straightens her spine, and she jogs off in front of me. "Come on, Elf Boy, stop being such a little bitch," she calls out.

"I like this view," I tell her, watching her ass bounce in her shorts.

She's no longer the skinny girl that I followed into town two months ago. She's lean and tanned and just as alluring to me now as she was then. Only now she's happier, healthier, and she's fucking mine.

WHEN WE MAKE IT HALFWAY she nearly collapses at my feet. I carry her back down because I'm legitimately worried she's going to pass out. When we get back, I let my magic run over her and lessen the soreness in her muscles. My little Fox is exhausted and falls asleep before dinner, but I don't wake her. She's cute as fuck when she's sleeping, especially when Pants curls up into the crook of her arm like he was made to fit there.

I stroll into the living room and everyone stares at me.

"What?" I snap.

"I almost feel like we should applaud or something," Emery says, looking at Ellison.

Ellison wipes a fake tear from his eye and walks over to pat me on the back. I tense under his touch. "We're so fucking happy for you, buddy," he croons.

"Realm, save me," I mutter, and take a seat on the couch.

Torin, Idalia, and Pippa are playing a game at the table, but I look at them waiting for them to say their fucking piece.

"She's good for you," Torin says genuinely.

"She's great for him," Pippa corrects.

Idalia goes back to the game, ignoring the conversation. Fox told me what she said, but as far as I'm concerned, it doesn't excuse any behavior she's had toward her. I dropped it quickly, though, because it's not like I've been innocent through all of this.

"So she's staying?" Pippa asks.

"For now," I mumble. I'm trying not to think about it. When I do, it's like a bomb has gone off in my chest.

Emery and Ellison exchange silent looks, and I grind my teeth.

"Come on, Atlas," Emery says, walking toward the door, Ellison on his heels.

"No." I don't want any part in whatever madness they think I need to participate in.

"And here I thought all that sex would put him in a better mood," Emery says to Elli.

"Maybe she's not that good." Elli shrugs.

I'm pinning him against the wall in seconds as he laughs down at me, the side of my forearm shoved into his throat.

"Why do you insist on pissing me off?" I growl, loosening my grip.

"You make it so easy, dude," he says with a strained smile.

I shift my weight but keep him against the wall.

"Would you rather I have said that she sounds like a fucking dream and I beat off to her moaning?"

"Ew!" Pippa exclaims from across the room.

"Fucking children," Idalia says with an eye roll.

I push my arm into his windpipe as he chokes on a laugh. "Relax, dude. You know I won't go near her."

"I'm not sure *relax* is a word in Atlas's dictionary anymore," Emery says from the doorway. "Hurry up, we got shit to do."

My curiosity gets the better of me and I let go of Elli, sending a wave of healing magic into him just in case I actually hurt him.

"Love you, big boy," he says with a wink, and follows Emery out.

A smile involuntarily crosses my face.

We wrap around the house and walk a few paces into the mountain. There's a cave back here that we explored when we first arrived. It's empty and dark and not very exciting, so I promptly forgot about its existence. But now, as we walk back there in the dark, I can see a faint glow, and as soon as we cross the rocky arched entrance, my brow furrows in confusion as I take in the scene.

There's a carved out rectangular, shallow pool in the center. Breaking through the surface are various platforms of different sizes and spaces apart. On the opposite side of where we're standing are big metal hoops—some tall, some short, some close to the water and some farther back toward the cave edge. Neon blue lights glow from the ceiling, illuminating the water just enough for me to make out what this is.

"How ... where?" I'm fucking speechless.

Emery smiles, his sharp teeth glowing in the sparse lighting. "We've been working on it for a while."

"We wanted it to be a surprise," Ellison pipes up.

My heart is both full and breaking at the same time. I don't deserve anything I've been given.

"It's not like the one we have back at the castle, but the water is cold as fuck and the platforms are hella rickety," Elli says with a grin.

It's a game I invented when we were little. The floor is lava and you have to jump from platform to platform while shooting a big ass metal ball through the hoops on the ground. It took me months to carve out the earth enough in the woods behind the castle, back when my magic was volatile and new. As we grew up, we made it into a drinking game and switched out the lava for freezing cold water because with the alcohol, we fell a lot more and healing lava burns is really no fucking joke. Every now and then I'd switch up the material of the platforms—sometimes they'd be ice, sometimes they'd be mud. The sketchier the better. We'd spend a full day playing this shit and passing out on the lush forest floor. Fucking stupid, but it was fun and it was ours.

With my magic, making something like this was easy, but it must have taken them weeks to do it. I'm still not even sure how they pulled it off.

"Harper helped," Emery says, reading my mind.

"What do you mean?" I ask. There's no way she could have shared her magic with them.

"She's been practicing using her magic to manipulate things other than time. She's shit at it, but for whatever reason, I'm able to control it once it's out in the world. Maybe because I have so much practice with yours," Emery says.

She's been practicing without me? My sly little Fox.

"What can she do?" I ask, genuinely curious.

"Nothing really. It's a whole lot of earth trembling and water seeping from the ground, but when Emery coaches her through it with his magic, she can get pretty far," Ellison remarks.

I'm almost angry that I haven't been privy to this information, but the gesture is too nice for me to get upset.

Tears prick the back of my eyes, but I'm not going to fucking cry. I'm gonna get fucking hammered with my friends.

"Shall we?" Emery says from a corner of the cave. He's standing next to a cooler made of ice with bottles of ale sticking out.

I jump onto the first platform, nearly falling over as it sways back and forth. Perfect.

"Let's fucking do it," I say with a genuine smile.

Fox gets up every morning with me and runs the mountain. She fails every time to make it to the top. It's been a week and she still can't do it, but I've never been more proud. She's a fighter to the core. The bravest creature I've ever met and the most beautiful soul I've ever known. Every day I wake up to her warm body wrapped around mine and I feel like I've been given a gift I don't deserve, but I'll find a way to give back to the Realm if only so that I can keep her with me as long as possible.

We don't speak of the future or the past. Through her, I'm gaining the courage to tell my family everything, but she doesn't push me. She's a constant source of comfort and holds my secrets with the strength of a warrior.

Fox never says if she wants to go home and I'll never bring it up. It's her decision, but I try not to think about what my life would be like without her and how I'll never be home unless she's with me. It's fucking insane. Loving her is turning me into a completely different beast. I'll never look back.

"How you doing, Fox?" I ask her on the mountain. This is the point we usually turn around.

"Fuck off, we're going to the top today," she pants. She doesn't look at me, her eyes determined and focused on the rocky incline ahead.

Her persistence is making me hard and I can't help but think that if we really do make it to the top, I'm going to fuck the breath from her lungs. "Damn right, baby."

That earns me a smile, and I refrain from kissing her as she pushes ahead in front of me. We don't stop, she keeps going despite the fact that her little feet drag and her breathing turns ragged. I don't dare ask if she wants to turn back.

When we finally crest the peak, she lets out a little holler of triumph that has me grinning like a fucking idiot. She stops dead in her tracks when she spies what I've set up here.

Her wide eyes find mine and I watch her closely as she approaches the blanket and picnic I've set up. Everything is spread out over the tip of the mountain so that all of Calamity is laid out before her. I never wanted to be a king until I let her in. She makes me feel worthy of the title and I'm ready to give her anything. If she wants to be a queen, it's done. Crown or not, I'll kneel before her every day of the week.

"I didn't make the food, don't worry," I tell her.

Fox doesn't speak, her hand over her mouth as she takes in the view. I watch her carefully, but the longer the silence stretches, the more I worry this was the wrong thing to do.

When she turns to me with glossy eyes, my heart flips in my chest. "How ... how did you know we'd make it up here today?"

An easy smile spreads over my face. "I didn't. I come up here every morning and set this up just in case. But I'm glad today was the day— I'm pretty sure Elli is ready to murder me in my sleep for turning him into a sandwich maker." I nod at the basket filled with food.

Fox giggles through a sob and runs into me, wrapping her arms tightly around my waist and pushing her magic into my soul. "Thank you," she whispers.

"It's nothing."

She tilts up and looks at me. "It's everything. You've never stopped believing in me."

Lifting my hand, I brush a piece of hair out of her face. "You're unstoppable, baby."

379

Fox reaches up on the tips of her feet to kiss me and warmth spreads through me like lava heating the earth.

Before I can rip every piece of clothing off of her, I pull back. "There's one more thing." This part I'm actually nervous about.

She cocks her head as I walk over to the blanket and sit down, removing my gift from the basket. I quietly thank the Realm for letting the sun shine brightly on us. The green hills of my land spread out below us as the sea sparkles in the distance and this mountain's sisters stand proudly in the light. Tiny houses pepper the landscape and the spires of the castle gloom ominously to the north. I ignore the pang of sadness that enters me as I turn back to the stunning creature beside me. She takes the seat next to me.

"Close your eyes," I command.

"Is this a kinky gift?" she jokes.

I groan at the thought. "Not yet. Hold your hands out."

She opens her palms eagerly, and I place the notebook in them. I wasn't sure if it would work or not, but her glowing skin confirms my assumptions as a tiny gasp comes out of her perfect lips and she opens her eyes despite my instructions. The need to touch her is irresistible. As I place my hand on her thigh, magic rushes through me.

"Is this ... is this bark from the Reign Tree?" Her palm caresses the cover of the notebook, its white wood regenerating our magic.

"Yes."

She frowns. "Seems kind of sacrilegious."

I roll my eyes. "It's made from the branches and it will grow back, Fox. It's a piece of you and me. It belongs to us."

Fox bites her lip a little unsure, but in the end believes me as she flips through the blank pages.

"The pages are not from the Reign Tree. Like I said, I only took enough to make the cover."

"It's beautiful, Atlas ... but what am I supposed to do with it?"

"Write your poetry," I say.

Her body stills as her gaze finds mine. I worried about overstepping, but I know she needs this.

"I can't fix what's broken inside you. I can help you find the pieces, give you some of mine, show you how beautiful you are, love you with everything that I am. But only you can make yourself feel worthy of it all." I reach out and hold her hand in mine. "Write it down, Fox. Tell your story and find yourself between the lines."

Her eyes gloss again and I can't decide if it's normal to make someone you love cry this much.

"I wrote something the other day actually," she says, her attention turning back to the notebook. "About anxiety. Do you want to hear it?" She flips her head back up to look at me, a vulnerability she doesn't usually let me see fills her eyes.

I nod silently, unable to find the words to tell her how much that would mean to me.

Fox takes a deep breath and closes her eyes. Her fingers run down the blank page in a rhythmic pattern as she speaks, "Okay, here it goes:

A darkened hallway haunts my dreams, it calls me when I sleep
It lights me up and fills this need that always makes me weep
And when I say no more, no more, I find myself back here
On my knees, just begging for a chance to taste the fear
Electricity will sweep me down a path that leads nowhere
Hunger pains and days of rain will forever leave me bare
I'm sick, I'm tired, I'm gone, I'm lost, a ghost who pleads for more
Don't trust, don't breathe, don't dare believe the demon at your door

... or something like that," she adds nervously when I don't say anything.

I still can't believe she exists. This person who reads the words of my soul and finds a way to make them seem beautiful instead of ugly and useless.

"You're perfect," I whisper, and a blush crawls up her cheeks.

"I'm not," she argues.

I drag her into my lap so that she's straddling me. Gently taking the notebook from her grasp, I place it next to us and cup her face in my hands. "You're perfect for me," I tell her before grabbing her lips with my own.

She moans into my mouth and I swallow it whole, capturing every bit of her she gives to me and storing it inside myself.

CHAPTER FIFTY-SEVEN

HARPER

OME ON, PLEASE!" I'M NOT ABOVE BEGGING, NOT
anymore.

"We have training tomorrow," Atlas says with a shake
of his head.

"We've had training every day for a week," Emery
argues.

"Don't make me go without you," I threaten.

Atlas glares at me, and it still sends a shiver of fear dancing along
my spine. "You wouldn't."

"Oh, I so would, Elf Boy." I don't think I would. I have no interest
in spending any time away from him. "Also, I ran to the top of the
mountain today, so I think I deserve a reward."

"Fine," he reluctantly agrees.

Pippa jumps up and down with a squeal, pulling me into happy-
dance with her in the foyer while Pants yips at our feet.

"I don't know why you're so excited about this. It's the same fucking tavern we normally go to," Atlas mumbles.

"Yeah, but tonight is Hollow Eve," Pippa explains like he's five.

Ellison found a box of glass masquerade masks in the basement. They're intricate antiques, each one made to represent an animal. There was even a fox one, so I'm obviously wearing that.

"This is my favorite holiday back home," I say excitedly.

Everyone turns to me, surprised. "You have this holiday where you're from?" Torin asks.

It's one of the first things my world and Calamity share. The fact that it's fucking Halloween just makes it even more enjoyable. I nod with a smile on my face.

"Let's go! We're going to be late."

Despite the fact that it's night, the sun is shining outside, which kind of ruins the spooky vibes I normally like to enjoy, but whatever.

I pull the mask from the table and put it on my face. It's heavier than it looks, and the smooth feel of the glass is cold against my flushed skin. Atlas comes around and ties the leather strap around my head.

I bite my lip. "I'm afraid I'm going to break this. I'm not the most elegant thing."

"We've noticed," Elli says from behind me.

I turn to smack him on the arm while everyone chuckles. "Bite me," I sneer.

"Don't even think about it," Atlas growls.

We all roll our eyes at his protective tone. I'll never admit to him that his overbearing comments get me all hot and bothered.

"I picked this one out for you, Big Fluffy Kitty." I hand him a black cat mask adorned with a pink little nose and white tipped ears.

"No," he states. There's little room for disagreement with his tone, but I've always been able to squeeze into tight spaces.

"Yes." I pout.

"This should be interesting," Elli mutters.

"Absolutely fucking not, Fox. I'm not wearing this."

Hands on my hips, I glare at him. "What do you plan on wearing, then?"

"This," Atlas gestures to his current outfit—black slacks and a deep maroon t-shirt. I briefly imagine everything underneath.

"Eyes up here, baby," he smirks.

"I've decided I liked them better when they thought they hated each other," Torin sighs.

"Too fucking bad," we both snap at him.

Giggling, I give him an apologetic look. I know Atlas hates Torin, but I'm not entirely sure why. He's never been anything but nice to me.

"Wear it," I demand, handing the mask back to Atlas.

He stares at me, nothing kind in his eyes.

Time to pull out my weapons. I lean up to catch his ear while everyone else picks out the masks they're going to wear.

"If you wear it," I whisper. "Then you can ask me to do anything you want."

Atlas chuckles darkly. "Anything?"

"Anything," I promise.

"Fine," he agrees. "But I'm going to make you sorry you ever offered."

"I'm counting on it," I breathe into his skin before pushing up farther on my toes and kissing him on the cheek.

A delighted groan rolls through him as he turns me and pulls my back into his chest, kissing the top of my head.

"I love you," he says softly before letting me go.

In the weeks since he's first said those words, I haven't said them back, and he hasn't pushed me. The truth is that I think I love him, but I'm not sure I know what love is. I've never had a single healthy relationship in my life—family or anything else. Being with Atlas is like nothing I've ever known. Instead of a give and take, it's a connection where we share everything. He's not trying to define who I am; he's proving to me that I've always had the tools to do it myself.

So saying *I love you* won't work, I've done it countless times and for what? They're just words. Atlas deserves more than words and empty promises. He deserves forever. If I'm ever going to tell him how I feel, I need to find the right way to truly express it.

I haven't kidded myself into thinking this is anything but a fairy-tale. An actual, living, breathing fairytale. I know I'm no longer in a nightmare, but I'm still afraid it's a dream.

WHEN WE GET TO STELLA'S, the tavern has been transformed into something more representative of the spooky holiday I'm used to. Halloween meets nineteen-twenties nightclub, if you will. The lights are dim, there's blaring music, and the occasional magic ball of light floats around. Unlike every other light orb I've seen since being here, these are neon colors.

Pippa and Idalia run off to grab a table as Ellison, Torin, and Emery go to the bar to get drinks. I'm about to tell Atlas my order when he drags me upstairs into a dim hallway. We pass a mirror on the way, our glamoured reflection sending a thrill through me.

"You're taunting me in this outfit," he growls, pushing me against the wood-paneled wall. Sharp splinters poke into my open back, but I'm numb to the pain, desire pumping through me like liquid nitrogen.

"It's just a dress," I mutter, looking up at his darkened eyes.

It's not just a dress. I spent forever trying to decide what to wear when Idalia said I could borrow it. It's skin tight and naturally pushes my boobs up. The open back dips to just above my ass and the silky material comes up mid-thigh. But the best part is that it's an obsidian color that makes my hair look even more like chocolate, and I knew Atlas wouldn't be able to resist ripping it off me. I warned her of that too—I mean, I didn't want to ruin the one nice thing she's ever offered me. Idalia had just shrugged, so I took it willingly.

Even though he's wearing this ridiculous cat mask, the black glass in the unlit hallway casts shadows on his face, making him look even more sinister than I already know he is.

"You're right," he says, lifting me up as I wrap my legs around him. His hand skims the hot flesh of my thigh and I shiver against his touch. "It's not the outfit, it's just you. Always taunting me."

"I think you like it," I say, lowering my voice.

"I fucking love it," he grumbles, pressing his mouth to mine.

The heat of his tongue pushes past my lips and roams freely, tasting every bit of me, as I moan at the feel of him pressing against me.

Someone walks by the hallway just as the noise comes out of me and he pulls back. Even here, where there's no light, I can see the shine of his white canines as he flashes them to me.

"Think you can stay quiet, little Fox? I wouldn't want someone coming in here and watching me fuck you."

"You wouldn't?" I say with my own smirk.

Atlas nips at my lower lip. "No, only I'll ever get to see the wild thing you become as you come around my cock."

"Seems a little selfish, Prince." I lean in to keep kissing him, but he pulls back and levels me with a serious stare.

"It's not selfish if it's fucking mine." With our eyes locked, he reaches between my thighs and strokes my clit through my panties. I'm certain they're already soaked and the noise of approval he makes lets me know I'm right.

Suddenly, he drops me to the ground and I barely catch myself from falling to my knees.

"Turn around," he demands.

I do as I'm told.

"Hands up against the wall."

My palms stretch out against the grainy wood.

"Spread those pretty legs, Fox."

Widening my stance, my body trembles in anticipation as he leans in and grazes his teeth over my racing pulse.

"Keep your hands on the wall like a good girl. If I catch even the slightest movement, I'll stop."

"What if I want you to stop," I breathe into the wall, the hard glass of the mask pressing into my temple.

Atlas's laughs quietly into my neck. "I think we both know that's never going to happen. You may be able to bend me to your will, but your body bows to mine. Understand?"

"Yes," I whimper.

His hands skim down the sides of my breasts, over my hips, and hike my dress up so that cool air passes through my legs. I gasp as he falls to his knees and sinks his teeth into the tender flesh of my ass.

Atlas groans, the sound muffled by my skin, and I'm ninety-nine percent sure that I'm legitimately dripping with desire.

His fingers dance delicately over my skin until he's spreading me open and pushing two fingers slowly into me. The sound of his mask dropping to the floor makes mine feel tighter, but I keep my hands still. I fight the urge to cry out, biting my lip so hard it draws blood.

"Fuck, you're so tight. How do you fit all of me in here?"

I honestly don't know. It's the best type of agony every time he stretches my body around him. I can hear how wet I am as he continues to pump his fingers into me and the sounds of the bar fade into the background. It's only him and me.

Pushing the flesh of my ass up, he doesn't stop his firm pace as he says, "I need to taste you, Fox. Should I suck my fingers or would you rather feel how hungry I am for you?"

"Please," I try to say quietly.

"Please what?"

"Please lick me," I beg.

His response is the hot pad of his tongue against the aching center of me, and my nails dig into the wood as I whimper against closed lips.

Atlas's sounds of pleasure as he fucks me with his tongue is my undoing, and I come, hard, as his grip tightens on my ass and he pushes more fingers into me until I'm drowning in overstimulation begging him to stop. He doesn't listen and soon enough I'm coming again, literally biting into the wood wall at the cruel waves of bliss that wash over me.

Finally, he pulls out of me and stands, pressing the outline of his cock against my skin. "You're a fucking masterpiece. Do you know that?"

I might blush if I had any idea who or where I was, but I'm still floating in the ether of life-altering orgasms. The clink of his belt, the pull of his zipper, brings me back as my body lights up again.

"Don't move," he commands, slipping the warm length of him between my thighs before shoving into me with one thrust.

I can't help it this time, I cry out and dig my nails into the wall.

Atlas chuckles, but it's a staccato of noise as he enjoys this just as much as I do. "I said quiet, little Fox."

All that comes out of my mouth is a muffled whimper.

He uses his hands to push my ass up again, so our bodies are pressed together as much as possible, as he drives his cock in and out of me with so much power I have to turn my head so that I don't break my mask against the surface of the wall.

"Fuck, fuck, fuck, Atlas. It's so fucking good." I breathe out the chant in a hushed voice.

"Can you feel it, beautiful?" he asks, my head fuzzy and having a hard time processing his words. "Can you feel how your body bends to mine?"

"Yes," I whine, and it's the truth.

"You were fucking made for me," he groans.

One hand lets go of me and slaps against my palm as his fingers intertwine with mine. He's squeezing my hand so tightly I feel like it might break, but I couldn't care less. I want to feel everything he can give me—pleasure, pain, love, hate.

"Fucking Realm," he snaps.

Atlas pulls out of me and spins me around to face him. My legs are gelatin as I wobble to stay upright, frowning because I'm one-hundred percent certain I'll die if he doesn't put his dick back inside me. With his hand wrapped around my waist, he grabs my leg and hikes it over his hip, as he lifts me and pushes me into the wall. His free hand presses against my throat and squeezes ever so slightly. There's something dark and dangerous in his gaze that sends a ripple of fear through me.

I don't have to wait much longer before he plunges back into me and my head falls back. "Look at me, Fox."

I don't comply. I'm in my own world where the only thing I can think and feel is my orgasm rising like a tidal wave.

"Look at me," he demands again, and the danger in his tone forces me to do his bidding. "I want you to watch as you fucking ruin me."

Keeping my eyes pinned to his unravels me as love and anger swirl into the dark pools that strip me down. My lips quiver with the need to make some kind of noise, hands locked over his forearms as the muscles in them flex beneath the surface of his skin. He feels so thick and big inside me, filling me with more than just his length.

As pleasure morphs into something undeniably possessive, I fight the urge to close my eyes and scream, letting him watch every emotion in me as I fall apart and bleed before him. Atlas's eyes glaze more, his jaw slackening as he follows, and I marvel at him pouring his soul into mine.

A sticky warm feeling slides down my thigh as he thrusts slowly into me a few more times and releases my throat. I'm still staring at him, mostly in awe. I'm not sure how every time we have sex I feel like he lights a fire in me that burns us both. It's not heaven, but it will fucking do.

He drops my leg but keeps his hand on my hips, holding me up. Covering my mouth with his, he kisses me with a surprising tenderness. We're a tornado of passion and fury. It's how both of us were forged, but Atlas has shown me just how beautiful it can be to be serene and calm.

"I'd happily worship you forever," he mutters against my lips.

Leaning in for more, I kiss him. Flicking my tongue along the surface of his mouth, I breathe in his citrus and warm scent that now feels so much like home. "I think that can be arranged."

CHAPTER FIFTY-EIGHT

ATLAS

THE PARTY

I wait in my room for Elrora, but she never comes and a hollow feeling carves its way into my heart. I want her to be by my side, but I guess there's a small part of me that's relieved at the drama I'll avoid. I walk into the common room that separates Emery and my bedrooms to find him waiting for me.

"Ready?" He's messing with his tie in the mirror, but it looks perfect to me.

"Yup," I reply.

"Thought you were going to have a date? Where's the mystery girl I keep hearing so much about?" he asks as we stroll down the halls toward the ballroom.

"Don't ask," I mutter, ignoring his questioning glance.

The room is resplendent as usual. Bright colors decorate the space in opulent furniture and silk hanging from the structural columns. Bulbs of magic illuminate the room unnecessarily, as a massive crystal chandelier hangs from the center of the domed ceiling. The room is filled with people dancing and chatting lazily. Fake laughter echoes off the walls and I glance to Emery as we both mentally prepare for another long night.

"Bar?" he suggests with a raise of his eyebrows.

"Must you even ask?"

A chuckle is his only response.

We walk through the maze of guests, sometimes pausing as one of them puts their arm on my tightly pressed black suit. "Your Highness," they coo and I smile politely and make casual conversation about useless shit while internally I'm dying to tell them to fuck right off.

I miss Pippa and Ellison. The four of us usually tolerate these events together by making fun of the guests and getting way too drunk, but Elli is off doing some shit for his dad and Pippa is visiting her friends on the coast.

We reach the bar and Emery orders as the staff rush around trying to make our drinks. Someone runs from behind the bar and dips their head low while offering my beverage to me. I want to tell them they really don't have to do that bowing shit, but that would be ridiculous.

"Thank you," I say, taking the glass from them.

I sip the drink, letting the burn of alcohol and the mild fruity taste wash over my tongue.

"Who looks good tonight?" I ask Emery, perusing the crowd.

"Atlas," he warns.

"Pippa's not even here," I argue.

He sighs. "I'm not interested."

I look at him by my side. "Fine. But if you're not going to go for anyone else, then you better tell her how you feel because eventually your cock is going to shrivel up and fall off from disuse."

"Fuck off," he says with a laugh.

"On the plus side, your forearms are looking pretty good. Is it so big you need both hands?" I joke.

He shoves my shoulder as a smile creeps over his face.

"I suppose you know everyone here anyway. The last thing you need is some needy female chasing you down at every event."

"Exactly. Though I don't know her," he says, pointing subtly with his drink.

I follow his gaze and my heart stops. When it beats again, it's to a fast and uneasy rhythm.

"I wonder who that is. She's ... she's faun."

Elrora lets out a hearty laugh at whatever Essen Reid is saying, his young son clinging to his tailcoat. I tighten my jaw.

"Well, whatever she is, she's barking up the wrong tree if she thinks Essen is interested in her," Emery says with amusement.

"Why?" I snap, not really paying attention to what he's saying. I'm too busy staring at the woman I love in the elegant red gown I picked out for her. The soft fabric flows over her curves, hugging every inch and glistening in the crystal chandelier's fractured rainbows.

"He's married to the Duke of Ashberg, Torin Reid. You know that. Essen's a professor at the University." I can feel Emery's eyes turn to me, but I can't stop staring at her. Her black horns twist up like spires above her head, and for the first time they look demonic to me. "Atlas? Is everything okay?"

"Excuse me," I say, without giving him any explanation.

Walking through the crowd, I target Elrora as she catches my eye. If she sees the fury or confusion on my face, she doesn't acknowledge it.

"You said Torin isn't here?" she asks Essen.

"No, he had to stay home to take care of some things. Always busy, that one," he replies with a laugh.

"Well, it's good to see you again, and look how big you are," she adds, looking down at the little boy.

"Oh, can you say thank you, Dorian?" he asks his son, who's definitely way too young to respond.

When I reach them, they both stop their chatter and look at me.

"Your Highness," they say in unison with a bow.

"Can I speak to you?" I ask her quietly, placing my hand on her arm.

"Well, of course," she answers, the necklace I gave her shining like a beacon. "Good to see you again, Duke. Please send Torin my regards."

I give Essen a bullshit smile as I pull her away and into a corridor. "What the fuck is going on?"

She frowns at me. "You seem mad."

"You were supposed to meet me in my room."

I don't realize I'm still gripping her arm until she looks down at it with a frown. I let go immediately.

"I was late, so I thought I'd meet you here." Something in my chest eases, but it still doesn't feel right.

"How long have you been here?"

"What is with the twenty questions?" she laughs. I'm not fucking laughing. "Atlas, relax. We're supposed to enjoy this night together." She slides her fingers down my arm in a calming caress and my heart rate slows.

"You just surprised me," I reply, leaning in to kiss her.

"I'm full of surprises," she whispers seductively, causing a grin to spread over my lips. Her tongue pushes into my mouth and I grip her waist, pulling her close.

When I pull back, my gaze drops along her body. "You look beautiful."

Elrora gently kisses the tip of my nose. "Thank you, my love."

"Come on, I want you to meet Emery." I move my hand from her hip and lace my fingers in hers, gently tugging her toward the party.

"Stay by the bar. I'll meet you there, I just need to use the restroom."

"Okay," I agree, watching as she hurries in the opposite direction. "Elrora," I call out.

She turns to face me.

"Other way."

Her laughter fills the hallway. "Silly me."

I shake my head and turn back to the party, finding Emery and making my way toward him. There are two females fawning over him.

Wow, I'm funny.

"Where did you go?" he asks after politely excusing himself from the attention.

I start to explain, but before I can say a word, my father steps onto the dais where his and my mother's thrones sit like monuments. They're both massive structures, made entirely out of a pale wood that glows with a golden hue. The bark twists and wraps itself in an intricate pattern, weaving the armrests and then towering high to a point on the back. Delicate green pieces of silk flow over the chair, cushioning the seat and adding life to the quiet tones. The room becomes silent, and everyone does a collective bow before their king.

"Thank you, everyone, for coming. This event, where we can all come together, is so wonderful. Where is my son?"

Everyone turns to me like a well-choreographed dance move, parting to make way for their prince. I walk up to the dais and stand by my father, who throws his arm around my shoulder and pulls me in for an uncharacteristically casual hug. My mother beams next to him and a smile pulls at my own lips.

"The Ravenwood Prince is to become king soon!" my father boasts, magic amplifying his voice so that it bounces off the gold-trimmed walls.

The crowd cheers, and I beat down a flush that dares to cover my cheeks, instead giving them a stern but friendly look.

"Even though our dear daughter, Pippa, cannot be here tonight, we are so thrilled to share this evening of drinking and dancing—"

His speech is cut off by a blood-curdling scream in the back of the room. My father stiffens, letting go of me. I can feel his magic flaring before it extinguishes and his face turns pale. Everyone turns as the screaming continues, murmurs and panic spreading like a rumor. That's when my own magic feels tempered, weak, like it's taking a nap. I make a move to investigate when a sharp pain pierces through my chest and my mother cries out next to me.

The pain turns dull, a firm pressure radiating through my body as my knees weaken, and I look down at the arrow protruding just below my shoulder. Poison pumps through my body with swift ease. My father grabs at me as guards swarm around us and into the crowd of people turning hysterical as the seconds pass.

I part my mouth to speak, but nothing comes out, and the room shifts in a blur of light and color. I'm aware that my mother is speaking to me, but I don't know what she's saying. I think I can hear Emery shouting, or maybe that's my father. My knees buckle and hit the floor, but I don't register pain anymore. Just a hazy throb that seeps into my body as everything fades away.

CHAPTER FIFTY-NINE

HARPER

FTER MAKING OUT FOR AN OBSCENE AMOUNT OF TIME,
Atlas and I decide we should probably spend time with
our friends. I kiss him on the cheek before heading to the
bathroom to clean myself up and pee.

What? Just because I'm in a magical world doesn't
mean I've forgotten about basic sex hygiene. Can you imagine how
embarrassing that would be?

Hey baby, can you heal my UTI? Thanks.

Fuck that.

The bathroom is nearly empty as I walk in, and a female faun walks
out of a stall. She looks so familiar, but I'm sure I've never seen her.
Her lack of floppy ears makes me wonder if she's half-faun like Emery.
I give her your typical tight-lipped smile. You know, the one you give
to randos. It says, *I'm a nice person but please don't talk to me.*

She clearly doesn't catch the signal as she says, "I love your mask."

With one hand on the stall, I turn my neck to look at her as she stares at me through the mirror washing her hands. "Thank you."

I catch my reflection, forgetting what I look like with my glamour on. Looking back at me is a young female elf with short, red hair and a fox mask.

"Where did you get it?" she asks. Her voice is melodic like Pippa's, but if Pippa's voice is salted caramel, this faun's voice is black licorice.

"It belongs to my friend's grandmother," I say, trying to escape the conversation by pushing into the bathroom stall.

I feel her next to me in an instant. "This is so weird of me," she says with a nervous giggle, and my hackles raise immediately. Why the fuck is this bitch invading my personal space? "I saw you with that guy. Is he your boyfriend?"

My cheeks flush as my stomach decides to try its luck as a gymnast. "I don't know what you're talking about."

The female laughs a forced laugh that has me turning to face her entirely, her long, Malibu Barbie hair falling down her back as she tilts her head toward the ceiling. I'm pinned between her and the stall door, trying to find a way around her. "Oh, come on. He's so hot with those dark eyes." She groans in delight and I clench my fist. Magic burns at my fingertips, but I try to remember what Atlas told me about keeping it hidden. "I love a guy with facial hair."

My heart drops at her words, realizing she's describing Atlas. My Atlas. She shouldn't know what he looks like because the glamour he's wearing doesn't have facial hair.

"Who the fuck are you?" I snarl, stepping into her instead of backing away.

If she's bothered by my sudden switch to anger, she doesn't show it. She just keeps smiling, her sharp canines taunting me. "Oh, must have hit a nerve. You're not, like, his mistress, are you?" She giggles again and my jaw tightens as I clench my teeth so hard I feel like they're going to crack.

"Get the fuck away from me before you regret it." It's pretty weak as far as threats go, but hey, she caught me by surprise.

For the first time in this bizarre confrontation, a darkness enters her gaze as her smile drops. "If you insist," she says, her voice dropping an octave that has a slimy feeling crawling its way up my back.

"I do," I snap back, but she's already turning away and skipping out of the bathroom.

I know I need to go tell Atlas and the others about that weird interaction, but I'm still really uninterested in getting a UTI, and I swear that shit actually happens, so I hop into the stall and pee really fast before rushing out.

When I do, I let out a startled scream. Elijah, the half-kangaroo, half-goat thing, is staring at me by the door. He's perched next to the sinks with a little maid outfit on. A small pink table with a glass top is next to him, holding tampons and hard candies.

"Don't forget to wash your hands. Wouldn't want to get those nasty germs everywhere."

I pick my fucking jaw off the floor and glare at him. "This is the female's restroom. What the hell are you doing here?"

"What's that supposed to mean?" he says with a snippy tone, and then his face softens. "Ah, you must be Harper."

I scream again, this time in frustration. "Of course I am! We've met three times!"

He scratches his head and purses his lips. It's a fucking sight to be seen. "If you say so," he says with a shrug.

Closing my eyes, I will my patience to the surface, and take a deep breath before walking over to the sinks.

"Funny thing about meeting you here," he starts.

"You're fucking following me," I snarl as I rub soap between my palms.

"I don't think so," he says genuinely. It only makes me scrub my hands harder. "Hey, I lost something out back. Could you help me look for it?"

My head snaps to him so fast I cringe at the muscle that's surely torn. "What?"

"There's something out there. We can take the back door and you can help me find it."

"Absolutely not," I say without hesitation. "I don't know you. You keep showing up randomly. What is your deal?"

Elijah ignores me. "Well, worth a shot. Towel?" A fluffy white hand towel appears in front of my face and I reluctantly grab it.

"Thank you," I growl.

I rub my hands on the fuzzy cloth and look back at my reflection one more time out of habit. Elijah starts humming the melody of "Vienna" by Billy Joel and at first I start singing the words absently in my head and then my breath catches.

"How do you know that song?" I ask him with wide eyes.

He smiles like he might let me in on a secret. "I know lots of things."

"Who are you?" I mutter.

"Shouldn't you be asking yourself that question? Who are *you*? How did you get here? How do you move forward?"

I cross my arms and roll my tongue over my teeth. "I ask myself that every day, but no one has given me any answers."

He scratches his chin again and looks out the door like he's checking we're alone. "Maybe that's because you haven't been listening."

I narrow my gaze at him, trying to understand what the hell he's getting at. But, my friends are waiting and something isn't right here.

"Do you know how I got here? Why me?"

Elijah reaches into his pocket, still humming the tune to one of my favorite songs. He pulls out a pocket watch and then another, and another, until he's holding ten or fifteen and sorting through them. I'm too mesmerized by what he's doing to repeat my question. Are they regular pocket watches or are they the special kind Atlas told me about?

"Funny thing about pocket watches," he comments, juggling the ones in his hand. "I find they're always getting stuck." He looks up at me, fingering the knob on the top of the watch. "One twist of this little dial, though, and you're right back where you belong."

My heart pounds as I take in his words. "Are you saying—"

"Ah, here's the one," he interrupts. Popping one open, he shoves the rest down into his skirt pocket. "Yes," he says as if he's pondering something. His eyes snap to mine and the silly creature is gone; there's nothing but concern in his gaze. "You've made your decision." He waves the pocket watch at me. "Time is running out."

I open my mouth to speak when I hear someone screaming from the tavern and the music cuts out. I'm torn. I know this moment is crucial, and he has the information I desperately want, but I need to help my friends.

"I have to go," I say under my breath.

"Yes, yes," he agrees. "Fuck right along now."

I give him a tight-lipped smile and hurry out into the hallway.

I still don't have answers, but I have a lead. I know Elijah will be back and that will have to do.

CHAPTER SIXTY

ᴀTLAS

THE AFTER PARTY

When I come to, my head throbs in time with my slow but steady pulse. My tongue feels like a brick of sandpaper and there's a searing pain in my chest. My eyes snap open when I realize my hands are restrained and I blink as shades of red fill my vision.

There's blood. So much fucking blood everywhere. Painting the golden walls and seeping into the pores of the white marble floor. It reeks of death and, as I survey the room, I take in the gruesome scene. There's not a single living person amongst the bodies that cover the floor.

No. No. No. No.

I let out a helpless yelp. I can see my mother laying face down as her blood pools, dark and thick around her and my father. He's staring up at the ceiling, eyes wide and unblinking, his crown cast aside like a cheap replica. Everyone is someone I know and yet entirely unrecognizable as their flesh rots before my eyes. I try to catalog who everyone is, searching the room for Emery as tears roll down my face. I fight against the restraint and yell, my world blurring as anger burns through me and the beast beneath my flesh tries to escape. My mind is swirling. My heart, racing. I feel like air is escaping me even as I watch my chest move up and down. Worst of all, my magic is empty and distant.

"He's awake!" a voice calls out.

I try to spin around to look where it's coming from, but my head feels like it's going to split open and I close my eyes against the horror in front of me. Hoping, begging the Realm to tell me it's all a nightmare.

"Good," she says, and my eyes fly open at her voice.

Elrora stands in front of me, entirely unharmed. She twists her silky hair innocently around one finger before picking my father's crown off the floor and placing it on her head. I can't fucking breathe. She plops down onto the blood-soaked floor beneath me like it's a cushioned seat.

"What ... what are you doing?"

"Oh, this and that," she says casually.

I scream. And pull. And scream. And pull with all my strength, with everything in me, but I can't move.

"My love, please. You're going to hurt yourself," she says as my energy runs out and I heave for a breath.

"What did you do?" My voice cracks as my heart shreds itself into big, meaty chunks.

"What I had to do. What I always planned on doing," she says simply.

She looks so pretty sitting there, so docile and yet, something dark hangs over her. Elrora gets on all fours and crawls over to me, blood soaking into her red dress and darkening it to a port wine color. It soaks into the ends of her moonlight hair, dying the strands strawberry. It coats her fingers and hands as she wades through puddles of it, and my eyes widen in horror before she comes close enough to touch me.

I flinch back from her and then try again to break my restraints as she reaches out and trails her bloody finger down the side of my face. I yell as loudly as I can at her, but she doesn't even blink.

Tears blur my vision as I try desperately to grab on to something normal. "Please tell me this isn't real," I beg her.

A shadow of a frown passes over her face, and then she lets out a groan of impatience. "You are mad. I hoped this wouldn't happen, but here we are." Throwing her arms in the air, she stands back up as the blood of my family and friends drips from her arms, her legs, the fucking dress I had made for her.

Ignoring me entirely, she paces before me with a skip in her step. "At first I was nervous you wouldn't let me come. I had to find a way to be here. This night. It was the perfect night." Her eyes gleam with tears when she turns to me. "Then you told me you loved me and I knew you meant it. Oh, Atlas," she sighs, tilting her chin to the ceiling, a hand above her heart. My head spins.

"You bought me this dress," she says, twirling around, blood spraying out with her turns. "And the necklace!" Her hands clasp over the ruby sitting above her breasts. "The necklace was everything."

I'm barely aware of the obscenities and screaming that erupt from me. Everyone is dead. Everyone is fucking dead, and it's my fault.

Elrora dances around me to a silent tune before kneeling between my legs and gripping my thighs. Her nails dig into my flesh as she stares deeply into my eyes. Her own aren't even green anymore, they're empty. A colorless black that feels like it might swallow me whole.

"Don't you see, my love?. The high elves have been ruling over faun for millenia. We've never been raised any higher than common folk. I had to. For us, for our children. Now we can rule in peace. You and I, King and Queen of Calamity." She looks at me with sincerity, truly believing the shit she's spouting.

"You're half elf!" I stutter.

The twisted kindness drains from her eyes before she closes them and lets out a piercing scream. "Don't fucking say that!"

I don't even know who she is.

"*I would never marry you,*" *I snarl, letting my venom coat my mouth and then spitting in her face.*

Her body stills as her nails retract from my legs, but she doesn't cry out, she doesn't scream again, and my eyes widen in horror.

"*What the fuck are you?*"

Slowly wiping my spit from her face, I watch as little burns work their way through her flesh and then heal before I can blink. She lets out an impatient sigh and then backs away from me.

"*I hoped it wouldn't come to this, but ...*"

I wonder if she's going to kill me now. I hope she fucking does.

Elrora snaps her fingers and a creature wearing a cat mask wades through the blood and bodies, stepping on and over them like they're not even there. It's not just any cat mask, it's my panther with a creepy ass grin from ear to ear. I scream out again, but it's futile.

I calm my breathing and try a different tactic. One it's likely too late for. "*Elrora, baby.*"

She blinks through what I assume are tears, but when she started crying, I'm not sure. "*Atlas?*" *she asks, like I've just come to my senses.*

"*Baby, please don't do this. Untie me and we can figure out a solution to all of this.*"

This female, this demon, bites her lip like she's considering my proposal. She even does a little shuffle of her feet. "*I can't, my love. You're too angry. But you'll see. With a little time apart, I know you'll come around.*"

I roar at her. "*I'll fucking kill you, you stupid fucking bitch!*"

Elrora smiles nervously at me. "*Mmmm ... I don't think so,*" *she decides.*

The creature stands tall before her, handing her a pocket watch, and my stomach churns before finally turning to lead.

"*Here's the deal, baby. You get one year away from me to clear your head and then you come back to the castle by my side. Deal?*"

She's giving me an out, an escape. It must be a trick. "*Where is Emery?*"

Elrora rolls her eyes. "*He's alive. I was worried if I killed him it might kill you. I don't fully understand your bond.*"

Relief floods through me as my heart starts beating again.

"He's actually knocked out and tied up behind you. I didn't want to ruin the surprise, but see! I can be nice. Just remember how much you love me!" she pleads with childlike eagerness.

Bile rises up my throat because I do, I do love her even though it feels forced, as if every part of me is fighting against it.

Like the switch of a light she's sad again, angry actually. I can't fucking keep up. "It's a shame your sister wasn't here. I don't like the idea of you being with other females and I just know you're going to be so eager to find her.

"Don't you fucking touch her." Also gross, she's threatened by my sister?

But Pippa. Pippa is out there. I can get to her and maybe we can find a way to fix this. Fuck, this is so fucked.

"A year isn't enough time, Elrora. I'll still be mad. I know I will. Give me five."

"No," she snarls like the monster she is. Her voice changes to sickly sweet so quickly I can barely keep up. "I miss you already. That's too, too long."

"Four," I beg.

"Six months," she growls.

"Three, please."

She seems to think about that, her lower lip quivering like she might start crying again. "Two," she offers.

Not like I have any fucking choice. "Two," I agree.

She swings the pocket watch in front of me like a pendulum. "Swear it?"

"Yes," I promise.

"One more rule," she says, stilling the movement of the watch and walking closer to me. "Do whatever you want with other females. I don't like it, but I know what an animal you are." She winks. "But keep it to sex, okay? Don't get any ideas about falling in love with anyone else. I know I'm the only one for you."

Before I can avoid it, she's in front of me, pulling my face to hers and shoving her tongue in my mouth. I can only taste blood and death. A sick feeling surges through me as her serpent tongue licks the roof of my mouth.

"Promise," she whispers as I try to get out of her impossibly strong hold.

"I promise," I say through gritted teeth.

"See you soon, my love. Stay out of trouble." With her words, a cracking sound rips through my skull and the world turns black.

CHAPTER SIXTY-ONE
ATLAS

DO I EVEN WANT TO KNOW WHERE YOU WENT?" Pippa asks.

"Probably not," I shrug.

She crinkles her nose in disgust and I laugh, sliding into the seat next to Emery.

"Here," he says, pushing a mug of ale in front of me. "Drink up, Prince."

I smile, taking the mug and bringing it to my lips when something flashes out of the corner of my eye. A figure. A monster. I turn my head, but no one's there and I try to calm my spinning mind.

"Looking for me, love?" she whispers into my ear. Her hands move sensually over my shoulders, but it feels like someone is rubbing a razor blade over my back.

She comes up from behind me—a tight red dress barely covering her body—as Emery furrows his brow in confusion. Elrora sits on the table surface, her legs on the bench as everyone becomes silent. She's as beautiful as I remember, but that unnatural ache and longing I felt whenever she was around is gone. In its place is thick, slimy repugnance.

"Who's this?" Elli says standing next to me. I can feel him tensing.

"Oh, hello," Elrora purrs, twirling a lock of hair around her finger.

"Let's talk outside," I demand in a low voice.

She laughs, tilting her head back so that her hair cascades over the table and into Emery's drink, but she doesn't notice as she whips it back up.

"Who in the Realm are you?" Pippa snarls.

I glance at her with a silent plea to shut the fuck up.

"Who am *I*?" Elrora asks her, her gaze turning to black ice. She stands on the table as the bar's ruckus turns to murmurs. "I'm your fucking queen!" The tavern falls completely silent.

I don't know where Fox is and I'm panicking. I won't lose her. I fucking won't.

"Atlas?" Pippa pleads.

"El, please. It's me you want; let's just talk outside."

The demon witch stares down as everyone's eyes shift to me. "We had a deal, Atlas. But as usual, you're such a troublemaker." She jumps down off the table to stand next to me and the building shudders unnaturally. "Is it because you just wanted to come home?" Her eyebrows quiver as her face switches to serene.

"What is she talking about?"

Elrora shifts to my sister and smiles. "Oh, you didn't tell her? That's *good*. Good boy."

"Pippa ... I ..."

"Atlas?" Emery asks. His hands gripping the table as his knuckles turn white. He's moving closer to Pippa and I'm grateful.

"Shift," I breathe, and they do at my command until our table is surrounded by everyone in their derax form.

Elrora turns to me and narrows her gaze. "I really wish you didn't do that," she hisses.

I see Fox pop out from the hallway to the bathroom, looking at the scene in horror and linger on her for too long. She's everything. Fucking everything, and I didn't have enough time.

Elrora turns to her, and her smile is back, like the face on her masked sentinels. "Don't worry. We've already met a few times, actually."

My heart sinks, but I refuse to believe her. Fox can't know her. She wouldn't do that to me.

Not again. Not again. Not again.

I'm fucking losing it. This can't be real.

"Do you really love her?" Elrora asks me.

"No," I lie, and Fox's face contorts painfully before she schools a mask of indifference onto her face. Good girl.

"Is she really a *human*? Don't answer that, I'm going to kill her anyway."

"No!" I shout, reaching for magic that isn't there. I can't lose her. I won't. I'm brought back to the worst night of my life. Reliving all the horror, the blood, the empty eyes and frozen flesh.

Emery breaks the silence by snarling, his serpent tongue cracking like a whip in the air.

"Don't." I command, forcing him to heel.

Pippa caws from a rafter above, the black feathers of her raven wings ruffling angrily.

"It's cute you didn't tell her. Was that to protect me?" Elrora reaches out and grazes her hand down my face.

"Don't you fucking touch him," Fox spits.

Her magic echoes along the walls, somehow not tempered by whatever monstrosity stands before me. I'm so fucking scared for her, but looking into her eyes, I find a strange kind of safety. A warmth I don't deserve. A love she hasn't admitted to yet, and maybe I'll never get to hear her say. But in this moment she lets me see it and I'm so fucking grateful.

Be brave.

CHAPTER SIXTY-TWO

HARPER

ELRORA NARROWS HER EYES AT ME WITH SO MUCH hatred it almost stops me in my tracks. In return, I give her my best snotty little smile. You know the one—the fuck-you sneer. Two can play the crazy bitch game. Yeah, she might be some powerful sorceress or whatever, but she doesn't scare me.

It wasn't until I saw her standing next to him that I remembered the other time I've seen her. In the Backwood. A room with bleeding hearts and endless shadow. The memory escaped me until now and I wish more than anything I had thought of it earlier. She warned me she was coming. I could have stopped this. But the memory was a blur, indecipherable until she showed up. How fucking convenient.

I feel her magic swirling toward me and throw up a shield. It envelops me as the darkness coming from her tries to find a way in. Her face turns to one of anger as she realizes she can't touch me.

Don't get me wrong. It's hard. It's fucking painful to focus this much energy into it, but I grit my teeth and deal with it.

Elrora lets out a scream of frustration, and I've never smiled so big. I shouldn't be enjoying this, but I am. I hate how beautiful she is. I hate that she's touched Atlas. That he's been inside her. Loved her. I want to murder her for that alone.

"What the fuck is she?" she snaps at him.

"Leave her out of this," he growls.

I stalk toward her, pushing my magic out into a shield that encompasses my friends. "Your worst fucking nightmare." *Okay, I've just always wanted to say that.*

Glancing around, I note that everyone is an animal now, but I can't focus on that. Some dude shouts from the back of the room and makes a run for it. Elrora snaps her fingers, and the guy drops dead. I don't need to look to see it because an actual fucking heart appears in her palm.

Beating once.

Twice.

Blood drips down her pretty, pale wrist. She looks at it with curiosity before tossing it over her shoulder like it's a piece of garbage, the wet thump of it splattering against the floor. It's entirely disturbing and just the distraction I need to push back.

Stop, I whisper. Time slows and I charge toward her, grabbing the dagger from the strap around my leg and forcing it through her heart. Time speeds up and she gasps, but no blood comes out. She looks down at the blade in her chest and laughs. It's a laugh that sounds like nails against a chalkboard and it's then that I decide I *am* fucking scared of her. She's something made from nightmares and broken dreams.

"You can't kill me, you fucking bitch," she snaps at me.

I quickly throw the shield into place as Atlas grabs my hand. "Run, Fox."

"No," I respond immediately. "I won't leave you with her."

Elrora sighs like a child on a fucking roadtrip who's asked, *"Are we there yet?"* for the fifth time in twenty minutes. "I'm bored of this. Come with me, baby, or I'll kill all your friends," she says plainly.

"Atlas," I plead, but my magic is waning and I can't even feel his.

"I come with you and you leave them alone?" he asks.

"No!" I scream.

"For now." She lifts her shoulders up and down with true boredom.

This can't be happening. He told me we'd fix this. He promised me forever.

"No, please don't take him," I beg.

Emery whines behind me and nuzzles up to my hand.

"Fox, it's okay," Atlas says, squeezing my hand.

It really isn't.

"Stop touching her," Elrora snarls and he lets go of me. The absence of him is everything I can't handle. I can't breathe. I can't lose him. But I feel it. Time *is* running out, like a clock face *ticking, ticking, bong.* My magic drains faster and faster.

"I'll fix this," I whisper like an idiot. It's not like she can't hear me.

"Not if I kill you first," she says in a singsong voice.

I hope the look I'm giving her has enough hate to melt her, but unfortunately, it doesn't work. She smiles back at me as she weaves her fingers through Atlas's and tugs him up from his seat. It's like an ice pick to my heart, the last punch that shreds whatever bits had healed back together.

Atlas gives me this look like he knows he deserves this. One that asks for forgiveness even though he's unworthy of it. But he's so wrong. He deserves everything good, and I should have told him that more. I should have told him that I'm his forever.

I love you, he mouths silently, but I hear his voice ringing through my head.

I can feel his touch lighting me up with electricity and my soul begs me to do something, anything. The pocket watch feels like a lead weight around my neck. I could turn back time ... but who knows what consequences that would have or where I'd end up? My head spins.

I always thought of myself as a lone wolf, not by choice but by circumstance. As I juggle my decisions, and consider how they may affect those around me, I realize that before I came to Calamity, I wasn't cool or edgy for pushing everyone away. I was just ... selfish. And sure, maybe some circumstance and my good buddy, depression, had a lot to do with it, but as I look at all the friends I've made and the need to protect them tugs on my soul, I finally understand that I never had to ask anyone to save me, I just had to find people who were willing to trudge through the darkness to help. And most of all, I had to let them.

"It's Harper, right?" she asks, breaking me from my reverie.

Atlas pulls his hand from hers, nothing but the promise of a slow, painful death in his stare. "Don't speak to her," he says to Elrora.

She holds up one finger to shush him. "We're talking, baby."

I watch him grind his teeth to the sound of my own. "Yes, my name is Harper. Remember that for later. I'll so enjoy hearing it come from your lips as you beg for your life."

She smiles at me and if we weren't in this situation, I might actually believe she's nice. "I do see why you like her," she says to Atlas. "Listen, Harper. He's mine. And we're going to fuck every day and have a million babies and rule over Calamity happily. After a while, he won't even think of you."

I watch as Atlas's fists clench and unclench at his sides.

"Leave him alone," she explains, like we're talking about the rules of a board game. "And I might let you live out your miserable existence in peace."

"Fox, please," Atlas begs.

He's actually afraid of her. Truly scared. For the first time I see him as something penetrable, breakable, a boy who loves with all his heart. It only makes him even more beautiful.

I try to take in every feature of his, memorizing the lines of his face and the way his eyes speak all the words he can't say. Does he know that I'll never let go?

She yanks him through the crowd, and he pulls out of her grasp to walk beside her.

"You're fucking insane!" I scream at her, my anger painting the world crimson.

Elrora turns and dismissively clucks her tongue at me. "Haven't you learned, Harper? We're all mad here."

TO BE CONTINUED...

ACKNOWLEDGMENTS

Authors always say that it takes a village to write a book. And while it feels so generic saying it, I'm gonna do it ... because it's for real.

It takes a village to write and publish a book. Here's mine:

To my wonderful husband, Adam—my biggest fan and pushiest advocate. Thank you for always believing in me when I don't believe in myself, for taking me down a peg when I believe a little too much, and for loving me despite so many nights of me ignoring you in favor of Atlas. I love you more than words could ever describe, so instead, I'll promise you forever.

Thank you to all of my furry children—Penny, Taylor, Bixby, Mako, and Azula for endless cuddles and pick-me ups. But most importantly—yeah, I'm not afraid to admit I have a favorite—Jameson. My Pants. My fuzzy, orange companion. My lifeline. Thank you for finding the broken parts of me long ago and loving me until I was whole again, and then some. There isn't a star in the sky that shines brighter than you do in my heart.

I owe so much to my mother, who raised me to believe that I could accomplish anything and everything I set my mind to. Who taught me to believe that women can rule the world and that a heroine is just as likely as any hero to save the day. Who knew I'd be a writer long before anyone else, especially me. I love you.

To my amazing friend Kayla, who believed in my writing before it ever existed. Who pushed me out of my rut and helped me find myself again. I truly believe this book wouldn't exist without you.

Katelyn, Kate, Kit—Atlas wouldn't be Atlas without you. This story wouldn't be the same without you. I'm so incredibly grateful for our friendship. The list of things you did to help make this book a reality is endless. Thank you for encouraging me when I thought this wasn't worth writing, and thank you for loving Atlas and Harper just as much as I do. You are my Calamity muse.

To my beta readers and dear friends—Malory, Sarah, Evy, Lindsay, Gracie, and Lydia. You girls inspire me every day and listen to me complain about anything and everything. My hype team and soul sisters. Thank you for keeping me grounded and always making me laugh.

Endless gratitude for Zandy, my veterinary partner in crime. Thanks for keeping me sane into the late hours of the evening on all our overnight shifts, for being the very first reader of this book, for always assuring me that everything would be fine, and for making being a doctor and an author fun despite the overwhelming stress that both of those jobs bring. All three of my personalities love you immensely!

To Nicole, who edited this book in its infantile stages. Thanks for teaching me my new favorite word—sibilance—and the difference between blonde and blond. Most importantly, thank you for helping me based on our decade-old past and nothing more. I love you more than Jesse Lacey.

Thank you to my wonderful editor Taylor for your hilarious comments and thoughtful ideas. For helping me understand the nuisances of commas and inadvertently helping me build my playlist. I'm so grateful for the way you truly understand the characters I created, and I wouldn't want any other crochety old hag to bounce ideas off of.

Will Hatch & Virginia Allyn—holy fucking Realm—the art you did for this book quite literally made my dreams come true. Thank you and I look forward to all our projects in the future.

To Greg and Natalia at Enchanted Ink for turning this book into a reality and helping out a first-time author with a million questions and a terrible email response time.

To the endless well of family and friends—there's too many of you to name. Every sweet text, or dose of encouragement, sharing in the excitement, and reminding me how loved I am—you all pushed me to keep going when I really wanted to stop. Thanks for helping me get here. I feel like the luckiest girl in the world.

My very biggest thank you to the readers. Thank you for picking up this book and giving it a chance. I hope you loved it and I'm so excited for a future with you all!

Insert Elle Woods saying, "We did it!"

TALARA TATE

is the author of *All the Jagged Edges*, the first book in the Kismet and Coincidence series.

She has always had a love for reading and writing, but took the leap in writing her first book in 2022. She is a big fan of all things dark romance, fantasy, and sci-fi.

In her free time, she enjoys frequenting bookstores, reading, and exploring the beautiful Pacific Northwest with her husband, four dogs, and two cats.

WWW.TALARATATE.COM

instagram: @talaratate.writes

Made in the USA
Middletown, DE
16 September 2023

38476825R00260